Art-school dropout Chandra would do an  her wife's coma—including enroll in the first internet-access brain implant.

At first, the secretive research compound is paradise, the perfect place to distract Chandra from her grief. But as she soon learns, the facility is more prison than resort, with its doctors, support staff, and her fellow patients all bent on hatching plots of their own, no matter how invested they might seem in helping her communicate with her wife.

Making matters worse, a dark wave of uncertainty crashes down on the compound, forcing Chandra to become an unlikely but pivotal player in conspiracies stretching from the highest levels of the North American Union government to the lowest dredges of its shadowy hacking collectives.

To save herself and her wife, Chandra and her newfound friends from the study will have to overcome the scheming of a ruthless tech magnate, the naïveté of an advancement-hungry administrative assistant, and the relentless pursuits of an investigative journalist, all of whom are determined to outpace the others in their own quests to resurrect lost love, cover their tracks, and uncover the truth.

A twistedly delightful clockwork of intrigue and suspense, *Imminent Dawn* is an electrifying sci-fi debut from author r. r. campbell.

IMMINENT DAWN

EMPATHY, Book One

r.r. campbell

Virginia,

A new day breaks!

Thanks for your support,

A NineStar Press Publication

Published by NineStar Press
P.O. Box 91792,
Albuquerque, New Mexico, 87199 USA.
www.ninestarpress.com

Imminent Dawn

Printed in the USA
First Edition
January, 2019

Print ISBN: 978-1-949909-98-2

Also available in eBook, ISBN: 978-1-949909-92-0

Warning: This book contains depictions of suicide, gun violence, and elements of medical horror.

for my father

Chapter One

CHANDRA

Chandra didn't kill her wife, but she may as well have.

Now, as Chandra herself struggled against the darkness, against the paralysis that gripped her, she accepted no punishment was more fitting than the one that seemed to have found her on the far side of her install procedure.

"That's what I heard," said a man's voice, quiet but tense. "Comas. Seizures. Electrocution. All of that."

Chandra's pulse blared in her ears, her throat. She tried to wiggle a finger, but it remained still.

"No way," a different man responded. His voice thick, Chandra imagined him to be much larger than the first man who spoke. "If there were patients not waking up after the procedure—"

"Do you honestly think Halman would care?" said the first man. "Think about it. Would Wyatt Halman really put an end to this study over a couple of schmucks like you and me going brain dead after our installs?"

Brain dead. Chandra would have shivered were she able. But she couldn't be brain dead, no—at least not in any way the doctors used the term. She could hear, understand. Her wife, for all Chandra knew, was no longer capable of even that—deaf even to Chandra's whispers of apology.

Grief clutched Chandra as she tried to call out into the void. She managed only a gurgle.

"You hear that?" the larger man said. Bedsheets rustled against a symphony of beeping medical devices. "She's coming to."

Chandra's eyes flashed open to a world of white.

She lurched forward, hands trembling. Across from her, the two men—patients like her if their lavender-colored scrubs were any indication—sat propped up on gurneys of their own. To the left, a doorway opened into a long, vacuous hall, a nurse's station just visible at the end of it. To her right, a wall-length window opened to the colors of spring, to the pinks of blossoming cherry trees, and the brown branches of a twisted oak.

"Hey," the larger man said. "What do you know?"

The terror that had launched Chandra forward subsided, the weight of the anesthesia claiming her once more. She settled back against her bed, the pillow now more reprieve than prison.

"Come on," the first man said. "Leave her alone. She just woke up. Probably not thinking straight."

Chandra forced a dry swallow, thankful she had at least survived the install procedure. With her EMPATHY nanochip now installed, all she had to do was wait for it to start working. Then Kyra could get hers, just like the ad promised all immediate family members of study participants. Only then would Chandra know whether Kyra could hear, could understand her apology through their direct internet connection. With any luck, EMPATHY might even bring Kyra completely back to her.

"That's what I'm trying to tell you," the smaller man said, apparently responding to some bickering Chandra missed. "The nanochip isn't working for *anyone* yet. They've been doing these installs for months, and—"

"Wait," the large man said. "How could you even know that?" He took the words from Chandra's pasty mouth. "The compound has been on lockdown since the study started, and Wyatt Halman has been perfecting this technology for years."

"Look, man," the smaller of them said. "Believe me or don't. That's up to you. All I'm trying to say is even if the nurses come in here and tell us our installs were successful, that doesn't mean EMPATHY will ever actually work for us."

Chandra's fingers coiled inward. If that were true, she'd given up being at her wife's bedside every day only to get nothing but months of hopeless isolation in exchange. And to fail to return Kyra to something resembling consciousness via EMPATHY... no, Chandra couldn't bear to think of what that might mean.

A dull throb took hold along where the surgeons made the incision near her temple. She raised her hand to massage the area, still unaccustomed to the lack of hair there—or anywhere on her head, for that matter.

"Don't touch it," the large man said. Chandra lowered her hand. "The nurses said so. That's what they told us, anyway."

Chandra managed to sit. She opened her mouth to thank him, but before she could respond, a nurse strolled into the room.

Her periwinkle scrubs matched those of every other nurse Chandra had seen since arriving on the compound yesterday. The woman looked hurried, haggard—as if she hadn't slept in weeks. She leaned over the armrest on the side of the smaller man's gurney and spoke in hushed, inaudible tones.

Even the most casual glance at the man's drooping expression told Chandra everything. A failed install.

Without so much as a response from the patient, the nurse unlocked the brakes on his makeshift bed and wheeled him from the room.

The hospital equipment whimpered in three long, digital sighs before the man across the way finally spoke again. "I guess it's just me and you now."

The throbbing in Chandra's temple accelerated, the pressure immense as it pressed against her left eye. Her hands gripped the railings on the side of her gurney as she collapsed back onto her sheets.

"You okay?" the man said. "Want me to get some help?"

She pulled in a breath between her teeth, bracing herself against a pain so fierce she sincerely wondered if someone was taking an ice cream scoop to her brain.

"All right," the man said. "I'm calling a nurse." A tinny-sounding buzzer hummed as he depressed the HELP button.

A new feeling gripped Chandra. Painless now, she felt as though she were outside her own body, rising from her own chest and drifting toward the ceiling.

Her trembling ceased, though her eyes danced beneath her eyelids. When she opened them, an awareness of the tangle of bedsheets now twisted around her settled in. She unsnarled herself and brought herself upright, resting her back against her pillows, her head against the wall.

A flash of white struck in and out of her vision. The quivering returned, the hair on the back of her neck rising.

Across the way, her fellow patient had gone paler than the wall behind him. "Lady, can you talk? What's going on? Nurse!"

Chandra, too, meant to plead for help, to relay all she felt, but the flash crashed into her vision once more—and this time, it remained. When she dared lower the shield she'd created with her arm, the softness of the lingering light surprised her. It wasn't a light at all. It was a rectangle. No, a perfect square.

It hovered before her, fixed in the center of her vision, stirring some familiarity, the alluring awe of a daydream, a memory. And there, in the upper-left-hand corner, a thin vertical line blinked on, blinked off. Blinked on. Blinked off.

Finally a nurse stumbled into the room, his cheeks red, his chest heaving.

"Something's happening," Chandra managed. "There's this white thing floating here, hanging here."

On the far side of the translucent sheet, the nurse scampered back into the hall, his voice echoing as he called for support.

Disbelief consumed Chandra. How to describe what hovered before her? She drafted a description to remember for later, but even her best attempt failed to do justice to the moment. She shook her head to clear her mind and typed a description of the image.

Typed. No, it couldn't be.

The words crawled across the sheet of white, the cursor trailing her thoughts as they gathered on the screen. And as the textscape grew, so did her excitement—as well as her concern. She paused to calm herself, and the cursor halted in its march from left-to-right.

Her chest grew light, her skin tingling. It worked. EMPATHY was actually working. She wanted to leap from bed, to tell anyone, to tell the world, to tell Kyra most of all.

But before she could speak another word, the screen vanished into a single, impossibly distant point. All the same, something told her its contents had been saved forever.

Footsteps approached from the hall, the urgent pitter-patter of a herd of help on the way.

And help was on the way, all right—help for Chandra, yes, but more importantly, help for Kyra. Once the research team confirmed EMPATHY had taken for Chandra, they'd have to give Kyra the install they'd promised.

It would only be a matter of months, maybe even weeks before Chandra could apologize to her wife, could tell her she loved her again. They'd be back to squabbling over what to plant where in their garden, to bristling at bedtime ghost stories—even if Kyra's coma only allowed her to do so over EMPATHY.

Then a memory of the rumors returned, the smaller man's whispers of seizures and install recipients who themselves slipped into comas after their procedures. Chandra's stomach clenched at the thought.

She supposed the man had also said that after months of install procedures EMPATHY still hadn't taken for anyone, and Chandra had already disproven that rumor. Perhaps she was the exception. At least she hoped she was.

Her fate and that of her wife depended on it.

Chapter Two

WYATT

Doctor Wyatt Halman ground his teeth as he checked his pocketab. "You said they were meeting us at three."

"*They* said they were meeting us at three." Lars Alfreðsson, Wyatt's lawyer and late wife's brother, pulled at the lapels of his suit jacket. "Maybe the North American Union has finally accepted the truth; your life's work can't be purchased at any cost."

Wyatt picked at his mustache with his free hand. In the corner of the cramped, basement meeting-room of this otherwise opulent Liberty, Texas hotel, the youngest of his three adult children, Alistair, leaned against the wall. "And what do you think?" Wyatt said.

Alistair put on a smug expression. "I think the NAU is playing you at your own game."

As comments went, Alistair's was presumptuous. Sharp. Digging. In a word, perfect. "And what do you mean by that, exactly?"

Alistair narrowed his eyes, that self-satisfied grin still pulling at the corners of his lips. "It's your classic power play. He who arrives last controls the room when he arrives. Especially if the rest can't begin without him."

So Alistair *had* managed to learn something from his old man—and in fewer years than either Heather or Peter, his elder siblings—well, half-siblings.

Wyatt directed his response to Lars. "Look at that. You're nearly twice his age and half as wise." Sour as Wyatt's mood was, he still couldn't resist some playful ribbing of his brother-in-law.

"Twice his age? Hardly." Lars adjusted his cobalt tie, an eerie match to the color of his eyes. He had nothing more to say, apparently.

The end of Wyatt's digipen clacked as Wyatt returned to gnawing on it. Tardiness for the sake of control was one thing, but given Wyatt and Alistair themselves had landed on the hotel's helipad some thirty minutes after the meeting was to have started, whatever the NAU played at was something else entirely.

"I don't have time for this." Wyatt lurched forward. "*No one* has time for this." He stood, nodding for the others to join him in abandoning the room. "It's the final day of installs, for Turing's sake. We should be on the compound, Alistair. And you," he said, pointing squarely at Lars' chest, "should get a hold of your contacts at the NAU to tell them they can go piss in a—"

The door swung open. Wyatt stopped mere feet from the man and the woman who stood on the far side of the threshold.

"Doctor Halman," the man said, extending a hand. "I believe we've already had the pleasure."

They had, what little pleasure there had been. Senator Gareth Sinclair was a brutish, hot air balloon of a man whose waddle would have been comedic were his tone not always so menacing. With a demeanor like his, how he'd won the New Texahoma senate seat for three terms running was anyone's guess.

And, if Wyatt *did* have to guess, he would posit each election had been rigged—perhaps not through vote counts themselves, but rather the systematic voter oppression of demographics more favorable to competing parties. That, along with election day poll-book purges that all-too-conveniently affected voters who, again, would have been most likely to vote against Sinclair's interests... well, Wyatt supposed it was easy to see how his party maintained such a stronghold after that farce of a war.

"You can cut it with the campaign pleasantries," Wyatt said. "We all know what this is about."

The eyes of the woman on Sinclair's right grew wide. "I apologize for our late arrival," she said, much to Sinclair's apparent dismay. Her tone remained bright—painfully so—and something about her evoked a sense of familiarity. She extended her hand. "Beatrice Soved, NAU Secretary of Technology."

That's why he'd recognized her. Were any other party in power, Wyatt would already be more than familiar with the Sec of Tech, who in the old days was often a former Human/Etech higher-up. But since Chief Executive Gleason had stuffed her cabinet full of donors and kleptocrats, it was no wonder he'd never crossed paths with this—"Soved, is it?" He shook her hand with both of his.

"My friends call me Betty," she said. "It'd be great if we could be friends."

Wyatt released her hand, the taste of bile creeping up his throat. "I don't keep many friends among your ilk."

Her smile wilted.

"Told you," Sinclair said, stepping toward Alistair and Lars.

The rest of them exchanged names and handshakes as if any of it were necessary, and by the time anyone bothered to address Wyatt again, the four others had seated themselves at the tiny table in the room's center. "Won't you take a seat, Doctor?" Sinclair said.

"I'm an old man now. I need to stretch my back when I can." He also needed to loom over the rest of them as to assert authority over the proceedings, but he left that unsaid.

"Obstinate as always." Sinclair's tone suggested it was meant as a joke.

Secretary Soved paled at how brash it had come across. "Senator, we're here to treat with Doctor Halman as allies, not dismiss his concerns as a—"

"Madame Secretary," Wyatt said, "there's no need to dance about the topic. How much this time?"

"I'm sorry?" she said.

"How much? What's the offer?"

Lars bowed his head while Alistair did his best to conceal his amusement.

"Well," Sinclair said, the chair beneath him groaning as he leaned forward, "before we discuss anything offer-related, I think there's something you ought to know."

Wyatt steeled himself, arching an eyebrow.

"We know what makes EMPATHY tick."

His brow drooped. Impossible. He and Eva had accidentally discovered what would become EMPATHY's missing link decades earlier, and it wasn't until last year that Wyatt had teased out precisely how to make use of it—well, not that he had any actual evidence to prove himself right yet.

"I see," Wyatt said. He said nothing more, aiming to call Sinclair's bluff.

The senator clasped his hands in front of himself. "Whatever element it is that bridges the gap between the biological and technological, you can bet the Union's top scientists will have synthesized it soon enough."

"Hm." Wyatt forced himself to glower when he would have rather smiled. Synthesize astium? A comical notion. Eva had spent the first few years after their—well, *her*—discovery of astium attempting to synthesize it herself. Doing so was preferable, in her mind, to mining it from the Icelandic volcanoes where they'd first found it.

Her memory clawed at him, the sight of her kneeling at the base of that crater tearing at his throat. *Ást án enda.* Eva's voice was sweet still, even after all these years, even if only in his mind.

"I suppose," Wyatt said, keeping his expression grim, "that if you're so close, I can't imagine your offer has *increased* since we last met."

Secretary Soved seemed to sense it was her time to shine. "You'd be surprised." She tapped at the screen of her pocketab. "We have the document right here. It's... uh, well, I had it just a moment ago...."

Sinclair had to look away.

"Ah, here it is," Soved said. "In exchange for complete access in perpetuity to any and all biological, neurological, and technological findings or developments produced by Human/Etech singularity projects— in this case, namely EMPATHY—the North American Union would like to offer two hundred fifty billion ameros...."

She went on, but Wyatt ignored her. That many ameros would be enough for the NAU to build a military base and keep it operational for Tesla knew how long. If they were still offering that kind of cash, they were far less confident they could synthesize astium than Sinclair suggested.

Ordinarily, this was the part where Wyatt would excuse himself and march for the door. What Lars had said earlier was true; Wyatt had no intention of selling EMPATHY to these scoundrels—or anyone at all, to be frank—especially since their primary motivations to control EMPATHY were to weaponize it and, presumably, keep the general population pulling figurative levers for the Right for the Union's candidates when in the voting booth.

Simply put, so long as EMPATHY remained in Wyatt's control, it was a threat. To them. To their power. Perhaps to the Union itself insofar as they were concerned.

Soved finished rambling and looked up from her pocketab.

It took all Wyatt had to not storm out. He bit the inside of his cheek, placed his hands in—and then removed them from—the pockets of his lab coat. He knew better than to give these Hawking-forsaken politicos a taste of victory, but he'd permit himself this indulgence. "Two hundred fifty billion ameros?" He shifted his glance toward Lars and Alistair as if looking for their approval.

Lars knitted his brow, apparently concerned Wyatt might be taking the bait. Alistair, however, scratched the bridge of his nose to hide his exuberant expression. He seemed to sense a trick was afoot.

"I don't know," Wyatt said. "It's tempting in light of what you've shared with me today."

Soved scooted forward in her seat. Sinclair remained perfectly silent, perfectly still.

"But it's still a 'no,' I'm afraid. Gentlemen," Wyatt said, nodding to Lars and Alistair, "we'll be leaving now." He made for the door.

The sound of chairs squeaking behind him meant Alistair and Lars, too, followed Wyatt.

Sinclair hollered after the three of them. "You should be doing this as a service to your country. You're lucky we offer you anything, Halman."

Wyatt halted. He spun on his heel, the tension tight in his neck. "*I'm* the lucky one? Me?" Soved cowered as Wyatt stepped back toward them, spittle flying from his lips. "Might I remind you the purpose of EMPATHY is to unite all people on one network, to break down communication barriers, to build actual, worldwide empathy among all people?"

Soved leaned away. "I don't underst—"

"Oh, so you've forgotten?" Wyatt snarled. "You've forgotten you NAU-types have limited the future sale and distribution of EMPATHY to within the Union itself? You've forgotten you and your gang of political thieves have already robbed this study—robbed the world—of its true purpose?

"You can come to me time and time again with offers like these, promising 'to combine our resources' and 'create public-private synergy,' but don't for a second try to convince me that's what this is really about."

Soved looked past Wyatt and at Lars. "Enlighten us," she said. "Why would the NAU make such generous offers if we weren't sincerely interested in helping you develop your work more expediently? From what we've heard, you've had little success on your own thus far."

Wyatt ignored the truth behind her barb, that after months of installs and decades of development, they were still without a single cerenet-connected subject as the study's final patients were being induced some hours earlier. At least there had been no direct leaks to the press, which would spell disaster to be certain. Whatever she had heard had been rumor alone, and rumor was worth about as much as a promise from any of these two-faced con artists.

"This is about a victory," Wyatt said. "Not for the people of the Union, not for me or for us as 'the team' you might preach about. This is about you, your party, your government's desire to weaponize EMPATHY to get back at the Federation."

Sinclair opened his mouth to speak, but Alistair cut him off. "Getting us to sign an agreement would also be a nice narrative to distract the people from, say, any number of ongoing scandals within the Gleason administration."

Good, good. Wyatt nodded Alistair's direction. "My son is right. With another round of elections next year, I have to imagine you'd be rather pleased if you could take the focus off your Chief Executive's indirect support for the slaughter of schoolchildren."

Soved wagged a finger. "There has been no evidence found to suggest—"

"Let's drop all pretense," Senator Sinclair said. He waddled out from behind the table. "We've come this far. We may as well speak frankly." He clasped his hands in front of himself, stepping ever nearer to Wyatt as he spoke. "You're right, Wyatt. Gleason needs a win. The administration needs a win. Our party needs a win."

Wyatt fumed. "If you think I'm going to be the prop that delivers—"

"But the NAU needs a win, too." Sinclair was inches away now, the grease of his skin shining from the lights overhead. "In light of the war, people need someone to deliver them a sense of purpose, of safety, of resolve. They—or rather, we—need to recapture the pride that once came with standing alongside our fellow countrymen, of knowing where we stood in the world, of believing again that our way is the righteous way."

Wyatt sneered. "And you believe the weaponization of EMPATHY would provide that pride? You believe using EMPATHY to control the populace would provide the security you claim the people long for?"

"You act as though it wouldn't."

"Whether it would or would not is beside the point. EMPATHY was created to provide all you're asking for and more without using fear or intimidation to prop it up."

Sinclair snickered. "Here you go again, pretending your goals are benevolent, that you're free of deviousness yourself."

Lars piped up. "If you're going to slander my client—"

Sinclair held up a hand. "Earlier you complained about EMPATHY's eventual sale and distribution being limited to within the Union itself, but don't pretend you received nothing in exchange for that condition. If I recall correctly, you came to the Union Research Council with a study design that came up somewhat short of ethical—"

Wyatt wouldn't stand for that, no. "The design as presented and executed is essential to ensure my team can thoroughly evaluate—"

"Listen to yourself," Sinclair said. "You can preach all day about how you loathe 'our ilk,' but at your core, you're just like me. You're just like Secretary Soved here. You're just like every last one of the politicos you despise, clawing your way through this world and convincing yourself of your own righteousness at every turn.

"If I had to guess," Sinclair continued, his breath now hot on Wyatt's face, "beneath your facade of generosity is a man driven by his own self-serving desires. His own egomania. His own secrets."

Thoughts of Eva teased him again. "Perhaps you're right, Senator. Maybe beneath it all, I'm just like you—desperate for safety, for pride, for a win. There's one thing you've forgotten, though, one thing you'll never have that will ensure you fail where I succeed."

"Oh, and what's that?"

"I'm the only one who knows the true nature of the element that will make this version of EMPATHY work. I know what it is. I know how to put it to use." Wyatt narrowed his eyes. "And you? You know nothing. Less than nothing." He shrugged. "So, yes, we both need a win, but only one of us knows which game we're playing."

Wyatt nodded to Secretary Soved. "Now, if you'll excuse us, there's much to do back at the compound. If I'm not mistaken, I believe we have a celebratory banquet to prepare for."

"Celebratory?" Soved said. "Good news from the compound, then? EMPATHY has finally taken for one of your patients?"

Lars intervened. "If my client wanted you to know the reason for their celebration, I'm sure he would have said as much outright."

"That's okay, Lars," Wyatt said. He gestured broadly toward both NAU representatives. "We're actually celebrating not having to speak with either of these fools ever again."

Senator Sinclair offered Wyatt his hand. "You can't blame us for trying, can you?"

Wyatt took the man's hand. "I suppose I can't, no."

"I'm glad to hear it." Sinclair tightened his hold, a python choking its prey. "Because if there's one thing you should know about my boss, it's that she always gets what she wants in the end."

"Really? I don't see another term as Chief Executive in her future. Is *that* something she wants?"

"Meh," Sinclair released his grip and placed a hand on Wyatt's shoulder. "The elections are over a year away. We have plenty of time before then to learn all about this mystery element of yours, to find our way onto your research compound."

Wyatt paled. Was the NAU really threatening him? Here? In front of his lawyer?

"Who knows?" Sinclair said. "Maybe we already have."

Chapter Three

MEREDITH

Brad Mellocks, Meredith's coworker at the Austin *Star-Globe,* ran a hand through his shock of blond hair. "I don't know how Kathy expects us to go through this material any more quickly. There are thousands of these emails. Thousands." He plopped into the chair opposite Meredith at the e-paper's conference-room table.

"I wouldn't worry about it," Meredith said, eyes glued to the soft glow of her pocketab. "Kathy's disappointed if we fail to break news *before* it happens."

"Sometimes I wonder how long I can keep working for her."

Meredith snickered. "Hang around for a couple of decades and then come talk to me."

"That's... fair enough." Brad rolled up his shirtsleeves. "You find anything of note over there yet?"

"Not really, no." If she were honest, she *had* found something suspicious on day one of their comb-through of the emails the Merry Hacksters had leaked to the world, but she dared not tell Brad of it. Meredith had been burned far too many times over the course of her career to trust someone as advancement-hungry as Brad.

A new email hit her inbox. Her eyes narrowed at the FROM field: WITHHELD.

"Maybe we can't find anything because there's nothing here," Brad said. "Chief Executive Gleason could be telling the truth. She might have had nothing to do with the arms scandal cover-up, after all."

Meredith had a hunch he was wrong but couldn't be bothered to correct him. Her elbows on the table, she leaned in as she read the new email a second time.

To: "Meredith Maxwell"

From: <WITHHELD>

Subject: Human/Etech—EMPATHY Study

I am on the inside.

Prove you can be as valuable to me as I can be to you.

-Q♠

"Even if the weapons the Altamerican Militia used to kill those school kids were from her Civilians In Arms program," Brad said, apparently intent on talking to himself, "you have to think of how many lives were saved by arming the whole west coast against the Federation. It sounds cold-blooded, but it's a fact."

Meredith rubbed her temples. "I won't say you're wrong if believing so helps you sleep at night." Whatever Brad's focus might have been, her thoughts remained on the EMPATHY study, on this new email. If only this Queen of Spades had gotten in touch with her months ago! She'd spent the better part of the last two years attempting to plant moles in Human/Etech's first round of human trials for EMPATHY. Every candidate she found, however—no matter their background or how much Meredith prepped them in advance—failed to be granted admission to the study. Meredith didn't know how, but she had a hunch Human/Etech had some way to identify and reject would-be press informants. The study had started months ago, and not a single news source—not even those story-stealing S.O.B.s at *The Courier*—had been able to get a scoop.

She inhaled before talking herself down. Faux tipsters had defrauded her in the past, every one of them out for something. Fame. Notoriety. A few extra ameros in exchange for completely fabricated information. Meredith wouldn't allow herself to be duped. Not this time.

To: <WITHHELD>

From: "Meredith Maxwell"

Subject: Re: Human/Etech—EMPATHY Study

I'm intrigued, though I would need some proof of your credibility before I commit to anything.

Best,

Mer

"Do you want my real opinion?" Brad said.

Meredith looked up from her screen. "Is it going to ignore that nearly all the perpetrators of the attack just somehow managed to escape and never be found?"

"It's a long debunked myth the government let the militia get away to keep another boogeyman on the streets."

"Or," Meredith said, shifting in her seat, "what if instead of letting them off the hook 'to keep another boogeyman on the streets,' Gleason's administration never tracked them down because she enjoys going out of her way to sympathize with ethno-nationalists?"

Brad shook his head. "I'm not saying I agree with what the Altamerican Militia stands for or what they did, but to obsess over conspiracy theories—"

"Fine." Meredith sighed. "But you can't ignore that the weapons seized from the one attacker the SWAT team did gun down were checked into evidence with serial numbers, all of which were scrubbed at some point while in the care of the FBI."

"That doesn't mean Gleason told them to do it."

"You are out of your mind if you think that's something the FBI would have done on its own. Gleason had everything to lose if it turned out some of the weapons she'd put in civilian hands were later used in a school massacre."

Brad went silent.

Meredith returned to the lead she had been attempting to follow since earlier in the week. The emails from Executive Gleason herself weren't the ones that most caught Meredith's eye, but rather a veritable library of emails from a Susan Dunham. This previously unheard of woman had been in communication with the FBI Director, Gleason's Chief of Staff, and the Secretary of Defense all those years earlier during Gleason's stint as U.S. President. No matter how Meredith tried, however, she couldn't figure out what role this Dunham lady played in the Gleason administration, or why her contact with the then-president was always indirect and also limited to a narrow window of time following the Academy Shooting. Something about the whole thing seemed off, but Meredith still wasn't quite sure what. If she were able to tie the current Chief Executive of the North American Union to a botched arms-disbursement cover-up, well, that would be the kind of thing that could oust someone from power.

Oh, and get Meredith's own career finally moving in the right direction.

"What do you think Kathy would do if we told her we both wanted a raise?" Brad said.

"I don't know, Brad."

"What if...?"

Meredith didn't hear what came next. Another new email hit her inbox, again from the Queen of Spades.

> To: "Meredith Maxwell"
>
> From: <WITHHELD>
>
> Subject: Re: Human/Etech—EMPATHY Study
>
> See attached.
>
> The first one is always free.
>
> -Q♠

Meredith poked at the screen of her pocketab, navigating to the email's attachment—a video. She considered waiting until she was back in her own office before viewing it, but with Brad still playing at hypotheticals, she just made sure her pocketab was on mute before hitting PLAY.

She brought a hand to her mouth as the images danced before her. Seemingly recorded from a pair of cyfocals, a sprawling cafeteria of table-and-bench seating stretched out before the person doing the filming, a high ceiling looming overhead. The space brimmed with individuals of all ages, each of whom wore various colors of hospital-style scrubs. It wasn't the scrubs or the sheer quantity of people that stood out most, but rather the number of them whose heads had been recently shaved. Not only that, but the bald heads belonged mostly—no, exclusively—to those wearing lavender-colored scrubs.

"If the *Star-Globe* did that," Brad said, "it wouldn't be in this financial mess at all. Rather than cutting staff, it could probably—"

"Shh," Meredith said.

"What?"

"Stop for a minute. I need to think."

"What is it?" Brad slinked to her side of the table, a hop in his step.

"Call Kathy." Meredith started the video again and kept an eye out for any new details.

"Can you show me what you're looking at first?"

"I'll show you when I show Kathy." Her editor would be furious if she found out she wasn't the first to see this after Meredith.

As Brad dialed Kathy, Meredith shrank her pocketab before calling her intern, Alvin. He answered on the second ring. "Hey, Alvin."

"Yeah?"

"Can you come to the conference room?"

"I'm working on that slideshow right now."

"Can you stop working on that slideshow and come to the conference room *right now*?"

A pause took the line. "Yeah. On my way."

Meredith thumbed her screen to end the call. She would want Alvin here to take notes once Kathy saw the video; surely there would be some task he could take on to support this story.

"I don't know," Brad said into his pocketab. "Meredith told me to have you come to the conference room. Yes. No, on the fourth floor. What do you mean?"

Meredith made a gimme motion with her hand. Brad turned his device over. "Kathy?" Meredith said into the receiver.

"If you need me to meet with you, call me yourself."

"I would have, but I was a little too busy rewatching this video taken on the EMPATHY compound."

"Wait, what?! Never mind, I'll be right there."

Kathy and Alvin arrived within moments of one another, the former wearing an expression of you-better-not-be-yanking-my-chain, the latter a posture so lacking in enthusiasm one couldn't help but wonder whether he had osteoporosis.

"What's this all about?" Kathy folded her arms across her chest.

"Get your pocketabs, all of you." Meredith placed a finger in the upper-right-hand corner of her own device, stretching it outward to enlarge it once again. Then, placing the same finger over the video file, she flung it in the direction of each of her colleagues so they could watch it as she manipulated it on her own screen. "I got this video from someone who claims to be on the Human/Etech research compound. Tell me what you think vis-à-vis authenticity."

Alvin seemed incapable of getting the video to play on his own device. Instead of troubleshooting, he crouched close to Meredith, heaving hefty breaths of coffee stench in her direction. "Looks like lunchtime in a hospital to me," he said.

"Yeah," Meredith said, "except most of the people have their head shaved." All nodded except Alvin—who remained slack-jawed—as Meredith posed her hunches to the room. "Do you think they're study participants? They'd have to get their head shaved before having the chip installed, right?"

Kathy placed her free hand on her hip. "You'd know better than any of us."

Meredith did. Or should have, at least. EMPATHY was a nanochip, that much she knew, but knowing how it might have been implanted was anyone's guess.

Despite the footage, Kathy remained skeptical. "How do we know the video is authentic? It could be a setup."

Meredith raised a finger. "I—"

Alvin interrupted. "I don't think it's a setup."

Kathy scoffed. "What makes *you* qualified to make that assessment?"

Alvin pointed to Meredith's screen with a lone skinny finger. "Isn't that the guy?"

"The guy?" Kathy shifted her weight.

"You know," Alvin said. "What's his name? It's on the tip of my tongue. The one in charge of the study."

Even without context, Meredith knew who Alvin meant immediately. She didn't know how she missed him the first times she watched the video, but there, clad in his trademark white lab coat, was Wyatt Halman. "It's him. It's Halman." The room flittered with excitement.

"Except he has a dumb mustache now," Alvin said, laughing. "Look at that thing."

Kathy tapped two fingers against her lips. "This is—this has got to be real." She narrowed her eyes at Meredith. "Who did you get this from?"

Meredith's chair rolled across the carpet as she stood. "She signed the email as the 'Queen of Spades.'"

Kathy clapped her hands once. "More. I want more. Tell the Queen of Spades you want background. Details. Images. More video. You know what we need. Brad, you take over the Gleason project while Meredith follows this lead."

"You're joking," Brad said.

"You know I was born without a sense of humor." Kathy exited without another word.

As Brad fired off complaints and Alvin salivated over getting involved with the EMPATHY project, a warmth trickled through Meredith's chest. She had done it. She had finally landed the once-in-a-career story that could again have the *Star-Globe* back in the black—the kind of story that could salvage her shipwrecked career.

Chapter Four

ARIEL

Ariel Commons stood before the research compound's primary server, her pulse rifling through her fingertips as she fretted a mission she didn't understand, a keycard that wasn't her own, a job she didn't deserve.

"All right." She gave the W-USB in her hand a squeeze, keenly aware of how little time she had to accomplish her task. "Please just work." Ariel closed her eyes as the data transfer device clicked into its port beneath the eerie white glow of the monitor.

She opened her eyes. Nothing on the screen had changed. "No no no no no." Was failure on step one really how this was going to go? She supposed she should have expected as much. She had about as much business working as an administrative assistant to Alistair Halman as a squirrel does working as a gravedigger.

Weird. Morbid.

Maybe it was better put this way: she had about as much business doing this as she had studying computer science in the first place, which, if her abysmal grades from Southern Texas Franciscan University were any indication, had been absolutely none.

Ariel winced as she slid the W-USB from its port to inspect it. She turned it over in her hand, the oppressive hum of the server farm's HVAC system bearing down on her. There, on the opposite side of the W-USB, she saw it—the LED light blinking in bright red flashes. An incoming data transfer? Why would she be getting new code now?

She shook her head and retrieved her pocketab from the breast pocket of her canary-colored scrubs, prepared to text Alistair for clarification on whatever it was he thought he was doing. By now, he should already have been at the banquet celebrating the study's final installs. What was the point of them—well, *him*—using the banquet as a distraction for the upload of this code if he was just going to work the whole time he was there?

When she slipped her pocketab from her pocket, the message already on its screen knitted her brow.

>> This new code replaces Alistair's. His has already been deleted.

A lump clotted her throat. This was neither an expected message nor her normal messaging program. Maybe there'd been an update? The Human/Etech programmers were always pushing through new features. She typed back, but whoever had messaged her seemed to anticipate her response.

>> This stage is to serve as another layer of blindness, a check on Alistair. He is not to know.

Another layer of blindness? Alistair had said his code—which she was supposed to be uploading right now—was already meant to serve as a check on the work of his siblings. Half-siblings. Whatever.

And of course, he'd only taken on this task after receiving explicit instructions to do so from his father, or at least that's what Alistair had told her.

<< Who are you?

>> The one person capable of keeping his children from bumbling their way through this study.

Ariel's cheeks flushed. Wyatt Halman—*Wyatt Halman!*—had reached out to her to help keep his children in check. It was almost too much to believe, though Wyatt's constant demand for control could have driven him to do this, she supposed. The more she considered it, the more some elaborate plot seemed likely. Wyatt embodied one persona during advisory board meetings, another when in public. That in itself was a kind of deception. It shouldn't have been surprising to learn his flagship study was full of similar guile.

>> Well, perhaps I should clarify. I'm not Wyatt himself, but rather an extension of him.

Ariel noticed the LED on her W-USB had stopped blinking, instead glowing a vibrant green. Before she reinserted the W-USB at the primary server, though, she needed to know more.

<< If you're an "extension" of Wyatt, then you know we don't have much time. Tell me who you are and what this is.

>> My apologies for being vague. You can call me M3R1. Wyatt has programmed me to assist with matters better kept secret from those who might find them disagreeable.

M3R1. What spoke with her from the other side of her pocketab wasn't human at all. It must have been some AI, an app Wyatt devised to manage this component of the study when he was unable.

This was all happening so fast. Simply working for this study felt like she had caught lightning in a bottle, but the events of the last couple days made her feel as though she would end up with a shelf's worth of lightning-bolt-filled jars by the time the study was over.

<< Sorry for having questioned you. Am I okay to upload this code now?

>> Don't worry. A questioning mind is an asset, not an inconvenience. But please, hurry along with the code.

The messaging program pixelated out of existence, revealing her pocketab's normal background square by square.

Ariel slipped the W-USB into the port beneath the monitor, which triggered a menu to pop up on the screen.

USERNAME:
PASSWORD:

The keys of the keyboard clicked as Ariel's fingers danced about it. Once she entered her username, she tabbed into the password field, stopping when her pocketab vibrated.

>> Wait. Do not use yours. Give it a minute.

She huffed, though she regretted doing so a moment later. If M3R1 were to log in Wyatt with his username, no one would question Ariel about the upload. Any inquiries would go to Wyatt instead, and no one—well, almost no one—questioned him.

The username and password fields populated left-to-right simultaneously, each character a dot concealing the characters they represented. When the initial menu disappeared, a new one replaced it, this time a simple progress bar displaying zero percent completion. Above it, the words LOADING THE BUS consumed most of what screen remained. More quickly than Ariel anticipated, the progress bar zipped to one hundred percent before resetting to zero, the phrase FURTHER DEVELOPMENT taking its place.

The upload's progress froze at five percent. Ariel swore under her breath when another line of text appeared below the progress bar—about fifteen minutes remaining.

>> All good things come in time.

Ariel leaned against a nearby server. "Wait. Can you hear me?"

>> See the blue light?

Her eyes fell to her pocketab's indicator light, illuminated in blue. "So it was you listening to me. You're the reason my device has been all wonky." Her pocketab had been sluggish for weeks, sometimes even opening and closing apps without her consent. It had made remaining productive near impossible and compromised any enjoyment she might have gotten out of playing the puzzle game *Dallas* in her spare time.

>> Speaking directly to your device should be more efficient than typing.

Again, this was more fantastic foresight from Wyatt. Playing secret agent with the world's most respected name in biofusion was like something out of a movie. She could get over having a slow pocketab if it let her work with Wyatt so closely, even if indirectly.

"Very smart," she said. "Still, I don't know if we have fifteen minutes. The system administrator could be here any minute, and—"

>> Relax. I will alert you if Heather is on the way. Why don't you play some *Dallas* to pass the time while you wait? :)

The messaging program dissolved, her screen now displaying the start menu for *Dallas*. Ariel considered protesting further, but what choice did she have, really?

She looked about for a comfortable place to sit, but between the foreboding red of the overhead lights and the eerie blue glow emitted from row after row of servers, the place wasn't exactly designed for relaxation. The best she could manage was a spot on the floor with her back pressed to one of the stacks, the primary server still in sight only a few yards away. Ariel thumbed START on her pocketab's screen and let a new game begin.

She made it to the sixth level before she snapped out of the pseudo-hypnosis into which the game's soundtrack had lulled her. After pausing her game and checking the time, she eyed the primary server. Phase two of the upload had begun.

"M3R1, are you there?" The blue light on her pocketab suggested as much.

>> Yes, Ariel?

She bit at the thumbnail of her free hand. "There has to be a way to speed this up." Ariel stood, stretched, and crept her way toward the primary server's monitor. "It makes me nervous that there are still seven minutes left."

>> You will be fine. Heather's maintenance will likely be delayed if she's enjoying herself at the banquet.

Heather Halman enjoying herself? The absurdity of Heather even cracking a smile was enough to make Ariel laugh. Ever since arriving on the compound, Heather—the Halman sibling in charge of network and compound security—had been nothing but dismissive of Ariel, who was already more than aware she was the least qualified of any of the Halmans' administrative assistants. Still, Heather's glares and off-handed verbal barbs only worsened Ariel's feelings of self-worth, which she was totally capable of diminishing on her own, thank you very much.

And Alistair had made it plenty clear; Heather could not learn of this scheme, nor could the oldest Halman child, Peter, whose code provided the backbone for EMPATHY in the first place.

"I'm sure you're already aware," Ariel said, "but if Heather finds us—well, me—down here tampering with the servers, we're... I'm..." The words didn't come. She wouldn't just lose her job—though that went without saying—her future itself would evaporate before her eyes. Gone would be the dreams of quietly rising through the Human/Etech ranks, learning all she could at every step to prove the world and herself wrong about the girl who'd barely managed to graduate Southern Texas' lackluster program in CS, wrong about the girl whose naiveté had already once cost her a chance at a brighter future.

>> Please, Ariel, leave this step to M3R1. If Heather were to leave the banquet early, I could track her progress through the compound via her keycard.

She supposed that was likely true. Alistair had given Ariel a new keycard to use specifically when on these missions. He refused to provide the person in whose name he'd programmed the card, and Ariel quickly learned asking questions only led to conflict between her and Alistair, the one person whose recommendation could help keep her on the Human/Etech payroll once the study concluded.

As reassuring as M3R1's comments on the keycard should have been, Ariel still found herself fidgeting when she checked the time once more. If M3R1 were wrong, Heather could be here any moment. "What if I remove the W-USB and we wrap up the rest of the upload at another time?"

>> That could be disastrous for this code. You would have to begin the process again the next time you visited, and who knows when that might be? It's not often the compound is as distracted as it is tonight.

Again, valid points, but anxiety had already taken hold. Every clank or beep or sigh from a stack of servers had Ariel looking over a shoulder, a prickling sensation grating the back of her neck. "All right. I don't care. We have to take this thing out now."

She reached for the W-USB. Her pocketab bleated a raucous alarm.

>> Remove the W-USB and you forfeit all possibility of enrolling at the Trade Facility once the study is complete.

Ariel's hand froze inches from the data transfer device. Halfway through her senior year of college, Ariel had received a letter of acceptance from the Wisconsin Trade Facility's prestigious MBA program. For as hopeless as she was in computer science, she'd actually become an effective writer, and the recommendations she secured from working one-on-one with her professors to help her pass her classes must have been just enough to give her an edge in the enrollment process.

So, naturally, she had to accept the admissions offer—well, would have—had her then-boyfriend, Grant, not made a suggestion of his own. "Why don't you defer enrollment for a year?" he said. "That way we can graduate and start our lives together at the same time."

When Ariel asked the school if this was possible, they rescinded her offer. Perhaps the spot would be best filled by someone who had the dedication to begin immediately, they said.

Without explanation, Grant broke things off with her not long afterward.

But she had let that go. She had to. Whatever happened between her and Grant was in the past.

Ariel bit her lower lip. There was no reason M3R1 should have known all of that. "How do you know about the Trade Facility?"

>> You mentioned the Trade Facility on your interview paperwork. Wouldn't it be convenient to have the recommendation of a Halman to secure your place at the school once the study is complete?

"Are you saying I won't be able to work for Human/Etech once we're done on the compound?" That had become her new dream since starting here, anyway.

>> Though working for Human/Etech during this study bolsters a candidate's prospects for continued employment, there are no guarantees. Imagine, however, that you have an opportunity to further your education after collaborating so intensely with the Halmans. Experience like that would be hard to compete with. Once done with school, you may apply and find yourself in charge of an entire biofusion division.

Ariel rocked onto her tiptoes. Ariel Commons, Division Head for Human/Etech Biofusion Enterprises—that had a nice ring to it. More importantly, being in a role like that would allow her to introduce socially transformative technology like EMPATHY to the public. She could imagine nothing better. "You would really do that?"

>> Yes, assuming you can manage the tasks asked of you while on the compound.

Right. Patience. Ariel took a deep breath. She had to trust M3R1. It was an extension of Wyatt, after all, and if she couldn't let herself trust him, could she ever trust anyone?

Besides, now that she checked the primary server again, she saw the upload had advanced to a new stage—TAKING A BRUSH TO THE SNOW. One and a half minutes remaining.

>> The final stage.

"Good. I'm still hoping to get to the banquet before it ends."

>> You should be thankful this last component has been added to the code.

Before she could ask why, M3R1 followed up with a second message.

>> Apologies. My lack of attention has compromised us. Heather's security card suggests she has boarded the elevator for the basement floor.

Ariel flushed with panic. On the monitor, it still showed thirty seconds remaining. "This has to be done. Now."

>> You can afford to wait a few more seconds. Heather's card has only just been swiped to open the elevator doors on the basement level.

"Can you speed this up? Is there any way at all?"

>> This last upload is what preserves the secrecy of this stage of the study. Removing the W-USB before the upload completes will allow Heather to see someone visited the server.

Ariel felt her throat constrict. "If Heather finds me here twiddling my thumbs, the secret won't last long anyway." Adrenaline pumped through her as she waited for the upload to complete.

>> Further apologies. Again, mistakes were made. Heather is now inside the server farm.

Sweat collected in the spaces between Ariel's fingers. She opened her mouth to respond before thinking better, worried her voice would betray her presence in the stacks—even given the thrum of the HVAC system.

Ariel reached for the W-USB. She needed to be in position to remove it the second the upload ended. Checking over her shoulder and, seeing no one approached, she waited out the final seconds.

Three.

Two.

One.

The screen flashed the words UPLOAD COMPLETE before returning to the blank white display Ariel had found on arrival.

She snatched the W-USB and slipped it into her pocket. Rather than head the direction from which she came, she scurried off to the right of the primary server, careful to keep her shoes from squeaking as she stepped. She ducked behind a row-end server, confident she heard Heather in another aisle.

Heather took less care about the sound of her shoes as she strutted. A faint squawk echoed at the far end of the row where Ariel had hidden. With her back pressed to one of the servers, Ariel leaned to her right and looked down the aisle. Heather sipped from her thermos as she rounded the corner out of sight, headed into the aisle of the primary server.

Ariel drew in a tense breath.

Her feet carried her away, taking off without her consent. She padded toward the exit like a rabbit through the brush, frightened by a predator that might have not even known she was there. As she ran, the general EMPATHY servers flitted past on her left, and on the right, those labeled with participant numbers rushed by—the patients' personal backups and connections to the primary server once EMPATHY started working for them. Legs weak, panting heavily, she cursed herself for not having worked out more since arriving on the complex.

When Ariel reached the final row of servers, she dashed for the blue steel door, the exit from the server farm. After casting it open, she had to catch it before it slammed shut behind her. Despite her effort, the sound of the latch locking into place reverberated in the hall.

Ariel wiped away the stray auburn hair that had become mired in the sweaty sheen on her brow. After a moment's rest, she pushed herself at a steady pace in the direction of the elevator.

Once inside it, she scanned the keycard Alistair had given her to head for the first floor. Her shoulders relaxed as she leaned against the back wall. She had gotten in. She had gotten out. Now all she had to do was stay quiet. Avoiding Heather was a critical part of that third and final step, but assuming M3R1 had been successful in taking a brush to the snow, Ariel figured she had little to worry about.

As she checked her pocketab for the AI's presence, Ariel admired how flawless Wyatt's plan for this stage of the study truly was. In tasking Alistair to test the work of the other Halman children and then creating an AI bound to protect Wyatt's intended goals against meddling from Alistair, Wyatt had all but guaranteed the study's success. If Ariel simply did as M3R1 told her, it seemed Alistair would be none the wiser, which would prevent conflict between the two of them, too. All of it made for a masterstroke, the kind she would need to learn from if she were to set herself up for long-term success.

The elevator slowed as a new message appeared.

>> Thank you, Ariel. You did excellent work today.

Her face brightened. "Thanks," she said. "But hopefully future missions have a lower risk of us being found out."

>> So long as you obey there will be no need for concern.

M3R1's phrasing disheartened Ariel. "Obey" seemed like a strong word for something in which she felt more of a partner than a servant. And "concern?" She opened her mouth to question the AI, but the blue light dimmed and the messaging app disappeared.

The elevator halted, its doors parting. Ariel's breathing quickened as she exited, wondering whether M3R1 was really all it had claimed to be.

Chapter Five

CHANDRA

The nurses came and went, the entire hospital wing abuzz at the news of Chandra's experience. Her own nurse interviewed her about it, then another, then another still. After an hour or so, however, it was as if some great plague swept through the hospital wing, a near silence dampening the entire floor. From down the hall, the sound of every dropped digipen and every echoey cough survived long enough to make it to her room, and after a time, the soft crinkling of her own sheets grated her amid the unsettling quiet.

"When can I leave?" Chandra said to a nurse who came to monitor her vitals.

"No one leaves until the study is complete."

"I mean when will I be able to go to my real room?" They certainly weren't housing every patient in the compound's hospital wing.

"You'll get your private housing, same as everyone else. We're just waiting for the chain of command to approve your relocation." The nurse scribbled on the surface of his pocketab. "Is there something I can get you to help you pass the time?"

A half hour later, a different nurse returned with a sketchpad and a charcoal pencil, just as Chandra had requested. If she had to be stuck here alone, she figured she may as well pass the time as best as she knew how.

Chandra flipped to a fresh page and turned the pencil over in her hand. The grit of it dusted her fingertips, the ashy powder it left behind the most real-feeling thing she had experienced since arriving at the research facility.

Before the pencil could hit the page, the words of that gossiping would-have-been patient returned to her. What if they weren't releasing her for fear EMPATHY might fry her brain? What if she already *had* been fried, that experience with the screen nothing more than a hallucination from the nanochip as it short-circuited?

Calm. She had to remain calm. Those questions were for later, for as soon as she worked up the courage to actually ask someone when they returned to check on her. After pushing those thoughts aside, she adjusted her grip on the pencil and put herself to work.

At first the lines came easily—the oval frame of her face, the curve of her chin. The dimple found its proper place, languid along the curve of her lips.

Her eyes were the most difficult. Charcoal could never match their deep, mossy green, a shade kept from Chandra for months. Behind the ear she tucked a flower, a yellow rose, drooping softly against the sepia of her skin. Then, billowing behind her, Chandra shaded the suggestions of a wispy cloud, the product of the vape pen she almost always had within arm's reach.

A choking sensation climbed in Chandra's throat. Enough. So much for keeping calm.

In the corner of the page, Chandra scrawled the name. Kyra.

"Chandra?" A nurse called from the entrance to the room.

Her eyes darted to the door as she lowered her pencil. "Yes?"

It was then she realized it wasn't a nurse at all, but rather a doctor. Instead of periwinkle scrubs, he wore a cream lab coat similar to those of the other doctors she'd seen. The robin's-egg blue of his eyes beamed a hopeful stare in her direction, and his broad frame made the room feel smaller around him.

"Do you feel well enough to stand?" he said.

Chandra closed her sketchbook and tucked it and the charcoal pencil into the front pocket of her lavender scrub-bottoms. After a pause to stretch her legs, she joined the man near the door. "Can I ask you a question?" she said, that untempered gossip clawing at her once again.

"You can." The doctor led them from the room at a brisk pace, a surprising lightness to his steps. "I hope it's a question I'm able to answer."

"I heard a rumor..." Chandra, her legs tight from the hours spent in bed, struggled to keep pace. "Well, someone said some EMPATHY chips have gone berserk and left patients in comas. Or with seizures. That kind of thing."

The doctor's eyes widened, but he quickly lowered his brow. "Do you believe every rumor you hear?"

A nonanswer. He didn't say yes, exactly, but he definitely hadn't said no, either. "It's not true, then?"

"Even if it were, I couldn't discuss other patients' health with you unless I have their consent."

Chandra nibbled at her lip. "But it's safe? What I saw earlier... it wasn't because of some sort of malfunction or—?"

The doctor looked down at her, the neatly combed blond of his hair bouncing slightly as he walked. "We're actually off to look into what you saw earlier in a bit more detail."

"So you think it's working? You're sure EMPATHY caused that vision?"

He appeared to do his best to keep a straight face, but his boyish zeal betrayed him. "Again, that's what we'll be looking into shortly." They passed a nurse's station before rounding a corner that directed them away from the hospital wing entirely.

Moments later, the two of them entered an elevator, the doctor pressing the button for the fourth floor before scanning his keycard.

A tingling sensation took Chandra's shoulders at the awkwardness of the pause in conversation. She had so many questions, but didn't know what she should or shouldn't ask. The elevator lurched into motion.

"Oh my goodness," the doctor said. "I haven't introduced myself, have I?"

Had he? Had Chandra simply forgotten? She shrugged.

"I feel terrible," he said, extending a hand. "I'm Doctor Halman."

Chandra felt her hand go clammy as she took his hand in hers. "Wait. Halman as in—?"

"Oh, heavens no," the doctor said. "That is to say, I'm not *that* Halman. I'm Peter. Wyatt is my father." He released his grip. "I suppose it's for the best if you just call me by my first name."

Chandra wiped her hand on her scrub bottoms. First name, last name—it made no difference what she called him. This man was a Halman, one of the most important people on the compound. If Peter had come for her, whatever she was about to be part of must be exceedingly important. Beyond that, Chandra realized, he might be able to answer some of her most pressing questions.

The doors to the elevator parted and Chandra let loose. "The immediate family members of patients get their own installs, don't they?"

Peter laughed to himself. "I thought you might be more curious to know where I'm taking you." He gestured for her to step from the elevator and onto what must have been a doctors-only floor. The cream lab coats walking about—and the absence of periwinkle, black, cobalt, or burgundy scrubs—suggested as much. Chandra's patient-standard lavender seemed to induce wide eyes and sidelong glances from all who passed... until they saw who accompanied her.

"I ask because installs for family members are why I'm here," Chandra said.

"Immediate family members are eligible for their own installs, yes."

"When do those start?"

Peter nodded down a broad hall with a black set of double-doors at its end before leading them in their direction. "We've only just completed installs for participants." He cleared his throat. "And my apologies, by the way, for the delay in coming to get you. Most of the staff was at a group dinner this evening. It took the hospital wing's skeleton crew some time to get in touch with me, and a bit longer for me to review their notes."

Chandra ignored his apology. "But we can start soon then? With the family installs, that is."

"That depends on a great number of factors, the first of which is making sure EMPATHY works for those who have already had it installed."

"So if it works for me we're all good?"

Peter remained silent until they arrived at the double doors at the hallway's end. He stopped and held his tablet-size pocketab to his chest. "Let's take this one step at a time." He reached for the door handle.

"It never hurts to plan, though, right?" Chandra gave him an eager look—a wrinkled forehead, a tight-lipped smile.

"Let's... well, let's get through this exam first." Peter pulled open the door. "Shall we?"

On the other side of the threshold was a room of blinding white light, a long slender table with three plastic chairs around it toward the front. Off to the right, row after row of stadium-seating ascended toward the back wall.

Chandra kept her feet in place. "Tell me there won't be that many people watching me take this exam."

Peter hung his head, though he maintained his grin. "The only chairs we're going to be filling are one for you, one for me, and one for a special guest."

She raised an eyebrow at him.

"Why don't you look for yourself?" Peter said.

Chandra craned her head into the room. There, staring into the glow of his pocketab from behind a previously unseen podium, was Wyatt Halman. A feeling of faintness took her.

Wyatt failed to notice her at first, slouching in his famous white lab coat from all the pocketab commercials. He perked up when he saw her. "Chandra, my dear. Come in, come in."

She did as he asked. Peter filed in behind her.

"And try not to look so grim!" Wyatt laughed.

"Sorry. I'm nervous is all."

"There's no need for any of that," Wyatt said. He made his way over to her and offered her his hand. She took it. "We have a short exam for you. A few questions. Nothing more."

"Put it this way," Peter said, "if you're unable to answer our questions, it will say a lot more about me and my neuroware engineers than it will about you."

They made it sound so simple, as if failure would affect them and only them; they had no idea what failure would mean for Chandra, for Kyra.

Chandra forced down a swallow. She couldn't let it get to her now. She had an exam to pass, a goal to meet.

She had an apology to make.

Chapter Six

MEREDITH

Meredith hurled the tennis ball toward the far side of the dog park where it skidded once on the browned grass before whapping into the chain-link fence. "I don't know what I expected," she said, "but part of me still can't believe it."

Brad Mellocks stepped into the late afternoon shade of the oak tree at their backs. "You didn't know better? Really?" Woodward, Meredith's aging Japanese Akita, fended off a tiny mutt near the fence line as he retrieved his ball. "Ethics issues aside, Kathy's purse strings are as tight as they've ever been. There was no way she or the board of directors would cough up four thousand ameros for an uncertain lead."

A strange world, this—one in which Brad lectured her on ethics and not the other way around, but such was the state of the industry. As the decades—and the state of journalism—had worn on her, Meredith had slowly come around to occasionally surrendering her ideals in exchange for leads like the one she'd stumbled her way into now. But even that wasn't entirely true. *No* lead had ever been like the one she now had with the Queen of Spades, and Meredith was determined to follow it.

She clapped her hands twice and whistled for Woodward to stop taunting the other dogs on his way back to her with the ball. He was surprisingly spry considering the hour; it was nearly time for him to take his kidney medication again. On most days she would've given it to him before coming to the park, but Kathy's refusal to pay QS had Meredith's mind aflutter with distracting thoughts.

"The Queen of Spades isn't an uncertain lead," she argued, turning to Brad. "We all saw the video. If we don't take advantage of the connection, *The Courier* and WVN certainly will."

Brad laughed. "Your Queen of Spades is probably selling to the highest bidder. Even if you *did* have the four grand necessary for a story, what's to stop her from selling the same story to someone else? The whole thing is a racket."

A racket? Maybe for Brad, anyway. Meredith scratched the back of her neck as she tried to remind herself why she'd invited him to take a break from work and join her here in the first place. For his pointed, critical analysis, no doubt, but his contrarian disposition was again outshining his brilliance.

Sharp as he might be, this time both he and Kathy missed the point— four thousand ameros would be an investment, not a downright loss. Everyone was covering the Gleason story. EMPATHY was their exclusive scoop.

Meredith groaned as Woodward barreled over a dog half his size. "Woodward, what has gotten into you today? Leave him alone. Come here."

Her dog, seeming to recognize *that* tone of voice, hung his head and trotted toward her.

"Think of it this way," Brad said, "since the EMPATHY well has dried up, you can come back to working on Gleason with me."

Meredith placed her hands on her hips as Woodward arrived. "Sit." He sat. "Drop it." He dropped it. "Good boy." His tail wagged, though Meredith could tell he was gassed. Last year's kidney operation hadn't exactly invigorated him in his old age. "One more throw, boy?" He rose from his sit, turning in the direction Meredith last threw the ball. "All right, go get it." She released the tennis ball into a high-arcing trajectory, glad to be relieved of the grass and grime that had clung to it.

"How's that coming by the way?" She wiped her hand on the back of her jeans. "The Gleason thing, I mean." Meredith had wanted to keep following the story on the side, but the previous day had been an exercise in refamiliarizing herself with the EMPATHY notes she had taken over the last two years. At one point she had considered tipping off Brad to the suspicious Susan Dunham emails, but in case she ended up covering Gleason again, she resolved to say nothing—another ethical faux pas, another degradation of her integrity.

"The Gleason thing?" Brad said. "Let's put it this way—it's going poorly enough that I have no idea why I agreed to leave the office and join you at the dog park."

Meredith rolled her eyes. "You needed a break and I did, too. You'll lose your mind if you don't step away once in a while."

Off near where the ball had landed, Woodward and a dinky mutt had taken to sniffing at one another rather than pursuing the ball. The mutt's owner was trying to leash him, but Woodward seemed intent on preventing her from doing so.

"Ugh," Meredith said. "We should probably get going. I need to give Woodward his meds and I owe Kathy two hundred words on the EMPATHY video." She whistled for Woodward to return.

"At least you'll be working from home." There was a pause, a shift in his tone. "Oh no. No way."

"What's that?"

He glowered at his pocketab. "Alicia Melendez at *The Courier*. You ever meet her?"

"Once, I think, at the TJA dinner."

He passed her his pocketab. "Dead. Found this morning in her home."

"What?" Meredith expanded the device. "She had to be—"

"Thirty-four." Brad leaned back against the trunk of the tree. "Investigation is ongoing, but the way it's written suggests a suicide."

"Jesus," Meredith said. "That's... I don't know what to say." It was terrible news to hear anyone in the community passed away, but Alicia Melendez? A suicide? Last Meredith had heard, Alicia was up for a Hewlitzer for the investigation that led to the Merry Hacksters disseminating Gleason's emails in the first place. Things seemed like they were going incredibly well for her. Meredith covered her mouth with her hand, wondering how many others might be suffering silently, the success a shroud for something darker beneath it all.

Brad took his pocketab back and reduced its size. "Well, one thing we can say for sure is *The Courier* will be hiring."

There he was, the loathsome opportunist. Meredith might have committed a faux pas or two in recent days, but at least hers had been with good reason.

The two of them said their goodbyes not long afterward, and some fifteen minutes later Meredith pulled into her driveway. The crisp spring air of suburban Austin greeted her as the sound of a city bus roared in the distance. An older neighborhood, Meredith always loved twisting her way through its winding streets of modest ranch homes, each lawn patched in dull green and brown from the recent drought.

The tags on Woodward's collar jangled as she unlocked her front door with her pocketab. She had about a half hour to get Kathy the two hundred words she requested—well, that chairman of the board Chang-hoon Lee requested—in order to publish the video the Queen of Spades had given them the previous day. Meredith didn't exactly appreciate the candor with which Kathy informed her of the chairman's refusal to pay the Queen for a story, but there was little she could do about that.

Human/Etech still hadn't returned any requests for comment, either. But why would they? Maybe Halman figured ignoring Meredith's attempts to reach out would undercut the video's credibility—as if it could possibly be in doubt, anyway.

After refilling Woodward's water bowl and making sure he got his medication, Meredith attached her keyboard to her pocketab and propped it up on the kitchen counter. She watched the video again.

Two hundred words? With all that was said and unsaid in the video, Meredith was sure she could have written a lifetime's worth of stories.

It was then the idea possessed her, swift as some stealthy poltergeist.

"Where is this damn—here it is." She opened her most recent email from the Queen of Spades—the one in which she made her four-thousand-amero demand—and navigated to the attachment. Expecting simple instructions on how to do a wire transfer to the Queen of Spades' account, what she saw instead left her brain feeling as though it had been scrambled.

CRYPTOCOIN CURRENCY CONVERSION
"If it ain't crypto, it ain't hip, yo."

Meredith had heard of cryptocurrencies of course—Bytecoin, Memecoin, even the adult film industry allegedly had its own cryptocurrency to keep payer-recipient information private—but Cryptocoin made her wary.

Aside from its transparent name, the document's tagline left her uneasy as well. It ain't hip, yo? What kind of amateurs was she dealing with? Regardless of her reservations, she knew she would have to act quickly. She had twenty minutes to either get Kathy that story or get something tangible from QS. After poring over the instructions on how to convert ameros to cryptocoins, she navigated to her account information on her bank's website.

She gnawed at the nails on her left hand. With only around four thousand four hundred ameros in savings, converting four thousand of them—nearly ten percent of her yearly pay—into an unheard of cryptocurrency was ill-advised. Hoping a stranger on the internet would keep up their end of the deal in exchange for them was downright dangerous.

Meredith pressed her palms onto the counter. How could she justify taking that risk? What if Woodward's medication costs increased? What if the *Star-Globe* cut her salary again, or worse—what if it had to close its doors entirely?

But what if she didn't take this chance? The Gleason story was all fine and well, but EMPATHY? That was the career-maker. Besides, if she could write an article that created a great enough uptick in web traffic, the *Star-Globe* would certainly pay her back. They would want more stories, wouldn't they?

She nabbed her pocketab, swiping, typing, and checking the necessary boxes as she converted the bulk of her savings to cryptocoins. All the while, a vexing inconsistency pricked at her. She had spent her whole career at least *trying* to play by the rules, by waiting for the right story to come along. Now, with the right story only a few minutes away, was she really going to shelve all ethical consideration? She huffed. EMPATHY couldn't be passed up. The ethicists could be damned this time around.

Within minutes she turned four thousand ameros into more than seventeen thousand cryptocoins. She followed the Queen of Spades' instructions to forward them to her encrypted account before jumping back into her email and firing one off to QS.

It was only then that reality's claws mauled her with the truth of the gamble she had taken. She read the time from her pocketab. There were still two minutes before Kathy's deadline, which meant she had twelve minutes before she could expect a call from her predictably caustic editor.

Five minutes passed, then ten. Try as she might to focus on cobbling together two hundred words, Meredith ended up checking her email more often than she managed to type a word. After another unfruitful check of her inbox, Meredith cursed.

Woodward lay napping on the floor near her feet. "I think Mommy ruined everything. I think—"

Her pocketab rang to life. Meredith almost knocked it from the counter as she reached for it.

But it wasn't an email, no. A call. From Kathy. Meredith shrank her device and answered.

"Hey," she said. "Sorry I—"

"Send me whatever you have. I'll tweak it if necessary, but at this point we really have to get this thing done."

"I don't have much. I actually—"

"Don't have much?" Meredith had to hold the pocketab away from her ear. "I can't believe what I'm hearing. From my *senior reporter*? I—"

Kathy ranted on, but Meredith blocked her out. Her pocketab had vibrated. Her eyes widened when she saw who the email was from.

To: "Meredith Maxwell"

From: <WITHHELD>

Subject: Re: Human/Etech—EMPATHY Study

You like me. You really like me. *swoon*

See attached.

-Q♠

Meredith's jaw loosened as she downloaded the file. Despite its size, the download rallied to a quick finish. The folder contained—no, it couldn't be—a few hundred files? A document labeled SUMMARY.WRD seemed the most prudent place to start. She tapped the file open with the tip of her finger.

HUMAN/ETECH EMPATHY STUDY SUMMARY

1,061 PATIENTS ADMITTED

908 SUCCESSFUL INSTALL OPERATIONS

ZERO PATIENTS WITH CERENET ACCESS TO DATE

attached: install schedules, employee application materials, participant profiles, various photos

Kathy's wrath boiled on as Meredith reread the Queen of Spades' summary. "You still expect me to stick up for you? You still expect—?"

"I'll call you back." Meredith hung up, the silence beatific. She expanded her pocketab and dove into the files.

She fanned herself at the quantity of information. If she were to put any sort of story together, she'd need help organizing all she had just acquired. She called Alvin, talking as she typed.

"Hello?"

"Alvin, it's Mer. Are you at the office?"

"I went home to walk Finster. Why?"

Meredith strangled an invisible person at her side. "Can you turn your walk into a run? I heard back from QS. I need your help sorting through photos. Work on this from home once you're back. You have my permission."

"That is so meme."

"I don't know what that means and I refuse to respond to it." Meredith emailed copies of the photos she had received over to Alvin. "When you get home, I need you to look through the photos I sent you and pick out the ones that best show 'hope in a time of despair.' Or maybe 'despair in a time of hope.' I don't know. Either one. Hope and despair. Play them off each other."

"Despair? Did something happen at the compound?"

"No, nothing's happened at the compound. EMPATHY isn't working for anyone. That's what the article is going to be about."

"Damn. I bet The Mustache is pissed."

"That's not the point. Can you get me some photos in forty-five minutes? Ten ought to do it."

"Yeah, I can probably—"

"Don't probably. Please just do it. Thank you." Meredith thumbed the END CALL button. She cracked her knuckles before scooping her pocketab from the counter and heading for the couch. If she were going to crank out her goal of a quality thousand-word article in the next forty-five minutes, she'd need to get comfortable.

As she made her way to the living room, Meredith granted herself a heartbeat-long moment of celebration. The bulk of the work still lay ahead, but Meredith had taken a gamble and won. She needed a queen to complete her royal flush, and it was a queen she had drawn from the deck—assuming that made sense, anyway. Until now, she had never been much of a gambler.

Once forty-five minutes and one thousand words had come and gone, Meredith checked her email. Alvin had not only sent her a selection of photos, but he'd done so ten minutes before the deadline. Meredith nodded as she examined his selected shots, attaching each to an email that included her story.

Alvin hadn't done too shabby of a job. One photo showed a number of participants looking up at Wyatt Halman as he spoke from atop one of those cafeteria-style tables—not unlike in the video. Another one, much smaller in its scope, depicted an older woman in an off-white lab coat staring at the tiled floor of a broad hallway as she walked. Her lab coat fluttered behind her, creating a sense of urgency. A third photo was shot in a wide-set, darkened room littered with television screens, dozens of participants seated or standing as they watched what seemed to be one of Halman's sons—Alistair, judging by his dark hair—give a speech from a stage somewhere.

The other photos gave a sample of the compound's apparently diverse environments—one was even shot outdoors on a trail disappearing into a dense plot of trees—but the one thing each photo had in common was the presence of numerous bald heads. Meredith figured whoever the Queen of Spades might have been, she was either tasked with working very closely with patients or a patient herself. Meredith made a note to keep that in mind when considering the kind of information she asked for in the future.

She dialed Kathy after forwarding her the draft article, ready to boast of the spoils of her hunt.

Kathy was not expecting good news, apparently. "So now you call me back?"

"Check your email."

"It's a little late for those two hundred words. Chang-hoon is demanding I publish the video without your commentary. That's a missed opportunity for you, Mer. Having your name in that byline would have been—"

"Check. Your. Email."

"Excuse me?"

Meredith kept quiet. She heard Kathy tapping at the screen of her pocketab on the other end of the line.

"What is this?" Kathy said. "Did you—? Is this from—?"

"The Queen of Spades, yes. There are photos attached, too. Alvin helped me—"

"You got a response from the Queen of Spades and didn't tell me?"

"You were a little distracted at the time, saying something about how I was useless. I didn't want to interrupt."

The dig did not seem to faze Kathy. "This looks great. You've made a story out of a 'nothing to report' situation, which is something." Meredith ignored the noncompliment as Kathy continued. "I'm going to give this a few read-throughs and call you back with edits as soon as I can." The call ended abruptly as it had begun.

A tedious quiet consumed her home. Meredith called to Woodward, whose claws clacked across the linoleum as he found his way from the kitchen to the living room.

"Want to come sit by Mommy?" She patted her hand on the couch cushion to her left.

He leaped and curled up next to her, his tongue lolling as he leaned in for a rub behind the ears. Judging by his reaction, being on the couch was an honor on par with a state dinner.

"Oh, look at you," Meredith said. "You've wanted this attention all day, haven't you? Is that why you were so naughty at the park?"

Her pocketab rang. She answered immediately. "All right. What do you have for edits?"

"You got screwed, Meredith," Kathy said.

She must have not heard correctly. "Screwed? How is something of this magnitude possibly 'getting screwed?'"

"The story broke before we could get it out. Someone else had the same information as you."

Meredith felt her skin tingle. "How? Who? *The Courier*?"

"Some C-list blog. It looks like the Queen of Spades' sale of information wasn't as exclusive as you thought."

So Brad was right. She abandoned Woodward, standing and pacing before leaning against the sill of the open window that looked out into her backyard. Kathy buzzed on in her ear, crickets chirped, and the setting of the sun had started to paint the sky with colors of violence—blood reds and bruising purples.

The opportunity EMPATHY promised wasn't just a story, but something much more a part of her. Losing its exclusivity felt as though an organ had been removed, one she could live without, but without which life would never be the same. She felt its absence in her gut, the operation having ended and the anesthetic worn off earlier than expected. As the acid rose in her stomach, Meredith managed two words. "Which blog?"

"I'll send you the link," Kathy said. "When you come in tomorrow, I want you to meet with Brad and get caught up on whatever progress he's made on the scandal."

"Please send the link." Despondent, Meredith placed her pocketab on the window sill and rubbed her temples.

When her device chirped, Meredith swiped at it three times to get to the link Kathy had forwarded.

> More formally known as the Electronic Mechanism Purposed for the Achievement of a Truly Hybrid Yield (EMPATHY), the device improves upon its predecessor CompASSION by allowing users to both send and receive data over wireless networks....

Hot fury pumped through her veins. The text of the author's post, far less sophisticated than her own, contained but one detail previously unknown to the public at large: that EMPATHY still had not taken hold for a single participant. And the selection of photos accompanying the post? Those were unmistakable.

She stepped outside to make the call. Once it connected, she spoke immediately. "I know whose blog this is."

"And what good does that do us?" Kathy said. "The information is already out there."

"It is, but it's because Alvin was apparently just as foolish as you always suspected."

"That's *Alvin*'s blog? How did he—?!"

"I sent him the photos the Queen of Spades gave me so he could sort through them as I wrote. It was the quickest way to get the story together under the circumstances."

Meredith permitted another long minute of one of Kathy's tantrums, every expletive-laden moment focused on Alvin's duplicitous stupidity. When Kathy seemed to have tired herself out, Meredith interjected. "I think I know how to get out from under this. After you've taken a minute to breathe, do you think you can call Alvin into an 'emergency meeting' at HQ tonight?"

"Why the fuck would I want to meet with him tonight?"

"To fire him. The meeting is an excuse—"

"Oh. Yeah."

"Maybe give yourself more than a minute to breathe before calling. I'm going to put together a press release we'll put out after he's been let go. There's a way we can play this. It's damage control, but there's a way out."

"I sure hope so, Meredith. You really can't afford another embarrassment."

Kathy had the truth of it. After forking over four thousand ameros for a story that would now have diminished returns, getting the *Star-Globe* to reimburse her seemed less likely than ever before. Embarrassment wasn't the only thing she couldn't afford.

Chapter Seven

CHANDRA

Chandra's footsteps echoed off the walls as she approached the table at the front of the room, each step heavier than the last. She felt as though she were bound and brought before a jury that would decide her fate, the pit in her stomach deepening as she realized that wasn't all that far from the truth.

Wyatt offered her a seat opposite himself and Peter at the small table. "I can't begin to describe my excitement when Peter told me we may have finally had a breakthrough," he said. Chandra sat as the two men snagged their pocketabs from their pockets and enlarged them to tablet size. Wyatt raised a finger. "I suppose I'm getting ahead of myself, but this exam should determine exactly what kind of breakthrough may or may not have occurred." He adjusted his lab coat to hang more loosely on his shoulders. "Now, no pressure if you don't think you know an answer. We're interested in best guesses, too. Understood?"

Chandra nodded, her palms dewy.

Wyatt looked down at his pocketab. A lifetime passed before he spoke. "Question one—are you comfortable?"

Chandra twisted her head to the side. "Am I what?"

Wyatt snickered. "A joke. I want to make sure you're comfortable. You seem tense."

Take a deep breath, she told herself. All was fine—or could be, anyway. "Yes, I'm comfortable. Don't worry."

"Wonderful," Wyatt said. "Now onto the real questions." After a few pokes on his pocketab, he cleared his throat. "What is your name?"

"Chandra."

"I'll need your full name for the sake of recording the exam."

"My name is Chandra Amritha Adelhadeo." Chandra picked at her scar.

Wyatt caught her in the act. She lowered her hand.

Peter spoke next. "Your age please?"

"Twenty-six." Seriously? Were these the questions they needed to be asking?

The reflection in Wyatt's gold-rimmed glasses showed him scrolling to the next question. "Who is the current North American Chief Executive?"

"Monica Gleason."

Wyatt typed away.

Peter followed up. "In what city are we now?"

"Austin. Or, well, somewhere outside it."

Peter typed.

"In what year was the amero introduced?" Wyatt said.

Chandra recalled the last time she had held United States dollars in her hand, the green grit of it on the tips of her fingers. That had been a handful of years ago—but how many? Nervousness clouded her memory. "I want to say 2023."

Wyatt entered the answer on his device, but neither Wyatt nor Peter gave any hint as to whether she was correct.

Chandra scowled as she looked to Peter for the next question. Wyatt spoke instead. "Who won the 1943 World Series?"

"What?"

He looked down his nose at her. "Who won the 1943 World Series?"

"I have no idea."

Wyatt rested his pocketab on his lap. "Guess, if you must."

Chandra eyed her scrub bottoms, the wrinkles in the lavender running north-to-south down her legs. She wracked her brain for any number of team names, but none came. As she shrugged, however, an answer exploded from her. "The New York Yankees." Her neck stiffened at the confidence with which she'd said it.

Wyatt remained expressionless. "And who lost that series?"

A knowingness crept up Chandra's shoulders. Even if it had been a lucky guess, the confidence pumping through her made her feel as though she must have been correct. Guessing who lost the series, though... how could she have any idea?

Again her fingers found her scar. Think of a team. Any other team. "The Saint Louis Cardinals." The same sureness rifled through her.

Wyatt nodded for Peter to proceed.

"Labaro is a suburb of which city?" Peter said.

"Rome." The words bolted from her, a near involuntary response.

"Which state has the only nonrectangular flag?" Wyatt said.

Were those even allowed? There can't be—"Ohio."

Wyatt made notes on his pocketab.

Chandra swiveled toward Peter. "What is the German word for 'badger?'"

She had to laugh. Chandra had minored in French and learned a little Hindi from her mother, but German? That was *plus facile à dire qu'à faire.* "What was the word again?"

"Badger."

She responded with a series of sarcastic-sounding gibberish.

Both of the Halmans laughed before Wyatt said, "Very nice, Chandra. But a real answer, please."

Chandra closed her eyes. A floating feeling took her as the word appeared in front of her, just as the screen had the previous day. "*Dachs.*"

Again, neither Wyatt nor Peter reacted to her answer.

Wyatt scanned his screen's contents. "Now I'm going to read an excerpt from a poem. I'd like you to tell me the name of the poem, as well as the name of the poet. We know this may take longer to look up, so please take your time."

Look up? There was a way she could look this stuff up? Almost everything she had said to this point had just popped into her brain. Chandra coiled her fingers around the edges of her chair's seat. What if this was the real test—making sure she could not merely use, but *control* her use of EMPATHY? If she couldn't get this right, would that mean she failed despite everything else? The blood bolted from her legs at the thought.

Wyatt read from his pocketab.

"*... drawn by the promise of imminent light,*
we lose ourselves in the eternal dawn—
the bridge between ourselves and that which we might become."

"Wow," Chandra said.

"Like I mentioned," Wyatt said, "this may take time to look up, so please don't—"

"Oh, no," Chandra said. "I know who wrote it." She had focused on the words, each one alone, then together. After a second's delay, the answer was delivered to her on what appeared to be a web browser in her mind's eye. "It's a lovely poem is all."

Wyatt raised his eyebrows. His son did the same. They exchanged a look.

"R. B. S. Alaska is the writer," Chandra said. "The poem is 'Ages Upon Us, of Us.'" She paused and took in the information on the screen she had summoned. "Looks like he wrote a few novels in the early part of the century as well."

Both took to recording their thoughts on their pocketabs.

After another ten minutes and many more questions, both Wyatt and Peter appeared satisfied. Wyatt held his pocketab to his chest as he stood. "Thank you, Chandra. I have one last simple test for you."

She bowed her head. Get on with it, she thought. Get on with it and let me ask when this can happen for Kyra.

"Remember the screen you described having seen earlier? The one you could type or write on?"

"Of course."

"I want you to envision that screen once more, if you can." He turned his pocketab around, its display facing Chandra. "Once you've recalled it, send a message to this address."

Chandra's eyes opened further. "That's a simple test?"

Peter intervened. "Simple is relative, but think about it. Would you have believed us twenty minutes ago if we had told you that you could recite the words of Shakespeare, mentally solve complex equations, or tell us who won the 1943 World Series?"

"Does that mean I got all of that right?" Chandra said.

"A perfect score." Wyatt swiped at his device.

The gravity of the moment returned the feeling to her legs.

Peter urged her onward. "Just think of the screen and send Wyatt a message."

Chandra's jaw hung loose, lips parted. "What would you like me to say, Doctor?"

"Anything you'd like. Anything at all. And please, call me Wyatt."

Chandra closed her eyes. With little effort this time, Chandra pixelated the screen into the forefront of her consciousness, her brain tingling as she focused on it. Just like before, the cursor blinked in the corner like the pulse of some digital heart. Moments later, her message trickled across the screen. She focused on her memory of the email address she had seen on Wyatt's pocketab and, after a moment, felt as though something left her.

The screen disappeared. Chandra opened her eyes.

She saw the grin on Wyatt's face—one that seemed to have become stuck there. He looked down to his pocketab and read the message aloud. "Wyatt, your shoe is untied. Best regards, Chandra."

Peter peered at the pocketab in his father's hands. Wyatt looked at his feet.

Both of them laughed in disbelief.

Wyatt turned to Peter. "Well it's no 'What hath God wrought?' or 'One small step for man,' but it will have to do." He knelt and reworked his laces.

"Doctor, er, Wyatt," Chandra said. "What does this mean?"

"Chandra," Wyatt said, righting himself and extending his hand to her. "Welcome to the cerenet."

Glee electrified her fingertips. "It worked? It really worked?"

Peter exhaled. "Yes."

"You seem to have cerenet connectivity, at least," Wyatt said.

Chandra felt as though she'd crossed the finish line in a marathon of emotional upheaval. She knew, however, this moment was a mere checkpoint. "When will it begin working for others?" She rocketed to her feet. "When can my wife have her install?"

"Ah." Wyatt set his eyes to the floor a moment. "I wanted to speak with you about that."

His shift in tone spiraled Chandra's spirits downward.

"After reviewing your file this morning," Wyatt continued, "I put a great deal of thought into your motivation for participation in this study. Very admirable. Astounding, really."

"Thank you." She said it at quarter-volume. Something about the way Wyatt spoke had drained all enthusiasm from her.

"Considering your wife's case, I thought to myself, 'How can we make the most out of this terrible situation?' I felt the answer was, 'Assure others of the good that can come from EMPATHY. Assure them that connection to the cerenet can have long-lasting impacts, including in the field of medicine.'"

"Are you saying this will work for her? Are you saying that with it, I'll be able to speak with her again?"

Wyatt paused for longer than Chandra would have liked. "There would be no guarantee of that. Peter, nor his team, nor I have done any testing in that realm."

Peter, hands behind his back, nodded with a cynical expression about him.

"What EMPATHY *could* do for your wife would be to assist with matters of memory, for example, once she has recovered from her coma. But to think—"

"Couldn't you try?" Panic surged through her, her vision blurring at the edges, her mouth dry. "What if I gave you permission? I could do that, right? You could give Kyra an install and—"

Peter stepped in. "We have hundreds of participants on-site for whom EMPATHY hasn't yet taken. You are the first for whom it has worked. Maybe someday we could attempt to help your wife in that specific capacity, but that might be years away."

"Kyra doesn't have years." The tears welled in her eyes—anger, frustration, and sadness forcing them out.

"That's not for us to know," Wyatt said. "Neither Peter nor I are familiar with the particulars of her situation."

Peter retreated to the podium a few yards away. Wyatt removed himself from behind the table and crossed to Chandra. He slid his device away before interlocking his fingers in front of himself.

Chandra thumbed away tears from each eye. Nothing. It had all been for nothing. She stared at the floor, wanting to bound from the room, to run and never stop, to cast herself from a fourth-floor window if it meant an end to the anguish consuming her.

"Thank you, Peter," Wyatt said. Chandra heard him take something from his son before Wyatt offered her a tissue. She grabbed it, dotting beneath her eyes before wiping her nose. "No one likes to bear bad news, but I felt it was important we be honest with you as soon as we were able. Even if we're unable to help Kyra, I want you to think of the good you could do for others whose lives EMPATHY could improve."

A hiccup escaped. "Me? Look at me. I can hardly help myself." Chandra forced down a laugh, surprised at her own reaction. Was she losing her mind? She was worried she'd begun to understand the madness that might lead someone to remove an ear.

"You can help yourself, Chandra," Wyatt said. "And even if you feel like you can't, Alistair and Peter and I and all the others—we can help you with whatever you need. We only ask one thing in return."

"What's that?"

"We want you to be the face of EMPATHY."

The sour cocktail of elation, grief, and surprise left Chandra with no inkling of how to respond. She went with the first thing that came to mind. "I suppose that's better than its butt."

Peter and Wyatt erupted with laughter. As the two doctors calmed, Chandra spoke up. "What would that mean, exactly—being 'the face' of EMPATHY?"

Wyatt caught his breath before responding. "We'd ask you to participate in promotional events with responsibilities like interviews and photo shoots. You'd be taking a prominent role representing EMPATHY in the media."

"You should really choose someone else."

"But your story gives you credibility," Wyatt said. "More than a face, your participation would give a heart to our entire program for assisting adversely affected populations. It has to be you."

"It can't be me," Chandra said. "I'm like deathly peanut-allergy adverse to speaking in public."

Wyatt took a step forward. "We'll pay for all of Kyra's medical bills. Past and future."

The offer floored her. Chandra had depleted her meager savings long ago, and Kyra's parents had already taken a second mortgage out on their home. Compensation from the study may have been fantastic—especially compared to the zero-salary life of a grad student—but even that would fail to pay off the debt accumulating in Chandra's absence.

"Take a day to think on it, if you'd like," Wyatt said. "I'm sure all this testing has left you rather tired. Besides, I believe some celebration is in order."

"It is," Peter said, "but we'd still like some time to monitor your egodrive's cerenet connectivity over the course of the next twelve hours before you tell anyone of your success. If you can, try to—"

Peter continued talking, encouraging her to refine her search skills as she explored the cerenet and the other features of the EMPATHY interface. While he went on, though, Wyatt's offer distracted her. How could she say no? Confronting her fear of the limelight was nothing considering what she would receive in return... but, then again, payments for medical bills weren't the reason she enrolled.

Chandra knew what she had to do. "I'll do it," she said.

Peter leaned forward. "What was that?"

"I'll be the face of EMPATHY—on one condition."

The brief jubilation they displayed shifted to consternation. "And what, might I ask, is your condition?" Wyatt's voice had become laced with venom.

"I want you to research whether EMPATHY can work for those in comas. Not years from now. Not when this study is over. I want you to look into it now."

Peter leaped in to intervene. "Our engineers are already thinly stretched as it is, and—"

"All right," Wyatt said.

"All right?" Peter and Chandra said it simultaneously.

Wyatt fingered his mustache. "We'll do the research, but only if you satisfy two of *our* conditions."

Chandra curled her toes.

"We're going to need your absolute cooperation as the face of this technology," Wyatt said. "We won't have time to negotiate the finer points of messaging or how we choose to take the product to market. You will have no say in that regard. Is that clear?"

"What's the second condition?"

"Even if Peter and his team are able to find a way to test for this, and even if we do manage to test for it on a reasonable timeline, I need to know you're committed to sticking with the promotional program even if the results come back negative. We won't be investing in this research if we won't be guaranteed some sort of return on it."

"Yes," Chandra said. "Whatever you need, I'm in." She would have agreed to his conditions if Wyatt had told her she needed to light herself aflame and tap-dance her way across a tightrope. So long as there was hope for Kyra, there was hope for her, too.

"Wonderful," Wyatt said.

"Doctor Halman," Peter protested. "Our engineers don't have the bandwidth—"

Wyatt put a hand on his son's shoulder. "We will find the bandwidth. We always do. Now, would you be so kind as to escort Chandra to her new room on the first floor?"

Peter raised a finger. "Shouldn't Alistair's team—?"

"Please, Peter," Wyatt said. "Your cooperation in this is greatly appreciated." His tone remained light, though he said it through his teeth. Wyatt wasn't to be questioned, apparently.

Peter drooped his head. "If you wouldn't mind following me..."

Chandra kept herself a few feet behind him as they walked. Neither of them spoke, the last hour apparently leaving both of them equally awestruck. At one point, Peter did mention she should reach out if she had any questions, but the highs and lows of the previous day had left Chandra numb to all but two questions.

How soon would the Halmans have an answer on whether EMPATHY could work for Kyra? And the face of EMPATHY—what had she gotten herself into?

Chapter Eight

WYATT

It burned in the veins of Wyatt's forearms, tightened the cords of his neck. Rage.

The call from Lars came mere hours after Chandra's exam, spoiling what had been an otherwise delightful day—the first since the study had begun, if Wyatt were honest with himself.

He had summoned Heather to his office immediately upon receiving the news, doing little but grinding his teeth until she finally arrived.

Dark bags sagged under her eyes, her dyed hair—a rebuke of the shimmering blonde her mother had left her—a disheveled nest. Predictable as ever, her thermos accompanied her.

"What the hell happened?" Wyatt's voice was deep, gruff. "I'm glad you had time to make coffee before getting here."

"I barely had time to read the blog and review the photos on the way over. I'm still trying to figure it out. I—"

"Good. I'm glad you're still trying to figure out how to provide this study with the most basic security. Fantastic." Wyatt Halman had never been more disappointed in his daughter. "Close the door."

She did so with her posture stooped before lowering herself into the seat across from him, her bangs shielding her eyes.

The unexpected summons had left her shaken, it seemed. Wyatt would have to change his tone. An anxiety-ridden daughter would not produce the effort he needed from her.

"Heather." He smoothed his voice out at the edges.

"Yes?" She brushed her hair aside.

His heart melted at the tears in the corners of her eyes. Tempting as it was to soften completely, a conversation this grave had to be treated with an appropriate degree of severity. "Let's start with this—what do you know?"

Heather drew an uncertain breath between her teeth.

"Was this the result of some external threat?" Wyatt said. "Foreign agents? The Merry Hacksters? The NAU?" Though the last of these was likely the source of the leak, this was no time to let confirmation bias take hold.

"After releasing all those Gleason emails," Heather said, "the Hacksters moved on to targeting First Union Bank. They've been too busy to harass us lately. They took a shot at our pocketab network a few weeks ago, but our firewall seemed to bounce it back without any issue."

Seemed to bounce it back? That was uncertainty Wyatt would not have normally tolerated, especially where the Hacksters were concerned. They had been nothing but trouble throughout the Union as of late, taking defense systems offline and interrupting broadcasts of the NAU's official news network, which they saw as nothing short of shameless propaganda. Wyatt may have privately supported such an assault on the NAU, but given the fickle nature of the hacking collective's targets, he knew the moment he applauded them they might decide to turn on him.

Still, he let it go. The Hacksters' attacks on Gleason followed by a pivot to First Union made them seem far more focused on political targets than private ones for now.

"And where attacks from government entities are concerned," Heather said, "we've seen nothing our standard security hasn't been able to rebuff."

"If not the Hacksters, the Union, or the Federation," Wyatt said, "then who? It couldn't possibly be an internal leak." He nestled a digipen between his teeth to keep from clenching them.

"We've seen no anomalies from patients using computers in the lab."

He removed the pen. "It wasn't a patient, then?"

"Not one using the computer lab, no."

"So it was a member of the staff?" Had the NAU really managed to buy off a staff member? Full betrayal.

"I'm sure even my assistant would agree given the blog hints at having proprietary materials." Heather took a long sip from her thermos.

Proprietary materials. Wyatt's blood congealed at the thought. Considering he left no data on astium on any hard drive or network anywhere, he should have felt reassured no hacker could ever thieve it from him. Regardless, he bristled as he darted his eyes to his desk's lower-left drawer where he'd locked away the safe. Even the shortest-lived consideration someone aside from his children might gain access—which would only happen upon his death—was enough to increase his blood pressure. The safe's paper files on astium and EMPATHY's use of it would allow them to carry on his legacy long after he was gone. For now, though, that secret remained best kept with him. His children's biosignatures would unlock the safe when the time came, and, despite his occasional trepidation, in the most self-assured recesses of his mind, he knew he needed not fret the possibility of anyone gaining undue access. The safe had been designed to perfectly accommodate the dimensions of the files stored within, and any attempt to force it open would lead to the immediate destruction of its contents. Had it been a bit much to indicate this on the outside of the safe? Possibly, but pesky thoughts—those of any one of his would-be mourning children carelessly attempting to pry it open and, by extension, erasing the family's legacy—had pecked at him relentlessly until he applied the label to the safe's façade.

"Realistically," Heather said, "that a staff member was behind the leak is the only option left on the table. If we follow the assumption that an internal source is responsible, I'd want to start with a scan of email and texts between employees."

And why, exactly, hadn't she already started that process? Wyatt blunted his displeasure. "How long would a scan take?"

"I could have preliminary results in twenty-four hours, but even then they would only cover written communication."

He bit the tip of his digipen. "The transfer of the photos had to leave some sort of digital trail. Even so, staff pocketabs only communicate with other on-site devices—save for those approved by me, of course." That left his own pocketab or his lawyer's as possibilities, and Lars had little reason to upend the study.

Heather hid behind another sip. "This wouldn't account for the photos, but there's the, uh, matter of the landline phones in each office."

Wyatt's breath caught in his throat. "I told Alistair those were a mistake."

"And I agreed wholeheartedly."

A white-hot iron of wrath pierced his chest as he recalled the conversation he and Alistair had during the design phase of the study.

"If you want to attract the best talent, you'll need to make sure they have opportunities to speak to their families once in a while," Alistair had said. "With your suggested pocketab jamming, landline phones might be the only way to let people talk to the outside."

"The best talent follows the money."

"Relationships matter. Money isn't everything to some people." Alistair had looked him dead in the eye as he said it. The words had stung even worse in light of the real reason behind the study, behind EMPATHY.

For a flash, Wyatt found himself thinking of Eva, of what she would do were she still with them. He discarded the thought. There was a crisis to resolve before he could let her memory take hold.

Wyatt eyed Heather again. "I want all communication with the outside cut, including incoming broadcast media. The landlines are to be disconnected immediately."

"Alistair would argue we'll have a riot on our hands. Rescinding the ability for staff to have contact with their families—"

"Is exactly what we must do to prevent further leaks." He would have no protests. Not now. "I'd also like for you to arrange a series of interviews. Anyone with access to install schedules, compound blueprints, and application materials is to be questioned regarding the contents of their landline conversations since their arrival on the compound. Seize their pocketabs for inspection, too. They can have replacements assuming you and Candace find nothing on their original devices that would have allowed them to leak those photos."

"Just to play devil's advocate—or Alistair again in this case—"

"In *any* case," Wyatt said. For as proud as Alistair often made him where matters of persuasion were concerned, he often lacked in discretion and, in far too many instances, common sense. The spitting image of his father at that age, he supposed.

"Right." Heather cleared her throat. "I'm sure he'd say something along the lines of 'cutting people off from their families and then interrogating them will only breed further mistrust.' Seizing pocketabs is a harsh measure. Alistair would probably question whether you have the right—"

Wyatt lashed out. "I have the right. I am the right. You and Alistair want to debate rights? You want to play politics? I hear the NAU could use some new blood." He found himself standing over his daughter.

She held her hands in front of her, a defensive gesture. "I was only making the argument so you're better prepared when—"

"Yes. Right. I'm sorry." He pulled at the lapels of his lab coat before returning to his seat. Losing control like this was so unlike him, but Chandra's story, her request—both had taken him places he hadn't expected to go emotionally, places he hadn't visited in years. "How soon can you start the interviews?"

Heather drew a sip from her thermos. "As soon as I can assemble a list of individuals with the levels of access you described. I'll also need their call logs compiled if I'm to have targeted lines of questioning."

"So by tomorrow morning?"

Heather adjusted her glasses. "In the interest of assuring each interview is worth the time invested, I'd hope for a couple of days to—"

"One day. Interviews are to start tomorrow afternoon." Wyatt brushed his mustache with his forefinger. He may have backed off his brutishness earlier, but that didn't mean he shouldn't be stern now. "This has to be treated with the utmost urgency. I will not tolerate any further leaks."

His daughter folded her hands on her lap. The hum of the air conditioning took the room. After a time, she nodded—barely.

Wyatt's chair squeaked as it slid out from underneath him. "Good. I'll keep an eye out for your reports. You may go." He buttoned his coat.

Now on her feet, Heather collected her thermos from Wyatt's desk. As she reached the door, however, she paused. "I think Alistair may be right."

Wyatt couldn't keep an eyebrow from raising.

"I understand the need for security better than anyone, but I think if we implement severe measures, they'll have an adverse effect on the people we work with. I'm not convinced—"

Wyatt scoffed. "Good thing you being convinced isn't a requirement for action."

In that moment, melancholy gripped his daughter—the slight dilation of her pupils, the pouting of her lip. He could have sworn she even shook her head before opening the door and stepping halfway through it. Before exiting, however, she stopped and turned, her eyes meeting his own.

"Please don't forget what this is about." She released a deep breath. "I love you, Dad." She slipped through the door. It closed behind her.

Don't forget what this is about. How could he? And what did Heather presume to know about the real reason any of them were here? The only people who knew that were Wyatt and—no, he still dared not think of her.

Wyatt peered out the window looking down into the courtyard, his eyes following the orange glow of the artificial lighting that illuminated the paths in the arboretum. The leaves shivered and a bough from a great oak bobbed in the wind.

"I love you, Dad," she had said, though as more of a question than a statement. But perhaps he was misremembering, distorting his daughter's tone. His heart anchored in his gut as he tried to remember the last time she had told him that.

The branch of the oak bowed once more as the memory washed over him. It was at the cabin in Minnesota. Heather was missing a tooth then. He had stood with her shin-deep in the crisp water, sand and mud seeping between his toes. Heather swayed at his side, fishing pole in hand, a small-mouth bass wriggling out of the water, still hooked to her line.

"Daddy! It's gross. Unhook it." Heather swung the pole in her hand, the fish flailing in Wyatt's direction.

"Whoa, settle down." He laughed and took the pole from her.

Heather watched, hands on knees, as Wyatt attempted to unhook the fish from the line.

"Does it hurt?" Heather said.

"Taking out the hook?" It had really stuck itself in there. "I'm sure it doesn't feel good."

"Then stop! Don't hurt the fish."

"We have to take it out, Heather," Wyatt said. "I'm sure it hurts, but it'll hurt even more if we don't." The hook refused to remove itself from the bass' jaw. "Sometimes we have to hurt someone a little bit to keep them from hurting more later on." Wyatt jerked the line and the fish bled, a trickle of red running from its mouth and onto Wyatt's palm. In apparent pain, the fish flailed again, this time at just the perfect angle to release itself from the line. Wyatt dropped the creature back into the water. It swam away, listless.

"Is the fish gonna be okay, Daddy?"

No. It will die within the hour. "Yes, I think he'll be okay."

Heather wrapped her arms around his waist. "Thank you, Daddy. I love you."

The memory evaporated and Wyatt found himself staring absently at his desk. How long ago that must have been... Peter is how old now? Forty-four? Then Heather is forty-one....

He shook his head. Wyatt was only a few years away. Once EMPATHY was up and running, he would turn his legacy over to his children, he himself then managing only matters pertaining to astium. They'd be busy, yes, but hopefully they'd have some time for their semi-retired father—assuming he was ever able to truly step away. Given the recent incompetence his children had displayed, Wyatt wondered if it really had been in his best interest to trust his legacy to them and them alone. Each of them had been afforded the best education available, along with access to more resources than most could ever dream of. Still, nepotism did tend to breed complacency and entitlement. Of that, there could be no doubt.

Wyatt tapped the fingers of his right hand on his desk, those of his left gripping tight to the leather armrest of his chair. Would he ever be able to tell all three of them why he really did this? For the improvement of society, yes, and for all the reasons he cited in public and more. But he had made a promise to Eva decades ago, one that would not let him rest until he had fulfilled it.

Thoughts of Chandra and her wife prodded him. Eerie. The similarities raised the hair on his arms. Wyatt had waited more than thirty years for his answer. Surely Chandra could manage a few more months, if not years. Perhaps that was too cold of him, though—would he not have jumped at the chance to be reunited with Eva mere years after she had been taken from him? If he could now give to Chandra what he had never been able to give himself...

He reached for his pocketab.

Peter answered on the third ring. "Hello?"

"That experiment Chandra proposed earlier—"

"Right to business, I see."

Wyatt ignored him. "How feasible do you think it would be?"

"Like I was trying to say earlier, time is a finite resource—"

"I've been on this planet longer than you have. You can save me your lectures on time."

Peter sighed. "It wouldn't be impossible to test for the sort of thing Chandra is asking for, but I'd like a few days to bounce ideas off Gary before we commit to anything."

"Don't think you're not committed. You're committed, all right, and sooner than you might realize." His son had no response for that, apparently. Wyatt pressed on. "It shouldn't be difficult, really. All Chandra's wife would need is an external power source for EMPATHY, something to compensate for her brain's diminished electrical activity." At least that was how Wyatt had drawn it up for Eva years ago.

"That's actually the path I thought I'd pursue."

Atta boy. Wyatt withheld his praise. "Then take a day to work something out with Gary. I'll schedule some time to discuss your proposal shortly thereafter."

Wyatt ended the call before Peter could protest. All the pieces were in motion now. Heather would stop the leaks to the press, Peter would find a way to resolve the matter of Wyatt's—er, Chandra's predicament—and Alistair would go about ensuring patients and staff remained in good spirits despite the slower than anticipated start to the study.

It all sounded wonderful, that was for certain. If only Wyatt were confident they could pull it off as he'd conceived it.

Chapter Nine

MEREDITH

It had taken far more time to find an actually functioning camera around the *Star-Globe* offices than it did to secure the interview. As the North American Union's most-watched morning talk show, *La Vista* provided the perfect platform for a softball back-and-forth that would allow Meredith to divert attention from Alvin's blog to the *Star-Globe*'s story.

She may have only been remoting in to the set, but even that was enough to induce acid reflux. She popped another antacid as she stared into the camera in front of her, a monitor to its side casting her own image back at her. Light purple bags hung beneath her eyes, her thin blonde hair up in a small bun. Errant hairs stuck out from it, but there was little time to fix them before her segment started after the commercial break.

Meredith scowled, too, at the backdrop Kathy had forced on her. She would have much preferred a window at her back, but Kathy felt showing the interior of Meredith's office would show "how hard at work" everyone at the *Star-Globe* was.

The depth of Kathy's insecurity really did mystify Meredith sometimes.

"And we're back," said a voice in Meredith's earpiece—Janet Barry, the host of *La Vista*. Applause from the in-studio audience welcomed viewers back to the show.

Though Meredith was sure her image was still not being broadcasted live, instinct led her to straighten.

Janet returned to Meredith's earpiece, her tone one of cringe-worthy uptalk. "Next up on the NAU's favorite morning show, we're joined by two guests—one with a number of questions and another with hopefully as many answers—regarding last night's breaking news from the Halmans' secretive EMPATHY compound."

Meredith's knees bounced. Two guests? She'd understood Janet was doing the interview. Meredith snuck in a clearing of her throat before the host could go on.

"Joining us live in studio for this segment is WVN's own Rénald Dupont, host of *Newsnight with Rénald Dupont*."

The acid surged in Meredith's esophagus.

"Ren and his team have been working for years to get anything out of those tight-lipped Halmans," Janet said, "so we're sure he'll have a lot to ask of our guest today. Ren, thanks for being with us."

The image on the monitor flashed from Meredith's own to that of the network's live feed, the colorful, couch-ridden set of *La Vista* nearly searing her retinas. Janet sported a red dress that made it look as though she and the chair on which she sat were one. Rénald Dupont, seated off to her right, wore a blue suit and white collared shirt with a straight black tie, a crisp contrast to the yellow, overgrown armchair he occupied. His black mustache was as thick as it had ever been, and the deep brown of his bald head reflected the light overhead. The angle of the shot wasn't the most flattering, but he remained handsome and genial-looking for a man his age.

Meredith caught herself nibbling at a nail before she snapped her hand away. No matter how genial Ren might have looked, with him joining them, the interview could quickly turn from softball to hardball.

"Thank you for having me." Ren's voice was rich, and with only a hint of his native Quebecois accent.

"No," Janet said, "thanks to you for taking the time away from your *Newsnight* prep to join us."

"It's nice to have a quick break. Despite its name, *Newsnight* is an all-day project."

A few in the *La Vista* crowd chuckled politely, its host doing the same. "Surely," she said. "But we're pleased you could be here."

Pleased? Honored was more like it. Ren had hosted *Newsnight* for Meredith's entire life—or as long as she could remember, anyway. She always imagined she would one day sit in his chair, or at least she had until the day-to-day realities of a career in "print" eroded the aspirations of her youth.

"Also joining us for this segment," Janet said, "is Meredith Maxwell of the Austin *Star-Globe*."

If such a thing were possible, Meredith further straightened her spine. She plastered on her best smile but held back enough to lessen the appearance of the crow's feet near her eyes. "Thanks for the invite."

"Meredith," Ren said, the broadcast image now a split screen of him at his post and Meredith in her office. "First of all, I want to congratulate you on this story."

Not a bad start. "Thank you. That means a lot coming from you." Meredith avoided clenching her teeth at the giddiness with which she said it. You're a professional, she told herself. Act like it. Be prepared for the curveball.

Ren brushed aside the compliment. "Now, I have to ask—some are accusing you and the *Star-Globe* of riding the coattails of a blogger who posted a story similar to yours only an hour before yours made it to your home page. What can you tell us about that?"

She shifted in her seat. "The blogger who published the piece in question had a working relationship with us. The post he published was actually a draft of the story later released through the *Star-Globe* site."

"The blogger in question *had* a working relationship with you? Are we to understand he has since been removed from his position?"

Removed was an understatement. If Kathy had had a pitchfork on hand when she and Meredith sat down with him, Meredith was sure she would have driven it through his heart. And given the sobbing with which Alvin reacted to his dismissal, one would have thought he had actually been mortally wounded.

"I'm in no position to comment on matters of employment at the *Star-Globe*," Meredith said. "What I can tell you is that this story is the product of years of digging behind the scenes, and is only the first of what I'm sure will be many articles regarding EMPATHY."

"This idea there will be more stories forthcoming—are viewers to understand the anonymous source you cite in your first article will continue to work with you?"

God, she hoped so. Before Meredith could respond, Ren barraged her with follow-ups.

"Can you give us any information regarding this source? What are their credentials? Are they on the compound?"

Meredith wouldn't be tricked that easily. "I was fortunate to receive enough material for a few stories. As for my source, I'm afraid I can't divulge that information."

"I thought I had you there for a second." The in-studio audience laughed, Ren's own smile wide. "Well, if you can, tell us what we can expect going forward."

Her heartburn dissipated. Ren had backed down, it seemed, the open-ended question an invitation to shape the story as she liked. Without a concrete idea of what she might find as she waded deeper into her source material, however, Meredith remained vague. After a couple of minutes' discussion, the host from *La Vista* intervened.

"And I'll have to hop in here. It's time for a break. Thank you, both, for joining us this morning."

Ren, ever graceful, responded as he did at the end of any segment. "Thank you and be well."

Though Meredith felt as though her pulse should be slowing, adrenaline still had its hold on her. "Thank you. I, uh…" She watched the monitor in horror as confusion marred the host's face. Even Rénald appeared bamboozled, his caterpillar eyebrows mushing together in the middle.

Say something or hope they cut to break. Say something or—"I want to, if I may…" Meredith dislodged something from her throat. "I want to congratulate you, Ren, on your upcoming retirement from *Newsnight*. The show won't be the same without you, but WVN will be in good hands with you as network president."

A pause ensued. Had Meredith been disconnected from the feed? Had they already cut her mic?

In the moment before the host started her pre-break bump, Meredith could have sworn she heard Ren say thank you.

When her connection to *La Vista*'s feed cut out, Meredith relaxed her posture, the tension leaving her in one gargantuan wave.

"Good," Kathy said from outside her door. "Nice."

"Oh." Meredith spun around. "I'm glad you think I did all right."

Kathy rested her shoulder on the doorframe, arms crossed. "Well, except for the oh-my-God-look-at-my-professional-crush stumble at the end."

"Don't tell me you wouldn't trade your firstborn for the career he's had."

Kathy stepped into Meredith's office. "My firstborn moved to Detroit to pursue a career as a DJ. Last I heard, he was washing dishes at a restaurant on the verge of going out of business."

Meredith had to look away to keep herself from rolling her eyes.

Kathy put herself opposite Meredith and extended her pocketab in Meredith's direction. "I thought you should know we got this treasure from Human/Etech today."

Meredith took Kathy's pocketab and read its screen. "A cease and desist?"

Kathy took her device back. "They're trying to claim we're putting proprietary information at risk—as if that would stop us. News is news."

Meredith was grateful they were in agreement on that, at least.

"What I'm really here to discuss are the tough personnel moments we've had lately," Kathy said.

"We did what we had to do," Meredith said. "Alvin's actions were unacceptable. I think—"

"I'm not talking about Alvin," Kathy said. "I'm talking about Brad."

"Brad?"

"He quit this morning. Walked right into my office and resigned effective immediately. He'd talked to Mr. Lee about it first, apparently, as if the chairman of the board of directors even knew who he was."

There wasn't enough antacid in the world for the surge that rocketed into Meredith's throat. Brad's disgruntlement was well known, but Meredith would have never expected him to drop everything with no notice.

"Did he say why?" Meredith said.

"WVN. *The Courier.* Something about an opening after the unpleasantness with Alicia Melendez."

The bastard. Meredith resisted the urge to release a snort of exasperation. What this might mean for her own career now? "Don't even think—"

"I need you to take over the Gleason story again."

"We just had a breakthrough on EMPATHY! Are you seriously shutting it down now?"

Kathy let Meredith's desk support her. "Shut it down? Absolutely not. I'm having the materials distributed among some of the part-time staff. They'll take over EMPATHY while you get back to sorting through those emails the Hacksters dug up."

"I'm off EMPATHY? After years of work, I finally have a breakthrough and—"

"You did well," Kathy said. "Web traffic is up six hundred percent since your story made it to the front page, but the vulture blogs and aggregators have already picked it up. Six hundred percent will probably be our peak. It's great, but not enough to—"

"Not enough to let your senior reporter stick with it? This is our exclusive. My exclusive. You'd rather have me toil on a story every other outlet in the Union is covering?"

"This isn't about want. It's about need. You're the most experienced person—"

Meredith shot to her feet. "I was the most experienced person *before* Brad quit."

"Right, but Brad was the only other individual around here capable of leading a team. You're all I've got now."

"It's not just me," Meredith said. "EMPATHY is all you've got—all we've got—to claw our way back into a reasonable market share. Do you even realize what I had to do to get the information I got?"

"Your job?"

Meredith's ears went hot. "Four thousand ameros," she said. "Four thousand ameros of my own savings had to be forked over in exchange for that story, for all of those documents."

"Your willingness to make that sacrifice is proof of how dedicated you are to our goals. Thank you."

"Sacrifice? Are you saying if I put that on my expense report—?"

Kathy scoffed. "I understand the position you're in, Mer. I do. But you have to understand where I'm coming from. We've lost a junior reporter—and the board doesn't seem inclined to hire a replacement—and you still somehow expect me to shake four thousand ameros from the amero tree?"

"Wait." Meredith put her middle and forefingers on her temples. "You're not going to replace him?"

"The money isn't there, Meredith. Like I said, all the leaves have fallen from the amero tree, blown away in the wind."

"Then how do you expect to pay for future stories from the Queen of Spades? She doesn't come free, you know."

"We'll take advantage of marginal returns." Kathy looked past Meredith, seemingly thinking out loud. "We can get by if we release stories over time based on the material we already have. I'll ask the board of directors to allocate revenue from those stories to buy additional ones going forward."

"But you won't ask that I be reimbursed for putting myself on the line for this paper?"

"Again, your choice. Maybe at the end of the year when bonuses—"

"Go," Meredith said.

"Excuse me?"

"Leave my office." Meredith took in a measured breath. "I have work to do if I'm going to get caught up on this Gleason stuff."

Kathy's lips thinned, her eyes wrought with fire. "Send me any and all correspondence you have with the Queen of Spades. The team will need it." She stopped at the door before she opened it. "And the next time you speak to me like that, you'll be lucky if you still have a job." She slammed the door behind her.

"And you'll be lucky to have a senior reporter in two weeks." Meredith lowered herself back into her seat, trembling. It was impossible, she knew, to put in a notice of resignation without any job prospects on the horizon. She couldn't afford to take time off between jobs either—especially not now—and being away from the only career she had ever known would perhaps be the worst of all.

She could always break away for freelance work with QS in tow—except any work she had cobbled together while at the *Star-Globe* would be company property. A protracted court battle was something she no longer had the means for either.

Meredith seethed as she opened the Gleason files Kathy had forwarded her. It had only been a couple of days since her removal from the case, but Brad had made sizable progress in wading through the emails. Still, nothing in his notes suggested he had even begun to consider that Susan Dunham character Meredith had such a strong feeling about. She had started reconciling her old notes with Brad's updates when she realized she hadn't yet forwarded Kathy any emails between herself and the Queen of Spades.

Once Meredith had them grouped in one attachment, she looked away as she fingered the send button. Then, in a separate email—just to make sure she protected her own interests—she forwarded the messages to her personal account, too.

The day wore on with little progress on the Gleason front. Hours later, as she reached into her purse for her pocketab to unlock her home, she noticed a small white piece of paper in the shrubs to the right of her door.

Oh, come on. There had been enough wayward litter in the neighborhood lately. The last thing she wanted was for it to become tangled amid the shrubs on either side of her stoop. Reaching for the paper, however, its true shape came into view—an envelope.

She rose from a crouch, turning it over in her hands. Unmarked but sealed, the envelope had a weight to it suggesting something thicker than a letter.

Meredith slipped a thumb beneath the envelope's flap, sliding left-to-right with enough care to avoid its sharp edge. Her eyes widened as she flipped through its contents—twenty blue, two-hundred-amero bills.

Her heartbeat throbbed in her neck as she dropped the envelope into her purse.

Try as she might to explain away the envelope's appearance as a gift from someone with knowledge of the situation, the only possible suspects were Alvin or Kathy. Fresh out of school, Meredith imagined Alvin had neither the resources nor the wherewithal to attempt this sort of apology, and Kathy, well—her lack of compassion over the course of years had spoken for itself. That left Meredith with one conclusion. She swallowed hard at the thought of it.

Opening her front door to the chirp of the crickets, Meredith slipped inside. Once the door closed behind her, however, not even Woodward's excited greeting could ease her concern.

Someone was watching her.

Chapter Ten

ARIEL

When Alistair summoned Ariel to his on-campus apartment, her stomach turned itself inside out. Heather had probably discovered M3R1 on her pocketab after she seized it, compromising her—well, Alistair's—operation and condemning her employment to an early end. With any luck, Alistair was simply planning to give her advance notice of her upcoming dismissal.

She supposed if she were fired there'd be no need to endure what would surely be a grilling from Heather about her off-compound communications—not that she had anything to hide given she'd made only maybe three calls since her arrival on the compound a couple of months back, each of those conversations brief and uninspiring exchanges with her mom in Arizona. Still, the thought of being one-on-one in a room with Heather was... well, she didn't dare think of how that'd make her feel.

As she stepped off the tram that had carried her to the employee housing, her new pocketab shifted in her breast pocket. She winced at the urge to verify whether M3R1 had finally appeared on it. If it had, perhaps it could reassure her all was well before her meeting with Alistair even started. After a moment's pause, she surrendered to the feeling and checked her pocketab.

Nothing.

She chewed at the inside of her cheek as she traversed the crest of a hill, Alistair's building now in sight.

Once inside and on the top floor, the hallway leading to his apartment underwhelmed her. She had expected a grandiose entrance for the Halmans' floor, but its well-lit, forest-green-carpeted halls were identical to her own building. She exhaled sharply before knocking on his door.

The pinprick of light shining through the peephole blinked and the door swept open not a moment later. "Oh," Ariel said.

"Oh?"

"I was expecting you to be in your lab coat for some reason."

The shoulders of his mauve T-shirt wrinkled as he shrugged, and he scratched at his taut, clean-shaven jawline before motioning for her to enter.

Unlike the hallway, the flair of Alistair's apartment was exactly the kind of thing Ariel expected.

The living room had the same standard-issue faux wood flooring of all the apartments, but he had covered the center with a gray rug that had a texture just short of shag. The couches—one full and one love seat—were wine red, arranged in a near-L that framed two sides of the rug. The end tables that completed the L—as well as the coffee table in the center of the rug—had similar glass tabletops resting on black steel supports. Along the wall to her right loomed three bookshelves, thick with colorful spines ranging from technical manuals to contemporary fiction. One title stood out from the rest.

"*Flowers for Algernon*," Ariel said. "I love this book." She pulled it from between a musty hardcover on twentieth-century computational theory and a mystery novel. "This was one of my favorites in high school." Ariel thumbed through it, scanning the text as it flew past. Surely she'd have plenty of time to reread her copy back at home once Alistair told her she'd been fired.

"Ariel," Alistair said, apparently uninterested in small talk. "EMPATHY started working for a patient yesterday."

The book slipped from her fingers. So this *wasn't* about Heather discovering M3R1. In fact, it may as well have been just the opposite; perhaps M3R1 and Wyatt's modifications at the primary server led to the breakthrough in the first place. "That's great."

"That's where I disagree." His expression went grim. "Can you sit for a minute?" He ran a hand through his tousled brown hair.

"Wait. What do you—?"

"I'll explain." He gestured to the love seat before seating himself kitty-corner from her on the couch.

Ariel lowered herself onto the leather. She hugged a throw pillow as she leaned against the couch back. "How could it possibly be a bad thing for EMPATHY to have started working?"

"How do I put it?" His eyes hit the copy of *Flowers for Algernon* on the coffee table between them. "Imagine you're Charlie. I'm sure you've done it before."

Ariel kept her lips zipped.

"What you have in *Flowers for Algernon* is a man with a severe cognitive disability, one who, with the help of the best science available, becomes one of the greatest intellectual minds on the planet."

"I know the story, Alistair. You don't need to—"

"I only draw the comparison because my father intends to do the same with EMPATHY."

She couldn't help but laugh. "If you're worried EMPATHY is going to begin working only for it to cause the same crash-and-burn that happened to Charlie in the book, I'd say that's pretty wild speculation."

"It would be wild speculation only if I intended EMPATHY to work in the first place."

A chilling sense of foreboding crept up Ariel's spine. She hugged the pillow that much harder. "I think EMPATHY's functionality has more to do with Peter and Gary's work than yours."

His eyes went adrift as he loosed a sigh. "There is no double-blindness to the study. The code I had you upload... it wasn't part of some new phase of the experiment, and it wasn't intended to test Heather or Peter, though it certainly will."

Or would have. M3R1 had overridden whatever Alistair had hoped to achieve, and it'd done so with Ariel's help. Wyatt Halman's genius was truly something to marvel at, she thought; had he not designed M3R1 to keep a check on Alistair, his son's scheme might have succeeded.

All the same, what reason could Alistair possibly have to contradict the will of his father? Curiosity inched her forward.

"I plan—or planned, really," Alistair said, "to stop EMPATHY from functioning for anyone for the duration of the study. I'd succeeded to this point, but now—"

"The whole point of EMPATHY is to bring people together," Ariel said. "It could change the very foundation of our society for the better. Why is that something you'd want to put an early end to?" The heat between her and the throw pillow warmed her just enough to lower the blonde hairs that had risen on her arms.

Alistair stood and walked toward the window, his hands on his hips. "Even my ideologue of a father knows EMPATHY can't possibly accomplish half of what he hopes it will. The product could work fine, sure, but it will tear us apart more than anything."

"Absolutely not." Ariel got to her feet and hurled the pillow back onto the couch. "If people have access to the same information, have the same capacity for memory, and have the ability to communicate across languages and cultures and vast distances all at the same time, there's no way it could do anything but create actual empathy between everyone on the planet."

"You certainly have the talking points down." He faced Ariel, his Adam's apple rising and falling as he swallowed. "But even if it did help everyone on the planet—which it won't—it would create a greater rift in the long run than anything."

Ariel wrinkled her brow.

"EMPATHY will only be available in the North American Union." Alistair approached her, each step as thoughtful as the last. "It was the only way Wyatt could get clearance for the study to proceed. Because of Union concerns about weaponization in international markets, he surrendered what he believed would have been true, worldwide empathy. Agreeing to sell only to NAU citizens let him get government approval to deny patients some rights—including the ability to terminate their participation at any time."

A disappointment, for sure. The very idea of a geographic limitation to EMPATHY ran contrary to one of the study's chief goals, but it wasn't worth sabotaging the study over. "Even if that's the case, EMPATHY would still have a net benefit for NAU citizens. It'd give us a leg up on the rest of the world, yeah, but that wouldn't be the worst thing given the last decade."

Alistair made a dismissive gesture with his left hand. "That would only be true if each and every citizen had access to EMPATHY, another impossibility. How affordable do you think EMPATHY is going to be? Anyone who wants it is signing up for voluntary brain surgery. And even if it were affordable, the option of selecting from one of three install tiers will create a further divide between haves and have-nots, even in the upper-most echelons of society."

Ariel looked away. He wasn't wrong, at least if what he was saying could be believed. "So you've decided to just undermine the project completely? Have you considered reasoning with your dad?"

Alistair laughed. "He doesn't take well to dissenting opinions."

"You haven't even spoken with him?"

"I have. He dismissed my concerns outright." A sadness lit his eyes. "The worst part about it is I could see it on his face. He knew I was right, but there's some madness pushing him onward—egotism, maybe. I suppose EMPATHY *would* cement his legacy."

Alistair's position was madness, but it appeared there was no convincing him. "You know your dad better than I do."

A quiet thoughtfulness consumed him. When he broke it, his words came as no surprise. "I'm going to need your help."

Of course he would need to rope her in, too. Not that it mattered—whatever he asked of her would have no impact once M3R1 was put back into the equation. By cooperating with the AI, Ariel could do no harm... assuming M3R1 ever found its way back to her. "What do you need from me?"

Alistair shined with a charisma to which even Ariel couldn't help but feel drawn. "If we're going to keep EMPATHY from working for others, I'm going to need some additional programming power."

Had he even read her transcripts as part of the interview process? "Programming was never my forte," she said. "I think you'll want—"

"Someone else, yes. A participant, actually."

She must have misheard. "What makes you think a participant would want to work against the very reason they're here?"

"It isn't a matter of whether he will. He already is."

"This is a test, right? Is this about my allegiance to the study or something?"

Alistair tsk-tsked. "Don't be so paranoid. Everything I've told you in this conversation is the truth."

In this conversation. What a qualifier that was. "How did you possibly convince a participant to ensure the failure of the very thing he's on campus for?"

A cocksure grin spread across Alistair's face. "He doesn't know. The (h)ARMONY syntax I've taught him is valid, but when it comes to functions—well, let's say I've taught those incorrectly."

"So he thinks he's doing A but is actually doing B?"

"C—as in 'correct.' Once he completes his portions of the code, I run them through some corrective algorithms I've developed and we get an end-product in line with what I'm trying to achieve—like the code you uploaded during the banquet."

This was real. It had to be. Still, she pressed him. "So you spent all that time creating corrective algorithms for the EMPATHY programming language but don't have the time to write actual (h)ARMONY code yourself?"

"The algorithms are simple. They recognize key strings of code and replace them with preprogrammed inputs."

Devious. So devious. Still, Wyatt and M3R1 would save her—save the study—in the end. For now, she played nice. "If it works like you claim it does, that's actually pretty clever."

"I thought as much, too." His cream lab coat lay crumpled in the corner of his couch. He reached into the coat's breast pocket, and when he turned to face her, he revealed a security keycard. "Participant T-1719. I'll need you to take this to his room." Alistair handed over the card. "His assistance working remotely from the lab has been invaluable to date, but I'll need to work with him more closely going forward. At 10:00 a.m. on Friday, you'll need to escort him to a private programming room I'll have reserved. I'd do it myself, but, you know, degrees of separation and all that."

She tucked away the keycard for safekeeping, her nerves running hot. "Why does he need a card to meet with you? I already have one to get us through security."

"He'll need one to start programming after hours. I don't want him doing it in the lab anymore. Too risky."

"Why not give him the keycard after I've brought him to the reserved room?"

"It's a token of trust. It'll get him to come with you," Alistair said. "He's used to me coming for him, after all. Plus, I want him to know the change in plans doesn't have anything to do with his performance. The keycard will show him I still have confidence in him, that I'm serious about this."

That still sounded more cockamamie than necessary, but Alistair hadn't accepted much in the way of criticism so far.

"Also," he said, "I have this for you." From the pocket of his jeans, he slid out a small bottle of eyedrops.

"I don't think I understand." She kept her hands at her side.

"You know," he said, "for the bioscans at the server farm? Did you really not get the message on that?"

She threw her hands in the air. Alistair could be real condescending for a guy who needed favors all the time. "Obviously not."

"New security measures. It's part of this whole clamp-down on possible sources for the leak. Only Wyatt, Heather, Candace, Peter, and Gary have access to the primary server now."

"That could be a bit of a problem."

He extended his hand toward her again. "A drop in each eye will allow you to bypass the bioscans once you get to the server farm. Patient T-1719 has already helped me with a patch I've sent to that W-USB of ours, and I need you to upload its contents as soon as possible. Make sure you check the maintenance schedule though first. Oh, and again—be sure to use the additional keycard I gave you—not your own—when approaching and entering the server farm."

Hm. If he still wanted her to use the secret keycard he'd given her for the first round of uploads, then it had to be in the name of one of those who still had access to the server farm. Her nostrils flared at the thought of anyone on that list having to take the fall for Alistair's misgivings about the study.

Well, except Heather. If he pinned this all on her, Ariel wouldn't exactly be heartbroken. Though if she did have to guess, she figured Alistair registered the secret keycard under either Candace or Gary. As Heather's and Peter's assistants, respectively, surely Alistair would prefer to risk their hides as opposed to those of either of his half-siblings.

But with Alistair, she supposed, there was never really any way to know for sure.

Regardless, Ariel snatched the eyedrops from him. She'd need them to assist M3R1 once—if—it returned to her pocketab. If it didn't show up in the next few hours, she considered she may have to go to Wyatt directly; it might become the only way to help him avert a disaster not even he could have seen coming.

"How do these work?" She kept the bottle of eyedrops faceup in her palm. "Where did you get them?"

His face suggested she shouldn't have asked either question. Alistair indulged her anyway. "The drops are proprietary. The retina scanner Heather had installed at the server farm accepts fuzzy matches for people with glaucoma or cataracts."

"Wait—these will give me glaucoma?"

Alistair covered his face with his hand. "No. The keycard you have specifically for server farm access is set up in the name of someone who *does* have glaucoma. The eyedrops are set to interact with the eyes in such a way that retinal input becomes obscured to the point of a fuzzy match for the person in question."

Another clue. Did either Candace or Gary have glaucoma? She thought to investigate later until she realized perhaps it was for the best she didn't know who she'd be betraying by using that second card of hers. Besides, it's not like it would matter once—if—M3R1 overrode Alistair's programmed shenanigans.

Ariel tucked the bottle of eyedrops into the pocket of her scrub bottoms. "All right. I'll get T-1719 everything he needs."

"And upload the code?"

"And upload the code."

"Good." Alistair put his hand on the doorknob. "And remember—10:00 a.m. on Friday. I need him at that time that morning." He opened the door.

She stepped into the hall and, after the door latched shut behind her, leaned against it, her heart racing with excitement—and dread. Now that she knew Alistair's endgame for this participant, Ariel was more confident than ever in her purpose, working with M3R1 against the two of them to secure the success of the study.

As she took off down the hall, she checked her pocketab for the AI, turning her device off and on again in a desperate attempt to summon the only covert defense the study had against Alistair's machinations.

Chapter Eleven

CHANDRA

It took hardly less than a day for the news to domino its way across the compound, one rumor toppling into another toppling into the next.

"I heard she can move things with her mind."

"Apparently they're keeping her locked up in the hospital wing. Like an animal, yeah. And they're running all sorts of tests on her."

"They had to install a second chip to get it to work, apparently. I know, right? So be ready for another surgery. I'm serious."

Chandra couldn't help but grin at it all, most of the gossip as comical as it was outlandish. It gave her some reprieve from plaguing thoughts of the rumors she heard when she first awoke, too. If the myths that had spread about her were so off-base, then surely the whispers of comas and seizures were just as exaggerated.

Now, seated by her lonesome at one of the cafeteria's long, mess-hall-like tables, she clenched her jaw as she mulled over how soon she could get a real answer to that question, still kicking herself for not having confronted Wyatt about the rumors directly when she had the chance.

"Is anyone sitting here?" a young man's voice said.

Two lavender-clad patients stood across from her, both holding gray, plastic cafeteria trays of their own. The one who had spoken—his dark, black hair long enough to suggest he'd had his install months ago—cocked his head to the side. Through his black-framed glasses, he narrowed his eyes as if he recognized her somehow.

Chandra glanced away, avoiding his stare. "No," she said. "I'm not expecting anyone else."

He threw himself onto the bench across the table, but the woman who accompanied him placed a hand on his shoulder. "Are you sure it's okay if we join you? We don't want to interrupt your..." She gestured to the sketchpad.

"No," Chandra said. "It's okay, really." If she were honest, she'd forgotten she'd been sketching at all. She slid her sketchbook aside and pulled her tray back in front of herself.

"Was that a drawing of the arboretum?" the woman said, gesturing to the place where the sketchbook had been.

"Yeah, I love it there."

"Outdoors. Gross," the young man said. He had to be among the younger patients Chandra had seen since arriving, hardly cracking nineteen years old, if that. "I'd rather be in the computer lab," he added.

"Well, I for one," the woman said, "love the arboretum. And your drawing looked great." Her shoulders rolled forward as she smiled. "I'm Sylvia."

Chandra dipped her head. "Chandra."

"Ty," the man said before immediately going on. "So are you like... *the* Chandra?"

Her appetite for what remained of her breakfast faded. Of all the rumor-mongers Chandra had overheard, none of them seemed to know her name or what she looked like; in light of Peter's request, it's not like she'd been the one blabbing about her experience. That this Ty apparently had some knowledge of her had her hands hugging one another on her lap beneath the table.

"I'm *a* Chandra, yes."

He leaned forward, his brow wrinkling as he spoke. "What's it like? Have you been able to master the GUI? Is the internet less censored here once you connect to it through EMPATHY?"

Sylvia put a hand over his mouth. "He's not exactly a charm-school graduate."

Ty shot Sylvia a side-long glance. "Sorry, I guess." He paused for only a second before taking a breath and returning to his questions. "But you're her? You're the Chandra whose EMPATHY is working?"

Chandra let her gaze fall to Sylvia, who had to be only a few years younger than herself. Sylvia crinkled her buttony nose Chandra's way, the anticipation seemingly too much even for her.

"I didn't know there was a Chandra whose EMPATHY is working," Chandra said.

Ty frowned before taking a huge bite from his blueberry muffin. As he lowered it, Chandra noticed a tattoo on the back of his left hand. Aside from being a clear outline of the state of Texas, the cube poking out from the state's northeast invoked some strange familiarity. Somewhere in the distance, the cadence of a snare drum tap-tap-tapped in a steady march.

"I take it you're an artist?" Sylvia said.

Chandra attempted to shake off the sound of the snare drum tapping about the back of her mind. "Yeah. I was working toward my MFA in painting before I dropped out to enroll in the study." A half-truth, but a truth nonetheless.

"That's great," Sylvia said. "I got my Bachelor's in Art History, actually."

"Oh, really? When did you graduate?" Chandra tried to focus, but whistling woodwinds now accompanied the snare drum beating inside her head. An entire choir called out.

"Oh, the yellow rose of Texas, it's her I yearn to see—"

Sylvia seemed to notice something was wrong but pressed on anyway. "A few months ago. I'm actually holding some informal ceramics classes on the compound if you think you'd like to be part of those. I'm sure Art and Supply has everything you'd need to paint, too."

Chandra heard Sylvia, but the ensemble roaring in her head pulled her full attention away from the table. The music was alongside her, behind her, inside her. A dizziness took her, her attention returning to Ty's tattoo.

"It's true my eyes do miss her, she fills me so with glee—"

"That sounds... nice," Chandra said.

"Is something wrong? Your eyes look all, uh, glassy," Sylvia said.

Ty stopped chewing a moment, each of his hands now resting flat on the table. "She *is* the one. I knew it. She's having—it's gotta be some sort of EMPATHY-related vision. That's what it is, isn't it? Am I right? Am I right?"

Chandra opened her mouth as the chorus bellowed on.

"She cried so when I left her that it like to broke my heart—"

The spinning of the room worsened. Chandra clutched to the side of the table for support.

"Ty," Sylvia said. "Stop. Chandra—"

The room fell away. Was this it? Was she about to seize, to wind up like Kyra on the far side of this dizzy spell? She felt herself stepping backward, balance failing her.

"And if I ever find her, we never more will part."

A cry rang out from the far side of the cafeteria. The lightheadedness left her, the sudden silence in her mind more alarming than the music's arrival.

Ty and Sylvia threw themselves to their feet, their attention cast in the direction of the commotion.

Someone called for help, the sound of sneakers squeaking on tile following the cry. Chandra felt as though she should have to stand, should have to peer over the crowd to get a sense of what had happened, but she didn't have to. She could *feel* it. "Someone else gained cerenet access."

Ty spun to face her. "What do you mean?"

It was as if the name of whoever had connected was on the tip of her tongue, known but somehow withheld from her at the same time. "I *am* that Chandra," she said. "And I've got to go. I have to tell a doctor about that feeling, the song."

Ty shouted after her as a nurse hustled toward where the patient had fainted, a side effect Chandra must have avoided during her own connectivity event. Before Ty could catch her, Chandra had darted from the cafeteria and headed against the current of patients angling for a better view.

A half hour later, Chandra was alone with Peter in an exam room of the hospital wing. "This is quite the turn of events," he said, eager as ever. He performed no tests, no scans. He merely asked questions and logged responses on his pocketab as fast as he could manage. "I'll be curious as to whether you continue to have this—what did you call it?"

"Knowing," Chandra said. "It was the same as when you have a word or a name or an answer you can kind of see in your head, but your brain won't fully give it to you."

His tongue stuck out the corner of his lip as he typed, his pocketab's clip-on keyboard chattering with a stenographer's intensity. "If I had to guess, that feeling will dissipate incrementally over time, perhaps decreasing after each first connectivity event."

"And what about the song?"

His fingers stopped flying. He scratched at the side of his head his digipen, his eyes fixed to the screen. "You're sure you didn't just have a song stuck in your head?"

"I've never heard that song before." Chandra let her legs swing a bit as she dangled them from the exam-room table.

"Do you recall the tune? The words to it at all?"

"It's like it's all there but not, same as that patient's name."

"I wonder..." Peter leaned onto an elbow at the counter where he'd set himself up, sliding his finger with fury across the screen of his pocketab.

"You know what's an awful feeling? When you know you have a file sitting on a drive somewhere, but you can't quite find it." He looked up and winked.

So that was it. If Peter was right, the name of the patient, that song—both were being sent to her over the cerenet, but Chandra simply hadn't mastered it well enough to recall or access the information in its entirety.

"You need to practice more often," Peter said. "Keep making use of the search feature and trying out the various apps. And, perhaps most importantly, keep your chin up. I think you'll be amazed at how fast you adjust. Our brains are rather elastic, even if that can be a bit freaky sometimes."

Freaky was right. She may have now had an explanation for receiving the name of the patient when they connected, but that Ty's tattoo had triggered hearing that song still disturbed her.

Peter made for the door. "Well, if there's nothing else—"

"Actually, Doctor—"

Peter stopped with his hand on the door. "Please do call me Peter, really."

"Peter, right." She nearly asked about Ty and the tattoo, but a more pressing thought barged its way forward. "The other day, I asked you whether some patients were seizing or winding up in comas, and you said—"

"I said all I could say on the matter. There's nothing more to—"

"But what about the fainting?"

Peter brought his hand to his chin. He chewed on the corner of his lip before responding. "Fainting may prove to be a side effect for some patients at the time they first connect, but that's far from the same as—"

"Why can you tell me about that, but not about the other conditions?"

Peter clasped his hands behind his back, his normally bright demeanor now one of stone. "You witnessed that firsthand. I'm not betraying private health information by confirming something you saw with your own eyes."

Chandra bowed her head, sure he was telling the truth—about the policy, anyway. She nearly gave in, but then she thought of Kyra and what she would do were she in the same situation. "But isn't it a betrayal of another kind to not tell patients what health effects they might see if—?"

"Chandra, enough." Peter's eyes went wide at his own reaction. "Sorry. I don't mean to sound like my father, but there are some rules we can't break. Truthfully, we can't break any rules, this one most especially. I thank you in advance for understanding."

Stern. Calm. Clinical. Peter sure seemed to have a knack for going from friendly to fierce as necessary. Asking doctors directly for more information seemed increasingly unlikely to get Chandra the answers she needed regardless of whether she channeled Kyra's directness or not. She'd have to find another way. "Got it."

"Wonderful. Please, though, don't misunderstand me—I want you to contact me whenever you have *personal* EMPATHY-related questions." He returned his hand to the door, opened it, and gestured for her to exit. "Now get out there and amaze me with what you can make EMPATHY do. Amaze yourself, if you're able."

Chandra exited after him and entered the hall, losing herself amid the controlled chaos of pirouetting periwinkles, shuffling burgundies, and jostling lavenders. She stood still for a moment, taking it all in. The world around her seemed to slow, and amazed she became.

Amazed at how far she had come in only a few days. Amazed at how distant she now felt from Kyra, when all of this was intended to bring them closer together. Amazed every single person dressed in lavender had little idea they might be a ticking time bomb.

Chapter Twelve

WYATT

Wyatt arrived at Peter's office to find the door open. His son should have been expecting him—he had been attempting to speak with him about Chandra's proposed experiment most of the week—but even so, the open door gave Wyatt pause.

He placed a hand on the doorframe and peered across the threshold for a tripwire. The last time he had entered his son's office, Peter had taken a crack at making a Rube Goldberg machine "to stimulate his creativity." Wyatt learned of it the hard way, tripping a wire upon entry that set a ball rolling past a bell on a counterweight that dropped onto a cheese grater over a mousetrap.... All of it seemed juvenile, but Peter's code had gotten them this far despite the shenanigans. Wyatt would let his son do whatever he wanted so long as he produced results. There was no need to fix something that wasn't broken—unlike Peter's Rube Goldberg machine, which, by the time it was done, had sent an entire jar of marbles skittering across the floor.

Still uncertain there was nothing he might trip over, Wyatt knocked. "Peter? I'd like to discuss Chandra's proposal—"

"Here, Dad." Peter stepped out from around the corner.

"What are you doing in nonstandard attire?"

"Oh, this?" Peter pulled at his tight, white polo shirt. A similarly colored headband cut across his forehead, and his shorts fell maybe halfway down his thighs. "I was about to play some table tennis. The rhythm of it should help—"

"Stimulate your creativity?"

Peter responded with a blank stare.

"All right then." Wyatt entered the room on the assumption he would have been warned by now of any Rube Goldbergs lurking about. "But do not let anyone see you in that while you're in the compound's halls. If the staff starts to think my children are receiving special treatment—"

"Something something anarchy, something something disrespect. I know. Let's get to the matter at hand."

Peter's insolence stirred a rage within Wyatt—until he recalled his recent exchange with Heather.

He had to ease up. They knew themselves better than he did. Upsetting Peter wouldn't bode well for what he had to ask of him.

"Here." Peter put a paddle in Wyatt's hand and pointed to the opposite end of the table. "I'll serve first." He bounced the ball once.

Once Wyatt was in position, Peter bent at the knees and prepared for a serve. Wyatt tensed. Before he could center his paddle, Peter had already sent the ball across the net with a thwack.

Wyatt flailed off to his right, his paddle cutting through the air. The ball hit the floor with a hollow tock.

"You know," Peter said, "taking off your jacket might help."

Wyatt resisted the urge to make another fist with his free hand.

"You've got your whole life to wear it," Peter added. "We'll probably bury you in it unless you object. Well, we'll probably bury you in it even if you do object."

Wyatt grimaced at his son's morbidity. "I—"

"Ugh." Peter produced another ball from his pocket. "Remember what we buried Mom in? That should have been the last time you trusted Uncle Lars with anything."

It had been more than three decades, but for a moment Wyatt felt her touch, the weight of her head on his shoulder as she clung to him while they slept. "Please, let's—"

Peter prepped another serve. "Oh." He unbent at the knee, his expression one of regret. "I'm sorry. I've always found humor helps."

"I understand." The sensation in his throat loosened. He slipped off his lab coat before he redirected the conversation. "I'm not here for your mother." As he draped his coat over the backside of a nearby chair, he realized how untrue that was. All of it had been for Eva, not that his children could know that yet, if ever.

Wyatt turned back toward the shiny blue plastic of the tabletop. He nodded. His son served.

"I'm here," Wyatt said, side-stepping to his left as he returned the serve with an awkward forehand, "because I'd like to know how your conversations with Gary went regarding the proposed experiment."

Peter swatted away his father's return with ease. "I could have guessed you would."

Wyatt reached to his right, far too out of position to make contact. The ball dribbled onto the tile. "So have you put any thought into it? Could EMPATHY work for individuals in comas?"

"You really shouldn't do that," Peter said.

"You're rejecting the idea outright? I thought you'd have more to say than—"

"No," Peter said. "Not that. You shouldn't side-step when you could easily return my serve with a backhand. Like this." A confident backhand smacked a fresh ball clear across the table.

Wyatt's arm locked up as the ball headed straight for his chest. He dropped his paddle and lurched out of the way. "Peter, please. I thought this was supposed to help you—"

"Focus. Yes. It does." He laid his paddle on the table and cracked his knuckles. "Gary and I talked about it, and both of us agreed it wouldn't be impossible for EMPATHY to have functionality for someone in a coma."

Wyatt bent at the waist and retrieved a ball from the floor. "You don't sound too confident." With Peter still cracking the rest of his knuckles, Wyatt hoped to take his son unaware. He swung his paddle at the ball, sending it flying toward Peter. It bounced off the net and out of play.

Peter chuckled, though Wyatt couldn't tell if in response to Wyatt's skepticism or poor form. "We could do an install," Peter said. "That wouldn't be a problem."

"I shouldn't think so."

"Do you mind?" Peter gestured toward the table.

Before Wyatt could respond, Peter had lifted his side of it, locking it in place at a ninety-degree angle with Wyatt's end. He pressed his weight against it to rotate the table, much to the screeching chagrin of the metal legs against the floor.

"What is this madness?" Wyatt said over the metallic cacophony.

"I'm making a new opponent." Peter slid the raised end against the wall before he arched his back and lowered himself into serving position.

"You were saying something about an install," Wyatt said.

Peter, seemingly deaf to his father's words, slapped a serve toward the new wall he'd created. Forehand to backhand, Peter worked in a fury, the ball thwacking in rapid rhythm from paddle to wall to table.

"Peter," Wyatt said. "Can you—?"

"After an install," Peter said, walloping another forearm across the table, "EMPATHY neurohardware feeds off the electrical activity of the brain itself—you said as much during our call." He stretched for a backhand and connected with the ball before returning to his rhythm. "My concern," Peter said, pausing with each strike, "is that a comatose subject would lack sufficient electrical activity to power EMPATHY."

Wyatt thumbed his mustache. "Don't pretend you came up with that yourself. That's precisely what we discussed—"

"Be patient." Sweat dotted Peter's hairline. "I'm getting to the new stuff." His tempo was unyielding. "With targeted magnetic stimulation, however, we could attempt to awaken the necessary neural pathways for EMPATHY to function independently of an organic electrical source."

Magnetic stimulation certainly couldn't hurt. "Do you think your chances are realistic?"

Peter smashed a forehand across his body, turning to bat it back with another deft backhand.

The rhythm ended. The ball had become lodged in the crack between the two halves of the table.

"I would say," Peter said, turning toward his father, "that the ball getting stuck in that spot was about as likely as the success of the experiment I've outlined."

Wyatt's throat sealed off. Eva.

Peter laughed as he reached for the ball. "That doesn't mean I won't try."

Wyatt forced the phlegm from his throat. "Yes. Yes, I'd like you to."

"Do you mind if I ask a practical question—one slightly outside the bounds of the experiment?"

The tone with which Peter spoke suggested he had planned on asking whether granted permission or not. Wyatt said nothing.

Peter took a step backward. "Why Chandra?"

"I'm sorry?"

"Why would you invest so much in a quixotic side-experiment to satisfy a single patient? Now that we have a couple dozen participants to pick from—"

"Because she is the first to have EMPATHY connectivity. Her story—her wife's story—creates a broad appeal. You couldn't make something like that up." Wyatt struggled to maintain eye contact as he spoke, knowing he withheld the real reason for his request on Chandra's behalf.

Peter supported his weight on the table. "Has she said anything to you? Anything about the comas?"

"Aside from her wife's, I can't imagine—"

"No." He pushed himself away from the table. "About the comas." He said it under his breath, as if the word itself were some kind of dirty secret.

Then it dawned on Wyatt. "Well, no. Obviously not. How could she? Those incidents were isolated and occurred as a result of CompASSION, not EMPATHY." Wyatt fiddled with his gold-rimmed glasses. "We've made much progress since then, and those cases were so few I'd almost forgotten them entirely."

"Dad—"

"Dad what?"

Peter pulled back and forth at the two-button opening of his polo shirt, airing out his chest as he spoke. "It... worries me when you don't remember. Those were peoples' lives who were affected for the *worse*, and—"

"Peter."

"No, listen."

Wyatt nearly erupted at the continued obstinance but was again reminded of Heather. He had to give his children a chance or they'd never make it without him one day.

Peter pressed on. "Whether those comas were a result of CompASSION or not, someone is out there spreading rumors EMPATHY could lead to the same thing. Chandra even mentioned something about seizures."

"Preposterous."

"I know, but—"

"Peter, please. I respect your concern and understand we should seek to minimize the damage done by any rumors floating around, but the moment we address any of them directly, we're setting a precedent that we'll do the same for any baseless quibble any fool on this compound might conjure. Let's not cause alarm where no alarm is necessary." Wyatt stepped forward and put an arm around his son's shoulder. Sweat pressed through the back of Peter's shirt and onto Wyatt's forearm. He pulled away. "Where EMPATHY itself is concerned, things are going well right now. Let's focus on the positives and maintain the momentum we've got going."

Peter stuck out his lower lip, his eyes on the tile floor. "And if Chandra asks me again?"

"Double down on how there's no need for concern, and change the subject to let her know we're working on this 'quixotic side experiment' for her."

Peter's eyes went wide. Wyatt winked.

"Right," Peter said. "I suppose we should talk about subjects for this thing." He sighed. "I could make some calls about testing this on individuals actually in comas, but I feel we'll get quicker results by medically inducing comas in rats. They won't know how to access the cerenet, of course, but we would be able to monitor for sustained activity in EMPATHY itself."

All thoughts of Chandra, of rumors, fell away. Eva alone—her flowered scent of lilac—clouded his senses. "I, uh—yes. Proceed with rats for now. That will make for a fine first step."

Again, Peter appeared to notice his father falter. "Are you okay?"

"EMPATHY has started to take for patients and I'm sure we'll have even more soon. I've never been better."

Peter said nothing as he shifted his weight. Wyatt took the hint.

His walk back to his office was interminable, the week's proceedings a weight on his heart. First, Wyatt had put off Heather, ridiculing her for her failure to prevent the leak. Peter, already suffocating in responsibility, now had even more thrust upon him. Only Alistair remained unmarred. Well, that was surely not the case.

Alistair had always been estranged, his mother a shadow of what Eva had meant to Wyatt. Grief had pushed him away from Eva's memory when it should have brought him closer. He had a third child to show for that mistake, a daily reminder of his shame.

Wyatt stood before the door to his office, his breath taken from him. He held his keycard to the door's sensor and disengaged the lock. As he stepped inside, he found himself not in his office, but rather his on-complex apartment. No wonder the commute had been protracted.

His apartment's white-washed walls loomed as naked as Wyatt felt. Though expansive, his living quarters remained empty except for the appliances and furniture provided standard with his housing—not much, but enough to get by.

A pang of responsibility gripped him for a moment. Wyatt made to turn back for the compound, but the distractions were too great. He needed to clear his head, to have a moment of peace. He proceeded into his apartment.

His footsteps echoed off the wood flooring as he headed for the kitchen. Head stooped, he retrieved a tumbler from a cabinet above the microwave before removing a bottle of scotch from an otherwise empty cupboard nearby. Two fingers' worth of the liquor had splashed into the glass before he sank into the robust, brown leather armchair of his living room.

The first sips were fire on his tongue, the smoky richness settling in on his third pull. Fingers clasped across his chest, his eyes gravitated toward the hallway that led to the bedroom. He resisted the urge to stand. He shouldn't. Not now. The secret his closet held was too grave to address in his current state.

Wyatt sipped once more. The burn razed away at the inside of his mouth, an odd comfort. When he swallowed, he found his eyes drawn to the hallway once again.

Eva. It had been some time since he last visited her. His earlier judgment be damned. A few moments with her couldn't hurt. He rose, his fingers holding loosely to his drink.

Each footstep added to the rhythm, slow and plodding, much like the grind of their previous work together. It was Eva who had pioneered the pocketab, really, though Wyatt had helped in his own way. Her raw knowledge of electronics exceeded Wyatt's own at the time, making her the driving force behind the century's greatest telecom innovation. Wyatt, despite his intimate involvement, often felt as though he were nothing more than a public-relations delivery vehicle—not that he minded. Taking the back seat to her allowed him to wave out the window, after all.

Wyatt's hand touched the door to his bedroom. Once he entered, he knew the closet was only a few steps away, and what lay on the other side of that door would force him to confront a choice he had until recently thought he wouldn't face for years to come.

Still, he pressed onward, his steps soft on the carpet, this time to thoughts of her absence. Her voice remained as real to him as any, his love for her still churning deep within his chest. Gone were the years where her memory visited him every hour of every day, but in all that time he had never stopped loving her—just become distracted. He knew that now more than ever. Why pursue EMPATHY, if not for love?

At the door to the closet, Wyatt sipped what remained of his scotch. Then, with his pocketab over the door's sensor, he placed his thumb on a bioscanner. The door slid open with a hum. The heat of the closet space swept over him.

A cramped environment, Wyatt only required two steps to reach the podium at the room's center. The lights glowed gold around the white plateau, inviting Wyatt's touch to the keypad at its side. He fingered a combination and swiped his thumb once more before a digital voice issued a prompt.

"Why do you do it?" The digital voice was cold, hard.

"*Ást án enda.*" Love without end. They were the final words she had spoken before she slipped away, the last time they would tell one another they loved each other in that stilted Icelandic she liked to speak, what little of it she retained from her childhood.

From within the podium, a gear set into motion, the top of the pedestal beginning to part. Inside, a platform rose, revealing a tank the width of Wyatt's chest. He waited for the platform to cease its motion before he placed a hand on it.

There. Eva was in there. Not all of her, but the part of her that made her, her. As he lowered himself to the tank's level, Wyatt failed to fend off the choking tide of emotion that always came with having the brain of Eva Alfreðsdóttir inches from his grasp.

Young as they had been, Wyatt and Eva knew where their destinies lay. The supporting technology wasn't available yet, but with the design and programming language they had conjured—the design and programming language *Eva* had conjured—EMPATHY was the direction in which their careers had been headed, even all those decades ago. It was for that reason they made one another the promise upon her diagnosis, a promise of which they would remind themselves every day until the end came.

Ást án enda. With the concept Eva had developed, the separation would only be temporary. Through EMPATHY they would meet one another again.

Wyatt narrowed his eyes at her, suspended there in a golden elixir of cerebrospinal fluid and an aldehyde solution, the constant oxygenation and glucose supply keeping her intact. A bittersweetness enveloped him as he accepted much more time had passed than either would have expected. At least now he finally knew what they'd both long suspected, that astium, truly Eva's greatest discovery, would definitely form the cornerstone of EMPATHY's success. Even if something were to happen to Wyatt, EMPATHY could go on as knowledge of the element was passed to their children through the safe he'd locked up in his desk. Regardless of whether Wyatt and Eva were ever reunited in life, the legacy they had developed would endure.

The scents of sterility choked Wyatt in the tiny closet. He removed his hand from the side of the tank and pulled at his mustache. He had wanted to wait for EMPATHY to be widespread, established, and safe before making the decision he now faced. In light of Chandra's story, however—and the realization he himself wasn't getting any younger—Wyatt now felt compelled to take a leap at a time he felt only safe enough to crawl.

Reaching into the pocket of his lab coat, he produced his pocketab and redialed the last individual with whom he had spoken. His son answered on the first ring.

"Peter?" Wyatt said.

"What's wrong?"

"Nothing, I—" Wyatt held his breath. He knew once he made his offer he couldn't take it back. "Forget the rats."

"How do you mean?"

"I found a different specimen. A better one."

Wyatt could almost see his son chewing his lip on the other end of the call.

"It won't be the same as a coma patient," Wyatt said. "But the same principles should apply I would think."

"What are we talking about here?"

"I have a brain, a human brain. It's been..." Wyatt struggled for the word. "It's been 'offline' for some time, but if we're able to install EMPATHY and stimulate the specimen similarly to what you suggested earlier, I see no reason why—"

"Even if the specimen has been well cared for, that's such a long shot, Dad."

Wyatt struggled against the rush of dolefulness that seized his chest. "Is it a longer shot than it working with a comatose subject?"

His son drew in a breath. "I'd say the odds are slightly worse."

"But the ball—it got stuck, didn't it?"

"What?"

"You said the chances of EMPATHY working for a patient in a coma were as likely as that ball getting stuck in the crack between the two sides of that table." Peter did not object. "It happened once, right? Who's to say it couldn't happen again?"

"That was a simple analogy. A—"

"I know it was a damned analogy, Peter! The odds are what the odds are. It's up to me to make decisions, you to do the testing, and God or science or interstellar dust to sort it out. Are we clear?"

Wyatt heard no breathing on the other end of the line. Then, full with contempt, a response came. "It sounds as though you've made your decision."

"I have. I'll deliver the specimen to your office this afternoon." Wyatt thumbed his pocketab to end the call. His hands shook from the rage, but it quickly withered to a pervasive dolor.

Wyatt could now go to Chandra and tell her there was a chance. He, too, now had more hope than ever for Eva to return to his life, but somehow an emptiness came with it. Distraught and hollow, Wyatt again touched the tank on the podium before plodding out of the closet and plopping onto his bed.

A stillness overcame him, and he wept.

Chapter Thirteen

CHANDRA

The arboretum's wooden footbridge creaked beneath Chandra's bare feet as she descended its far side. In the pond below, the koi swam over and around one another, the orange and white and yellow of their bodies twisting against one another in a pattern Chandra felt she could almost understand.

It was here over the course of the last two days that she'd come to distract herself from gloomy thoughts by working to master EMPATHY, improving her cerenet search abilities and familiarizing herself with the chat app—though she dare not message any of the dozen or so patients who now had connectivity. For as much as she wanted to practice chatting via EMPATHY for when Kyra had an install of her own, Chandra still preferred a quiet room to a loud one.

As the weeping willow at the center of her island of solitude grew nearer, though, someone finally reached out to her.

SYLVIA EDISON: Hey! Hope you're doing okay. I'm getting folks together for ceramics in about a half hour. Interested?

Chandra scrunched up her nose, concentrating on the words as she typed—no, thought—her response.

CHANDRA ADELHADEO: Sure. Art and Supply, right?
SYLVIA EDISON: See you there :)

Chandra read Sylvia's response three times over, a warming sensation taking her each time her eyes drifted over the emoji. Was she... was she actually experiencing the same satisfaction Sylvia had while typing it out?

She brushed the question aside, determined to not let it wrack her. If she were going to be mingling in Art and Supply not long from now, she'd need to gather her social strength.

A ray of afternoon sun cut through the foliage, warming the side of her cheek and the front of her neck as she neared the end of the bridge. Here in the heart of the arboretum, she found everything the rest of the compound failed to offer: a sense of humanity over the artificial sterility, fresh air over the intensely air-conditioned. As she walked, she wiped the sweat from her brow and shielded her eyes from the sun.

She stepped off the bridge and onto the grass, its blades tickling the spaces between her toes. How everyone else seemed content to keep their shoes on when walking the arboretum's trails, Chandra would never understand. She had nearly reached the edge of the willow's shadow when she first saw him. There in the grass, he lay with his hands behind his head, his eyes open, each one glassed over as if he were connected to the cerenet.

"Ty?" Chandra said.

He blinked. The pastel tones left his eyes, returning them to their natural, deep brown. "Oh, hey," he said. "Glad you finally came."

Chandra halted before entering the shade, her toes digging into the dirt. "How did you... have you been following me or something?"

He rushed to his feet. "Oh, no. Not at all." Ty brushed dried grass from his scrubs as he spoke. "When we met the other day, I saw your drawing, the one of this place. I thought it looked nice and figured it would be worth checking out."

"I thought you hated the outdoors."

"Yeah, I mean..." He fidgeted with his glasses. "Well, I figured I'd get over it if I ran into you here at some point. You know, since this place was worth it enough for you to draw. Is that weird?"

"No, I just—well..." Chandra looked away from him. She adjusted her grip on her shoes in her left hand. "It is weird, maybe, but I guess it's not like we can't both enjoy the same spot. I'm not staying long anyhow." The skin of her scalp welcomed the step into the shade.

Ty's shoulders dropped. "Ugh, thank you. You have no idea what a hard time I've had making friends here."

She shot him a knowing look. "You don't say."

"Come on," he said. "Not you, too."

Chandra slumped down at the base of the tree's trunk, the bark of it rough against her back. It may have dirtied her scrubs, but the compound seemed to have an endless supply of them; she could always request more. "It can't be that bad. Sylvia's your friend, isn't she?"

"She invites me to things sometimes. Well, all the time."

It wasn't until Ty sat alongside her that she really saw him for the first time. Behind those thickly rimmed glasses, he looked much less confident than she originally thought he portrayed himself to be. He wasn't anything to fear, no; he was just an awkward kid.

Chandra reached into her pocket for her sketchbook and pencil. "You're going to the ceramics thing, then?"

"I didn't plan on it."

She let silence speak for her. He didn't seem to understand. "I bet you'd make more friends if you took advantage of her invites more often."

"I would," he said, "but I have projects of my own to work on in the computer lab."

Chandra raised an eyebrow. "Even now that EMPATHY has taken for you?"

"There are some things I can only work on in there."

"I thought the cerenet was as equally censored as the on-compound internet."

Ty gave a single-shoulder shrug. "What I do is about more than the internet."

"Are you a writer or something? Can't you just use the word processor to—?"

"No." He exhaled sharply. "Let me show you."

TYCHO LEE WANTS TO SHARE HIS VISFIELD. DO YOU ACCEPT?

Chandra's hand left her sketchbook in her pocket. "How does this... how do these work?"

"Do you really not know? Has the Halmans' golden child forgotten she's not a nonny anymore?"

Her lips went flat. "What is that supposed to mean?"

"I heard this other nectee say it." He scratched at the back of his head. "Have you met Metal Dave?"

Ty might as well have been speaking a foreign language. "I have no idea—"

"It's simple. Nonnies are people who don't have EMPATHY connectivity, and nectees..."

Chandra responded with a blank stare. It all seemed unnecessarily divisive.

"I don't know," Ty said. "I thought it was kind of fun to say, anyway." He stopped scratching the back of his head and picked at the grass for a moment. "But the VisField request?"

"Oh, yeah."

"You just accept it and then you can see what I see on the EMPATHY interface. It's like sharing your screen."

Chandra concentrated on accepting his request, though she couldn't bring herself to follow through.

"It's okay," Ty said. "Sylvia and I have done this dozens of times already."

Chandra drew in a breath through her nose. She accepted.

Immediately a translucent display took the center of her vision, her own EMPATHY interface replaced with Ty's. It was white, all white save for a familiar design smack-dab in the middle of the screen.

The shape of Texas. The cube in the northeast part of the state.

"Your tattoo." Chandra said it on reflex. "But why—?" She ceased to speak the instant the music began.

An eerie tickle lurked in the back of her mind as the square-shaped drumroll of the snare drums rose in volume.

"Wait," she said. "This is... this is *Dallas*." Sure enough, a second later the game's name appeared beneath the Texas-shaped design, a 16-bit version of the song she had heard the first time she saw Ty's tattoo now raging on in the forefront of her consciousness.

"It is." Ty seemed pretty pleased with himself. "I helped program it into an EMPATHY-compatible app."

"But how did you—there's no way you could have..." A wave of memories, of guilt, crashed down on Chandra. How could she have forgotten? Or in the very least, how could she not have recognized what was apparently the original version of the game's theme song when she'd heard it two days earlier? For weeks the previous summer, Kyra's fanaticism for the game had overshadowed almost everything else in their lives.

Warmth seeped through Chandra's body at the memory of Kyra humming the game's theme song while they held hands on the way to the beach, as Kyra did her jerky shoulder dance in the kitchen, as she washed her face at night. That song! *Dallas* was even the reason Kyra had started wearing those yellow flowers in her hair by midsummer, no matter how much they might have clashed with her standard baggy T-shirt and shorts attire.

"For the record," Ty said, manipulating the interface to start a new game, "I got the tattoo *before* the game was all over the place. It was originally a simple project a friend and I worked on for school years earlier, but—"

"'The Yellow Rose of Texas,'" Chandra said. "That's the song I heard, that's the—"

"One I used as the basis for the game's theme song, yeah." Ty fidgeted with his glasses. "Nice touch, huh?"

His eyes narrowed at the bulge of the sketchpad in her pocket. "Why do you still carry that thing around?" he said. In the background—or at least over their private cerenet connection—the *Dallas* version of "The Yellow Rose of Texas" tinked and tonked onward.

"Why wouldn't I?" Chandra said. "Draw, paint—it's what I do."

"I'm not saying you shouldn't," Ty said, "but haven't you tried doing those things with EMPATHY yet?"

It hadn't even occurred to her.

"Let me show you something," Ty said. "Or, I guess... well, 'listen' to this."

The *Dallas* interface dissolved, restoring Chandra's vision in full. "I don't know, Ty," she said. "Maybe I should get going. I told Sylvia I'd make it to her ceramics session, and—"

"It'll only take a minute, I promise. Plus, you'll love how this changes things for—"

"Ty—"

"Come on. I've been working so hard on all these technical things lately, and writing music gave me a nice out from that intensity." He steepled his hands. "Please please please."

Chandra straightened her fingers. "Fine. Yes. Okay." She folded her legs pretzel-style alongside him. "But please never whine like that again."

"Just close your eyes and tell me what you think."

Chandra closed her eyes, her innards feeling as though they were tied in a knot.

A melancholy tension hovered in her ear, then the drip-drip-drip of a single piano key. The chords descending upon it were minor, a mournful viola accompanying them. As the instruments crescendoed, Chandra imagined—no, *saw*—herself walking next to a boy on a blisteringly hot day, the sun beaming down through the leaves of palm trees. She walked with this boy—maybe fifteen or sixteen years old—into what appeared to be a school, a security officer nodding to them along the way.

The score went on, the drip-drip-drip of the piano more urgent than before. The minor chords crashed more strongly the second time through the refrain, a cello underscoring the most doleful notes of the progression.

She sat behind the boy in a classroom, the teacher preaching to his pupils about code, about projects due, about best practices. The music Ty had written still underwrote the scene, though birds chirped through an open window and loose-leaf shuffled as it was passed between students in desks only a few rows away.

A long rest ensued in Ty's arrangement. Chalk scratched against the blackboard. A broom in the hands of a janitor whooshed past the open classroom door.

Glass shattered as a flash grenade flew through the window.

Chandra was on the floor, the piano thundering in her ears, screams and cries for help rising and falling around it. She heard the pop-pop-pop of a weapon being fired, the shooter shouting a racial slur over the frantic pleas of a teacher bartering for the lives of his students.

When her sight returned, Chandra rolled onto her stomach. Dressed head to toe in munitions, the attacker, despite having covered his face, had left his slickly combed gray hair exposed. He stood over her teacher at the front of the room, the patch on his arm emblazoned with the flag of the Altamerican Militia.

Her hands had become sticky with blood. Her own? No, that of her friend. That of the boy. "Dallas," she heard herself say with a voice that did not belong to her. In the corner of her vision, the attacker took aim at the teacher from point blank range. The weapon fired. Chandra collapsed into a heap on the floor, faking her own death.

Minutes passed. The sounds of gunfire echoed through the halls. Try as she might to keep still, Chandra's eyelids flitted, her hopefully empty stare trained forward on one thing. The boy. Dallas. The boy who had been her friend. The boy whose warm blood pooled beneath her, against her chest and her cheek and in her hair.

The crescendo broke, plummeting down down down into a vacuous near-nothingness, leaving only the drip-drip-drip of the original piano key behind. Then it, too, faded. Chandra heard only the sound of the birds through the window—no, in the arboretum.

Her eyes shot open. "Ty. What—?" Her hands scrambled across her body. Where had she been shot? Where?

"I know, right? It needs some work still, but—"

Her eyes darted about. "We need to run. We need..." The way he eyed her, she could tell he had no idea what she was talking about. She slowed herself down.

All was well. They were in the arboretum. Nothing more. "What was that all about?" she said. "The school? The gunman?"

The whites of his eyes expanded. "How do you know?"

"The song," Chandra said. "When I listened to the song, I—the images just came to me. I saw it, Ty. Was that... are you from San Diego? Were you at the Korean Academy Shooting?"

He sat and pulled his knees toward his chest. "I don't understand. Did you read my mind?"

"No." She averted her eyes, drawing in a deep breath of the humid, earthy air. How could she explain? It was then another image came to her, one not of Ty's creation but her own. She let herself shape it, the memory of Ty's song—of her own grief for Kyra—guiding the form it took on the digital canvas. Sketchbook be damned, Chandra wanted a way to explain what she had seen, and this was the best way she knew for now.

A black pit bore through the mass of white canvas. Bleeding shades of midnight, twisted finger-like trails oozed from it, as regular in their spacing as the drip-drip-drip of Ty's piano key. Each tendril was as thick as congealed blood, as dark as still wet tar on the highway. She thought of Kyra, of her accident, of what she could have done to prevent it. Somewhere in the depths of the pit at the center of the image, the black became pitch. Black-hole pitch. Coma pitch.

Ty wept. "It's not your fault."

Chandra started backward at the sound of Ty's voice. "What?"

"What happened to Kyra. I—I see... I feel it." He wiped his nose with his elbow.

Chandra stared back, mouth agape.

"I get it now. I know how you saw the shooting in my song."

Chandra hadn't even told Wyatt Kyra's whole story since arriving on the compound, but now Ty had found out? Lightheaded, she rested on her back. "So you saw it? The whole thing?" Could she control it? Was there a way to share what she created without the viewer experiencing what had driven it?

Ty sniffed. "I saw you pick her up outside a One Amero Only. It was nighttime. You put her bike into your trunk and her helmet into your back seat."

He elaborated on what he'd seen, but his words became lost as Chandra relived it herself.

She'd picked up Kyra after her shift, the sky in its *l'heure bleue* as the sun dipped beneath the horizon. The bike fit snugly in the trunk, her helmet tossed into the back seat.

The next morning Chandra scrambled to her car much later than normal for her Wednesday seminar. She struggled to unwedge the bike from the trunk, but once she had—dripping with sweat and cursing herself for not having woken Kyra for help—she locked the bike outside and took off toward the university.

She'd made it halfway to campus when she remembered the helmet in the back seat. But it was fine. Kyra wouldn't need it. Her ride to work was what? Ten minutes? She rode the same route every day. She knew what to watch out for.

"There was no way for you to know," Ty said.

The pressure built up behind Chandra's eyes. "I should have turned around. I should have turned around when I saw the helmet back there."

"The fault lies with the driver of the car that hit her," Ty said. "Not you."

The tears came with the image of Kyra motionless in the hospital hours later, her mangled body mostly covered, a scar above her ear where a flower should have been.

"All I want," Chandra said, "is to go back to before that day and tell her I love her and tell her I'm sorry and tell her I won't let it happen this time."

Ty inched nearer. "All right, tell me—where would you go if you could disappear from it all?"

"I—what?" She removed her face from the crook of her elbow.

"Where would you go? What would you do if you had the choice?"

Chandra ran the tips of her fingers over the grass. "I'd go... I'd probably farm, I guess. Maybe somewhere in Minnesota."

"And why?"

"Like, why Minnesota?"

"Why either?"

"Ty, I really don't understand—"

"Me neither." He shifted to sit on his knees. "I'd always—*always*—rather be right here, right now. We can only—I mean, truly—affect the present, so why not be—?"

"That wasn't even what you asked. How is that supposed to—?"

"Okay. Fine. It was a bad pitch." He mumbled something about not being a professional therapist. "I thought you'd say you'd want to disappear into the past, but, well, you can't go back to that day like I can't go back to the day of the shooting. Kyra is in a coma. Dallas is dead. I named the game he and I had been working on in his honor so I could move forward, and you're in this study to help Kyra in whatever way you can. All we can do is focus on the present."

She shook her head. "But I should be *there* with her now, not here. I don't know what I was thinking. Even if the Halmans can help her, being without updates is almost worse than—"

"What if you could get updates?" Ty said. "What would that change?"

"Is this another 'bad pitch' from an admitted nontherapist?"

Ty raised his hands. "I'm trying to help." He lowered them. "And no, this isn't another bad pitch. I really do want to know."

"Well," Chandra sniffled. "I can't imagine there'd be much to report, but at least I'd know the lines of communication were open. Even if I could tell my brother they're investigating if EMPATHY could work for her, he could whisper it in Kyra's ear and maybe she would hear and—"

"Then let's do it," Ty said.

"What do you mean? Like I can call him somehow?"

"No, but you could email him."

Chandra swallowed a laugh. "In case you haven't noticed, the cerenet is just as censored as the internet in the computer lab while we're here, and it's not exactly like we can march in there and start sending emails."

Ty raised and lowered his shoulders. "Yeah, but that's—that's exactly what we'd do."

"Don't toy with me." Chandra stood. "I'm gonna meet up with Sylvia and the others. If you want to come along—"

"*I'm* headed to the lab to email a friend. If you'd rather hang out with the other nectees than get in touch with your brother, that's up to you." He turned to leave, flicking his hair to the side as he stepped away.

"You're serious?"

Ty didn't break stride as he arrived at the wooden footbridge over the koi pond. "Only one way to find out."

"Wait," Chandra said.

He did.

Ugh, what was she thinking? If they got caught, she could lose everything. The Halmans were offering her the world—a chance to actually speak with Kyra—and she was going to risk all of that just to have her brother whisper in Kyra's ear?

Maybe she didn't have to send anything. Yeah, she could go and see what it was all about, couldn't she? Being in the computer lab was a perfectly reasonable thing to do. How could she be held responsible if Ty got up to no good while she was there?

"Can you give me an hour?" she said. The grass prickled the soles of her feet as she hustled toward him. "I promised Sylvia I'd go to her class. I can come find you afterward."

"I'll wait for you in my room. Tell the nectees I say 'hi.'"

Realizing she'd left her shoes at the base of the tree, she stepped aside to let him pass—but not before she got in another word. "I'll tell the nonnies you say 'hi,' too."

Chapter Fourteen

ARIEL

As she stood before the great blue doorway to the server farm, Ariel twisted off the cap of the eyedrop bottle. She checked her pocketab one last time. No sign of M3R1. Her skin crawled.

This was it, then. She was going to doom the study to failure, all in the name of personal advancement. Wyatt knew what was going on, though, didn't he? Even if it wasn't through M3R1, he must have some design at work, a failsafe for this kind of situation. He had proven himself to have a plan for almost everything else.

The wall-mounted bioscanner had two slots on either side of it, each glowing an ethereal red, two fires burning in adjacent caves. She thumbed the W-USB in her free hand. Its LED still blinked at her, the receipt of code still underway.

Ariel sighed. With her head tilted back, she pinched a drop of Alistair's elixir into one eye. It seared with a murderous sting, worse than any amount of sweat and sunscreen. Ariel cursed, blinking rapidly to soothe the burn. Still seething, she tossed her head back again to scorch her other retina before bending at the waist and clutching a thick wad of her canary-colored scrub-bottoms in the middle of her thighs.

The feeling passed. She used the back of her wrist to collect the tears running down her cheeks, then scanned her keycard—well, someone's keycard—against the scanner. It flashed green.

She jumped at the sound of an unenthused digital voice, one of Heather's new features, apparently. "Please present your eyes to the bioscanner," it said before adopting an awkward shift of tone, "Gary Eiche."

Ariel let her hands hang loose at her side. Gary, then. The system would show he had been working against the study all along.

She told herself to walk away. This wasn't what she came for. No one should have to take the fall for Alistair's scheming. What was it they'd said in that ethics course she'd taken? It wasn't all that long ago she'd sat in a discussion session, ready to strangle that fresh-out-of-high-school know-it-all who thought he was God's gift to philosophy. Whatever. He and the other "young" freshman were still probably swimming in debt, whereas she'd worked for five years after high school before enrolling in college. Who was "misunderstanding the fundamental premise of the question" *now?*

Ugh. Why was she letting herself get distracted? She didn't have time for this.

Her fingers flicked at the screen of her pocketab in search of Wyatt's number. Just as she found it, the screen froze. The darkest pixels of her device shifted one-by-one to white.

The pixelation accelerated along with the jitters in Ariel's stomach. When the blue light in her pocketab's corner illuminated, it all but confirmed her hunch.

>> All is well. Please proceed, Ariel.

Ariel pumped her fist. "Where have you been? I almost—"

>> Please enter the server farm. M3R1 will explain everything once inside.

"Will do. Yes." She aligned her eyes with the glowing red caves of the bioscanner. With Wyatt back in control via M3R1, she had no reason to abort the mission she'd been given.

A flash of unexpected green fired into each eye. She pulled away, shuttering her eyelids.

"Thank you, Gary Eiche," the sensor said. The door clicked open and Ariel reached for its handle.

"Hey, M3R1, Gary's not going to run into any trouble because of this, will he?

>> All that is done can be undone.

Ariel yanked open the server farm door. The purr of the HVAC system beckoned her, the dull crimson of the lighting a warm invitation to proceed. Even the alien blue emanating from the hundreds—no, thousands—of servers seemed to hold less malice toward her on this visit. If the animals on this server farm really were sentient, it pleased her to know they could recognize the good she was doing them. "It's feeding time, farm friends." She turned toward the primary server.

>> What was that?

"Nothing. Forget it." Ariel shook off her embarrassment. "You were going to tell me where you've been. I was worried you'd never find me again."

>> There has been no need for M3R1 to bother you. It has been busy preparing this new code. When your pocketab's GPS indicated you were nearing the server farm, M3R1's startup sequence was initiated.

"I would have appreciated it if you had let me know everything was okay." At least Ariel had survived Heather's interrogation about her phone records. It wasn't hard to defend her calls to her mom, and it's not like she had any brothers or sisters to check in on.

>> Why the concern? Wyatt wouldn't allow you to be found out.

An excellent point. Ariel inspected the W-USB as she stood before the primary server, narrowing her eyes at her next challenge. "Heather changed the setup here, too, I see."

>> Yes. Retina scans have replaced the username and password fields.

The urge to nibble at her nails tingled her fingertips as Ariel struggled to find the eye sensor. After a second glance, she noticed a button beneath the scanner itself. She pressed it. Tiny fire-like light illuminated within the sensor's caverns before it gave her—well, Gary—its instructions.

Her eyes handled the flash much better this time around. The scanner welcomed her to the primary server and its monitor flickered to life.

>> You may insert the W-USB now.

Did M3R1 honestly think she didn't know that? "I'm on it." The storage device clicked into place. "What are we uploading this time? Will it help more patients gain EMPATHY access?"

>> At this time, the foundations for GPS capability have not been laid across all egodrives. This serves to make GPS available to all patients should it be activated. The upload also consists of M3M3D17.exf and P47CoN7RoL.exf. These will take some time.

"If you say so." Just as last time, M3R1 set to LOADING THE BUS for a file entitled GPS.exf before advancing to its FURTHER DEVELOPMENT stage. The GPS upload completed in a matter of moments. Ariel pursed her lips. "I thought you said this would take a while."

>> That was the quick one. The others are more complex.

The white glow of the monitor flickered as M3R1 set to LOADING THE BUS for M3M3D17.exf. When the display changed to FURTHER DEVELOPMENT, the estimated time remaining indicated fifteen minutes.
"Please tell me this is as long as any of these will take."

>> The largest file is P47CoN7RoL.exf. It may take up to twenty-five minutes.

"I don't have that kind of time." If she were honest with herself, the amount of time she would have to spend waiting was not what concerned her most. Though there was no maintenance scheduled for the near future, the last thing she wanted was another unexpected close encounter with Heather. "What does M3M-whatever do? What do either of these do?"

>> That is none of your concern.

"You told me the first one was for GPS."

>> M3R1 must provide *some* assistance to the Halmans once in a while.

It felt as though a rope tightened around her throat. "What do you mean 'once in a while?' Wyatt designed you."

>> Wyatt knows nothing of M3R1. Nor does Peter, nor Heather, nor Candace, nor Gary. Alistair is clueless as well. It's just you and M3R1, Ariel.

"You said you were Wyatt." Her eyes flitted toward the monitor before darting back to her pocketab. "You said you were the only one who could—"

>> There is no need to remind M3R1 of its words. M3R1 remembers. M3R1 lied. Well, its parents did.

Ariel's attention snapped to the W-USB. "Tell me who you are or I'll stop the upload."

>> You may have been fooled, but you are not so foolish.

Her hand fired in the direction of the W-USB. In her opposite hand, her pocketab roared. Fear froze her before she could remove the device.

>> Ariel would not want to cross M3R1. M3R1 knows what Ariel has done.

"What I've done? I've done nothing. I followed orders. I thought you were Wyatt. I—"

>> Ariel has helped M3R1. If the Halmans knew Ariel helped M3R1, it would be a problem for them. For you.

>> M3R1 can't imagine Ariel would enjoy decades in Union prison. Your uploads from last time alone would be enough to earn that. This new programming would come with an even greater sentence.

"But you erased my tracks last time. You took a brush to the snow."

>> Today is a day of fresh tracks in fresh powder. And who's to say M3R1 cannot trek through snows of the past?

The upload for M3M3D17.exf inched onward at a glacial pace. A ding on her pocketab drew her attention back toward it.

>> Please don't, Ariel. You have so much life left to live.

The W-USB was only a lunge away if she dared defy M3R1.
Her thoughts shifted to her father, his absence the last twenty-plus

years. Her mother had never told her what he'd done to wind up in jail, and though she could have searched public records to get an answer, she'd never ventured to do so. The image she'd had of him before he disappeared was too pristine, too perfect. Why compromise it until she could hear the story from the man himself?

Ariel chewed on her thumbnail as a thought gnawed at her, one in which she spent half of her own life wasting away in a Union prison. For her, prison would mean no more Trade Facility. No opportunity to become a biofusion division head. No chance to see her dad on the right side of the bars when he was finally released.

Ariel removed her stare from the W-USB. Surely there was a way to defeat M3R1, but this was not it. Foolishness had brought her here. Further foolishness could only worsen things.

"You're right. I have a lot left to live for."

>> Then please... why don't you remove your mind from this for a time? Why not play another game of *Dallas* until the uploads are complete? You seemed to enjoy it plenty last time.

The game's overture emanated from her device, though its loading screen remained concealed behind M3R1's communication. "I don't know if I'm in the mood for games right now."

>> M3R1 is also not in the mood for games.

Though Ariel expected the theme from *Dallas* to fade, it did not. Then she saw it—the slow depixelization of M3R1 from her screen. After a few moments, M3R1's strategy for disappearing became apparent.

As the M3R1 dissolved, it ensured the most critical bits of its message remained visible longest.

>> no games.

The message could not have been clearer.

Chapter Fifteen

CHANDRA

The clay, warm and wet in Chandra's hands, did little to distract her from Ty's suggested visit to the computer lab. Her late arrival to Sylvia's class had also put her on edge; she would have to hustle to catch up on crafting the mugs Sylvia had been giving instruction on for some time. The urge to draft a message to her brother on the cerenet wasn't making things any easier, either, especially now that she knew what she wanted to tell her brother, what would make taking the risk worth it.

"Dave," Sylvia said, "that doesn't look like a mug to me."

The participant everyone called Metal Dave, seated directly to Chandra's left, adjusted his immense weight on the bench. "It's not. It's a dragon, see?"

Sylvia cocked her head to the side. Rumor had it Metal Dave's shenanigans once led to the staff threatening him with forfeiture and commission—having EMPATHY access denied and being reassigned to menial work on the compound until the study concluded. His offense? Repeatedly refusing instructions to stop defacing his scrub-tops by writing things like DRAGON'S BANE and DAMNED SOUL on them in marker. With the threat hanging over him, though, he eventually shaped up—mostly.

"What?" he said. "You don't see it? Here's the dragon, and over here is the Viking village he's about to torch." He looked around the table, shrugging. "You guys see it, right? Anyone? Anyone?"

"Wow, Dave," said Calvin, one of those with a cerenet connection among Dave's legion of friends. "You are *so* metal."

Metal Dave bellowed a deep laugh and flashed the sign of the horns with both of his clay-caked hands. Others joined in the laughter, which drowned out Sylvia's insistence his work would never survive the kiln.

Once the group settled down, Chandra kept at her work while the others, who were mostly beginning to shape their mug handles, went on chatting. Grandma Maribel fretted over being one of the only ones in the room without connectivity, while Nicolas and Gui—two of Metal Dave's disciples—bickered about whether anyone cared about Nicolas' asthma and why Calvin needed to stop using the cerenet to justify the scope of his dad's yacht.

Grandma Maribel, fragile-framed and beloved among the other patients, shifted her worry from her lack of connectivity to how she was missing the birth of her *nietito* Alejo's twins, which would make her a great grandmother for the first time. Chandra listened as her fingers bored into her would-be mug, misshaping it into a slender cylinder. She tried again to fire up the cerenet, to draft a message to her brother Ratan, but an incoming transmission from Sylvia put a stop to that.

SYLVIA EDISON: What's wrong?
CHANDRA ADELHADEO: Nothing. Tired is all.
SYLVIA EDISON: Did you have another dream about her?

She hadn't, not since the first time she had told Sylvia of her dreams of Kyra only a day earlier when they spent the afternoon chatting as they lounged in GenRec. Try as Chandra might to prevent herself from dwelling on it, the image of the painting she'd made to Ty's song pushed itself to the forefront of her mind.

Sylvia went from narrow to wide-eyed. The crease in her forehead deepened, her shoulders slackening. Her eyes hit Chandra's from across the room. Tears flooded them.

Could Sylvia see—could she feel—the painting over their cerenet connection?

No no no no no. Chandra must have unwittingly transferred the image to her. Sylvia choked back a sob while Chandra attempted to message her, but she couldn't unsend the image now.

Around the room, a quiet fell—at least among those who already had cerenet connectivity. Their eyes glassed over, smiles that became frowns that became open wounds of grief. If Chandra didn't know how to prevent sharing her painting, Sylvia certainly couldn't have either.

The somber gaze of every nectee in the room found her. They knew. They all knew about her wife, about Chandra's role in her condition.

She jumped as one of Metal Dave's mighty paws found her shoulder. "It's okay, Chandra. If you ever need to talk—"

"That's—I..." The words wouldn't come.

When Grandma Maribel hit the floor, they no longer had to.

"It's working," Sylvia said, the cheeriness in her voice a mountainous contrast to the canyon of woe in which the room had found itself moments earlier. "EMPATHY must be working for her."

Chandra felt Maribel connect to the cerenet for a flash. Then Maribel spasmed. "*Merde.*" Chandra hopped from the bench and knelt at Maribel's side. "It's a seizure. You," she said, pointing to Gui, "call for a nurse." Gui rushed from Art and Supply, shouting for help.

Maribel's seizing worsened, her eyes fluttering, her shoulders twitching. Metal Dave made to intervene. "Here." He put himself opposite Chandra, crouched near Maribel on the floor. "Let me help you hold her down."

"No," Chandra said. She had plenty of time to fret over the topic of seizures in recent days, and at one point had checked the cerenet for what to do when someone seized; holding them down made the list of not-to-dos. "Help me get her on her side. And someone start timing how long this goes on for." She used EMPATHY to start counting as well, just in case no one followed her instruction.

Within a minute, Maribel's shaking waned. A couple of nurses arrived, gasping for breath, and set to working with Maribel as she recovered. After getting her into a wheelchair, they ushered her from the room and toward the hospital wing.

Chandra stared at the crowd of lavender-clad patients before her. An image came to mind—a wall of slate, its texture rocky and dry, run through top to bottom with lines like the desperate scratches of fingernails. She wanted to claw through it, to reach whatever waited on the other side, but she knew that was impossible. There were no claws. There was no other side. The image was only in her head, another painting with another hidden message, another she hoped she could prevent herself from releasing by accident.

She felt a hand on her hip—Sylvia. "Chandra, thank you." Sylvia wrapped her arms around her, tears wetting Chandra's shoulder. A few others neared to pat Chandra on the back as they exited Art and Supply.

Chandra didn't know what she had done to deserve thanks. Anyone would have done what she had if given another moment or two. Still, while she remained limp in Sylvia's hug, something about the acclaim felt different than it would have in the past. She felt no nervousness, and the walls no longer felt as though they rushed toward her.

It struck her. Confidence. This was what it felt like to be confident again, even if it came in the face of her worst fears about the study. Her expression soured as she stepped back from Sylvia's embrace. "It's true, then," she said.

The others eyed her with confusion, suspicion, unease.

"What do you mean?" Sylvia said.

Chandra choked out half a syllable before she pulled back. It was plain to see now. Each patient was prepared to hang on every word of whatever she was about to say. As the first to have connectivity—and after what she'd done to help Grandma Maribel—she now had a responsibility to every patient on the compound, like it or not. She couldn't incite panic by being indelicate about what she'd heard days earlier. "It's nothing," she said. "I'll work it out with the doctors." She loathed herself for saying it, knowing full well how unlikely that was. There had to be something she could do, though; she just needed time to develop a plan.

"How about this?" she said to Sylvia. "I have plans to meet up with Ty. Do you want to come with for the walk? We can talk on the way and try to take our mind off things."

"We should really clean up," Sylvia said, gesturing to the room at large.

"I think the staff will understand we needed to step away for a bit."

Sylvia seemed to agree. The two of them headed for the exit, trailing Metal Dave and his companions. "Grandma Maribel will be okay," Chandra said through her teeth to no one in particular. "We've got good doctors here."

Metal Dave held the door for Chandra and Sylvia. Chandra offered her thanks as she reached for it, gesturing for Sylvia to go ahead of her.

The thud of another body echoed in the hall. Gasps fired from all directions.

There, in the corridor, Calvin writhed on the floor.

Chandra rushed to assist, one hand held to her scar. As she set to work, she groped for an excuse, for some way to dismiss whatever was happening to Calvin as a coincidence.

But deep down, she knew the rumors were true.

She wondered how long it might be before a seizure came for her, and if it did, whether it would take her farther from Kyra than she'd ever been before.

Chapter Sixteen

MEREDITH

> To: <WITHHELD>
> From: "Meredith Maxwell"
> Subject: Re: Human/Etech—EMPATHY Study
>
> QS,
>
> Heads up—I've been taken off the EMPATHY story, but some of my colleagues will still be working on it. Either one of them or my editor will reach out to you for more info via this thread I'm sure.
>
> Thanks for working with us.
>
> Best,
> Mer

> —
>
> To: <WITHHELD>
> From: "Meredith Maxwell"
> Subject: Re: Human/Etech—EMPATHY Study
>
> It's been a couple of days. I hope all is well. Maybe you just haven't gotten to my last email yet, but as a reminder you can get back to any of the others who have now responded on this thread. Let us know if there's anything we can do to help.
>
> Best,
> Mer

—

To: \<WITHHELD\>
From: "Meredith Maxwell"
Subject: Re: Human/Etech—EMPATHY Study

If you're no longer interested in this relationship, could you please let a member of my team know? We'll better allocate resources accordingly.

Thanks,

Mer

Elbows on her desk, Meredith pulled at her hair. "I don't know how much more I can really do."

Kathy seated herself on the other side of the desk. "Have you tried calling her?"

Meredith lowered her chin.

Her editor seemed to take the hint. "No number. Right."

"This might be a sore subject," Meredith said, tapping a digipen on her desk, "but I'm beginning to think Brad was right."

"That traitorous opportunist? Are you saying he was right to go take that dead woman's—"

"Alicia Melendez."

"—job?"

Meredith shifted in her seat. "No, though his social media posts suggest he's having the time of his life over at *The Courier*."

Kathy mumbled to herself as she wrinkled her nose, a bony finger pushing her glasses back up it.

"What I'm trying to get at," Meredith said, "is I think Brad might have been right about this Gleason material." Meredith scrolled through it at rapid speed. "Maybe there's actually nothing here." Even her Susan Dunham lead had proven worthless. No matter what records Meredith inspected, nobody by that name turned up in the Gleason administration. That in itself was suspicious, but hypothetical musings on who Dunham might be didn't seem like much of a story to Meredith.

"Surely you can find something."

"I'm not going to manufacture news, Kathy."

"Then the news can be there is no news. That's not too unlike your first EMPATHY story."

"EMPATHY was different. The fact there even *was news* was news in and of itself. We can't use that as an excuse to shift into the un-news business."

Kathy clamped both palms down on the armrests of her chair. "In case you haven't noticed, we're in the whatever-keeps-our-doors-open business right now, and since your Queen of Spades has stopped responding, we need to break something and we need to do it soon."

Meredith rapped her fingers once on her desk. "Fine. An op-ed. We can say—"

"No op-eds. I need news."

"I'm not going to let my name be associated with opinion presented as fact. All we have right now is opinion and speculation and—"

"Then we publish opinion and speculation. It's a to-the-second industry now. I'm not here to harass or antagonize you. That's not my goal. But I, too, have a job to do, and sometimes that means putting ethics on the back burner to make sure everyone—including me—still has a job in the coming months. If you stopped for one second to think—"

Fantastic. Another lecture. They had increased in frequency over the course of the last week, likely the result of increased pressure from Mr. Lee after the first EMPATHY story. Meredith understood where Kathy was coming from, but thought it ironic that Kathy was willing to sacrifice their journalistic integrity by publishing opinion as fact, yet wouldn't fork over any cash for stories based on *actual* facts.

Not that Meredith was one to criticize the integrity of others. She had compromised herself in paying a source, yes, but she had to draw a line somewhere. To step across the opinion-as-fact line would make her a full-blown fake-news generator.

"... which is why I am asking—no, demanding—you get me a piece on Gleason by tonight at five. Do you understand?"

Meredith understood, but that didn't mean she planned to abide. "If I can work from home the rest of the day—"

"Why? You said yourself you feel less safe there after that damned envelope showed up."

"I want to check on Woody. Feed him. Take him out."

"The dog. Right." Kathy folded her arms against her chest. "Well, so long as you—"

"Yes. By 5:00 p.m. Got it."

Kathy raised an eyebrow. "Even if it's because you're digging up a bigger, better story, please don't miss the deadline this time."

Meredith choked down the anger bubbling in her throat. She told Kathy she wouldn't miss the deadline, but didn't exactly promise to meet it either. In the next two hours, Meredith planned on making some very serious decisions about her future as a professional. Would it count as missing a deadline if she'd quit her job by then?

The drive home became a mental exercise in discerning how long she could survive before she found a new source of income.

Even with the four thousand ameros she had spent on the first story having been replenished from that envelope, she might last—what?—a month and a half before those savings were depleted. She supposed it came down to how badly she wanted to stay in journalism. There were plenty of coffee shops looking for baristas, surely. The pay would be less, but she never minded the high-paced environment of her coffee shop job way back when, and if things got bad she could always sell her house and—

An email hit her pocketab. The message routed through her car's center console. A preview of the message's contents flickered on the screen as she made a right turn.

"To: 'Meredith Maxwell' From: <WITHHELD> Subject: Re: Human/Etech…"

"It's about time," she said.

As she fingered the MORE button on her console, the entire message came into view. She read it as she came to a stop at an intersection.

To: "Meredith Maxwell"

From: <WITHHELD>

Subject: Re: Human/Etech—EMPATHY Study

You. It has to be you. I have no trust for the others.

I have something new. Big updates from the compound.

For 6,000 ameros it's yours.

-Q♠

Whatever hope remained to Meredith vanished in that moment. The *Star-Globe* hadn't been willing to invest four thousand ameros in the last story. Six thousand was out of the question; surely Kathy would reason that having been reimbursed for the first story was no guarantee the same would happen with the second. Meredith swore, her hand slamming against her hatchback's horn. A pedestrian crossing in front of her threw his hands in the air.

"Sorry," she mouthed. "Accident."

As the light turned green and Meredith's foot found the accelerator, a future where she spent a portion of her day writing peoples' names on to-go cups became all the more likely.

Meredith made up her mind only a block from her home. She would give herself one last hour, one last shot at going through the Gleason material before she forced herself to accept a return to the world of coffee pouring.

She scanned the street as she came within sight of her home. Aside from the Austin Electric employee going door-to-door for meter readings, all seemed quiet on Esperanza Drive.

Meredith retrieved her mail before pulling into her driveway. Once parked, her financial prospects continued to darken as she thumbed through several bills—until an unmarked envelope caught her attention.

The same size as—but with a different seal than—the one that had shown up outside her home, this one seemed of a similar thickness. As she broke the sloppily adhered seal, her heart climbed into her throat.

Four thousand ameros.

Meredith ignored the obvious questions, her eyes watchful as she made her way to her front door. If she did have a second stalker, she certainly didn't see them on her street.

Woodward yipped on the far side of the door. After unlocking it and pushing past her exuberant Akita, she plopped the new envelope on her kitchen counter. Once Woodward had everything he needed to be comfortable for a while—and after she double-checked she'd given him his pills—she put herself to work. "Mommy needs you to be good for a while, okay?"

She took his wagging tail as assent.

Her pocketab splayed before her, Meredith headed first for her bank information. With two envelopes apparently set to show up after every story, she could afford whatever was asked of her and still have cash to spare. It was a risky assumption, but one she was willing to make—even if the *Star-Globe* wouldn't have been.

After purchasing some twenty-six thousand cryptocoins with her credit card—she could go to the bank and deposit the actual cash later—she transferred them to the Queen of Spades' account before firing off confirmation to QS that her demands had been met. While she waited for a response, she set herself to digging through the Dunham emails for what she hoped would be the last time.

She had spent only a few minutes on them when her concentration broke. The intrusive thought was of an airplane, two strangers passing in the aisle near the bathroom. Meredith leaned closer to her pocketab, steeling herself against distraction.

The scene on the plane forced its way into her consciousness again some five minutes later as she skimmed through email after email. As the incident played itself out in her mind, she recalled an exchange between the two travelers, cordial but with a hint of sexual tension. Something about the thought made her snicker.

That was it! The scene was from a shoddily edited romance paperback she had purchased a few years ago. As far as Meredith could remember, she hadn't even considered the book's existence since she had abandoned it within hours of starting it. Now, though, its title wouldn't come to her. Ugh. This wouldn't stop bothering her until she could at least remember its name. Meredith crossed to her living room to stare at her bookshelf.

She spotted it immediately. Reaching for her top shelf, Meredith dislodged *Dreams at 35,000* from between a script by Victor Denisov and a thriller by Darnell Dylan. Turning it over in her hand, she understood why the book had been calling to her.

Sue Dunham. *Dreams at 35,000* had been written by a Sue Dunham.

Rushing back to her pocketab, Meredith threw herself onto the stool and set to searching. Web results suggested Sue Dunham authored hundreds of titles across dozens of genres in the course of her career, which spanned a seemingly impossible seven decades.

As Meredith looked for an author profile somewhere—anywhere—to figure out why this woman might have been involved with the Gleason administration, the internet continued to produce bizarre outputs. Then, on the fourth page of search results, she finally found it.

Sue Dunham. Pseudonym. The author's name was a homophone for pseudonym. Whoever had used the name Susan Dunham in Gleason's administration had intended to conceal their true identity.

Meredith zipped back into the Gleason emails and ran a master query to sort them by parties involved. Her search application confirmed what she had already known for some time, that Gleason and Dunham never appeared in the same correspondence. Was Gleason using the name Susan Dunham to communicate with top members of her staff? Why?

These were the hypotheticals that would have been enough to satisfy Kathy, but Meredith kept digging. Woodward, however, apparently had other ideas about letting her get to work, now sitting at her side and whining.

"What? You want to go out? Is it bathroom time?" She granted herself a moment to let him into the backyard but didn't bother to leash him. At his age, he knew better than to wander into the neighbor's yard.

Once back in the kitchen, she opened a group of exchanges between Dunham and the then-FBI Director. It was then Meredith finally found what she'd been looking for.

To: "Addison Little"
From: "Susan Dunham"
Subject: San Diego Branch

Addy,

San Diego to scrub. No civ in AS ev.

-sd

Meredith trembled with what she had read. "Civ" had to be a reference to the CivIA, or the Civilians in Arms program, and "AS" had to mean the Academy Shooting. If "ev" stood for evidence, this had to be it. The smoking gun. Sue Dunham—Gleason herself—had asked the FBI to tamper with evidence to remove any link between her armament program and the weapons used in the school massacre. If true, this would mean she had perjured herself before a special Senate committee as well.

She paced around her kitchen once, twice, a third time before she settled enough to take actual notes. After opening an email addressed to Kathy, Meredith let her fingers fly, typing all she had found and attaching emails as necessary.

Meredith was reading it all through one last time when Woodward barked. She shook it off and started reading again. If she were going to send these notes to Kathy, she wanted to make sure her findings were clear and direct. Rushing to send them now would be imprudent.

Another attempt to reread her notes got derailed as Woodward kept on yipping. "Oh, come on, boy. You've only been out there for like two minutes." She looked over her shoulder toward the sliding door. No sign of him. If he wasn't whining to be let in, then—

A man's voice, thin with nerves, said something from the side of her house. Woodward barked again, growled.

No. The Austin Electric employee.

Meredith shrank her pocketab and tucked it away, a hop in her step as she scooted toward the door. "Woodward!" She slid open the door, the sound of his growling off to the right and around the corner. "Woodward, no. Leave him alone."

As she stepped into the thin patch of browned grass between her home and the neighbor's, she saw the Austin Electric employee with his hands at his sides, attempting to back away. "Easy," he said. "Easy."

"Woodward." Meredith romped forward and grabbed the dog by his collar. "What is wrong with you? Stop it."

He whimpered at her.

"Bad. Dog." She looked to the man on the other side of her meter, his expression easing. "I'm sorry. I know every dog owner says this, but he's never like this. Ever."

"It's okay," the man said. His lip curled upward, his posture more boastful than Meredith would have expected. Whatever fear Woodward had instilled in him had shifted to strange, wry confidence. "It happens." His eyes darted over her shoulder.

Before Meredith could turn, the man's eyes widened, his smile even more cocky than before. She felt a prick in her shoulder.

Woodward, now turned toward her, howled as the Austin Electric employee pricked him from behind with something as well.

Yanked from her feet, Meredith tried to scream, to wrest away the hand that covered her mouth, but her strength had left her.

Then Woodward, the sound of traffic, all of it quieted as the world dimmed. Her limbs numb, her vision blurred, the last sounds she heard were those of a van door sliding open, sliding closed.

Chapter Seventeen

CHANDRA

"I really don't think there's anything to be alarmed about," Ty said as the three of them set off from his room.

Sylvia kept up with him as they walked. "You weren't there, Ty. When Grandma Maribel hit the floor, it was like... it was like..." Sylvia turned to Chandra, a half-step behind the others. "Tell him, Chandra."

Chandra fell in line behind them as a nurse slipped past. "It was pretty bad. And then when Calvin fell—"

"It's these chips," Sylvia said. "It's EMPATHY. I can tell. We're—"

"Inciting panic for no reason?" Ty led them around a bend and up some exposed stairs. "Up to ten percent of people who live to be Grandma Maribel's age will have a seizure at some point in their lives. They're not always big catastrophic things, you know."

Sylvia pressed him. "Yeah, but then there's Calvin, who—"

"Has epilepsy." Ty held the railing as they turned on the stair's first landing.

"How do you know all this?" Sylvia said.

"What do I look like, some sort of nonny?" Ty winked at Chandra from over his shoulder. "And contrary to what you two might believe, I have managed to make at least one friend here besides you."

Chandra drummed her fingertips against the sides of her scrub bottoms. Should she tell them? She'd withheld spreading possible misinformation when she was in front of everyone in Art and Supply, but confiding the rumors to only Ty and Sylvia seemed safe, almost prudent. If the doctors weren't going to be of any assistance, perhaps the three of them could take matters into their own hands. "What about... well, when I first got to the compound, I heard—"

"That people's brains were getting scrambled by EMPATHY?" Ty said. "That there were dozens and dozens of patients left in comas or with speech impediments or—?"

"Yes," Chandra said.

Sylvia swung her attention toward Chandra. "You knew and didn't tell us?"

"Hey, Chandra," Ty said. "Remember when you had your chip installed and it gave you the power to talk to animals?"

Chandra huffed. "Ty, that's—"

"Or wait, no. It was that you started speaking in tongues, only for the doctors to later realize you'd mastered every language on the planet."

"What are you—?"

"What am I doing?" Ty halted at a juncture in the halls. He gestured widely at passing mobs of researchers, nurses, and patients alike. "I'm trying to prove you can't trust everything you hear. After what everyone said about you when you first got connectivity, I figured you would have known that by now."

Chandra's hands curled into fists. For as little as she cared for Ty's making a scene at her expense, he was right. Chandra herself had similar thoughts only days earlier, but fear of never seeing Kyra again—or of finding herself similarly afflicted—had clouded her judgment.

"Well that's—just—you know..." Sylvia shook her head, though she seemed to accept Ty's reasoning, too. "We're only trying to look out for one another. And ourselves. You could be a little nicer about it, Ty."

He shrugged before urging them onward.

Sylvia spoke up as she returned to a trot. "Where are we going, anyway?"

"To the computer lab," Chandra said. If she were honest, she was still suspicious there was a link between the seizures and EMPATHY, but it was best to abandon the topic for now. She had to finally start drafting an email to her brother. "Ty has something to show us."

TYCHO LEE: Damn right I do.

Chandra felt her pace slow. Why not say it out loud?

Before she could respond, Ty looked at Sylvia. "You have anyone on the outside you want to contact?"

"Oh, you know, just, like, everyone." Sylvia rolled her eyes. "Why tease us? It's not like we'll be able to reach them."

"So says you."

TYCHO LEE: Check it out. My left hand.

From her position behind the two of them, it took little effort to see the white piece of plastic half-concealed in Ty's palm—one of the keycards the staff carried with them.

CHANDRA ADELHADEO: Where did you get that?

Sylvia remained focused on trying to convince Ty he was wrong. "Have you ever even been to the lab? The internet is super censored. It's probably just as bad as…" Chandra tuned her out as Sylvia continued needling him with arguments Chandra herself had used hardly an hour earlier.

TYCHO LEE: Someone dropped it off inside a bundle of fresh scrubs. I thought it was an accident at first, but then they left this.

An image appeared of an invite to a meeting, all written on the keycard itself. The ink had an unearthly glow, blue with a sort of light emanating from it.

CHANDRA ADELHADEO: Are you going to meet with whoever it is?
TYCHO LEE: It's not like I have any other plans tomorrow morning. Plus they're coming to my room to get me so I'm sure they'd find me eventually.

The situation seemed an obvious no-go to Chandra. Ty's cavalier attitude shouldn't have been surprising, but even so, she felt like he wasn't giving her the whole picture. Something else was up. This all seemed too natural to him.

As Sylvia berated Ty for his ignorance in thinking he could contact people outside of the study, Chandra decided this wasn't the time to protest.

CHANDRA ADELHADEO: Well, good luck.

He slipped the card back into his left pocket. "And we're here," Ty said. "Wait." Sylvia put her hands on her hips. "Let me finish. I think—"

"You made what you think very clear," Ty said. "If you don't want to be a part of this, don't be. Chandra and I have a mission, though, so if you'll excuse us—" He pushed his way through the lab's glass door and motioned for Chandra to follow.

She made a face as she passed Sylvia. "I want to see what this is about is all."

"Whatever." Sylvia tapped her foot on the floor. "I'll be out here waiting." She headed to the hallway's opposite wall and leaned against it with her arms across her chest. As Ty and Chandra navigated the lab's rows of desktop computers, Sylvia continued to scowl on the far side of the glass wall.

"Don't worry about her," Ty said. "If she wants to tinker on the cerenet while we have all the fun, that's up to her."

Chandra swallowed. "Where should we sit?"

"Back here. Away from the window."

She slid out one of the blue plastic chairs at the terminal farthest from the glass wall. Chandra reached for her mouse.

"Don't," Ty said. "Let me handle each of our logins."

Painfully aware of her breathing, Chandra kept her attention trained on Ty. With a couple of keystrokes, he changed the login menu to a black screen littered with green characters. He gnawed at his lip as he typed. Out in the hall, Sylvia's eyes had glassed over, a sure sign she was passing the time on the cerenet.

At Chandra's side, Ty jammed down repeatedly on the ENTER key.

"Is that really necessary?"

"Damn thing is stuck." He bashed it once more.

Though the lab remained empty save for the two of them, Chandra still kept her voice low. "Do you want to teach me how to do this?"

He nodded for her to check out his screen, littered with complex patterns of letters and numbers. "Do you think this is the sort of thing you could learn in just one session?"

Chandra almost scoffed. Had he forgotten she was a nectee? *Zut!* Now he had her using the term. "I guess not," she said, figuring it wasn't worth reminding him of her cerenet connectivity. Rather than let EMPATHY absorb the screen's contents in the hope of deciphering it in real time, she employed it to snap an image of his screen.

After he finished his last few lines of what was now obviously code, he shot out of his chair. "Switch."

"Switch?"

"Sit here." Ty motioned to what had been his seat. "You're good to go. Stay off social media, though, or at least don't post anything that would let the public at large know you're online."

Swapping seats, Chandra felt the gravity of the moment—and the possible consequences for getting caught—settling in. "That's it? I can email my brother?"

"Yes. Now let me get myself set up on this other terminal. I have work to do, too."

Chandra navigated the operating system as she would have on any other device, opening the web browser and logging into her email. She had a handful of new messages, all of which were medical bills or spam. Gripping the mouse, she clicked to open a new email.

The blank expanse paralyzed her. She knew what she had come to say, to ask, but her fingers had gone stiff.

Focus, she told herself. You know what you want to ask. Just let the words flow.

Then it began—a feverish outpouring of requests and reassurance.

To: "Ratan Mahadeo"

From: "Chandra Adelhadeo"

Subject: Hello

Brother!

I know I said I wouldn't be able to reach you once I was enrolled, but I've found a loophole, one that will let me contact you. I don't know how often I'll be able to reach out, but I want you to know I think of you daily.

How is Kyra? Are there any updates? Please let me know if her most recent scans showed any changes. If you run into any trouble with the insurance company, don't worry. There may be a solution for that also.

I write because our anniversary—me and Kyra's, of course—is coming up at the end of the month. Please, I know this might be a lot to ask, but could you plant a sunflower in the garden? We were going to plant one on our anniversary for every year we were together, but... please.

When Kyra wakes up, I want to take her to the garden. I want to take her to the garden and show her I always knew she would return.

Write soon, and thank you for your kindness.

Love,

Chan

P.S. Please don't go telling others I'm in touch with you. It could prevent me from reaching you in the future.

She fired off the message before giving it a read-through. The moment its status moved from "Pending" to "Sent," a wave of regret crashed over her.

Why hadn't she mentioned EMPATHY taking for her? How hadn't she asked Ratan anything about himself? She thought about typing a follow-up—until sense set in. If they were to avoid being discovered in the computer lab, they would need to keep their session short. She had already accomplished what she had set out to do, and even that had involved more risk than she should have taken on, Chandra knew.

"I'm done." She made the announcement with far greater volume than planned.

"Okay." Ty's response was more of a question than a statement.

"Can you log me off now?"

"I've got my own emails to send." He mumbled something about a bank account.

"What?" she said.

"I'll tell you when you're older."

"I'm older than you."

He shrugged. "That doesn't mean I can't tell you when *you're* older."

Chandra's fingers flitted on her knees. "Thanks for helping me set this up, but I'm going to go wait in the hall with Sylvia." The chair screeched as she slid it out from under her.

"No you're not."

She froze. "I'm not?"

"Give me a minute. I need to give a go-ahead for the drop-off..."

"I have no idea what you're talking about."

"Because you're not old enough yet."

"Ty, seriously, can we wrap this up?"

"Yes. Look." His monitor had once again become a dark screen with intricate arrangements of green type on it.

"What's the difference between what you're doing now and what you did before?"

His fingers clattered against the keys. "Who wants to know?"

"Do you think I'm asking for a friend?"

He sighed. "It's the same thing with the exception of a final line that resets the RAM log." Chandra squinted at his screen, the keyboard clacking as he hammered the ENTER key. The screen disappeared. The terminal reset to its login screen. "I'll show you as I reset your terminal, but I think it'd be best if you let me do this for you whenever you want to come by. One slip-up and—" He drew a finger over his throat.

Chandra slid out of his way. As far as she could tell, what he had typed up to that point had matched the image she had saved to her egodrive. Then the clicking of his typing slowed, the notable decrescendo in volume and intensity luring her eyes away from the screen.

"Ty!" Her outstretched hands fell short of catching him.

He hit the tile with a dull thud.

Sylvia bolted into the room. "What's going on? Did he—?" Her hand went to her mouth as she saw him, eyes back in his head, tremors wracking him.

"Help me get him on his side," Chandra said.

Sylvia crouched next to Chandra. "Oh no. Oh no no no."

With Ty in as safe a position as Chandra knew how to provide, Chandra darted toward the hallway to call for a nurse. Her feet screeched as she came to a stop. "*Mon dieu.*"

The terror in Sylvia's eyes made her look as though she might cry at any moment. "What? Go."

"I need to log off." Chandra threw herself into the chair at her terminal. "I can't let them find us with this open." She swore, attempting to recall what she had seen Ty type for a final line when logging off his own terminal.

Her fingers shaking, she pressed ESCAPE. Nothing happened. That wasn't it. She tried holding SHIFT before pressing F2. A familiar screen appeared. "All right," she said. "Now it's..." Chandra typed "reset_ram:81"—it was eighty-one, wasn't it?—and hit ENTER. The screen that appeared was black but for a cursor blinking in green in the upper-left corner. That felt right, though Chandra couldn't be sure. Her hands hovered over the keyboard. ESCAPE. Now it's ESCAPE.

After pressing the ESCAPE key, the terminal reset. "That's it," Chandra said. Whether it was or not, there was no time to linger. "I'll get help."

On the ground, Ty still shook. Sylvia remained as doe-eyed as ever.

Again, Chandra only made it a step. "*Putain de bordel de merde.*"

"Just go! Ty needs help."

Without a word to Sylvia, Chandra knelt at Ty's side and fished through his left pocket. After withdrawing the keycard, she took off into the hall, shouting for assistance.

Her voice cracked as she called out, her attention just as focused on keeping a list of the loose ends she'd have to tie once she found help.

Before she could forget, she deleted the image of Ty's code she had saved to her egodrive—who knew who among the staff could see what she stored there? It wouldn't do her any good now, and there was no guarantee she had even exited her terminal properly. On top of that, she now had a keycard that was contraband for patients, the same contraband someone expected to meet Ty tomorrow at 10:00 a.m. to discuss.

And now, with a third participant now seizing in less than an hour's time, all of that was the least of her problems.

Chapter Eighteen

ARIEL

Ariel slipped into the boardroom, scampering past Wyatt at the head of the table.

"Emergency," Wyatt said, "does not mean arrive twenty minutes after the meeting has been called."

Alistair, a half-step behind Ariel, apologized for the two of them.

Ariel plopped into her seat, the solemn expressions of the rest of the Advisory Board only fueling the frantic rate of her pulse. What had they been told that she had not?

His lips pressed thin, Wyatt looked at Peter. "Go."

Peter went. "Thank you for coming on such short notice. Some of you are already aware of the health concerns we've—"

"Don't sugarcoat it," Wyatt said. "Seizures. There has been a wave of seizures among the patients."

A geyser of nausea surged up from Ariel's stomach. M3R1. The new code.

"Well," Peter said, "I don't know if I would call it a 'wave' exactly."

Wyatt removed his glasses. "Whether it was a wave or a couple or a platoon's worth, it makes little difference! I thought we left this sort of thing behind when we abandoned CompASSION. What do you know about each case? Did EMPATHY play a role?"

Alistair glanced up from his pocketab. "As far as we can tell, it did not."

The geyser of nausea weakened. But then again... Alistair knew about the seizures? Why hadn't he shared anything about them with her? Both of them were responsible for patient welfare.

Alistair continued. "Two out of the three individuals to seize have cerenet connectivity. The third does not."

"But," Peter said, "I explained to Alistair this information alone is not enough to make a proper determination. Even if a patient doesn't have connectivity, EMPATHY pings the server every sixty seconds to attempt to establish a connection. If the seizure for this individual coincided with one of those pings—"

"Which it did." Wyatt returned his glasses to the bridge of his nose. "At least according to your report."

So this was it. Ariel had caused the suffering of three patients by letting M3R1 take advantage of her ambition, her desire to please. Her cheeks warmed as color surely flooded them, a cold sweat beading on her brow.

"Yes." Peter's voice conveyed how carefully he trod. "But one data point isn't enough to determine whether EMPATHY played a role in the seizing of that individual or all three patients."

"Especially considering," Alistair said, "the two with connectivity are also epileptic."

Ariel never expected she would respond so positively to the news of an epilepsy diagnosis. Still, like Peter had said, they had no way of knowing anything for sure with such little data available.

Ariel considered a confession. If she were to tell them of her experience with M3R1, to expose herself as possibly having assisted in the harm done to these patients, she could help the team make their determinations all the sooner. Lives might even be saved.

But, then again, what if she was wrong?

Her lip quivered as the panic spread to her toes, the tips of her fingers.

Peter pressed a hand to the side of his face. "I *told* you admitting epileptics could create confounding variables."

"Don't take that tone with me. We needed to cast a wide net," Wyatt said, "and we're not here to play 'I told you so.'" He ran a hand through his hair. "If the two patients who seized both have connectivity but are also epileptic, then why call us here? What's the damn point?"

Peter flinched, though only for a second. "The point—aside from that we shouldn't have admitted some of those patients at all—"

Wyatt practically growled. "I'm warning you, Peter."

"—is that though these events do not *appear* EMPATHY-related, we cannot rule out the possibility. Only one of the afflicted patients is completely responsive at this point. Whether EMPATHY or some other variable is responsible, we need to monitor the situation with care."

Heather narrowed her eyes at Ariel from across the table, training them on her right hand. Then Ariel heard it—the jackhammering of her own fingernails against the tabletop. She flexed her hand, forced down a dry swallow, and retrieved her pocketab from her breast pocket to stymie the fidgeting.

"Gary and I will investigate," Peter continued, "and report back as soon as we're able."

A light flickered to life in the corner of Ariel's eye. Her pocketab. The blue indicator light. Her free hand clutched tight to the cloth of her canary scrub bottoms.

Heather removed her attention from Ariel. "I have two critical updates to provide as well." She expanded her pocketab to tablet size.

"Do you want to maybe advise us of these agenda amendments by email *before* these meetings begin?" Wyatt rubbed his forehead.

"These determinations were made only moments before entering the room," Heather said. "And you're already aware of the trespassing situation."

With M3R1 now listening in via Ariel's pocketab, she wondered whether she ought to dismiss herself. Or what if... she ran her thumb over the device's plasticky bump of an on-off button.

Her tongue found the corner of her lip as she depressed the button for one second, two—

"Candace and I are pleased to announce we have determined the source of the leaks," Heather said.

Ariel's finger slipped from the on-off button as a digipen fell from Wyatt's mouth, clicking against the boardroom table and tumbling to the floor. "You have?"

Heather set down her mug. "Patient C-5417."

A patient? No. The news was almost enough to make Ariel forget M3R1 still listened in, that she had just been about to power down her pocketab—and M3R1 along with it—only moments earlier.

Wyatt was aghast. "Did you say a patient?"

Heather took another drink. "The patient accessed the uncensored web via a terminal in the computer lab. We were able to obtain a copy of an email she sent during that time."

"That's—that's Chandra's participant number," Wyatt said. "How could she have... you're sure it was her?"

Right. This was enough. Ariel had to shut off her device before M3R1 heard too much. Who knew what it could do with this or any other information that might be revealed during the conversation? Her thumb found her pocketab's power button again, but, after further consideration, she removed it just as quickly. She could—and probably should—turn off her device, but that would risk retaliation Ariel could not afford.

She hid her pocketab away.

Heather tapped the screen of her own device. "I've just forwarded you the contents of Chandra's email. My best guess is she somehow circumvented security in the past, but failed to protect herself from being discovered on this occasion. Laziness from overconfidence, I would suspect."

"No," Wyatt said. "Nothing about her indicates any sort of computing background." He lifted his pocketab to his face, his eyes scanning its screen.

Alistair glanced in Heather's direction. "Perhaps if we had the proper measures in place, we could have prevented her from reaching the outside."

"My security has been nothing but flawless," Heather said.

Ariel felt the blood racing through her veins. All of this was madness, but if she couldn't outright deny M3R1 the chance to listen in by turning off her pocketab, she had to at least find a way to leave the room, especially if she'd only be missing Halman-family bickering.

"I'm sorry." Ariel raised a finger, surprised at the sound of her own voice. "But I... I'm not feeling—"

"Please don't interrupt unless you have something to add," Wyatt snapped. "And surely you can wait out the rest of this *emergency* meeting."

"I'd rather—"

Alistair's hand found her thigh. Her skin crawled. "She can wait. It's fine."

"No," she said. "I'm—"

Wyatt ignored her. "Please, Heather, go on. What else—"

Ariel made to stand. "I'm worried I might be sick."

Wyatt pressed on. "—did Chandra do after bypassing your security?"

"Sit down." Alistair said it between clenched teeth. "Ariel."

She started for the door when Wyatt's voice boomed once again. "If you exit this room, don't bother to return. I'm sure we can find Alistair another assistant, and work for you in the kitchens to boot."

Ariel halted, her hand on the door. If Wyatt followed through, she may as well be back bagging groceries outside Tempe—though this time there'd be no magical call from Alistair to pluck her from obscurity after having already been turned down for a different job on the compound.

She muted a sigh. If she were booted from the Advisory Board, she'd be in a far weaker position to stop M3R1. "My apologies. I'll wait."

Wyatt repeated himself, not dignifying Ariel with a response. "Again, Heather, tell me what else Chandra did in the computer lab."

Heather scrolled along her pocketab's screen. "She sent an email to her brother, nothing more."

"You're positive?"

"Absolutely."

Wyatt coughed a gust of frustration as Ariel returned to her seat. "How is our luck so poor? We finally have EMPATHY up-and-running for a few patients—one with the ability to become an immense marketing asset, mind you—and she turns out to be a mole." He laughed to himself. "This can't be right. What if—?" He stopped himself, apparently midthought.

Heather sipped from her coffee. The others—Ariel herself included—leaned in.

"Heather," Wyatt said. "Could you intercept any return correspondence from Chandra's brother?"

"Yes." Her tone contained a mistrustfulness.

"Then this is the plan," Wyatt said as he squared his shoulders. "We monitor her activity in the lab and keep an eye on anything she sends or receives. Mind you, I would expect we intercept all incoming and outgoing messages. I would only want them released to either Chandra or her intended recipients with my approval. Could you accommodate that?"

"We need to revoke her cerenet access," Heather said, "and shut down her EMPATHY entirely. She's a liability we can't—"

"Answer the question," Wyatt said. "Could it be done?"

Candace answered for Heather. "Yes."

"Thank you, Candace." Wyatt retrieved his fallen digipen from the floor, tucking it back into his lab coat. "Then that's what we do."

Heather protested. "Doctor, we—"

"We can't afford to cast aside our first cerenet-connected patient. Besides, I'm willing to bet she wasn't the source of the leak. She seems far too risk-averse, and doesn't have the background to carry out what would have been necessary to make this happen. Heather, Candace—the two of you are to monitor all of her lab activity from here on out."

Peter picked at a fingernail as he spoke. "What if Heather is correct about Chandra having been able to cover up her activity in the past? Her team won't be able to track anything if Chandra doesn't make the same mistake in the future."

Alistair chimed in. "Can you track her whereabouts? Via EMPATHY, that is."

"Possibly," Peter said. "Gary did upload the necessary code to support GPS, but we've done no testing to date." He bowed in Gary's direction. "Thanks for that, by the way."

Gary, though notably starry-eyed at the praise, coughed up a very uncertain, "You're welcome."

Ariel tensed. Was M3R1 celebrating on the far side of this conversation, knowing its GPS upload would now pay off?

"Then that's it," Wyatt said. "Peter, can you and Gary recalibrate Chandra's egodrive from the server side to ping Heather, Candace, and me when she enters the lab?"

"We've been recalibrating every patient's egodrive to be more in line with Chandra's configuration since EMPATHY took for her," Peter said. "Doing hers again would require more resources, and—"

"And that won't be a problem, I'm sure."

Gary intervened before Peter could throw more snark Wyatt's direction. "It won't be a problem, no."

Peter shot Gary daggers as Ariel checked her pocketab. Ten o'clock. Her stomach turned. She was supposed to be meeting with that patient, T-1719. Amid all of the chaos surrounding the emergency meeting, she'd forgotten entirely.

She almost shot her hand into the air, but she reined in the instinct to ask to be excused. The meeting had to be about over. Surely the participant would wait a few additional minutes.

"One last matter," Wyatt said.

Ariel clutched at her thighs under the table.

"There's little any of us can do with the exception of Heather's team," Wyatt said, "and we've already discussed in detail what must be done to prevent further occurrences—"

Heather cowered.

"—but we had a breach of another sort in the early hours of the morning. One of those bums camping outside the compound hopped the fence and made a run for the complex."

Heather chimed in. "He was apprehended about halfway up the hill, arguing he just wanted to get in touch with his wife. He hadn't heard from her since we disconnected the phone lines."

Alistair dug in. "More protesters show up out there every day. I told you we would have a riot on our hands if we prohibited communication with the outside. The next thing you know, the staff will go on strike and—"

"I won't hear it," Wyatt said. "I will *not* hear it. I brought this up as an FYI only, not an opportunity to further bicker with your sister."

"Half-sister," both Alistair and Heather said, correcting him under their breaths in unison.

"Since you've all proven yourselves incapable, I personally will handle contracting additional security around the compound's perimeter. Now go," Wyatt said. "Do your duty. No more surprises, please. And report back to me as soon as you've each resolved all we've discussed today."

Everyone launched to their feet, Ariel quickest of them all. Alistair seemed intent on holding her back, but she slipped past and into the hall, eager to keep M3R1 from hearing any private conversation Alistair might want to have.

Besides, already late for her meeting with that patient, she figured she should hurry to get to their room. With a midshift transition in effect, the halls bloomed with burgundy, cobalt, black, and periwinkle as employees in their respective colors migrated from one area of the compound to the next, each group encumbering any kind of speedy journey from one side of the compound to the other.

Even given the increased traffic, it took less time than she anticipated to arrive at the patient's room. With the apartment door closed, Ariel thought she should at least knock before bursting in and apologizing for her tardiness.

She rapped on the door twice as a small pack of researchers slipped past. No answer came. She knocked again, bringing her ear closer to the door. Nothing.

Ariel cursed her luck. Alistair would already be furious about her attempt to abandon the emergency meeting, but if she failed to deliver him to Alistair's requested location... then again, what was she to do if the patient had grown tired of waiting and set off for somewhere more exciting than their room? She had to know for sure. As she reached for the handle, the door eased open. "Hello?" Ariel said.

A voice on the other side told her to come in. She stepped across the threshold.

Her mistake stopped her where she stood. Thick of eyebrow with eyes of dark russet and warm brown skin, this was not the patient she was supposed to meet. "Chandra, I'm sorry. I've got the wrong room."

Chandra held out a hand. "You're looking for Ty, right?"

Ariel turned her head to the side, fumbling with her pocketab. T-1719, that's who she was here for. "I... yeah. Ty. Is he here?"

"No," Chandra said. "But I wanted to give this back to you." In her hand, she held a keycard.

"Shit." Ariel felt herself lock up. "Shit shit shit."

"Should we... shut the door?" Chandra said. She reached behind Ariel to close the door and seal them off from prying ears in the halls. "All I want to do is return this to you and move on like it never happened. I don't even know your name, so it's not like you have anything to worry about."

Ariel forced herself to breathe. Whether Chandra knew Ariel's name was immaterial. She was only one of three on the compound to wear canary-colored scrubs, and one of two women at that. Identifying her to a higher authority would hardly be difficult, and it was apparent Chandra knew doing so would make trouble for Ariel especially.

She couldn't undo whatever mistakes she had made to botch this operation so far, but Ariel knew she had to at least get things back under her control. "That's okay." Ariel took the keycard from Chandra and tucked it into a pocket. "I'm Ariel, by the way. I don't want either of us to have anything to worry about."

Chandra arched an eyebrow. "How do you mean?"

Ariel hadn't meant for it to sound like a threat, but perhaps there was a way to make that work in her favor. "Who else knows about this?"

"No one. Just me and Ty, really."

"You and Ty, *really*?" Ariel said.

Chandra looked at the floor. "Just me and Ty. Only me and Ty."

Ariel forced strength into her voice. "Good." If Chandra were telling the truth—that no one aside from her and Ty knew about the keycard—it played right into Ariel's lap. She could get the keycard back to Ty once she found him, and Alistair, though upset over the delay in delivering him to the meeting room, would be none the wiser. But silence from Chandra was a must. And Ariel? She'd grown tired of being the one pushed around.

"Before you think of telling anyone about this keycard or me running into you here," Ariel said, stepping toward Chandra, "I need to make something very clear."

"I won't tell anyone." Chandra raised her hands in front of her. "I want this to go away as much as you do."

A pain clutched at the back of Ariel's throat, but the pent-up anger at the rest of the advisory board, at M3R1, at herself, pushed her forward. "I know about your escapade in the computer lab."

Chandra paled.

"But," Ariel said, "I haven't mentioned it to anyone. Yet."

Whatever confidence Chandra seemed to have left evaporated. "Please, I won't do it again. I—"

Perfect, Ariel thought, until she realized what that would mean. If Chandra never went to the lab again, Heather and Wyatt would never be notified of her presence there. A sudden lack of interest in a response from her brother might raise more suspicions than it would lower. "No. I want you to keep going."

Chandra blinked a number of times in quick succession.

"Keep going to the lab if you'd like. Consider it a trade."

"I don't want a trade," Chandra said. "I want this to go away."

"Then why come at all?"

Chandra raised an eyebrow. "What do you—?"

"You could have just as easily thrown the keycard in the trash or dropped it on the floor in an empty hallway."

"I'm trying..." Chandra bit at her lower lip. "I want to protect Ty. Whatever he's up to—whatever you're up to—can only lead to trouble." She shrugged. "I think so, anyway. I felt like I had to come in person to—"

"Coming in person could've meant trouble for *you*."

"I feel like the person handing out keycards to patients probably has a lot to lose, too."

Ariel steeled herself against that terrible truth. "If you want this to go away, it can and it does. Stay quiet about the keycard, and I'll do the same about your visits to the lab. I help you. You help me."

Chandra's hand went to her scar before she pulled it away. "I won't say anything."

The tension left Ariel's shoulders. "All right. In a minute I'm going to step back into the hall and we can pretend this never happened. Understood?"

Chandra nodded.

"Don't look so worried," Ariel said. "Silence is golden, like they say. Let's put this behind us and go on as friends."

Chandra shot her a skeptical expression.

"Maybe 'friends' isn't the right word," Ariel said, "but our arrangement can be friendly, at least." Without waiting for a response, she stepped toward the door, opening it a crack. "Remember, Chandra. Not a word."

Back in the halls, Ariel tried to reassure herself the encounter had shaken out as fairly as it could have. Going on as if it never happened was possible, whether Chandra realized it or not. In fact, it was more true for Chandra than for herself. She still had to find Ty and deliver him to Alistair's reserved meeting room. If she didn't know where he was, though...

That was it. There was a way to placate Alistair in this as well. All she had to do was shift the blame. With the mid-shift transition having ended, the halls had mostly cleared. Ariel leaned against the cool brick wall and retrieved her pocketab before noting its recording light was only just dimming.

In her haste to find Ty, she'd forgotten about M3R1 entirely. But what—if anything—had it really learned in the conversation she'd had with Chandra? Whatever additional dirt it might have on her as a result was nothing compared to what Ariel had done in the server farm. Going forward, she'd have to be more deliberate about when she had her pocketab on her. She'd be golden if she could find a way to deny M3R1 access to critical information without arousing its suspicion, but no—those were matters for another time. For now, she speed-dialed Alistair from her home screen.

His answer was immediate. "What is wrong with you?"

"What?" She pushed herself away from the wall, bringing her free hand to her face.

"During that meeting! You showed up uninformed, tried to excuse yourself, embarrassed me, embarrassed *yourself*—"

"Slow. Down." She took a short breath in between her teeth. "You know I had to get out of there in a hurry. I had that meeting at 10:00 a.m. Remember?"

"And how, exactly, did you plan on meeting with a patient in his room if he was in the hospital wing after seizing?"

Ariel shot down into a crouch. "What?"

"Yes. We actively talked about it in the meeting."

"His specific name or patient number didn't come up."

"Didn't you read the report?"

"You mean the one everyone seemed to have except me? I sure don't remember seeing it."

"Excuse me? Surely you saw it." His voice became more distant as he presumably checked the SENT folder of his email. "It's right here. I..." He grumbled something to himself. "Well, that's not the point. In either case, you can't go rushing away after an emergency meeting. We have a ton to discuss."

Ariel brushed his anger aside. He could deal with a bruised ego on his own time. "So what's your plan now? How are you going to work with this patient if he's in the care of the hospital wing?"

"He'll be out soon enough, but don't bother visiting him once he is. I'll take the risk of continuing to work with him directly. At least I can trust myself not to make any unforced errors." Alistair ended the call, apparently failing to grasp the irony of his closing words.

Ariel felt as though she should have been upset, but relief took her instead. Chandra had been dealt with, and soon enough Alistair would be working directly with Ty. Now Ariel had just M3R1 to worry about.

Just M3R1.

The relief dissipated. As she took off toward her office, Ariel clenched her pocketab, the feel of it filling her with dread. Sooner rather than later she would need a plan to undo whatever evil she had helped load onto the primary server.

Chapter Nineteen

MEREDITH

Meredith opened her eyes. Darkness reigned. What felt like a canvas bag prickled her nose.

She made her first attempt to move, but her hands, her legs had been bound. Her heart lurched into her throat, throbbing at the speed of a hummingbird's wings.

Don't struggle, she told herself. The longer she went without drawing her captors' attention, the more she stood to learn. The more she learned, the better off she might fare.

The hum of the highway rushed by outside. Then came the sound of breathing, her own and that of two others. Lying horizontally, the cool steel floor of the van pressed against her head, her shoulders, her back. She kept quiet, ever so quiet—until she heard a whimper.

"Don't hurt him," she said. They must have snatched Woodward after they threw her into the van. "Leave him be." She attempted to kick, forgetting her legs had been bound. As she rolled onto her side, strong hands took hold of her shoulders and pinned her onto her back.

"I don't remember asking you to talk," a man's voice said. His hands—seemingly double the size of a normal man's—pinned her tight to the floor. "A little help here?" he said to what must have been his accomplice.

Woodward's whimpers became yelps.

"Shut the fucking dog up, would you?" the man said.

"Which one is it—give you a hand or shut up the dog?" The second man's voice was thinner and more nasal, not unlike the one who had been posing as the Austin Electric employee.

"Don't hurt him," Meredith said again. "Just tell me what you want." She heard the second man smack his hands against steel, perhaps rattling the side of a cage. Rather than silence Woodward, it turned his yelps into full-on barks.

"What kind of idiot are you?" said the man holding down Meredith. "I said shut the beast up, not have him go full wolf-dog."

"What the hell am I supposed to do? He's a dog. I can't just ask him to pipe down."

"Give him a shot for all I care."

Meredith struggled. "Don't shoot him! Please." A fist collided with the side of her face. The pain throbbed in her jaw.

"Again, no one asked you to talk. You hear that back there? This lady thinks we're gonna shoot her dog."

The man farther from her laughed, a cackle not unlike one of Woodward's yelps. "We're not that bad. Probably."

"Here," said the man looming over her. "Maybe this will help clarify things."

She braced herself for another blow. None came. One of the large man's hands left her shoulder, and the soft swishing sounds of someone rifling through a duffle bag tickled Meredith's ears.

Something pricked her in the thigh. Another syringe. *That* kind of shot. "Why would you—?"

The canvas bag flew off her head. "We want to let you breathe a little easier."

Surprised her surroundings weren't slipping away as they had after the last time they pricked her, Meredith sat and looked about the van. No windows. A cage against the back wall. Inside was Woodward, whose barks became more frenzied at the sight of her.

Sure enough, the man nearest her—presumably the one who had been holding her down—clutched an emptied syringe in one hand.

"What was that?" she said. Meredith studied his face to remember as many details as possible. His bottom lip was much larger than the top, his forehead a broad, wrinkled mess. He had to be about forty, or maybe fifty, or twenty?

No. She had to be hallucinating.

The man near Woodward's cage—the one who she'd seen dressed as the Austin Electric employee—should have looked somewhat familiar, but though she had seen him outside her home, her memory of the moments before she was needled had become hazy at best. Now as she stared at him, too, his features seemed to shift with every second. What kind of drug had they given her? She spun back to the larger man, ready to demand answers.

"It'll wear off," he said. "Eventually." Whatever it was, it seemed to affect only their faces. "It's a targeted serum." He flicked the syringe twice with his middle finger. "Our bosses don't pinch pennies where research and development is concerned."

"They sure don't," said the other man.

Woodward still yelped in his cage, attempting to pace in what little space he had. "You're doing a pretty awful job with poochy over there," said the man with the syringe.

"Maybe this will do the trick," said the smaller of them.

His arm swung downward through a gap in the top of the cage. She froze at the sight of the syringe jutting from Woodward's neck.

"What kind of—?"

The larger man yanked her by the hair. She landed on her back with a crash. "Come on," he said. "I was just about to explain." He nodded to the smaller of them, who jerked out the syringe. "Can you believe this lady? People these days, they have no patience."

"No patience," said the little man.

"It's a short-lived sedative. We want him calm. We want *you* calm. If you can't keep him calm yourself, we make him calm. If you can't keep yourself calm—"

"I'll keep myself calm," Meredith said. "What do you want? Tell me who you are."

"Who we are?" The larger man laughed. "This lady wants to know our names. You think we should give her our NAUCID numbers while we're at it?" He chuckled again but turned back to Meredith. "Call me... I don't know. Call me Harold."

"And you can call me Buzz," the other man said.

"Buzz?" Harold said. "What kind of stupid name is that?"

"Like the astronaut," Buzz said. "You know—"

"That wasn't his real name, you moron."

"Are you sure? I could have sworn—"

"Guys," Meredith said. "Tell me what you want."

They fell silent. Outside, the empty rush of the highway droned on.

"I'd like to show you a picture," Harold said, "and you tell me the first thing that comes to mind." He reached into the pocket of his black jeans and retrieved a pocketab. After a few pokes at its screen, he thrust it toward her face. Meredith cowered, but he held it there, inches from her nose. "Recognize this lady?"

She stiffened at the sight. "Alicia Melendez—the one from *The Courier* who—"

"Suffered from severe depression. Can you imagine having to deal with something like that all by yourself all those years?" Harold looked at Buzz, his face now ancient. "Really a shame what happened to her." Harold turned to Meredith. Even as his face transformed, Meredith could tell what his expression meant.

"It was you. You killed her."

"Well," Buzz said, "not us. That was—what were their names that day? Simon and Garfunkel?"

Harold bellowed, stirring Woodward from his slumber. "It was. I could have smacked you across the jaw when you said 'Garfunkel' after I went with 'Simon,' but my God if that wasn't the funniest goddamn thing...."

Meredith scanned the van for anything she could use as a weapon. She may have still been bound, but she needed an escape plan should the opportunity present itself. Much to her distress, the floor was spotless save for her, the two men, Woodward's cage, and Harold's duffle bag—whatever else was in there. Unless she found a way to get into the duffle bag, her options were limited.

"So what then?" Meredith said. "You just kill me because I stumbled onto Gleason's 'Sue Dunham' alias?"

Buzz spoke first. "Wow, she's way more on top of it than that other gal was."

"The other one was playing dumb," Harold said. "This one knows she can't." He addressed Meredith directly. "And you should be grateful we got to you before you fired off that email to your editor."

Meredith didn't need to ask why. Something primal surged through her, some instinct she didn't know she had. Rather than beg, than plead, than tell them she'd abandon her work, she spat. "If you're going to kill me, just do it, you sons of bitches. All I ever wanted was to find the truth, and if you're going to deny me that—"

Harold's fist connected with her jaw once again. Meredith bit her cheek, releasing a taste of blood.

Dazed and on her side, Meredith struggled to right herself.

"Maybe she's not as smart as you thought," Buzz said.

Harold muttered something to himself before he gripped her by the ropes that bound her. He propped her against the side wall of the van. "If we were going to kill you, don't you think we would have done it already?"

Meredith, ready to spit in his face, managed to hold back. Right. They had killed Alicia in her own home, making her death all the more convincing as a suicide. Why abduct her if they didn't have to?

"Look," Buzz said, "she's getting it now. See, lady? We're not so bad—not as bad as Simon and Garfunkel, anyway."

Harold's lips—now those of a paunchy man in his forties—curved upward in a grotesque, toothless smile. "That's right. You see, you can offer us something our depressed friend could not."

"What?" Meredith said. "All the backing of a financially defunct e-paper? You would have been better off forcing *The Courier* to do your bidding."

"No," Harold said. "*The Courier* doesn't have access to your Queen of Spades."

That was the moment it hit her. "It's been you. You're the ones leaving envelopes outside. You want stories—more EMPATHY stories."

Buzz offered some of the most sarcastic applause Meredith had ever heard. "We have a winner."

Harold shrugged. "We were leaving envelopes outside, yes. We figured our bosses could bankroll this Queen of Spades better than you could." He sighed. "But, now that someone else is also reimbursing you for every story, I wouldn't expect any more cash from us."

"Why not go to QS yourselves? Why get me involved?"

"She doesn't respond to anyone except you," Harold said.

"So that's it then?" Meredith said. "I keep quiet about Gleason, write more about EMPATHY, and all of this goes away?"

Woodward twitched at what must have been a bad, drug-induced dream.

"Not exactly," Buzz said. "The people that sent us want specific information."

"Technical information," Harold said. "Our people—those great folks in R and D that I was telling you about—they've caught a whiff of something. Something special. They suspect they have an idea of what makes EMPATHY work, but these Halmans... they haven't been very forthcoming about confirming what that thing might be."

"And you want me to use my source to get that information?"

"Yes and no," Harold said.

Buzz clasped his hands together. "Knowing *what* separates EMPATHY from our own prototypes—and the one NanoMed's been developing—is only helpful if we know where to find the stuff."

"And of course," Harold said, "we'd also like to know how they're putting it to use. You know, to help us move along in our own development more quickly."

Not good. Not good at all. The Queen of Spades was presumably a patient; could she even get Meredith that kind of information? She needed to know more first. "All right," Meredith said, "but if you want me to confirm your suspicions about what this *it* is, it may be helpful for me to have more background than it's the 'special thing' that makes EMPATHY work."

Harold's smile disappeared. "Knowing you're searching for details on a previously undiscovered element should be a good starting point."

A new element entirely? No wonder it'd taken so long for Halman to progress this far. If Meredith had to guess, there was no way any patient— not even one like QS, if her hunch was correct—could get that level or proprietary information, and, well, it went without saying what the NAU might do to her if she failed to dig it up for them. She felt the urge to rock, to wiggle her fingers and tap her toes as anxiety took her, but she still had an out. Possibly, anyway. "Okay, but you said 'yes and no.'"

"What?" Buzz said.

"You trying to get cute?" Harold added. "We don't need—"

Meredith drew in a tentative breath. "You said 'yes and no' when I asked if you needed my source to get you the information you're looking for. What did you mean with the 'no?'"

Buzz turned to Harold. "Yeah, what *is* up with the 'no?' I didn't really underst—"

A backhand from Harold silenced Buzz in a hurry. "You're just as bad as the people we kidnap, I swear."

"Hey—"

"Hey nothing," Harold said. "Let me talk." He scooted that much closer to Meredith. She winced, but he didn't lash out. "This special sauce of the Halmans', so to speak—we've had it on our radar for some time." He let a pause linger.

"I'm listening," Meredith said. "Tell me what I can do." Whether she could do it would be one thing, but she couldn't do anything until she was released from their custody, and whatever it took to have that happen sooner rather than later was something she'd gladly consider.

"Let's say hypothetically," Harold said, "that for whatever reason your Queen of Spades can't get her grubby hands on the what, where, and how behind EMPATHY's secret. If that were to happen, well, in that case, we might be amenable to your source helping us pry that information from the Halmans' fingers via other means."

Before Meredith could ask what those other means were, Harold intervened.

"If you can help us force Human/Etech into surrendering that information..."

A pregnant pause took the back of the van, the iron-y taste of blood still in Meredith's mouth. Woodward's collar jangled in his cage, the sedative apparently starting to wear off. It was in the midst of the panic beginning to flicker in Meredith's chest again that Harold's implication clicked. "You want me to force an investigation," she said.

Harold leaned back, his face shifting from old to young. Despite the change, his smile was unmistakable. "Smart, huh?" he said to Buzz.

"She gets it," Buzz said. "And I guess I do now, too, but—"

Meredith cut him off. "If I can find you some dirt on the Halmans—"

"Specifically about the study," Harold said, raising a finger. "It needs to be about the study."

Wow. Wow wow wow. Rather than continue to try and steal the information themselves, they planned to make the Halmans deliver it to them directly. "You're going to subpoena their trade secrets and make them divulge everything about this element in court."

Harold cracked his knuckles. "That's the plan. You have your Queen of Spades get us the dirt we need to pounce on the Halmans—"

"Or as a bonus," Buzz said, "have her deliver to us exactly what we're looking for through you, and maybe we'll forget all about your little Gleason discovery this afternoon."

"So long as you forget about it, too, lady," Harold added. "All right?"

"All right," Meredith said, her pulse racing at the thought of a new mission, this new goal. "I'll get you whatever you need to force an investigation as soon as I can."

"As soon as you can?" Harold said. "How about with each of your next three stories? Our boss, you see, she's not very patient. The longer it takes the NAU to start weaponizing EMPATHY, the more likely the Asian Federation is to find a way to do it with their own technology first. That puts lives at risk, you know. Yours, mine, everyone else's on this continent."

Meredith clenched her teeth at the party-line jingoism of the ruling Right For The Union party. No one wanted another war less than the

Federation, but so long as a paranoid, defeated Gleason held sway over continental politics, there was always a risk of tensions boiling over again. "Three stories, sure."

"And get us *the good stuff*," Harold said. "Actionable information. Hearsay's not going to cut it. Time is of the essence here."

"So tick tock," Buzz chimed.

"Exactly," Harold said. "Get us something to justify an investigation in each of your next three stories, and we'll be in a good position to forget this ever happened. But if you fail," he said, shrugging, "well, you can expect to hear from us again—and I think we've made it plenty clear this is not something you should be looking forward to."

Meredith swallowed, the taste of blood now fainter than it was before. "I'll work with the Queen of Spades on this right away."

"Good." Harold made a fist.

Meredith flinched.

He pounded three times on the wall separating them from the van's cab. Her weight shifted as the van slowed. "Well, this is where you get off."

"Where are you leaving me?"

Buzz shrugged. "How should we know? We can see outside just as well as you can."

Woodward picked up his head. "I'm going to be real glad to get rid of Barky McBarkerson back there," Harold said. Then, to Meredith, "Please get us the information we need. If you can't do it or try to skip town, let's just say our watchful eyes will let us know and I'll have to come back for you and your puppy here. And if you want an honest self-evaluation, I'm not very good with dogs."

The van now at a stop, Harold reached past Meredith and slid open the side door. They appeared to be on the shoulder of a rural highway with nothing but farmland for miles in every direction. A deep ravine yawned between the van and the fence line of a bordering property.

Harold lumbered past her and out onto the gravelly shoulder.

"Anybody out there?" Buzz said.

"No. Let's do this." Harold reached into the van, putting his gigantic arms under Meredith.

As he lifted her from the van's floor, she attempted to barter with him. "Why leave me here? How am I supposed to force an investigation if you leave me tied up on the side of some country road? What does that prove? Why not—?"

"Lady," Harold said. "Slow down and think about it." He took a large step over a displaced log in the tall grass. Over his shoulder, Buzz struggled to carry Woodward in his cage a few yards behind them. The van beyond the two of them loomed white and without marking of any kind, the plates impossible to see from her angle. "You're probably smart enough to not call the cops once we get out of here, but in case you're not... we need to give ourselves a head start."

Meredith grimaced. "I won't call the cops. I only want to go home."

"Good," Harold said. "Calling them would be a waste of time anyway. You think they're gonna come looking for us once they find out who we represent?"

She figured the question was rhetorical. Meredith stayed silent until they reached the bottom of the ravine. "How will I get home if you leave me here like this?" She attempted to roll onto her side, but Harold held her down.

A moment later, the dog cage rattled as Buzz plopped it alongside her. Woodward set to barking.

"Dammit, Garfunkel."

"It's Buzz—"

"Who cares?" Harold pulled something from his back pocket, flipping it open. It gleamed in the light of the sunset. A knife.

"No," Meredith said. "Don't—"

"Don't cut you loose?" Harold said. "Listen, we don't have time to mess around. I'm gonna cut through the rope just enough so you can wiggle your way out once we're well down the road. Then you and poochy can wander back up the hill and call someone to come get you." He pulled her pocketab from his back pocket and tossed it into the muck in the ditch, just beyond her reach. "You're welcome."

As Harold started to cut through the rope, Woodward's barking intensified, each yap stronger than the last.

"Come on," Buzz said. "She can handle it from here."

Harold stood over her. "Now I don't want you to start trying to free yourself until we've pulled away, understood?"

"Yes. Please. Just go."

"Look at that," Buzz said. "She wants the same things we do."

"Yeah," Harold said. "A real match made in heaven." With that, the two of them trudged back up the ravine.

For fear they might look back, Meredith remained frozen until she heard the door of the van slide shut. Then she set to work.

Woodward's cries only worsened as she struggled to untie herself amid the dirt and tumbleweed litter at the bottom of the ditch. A quarter hour and a severe rope burn later, Meredith collected her pocketab before kneeling at Woodward's cage and unlatching its door to free him.

Unsure who else to call, Meredith dialed her editor. Kathy—at first pissed with Meredith for missing the Gleason deadline—almost seemed a different person once Meredith managed to make herself heard, rushing to arrive only a half hour after Meredith forwarded her GPS coordinates.

Though feeling safer in Kathy's car en route back to Austin, Meredith remained wary. Kathy's face grew fuzzy at the edges at times, no doubt the product of whatever serum remained in her bloodstream.

Kathy seemed willing to give Meredith time to breathe, but after a few minutes, the silence became too much to bear. Meredith spilled all the details she could—leaving out that she knew who her abductors were, and certainly withholding knowledge of the Gleason story she had uncovered earlier in the day.

Kathy's first response suggested her compassionate streak was to be short-lived. "I don't know how you're going to cover both EMPATHY and the Gleason Scandal." She turned her vehicle into the trickle of evening traffic on the outskirts of the city.

Meredith gave herself a second before responding. "They only want details on the secretive, inner workings of EMPATHY. It's that or dirt on the study as a whole. They said nothing about Gleason." Meredith brought her knees to her chest in the passenger seat, watching the orange streetlights strobe past overhead.

Kathy tapped on the steering wheel. "Do you think the Queen of Spades can even get you the technical info they're looking for?"

"Not likely." Meredith leaned her head against the window. "But hopefully she can get me something juicy about the study—assuming there's something scandalous to dig up at all."

"And if there's not, what's your plan?" Kathy took her eyes off the road. "You're not gonna run away to Central America, are you?"

Meredith sighed an almost-laugh. "Not yet, at least." If she were honest with herself, she had no plan aside from starting with QS. If it turned out she had no way to determine the mystery element at the heart of EMPATHY, Meredith would have to go after the forcing-an-investigation angle hard, banking on the Halmans' study concealing some dark or salacious secret. Her stomach reeled with the stress of it all. Regardless of the assistance the Queen of Spades ultimately lent, there was still the matter of her needing to be ready for reprisals from her abductors at any time. "Kathy, I need you to do something for me."

Kathy said nothing.

"I need you to talk to the board and ask Mr. Lee if they can cough up enough cash for personal security. I'd feel much more able to do my job if—"

"I don't know, Mer, there's hardly enough cash to—"

"For Christ's sake, your senior reporter was just abducted. Can you at least ask? Show some frigging compassion!" Neither spoke for a time as Woodward snored in the back seat. Then it came to her. Compassion, Meredith thought. EMPATHY. "I know how we get it. I know how I get what my kidnappers demanded."

"How's that?"

"We go straight to the source."

Kathy faced Meredith, her sarcasm apparent. "I'm sure Wyatt Halman would love to meet with you if you asked. He'll probably fork over whatever you want to know about his most prized invention."

Meredith unwrapped her arms from around her legs. "I'm not going to ask. I'm going to force his hand, make him give it away." She looked toward the Austin skyline as it rose on the horizon. "I'll leave him no other choice."

Kathy laughed. "How do you expect to do that?"

"I blame him for my abduction."

The rumble strips roared as Kathy nearly lost control of the vehicle. "Wait—you're serious?"

"What makes you think I'd be joking right now?"

"Going public with that story would only be setting us up for a lawsuit. I can't—"

"That hasn't stopped you before." Meredith clenched her jaw, her fingernails digging into her scalp. "And we don't have to be the ones who publish it. We get someone else to float it and—"

"No. Absolutely not. Even if we did, how could that possibly—?"

Meredith threw her back against her seat. "It gets Halman's attention and forces him to engage in a dialogue." It might also be enough to get some kind of NAU investigation of the compound started, or at least lay the groundwork for one. She wasn't willing to wager one of her three stories on that, but it didn't hurt to have others try on her behalf.

"For as much as you might want that dialogue," Kathy said, "the *Star-Globe* can't afford for it to be through the legal system."

Meredith's tongue explored the spot where she'd bitten her cheek. The taste of blood still lingered. She opened her mouth but thought better than to reply. Kathy wouldn't be moved. Not now. Not ever.

If Meredith were going to pull this off, she'd have to do it alone.

Chapter Twenty

WYATT

Wyatt poured himself another scotch and checked the time. The events of the last twenty-four hours had made him anxious—and frightened, if he were honest. His lawyer's tardiness wasn't helping, either.

His shoes knocked on the wood floor with each step across his living room. He stood before the unused fireplace, staring above the mantle to where a picture would have been mounted had he taken the time to decorate. Another hearty swig hit his throat. Wyatt had grown accustomed to the burn during his first drink; the second was going down much more smoothly.

As he swallowed, Wyatt thought of what he would have placed above the mantle. The image came to him immediately. *Ást án enda.* He would have hung that picture of himself and Eva from their first weekend at the cabin. They stood beneath a grove of balsam firs, the lake at their backs. Wyatt had said something, though he couldn't remember what, in the moment before the photo was taken. Eva threw herself forward with laughter, her long golden hair flopping over the front of her face. She had brought one leg up toward her chest and a hand to her mouth, only partially covering the crisp whiteness of her teeth by the time the photo was snapped. Wyatt had always loved that photo, but Eva forbid him from displaying it anywhere. She said the picture made her nose look piggy, though he never understood what she meant. Still, he honored her request, keeping the photo tucked away in his desk where no one would see it but him.

Wyatt pulled again from his tumbler. No, even if he had taken the time to place a photo above the mantle, it never could have been that one. Not only had Eva forbidden him from displaying it, but doing so would have also sent the wrong message. EMPATHY wasn't about the past, it was about the future... mostly.

A knock at his door snapped him into action. "Come in." It had to be Lars.

"Sorry I'm late." Lars closed the door behind him. "Your pilot got a little lost on the way to pick me up."

"At least the helicopter was an option," Wyatt said. "It didn't make you too sick this time, I hope?"

"Maybe a little," Lars said, "though not too queasy for one of those." He pointed to the scotch in Wyatt's hand. "Is that the fifteen-year Stenlivet?"

"Twenty-one." Wyatt gestured to the kitchen and Lars helped himself before joining Wyatt in the living room.

"I hate to do this to you," Lars said, "but as your lawyer, I have to ask— *did* you orchestrate that journalist's kidnapping?"

"You're going to come to my home-away-from-home in your pajamas and sling accusations?" Wyatt's nerves still prodded him. He felt so unlike himself.

Lars sipped his scotch. "You called me in the middle of the night, urgently needing my counsel. I figured after how long we've known one another we could set aside the decorum."

"I suppose." Lars was Eva's brother, after all. They'd been family, once. "At any rate, the answer is 'no.' That journalist was hardly on my radar after we served the cease-and-desist. There haven't been any more leaks since, so I could have cared less what she was up to. But now—"

"But now we have to do something about her... again. What are you thinking?"

What *was* Wyatt thinking? The ruthless strongman raged inside him, the man who had driven the study from idea to reality. That strength had dissipated in recent weeks, however, as thoughts of Eva and sympathy for his children had clouded his judgment.

Indecision. Indecision everywhere. Wyatt, unable to shake it, deferred. "What am I thinking? I think you're the legal expert."

Lars' tumbler tocked against the wooden end-table as he set it down. "I think we do three things. First, we issue a statement reminding the public of the great work Human/Etech has done in the community over the course of the last few decades—we're a force for good, sticking up for the little people, blah blah blah."

"I like the part about the 'blah blah blah.' That will really convince them."

"I'm no wordsmith." Lars scratched the side of his head. "Just rework the mission statement and then flatly reject Miss Maxwell's assertions as desperate grabs for attention from a paper that's been floundering for years. Well, maybe we don't need to insult her, but—"

"Just get to the next two suggestions." The snappiness felt like a return to his former self.

Lars seemed to take no umbrage. "Secondly, I think we need to sue for defamation."

Now there was a strong answer. Wyatt assented.

"The last thing I was thinking—and this is a bit of a wild card, so bear with me," Lars said.

Wyatt did not care for the manner in which Lars raised his hands at his sides, scooting back in the sofa as he spoke.

"I'd like to arrange an unofficial meeting with this Meredith Maxwell. I want to see what she wants. What is she really—?"

Wyatt nearly choked on his scotch. "No. Absolutely not." The alcohol singed his throat, preventing him from going on.

"I don't see the harm in it," Lars said. "If we figure out what she wants, maybe we can settle this privately and it all goes away. A few thousand ameros might be all it will take to—"

"No, dammit," Wyatt managed through the coughs with just enough strength to keep Lars from continuing. He stood and made for the kitchen as he spoke. "If your meeting with her somehow gets leaked," he said, holding a glass under the faucet to fill it with water, "it could seem like the deal we're trying to reach with her is intended to convince *her* not to press charges." He took a few slugs of water, clearing his trachea. His mustache absorbed some of it, water dripping from his upper lip as he laid the glass down on the counter. "The public is always more sympathetic to the victim, real or perceived."

Lars looked away. "I only thought—"

"Well, you're done thinking it now." Wyatt tossed what remained of the water into the sink before returning to the living room. "And as for your first point, we'll skip on that one, too. Addressing her charges directly will only demonstrate our concern, which may again make us look guilty in the court of public opinion." He eased back into his armchair, the leather still warm.

Lars' expression flattened. "So you want me to file suit against her?"

"The strictly legal approach worked last time."

"It did." Lars regained his composure—or at least attempted to show he had—by raising his tumbler to Wyatt. The doctor adjusted his glasses before gesturing in Lars' direction with his own glass. The two of them drank in silence.

Wyatt moved on. "I also want to know how you feel I handled the protester this afternoon."

Lars stifled a laugh. "Do you want my actual opinion or do you just want me to agree with you? I'm a pretty expensive yes-man."

"You bastard." Wyatt flashed an earnest grin.

"I'm just saying," Lars said.

"I know. I know." Wyatt took another swig and thought on it a moment. "Your real opinion. Please."

"Can I ask a question first?"

"You just did."

"Wow, a sense of humor. You should have tried on one of those decades ago."

"All right. Just ask the question."

Lars seemed to hesitate before he said it. "What did the kids suggest you do about the protester?"

The question floored him. Truth be told, he had been trying to forget about the farce of an email chain he'd started after the trespasser had been apprehended. Heather was predictably harsh in her recommendations, and Alistair unsurprisingly sympathetic to the protester's plight. Bringing it up in front of the whole advisory board in their meeting later had proven to be an error as well, as it only led to further bickering.

Perhaps this had all been a mistake—not EMPATHY, but the reckless nepotism with which he had decided to prop it up. Were his children truly the most qualified for the job? Their credentials said maybe, but their interactions while working together under high pressure said otherwise.

Whether they were the most qualified or not, though, they were the only ones he could trust with his legacy. With Eva's legacy. They were the only ones he knew wouldn't turn EMPATHY over to the NAU. Wyatt would turn in his grave if he knew those hacks had been allowed to pervert his life's work.

"All you need to know," Wyatt said, "is I took their input into consideration when deciding to press charges."

"Don't hate me for saying this," Lars said, "but I think we should back off on the trespasser, especially in the light of that journalist's accusations.

You can't seem like you're turning your back on the public you're allegedly hoping to serve."

"The man trespassed. It was madness. Those people can remain camped out there so long as they don't hop the fence line. I intend to make an example of him."

"And you did," Lars said. "But—"

"The charges stay," Wyatt said. "They stay." He put back what remained of his scotch before tapping his fingers twice on his thigh. There. The strongman. Wyatt still had it.

"They stay then." Lars finished his own drink. "But—and I ask this for the sake of contingency—what happens when more people jump the fence? What if they climb it in groups?"

"Let me guess. You have an idea?"

Lars leaned forward, elbows on his thighs, his hands clasped in front of him. "Put out a statement—"

"Not this again—"

"Hear me out. Put out a statement explaining why they haven't heard from any employees on the compound. Tell them for the sake of the study's integrity, we had to cut off communication with the outside. Maybe that will settle some fears and the protesters will head home."

Wyatt shook his head. "And what happens when they ask for proof? Then we've opened up a dialogue. We give them the idea it's okay to question us."

"You're going to want this to go away," Lars said. "Why not—?"

"They can protest all they want. That's their right. I may have to hire more private security to monitor the fence line, but that's hardly an inconvenience." So long as the security team remained outside the compound's border, Heather wouldn't have to give them any sort of on-compound security clearance. Convenient, to be sure.

"Further securing the border may only fuel the protesters' concerns—"

"To hell with their concerns. To hell with your reservations. The work we're doing here is far too great to get held up in a game of cat-and-mouse. Unless they have something to offer me aside from complaints, I will not let third-party groups dictate how this study is run." Wyatt found himself gripping the arms of his chair, a white rage twisted in his fingers.

Lars maintained a raised brow, rubbing his temple as he stared toward the wall at his right.

Silence. A sign of victory. Wyatt had nothing more to say on the matter. He would let Lars make the first move if he so chose.

When Lars finally did speak, his words took Wyatt aback. "Her birthday would have been next week."

All the rage and satisfaction turned to melancholy, a sweet candy gone sour. The strongman might have returned, but Wyatt should have known better than to use Lars as a punching bag.

"You're right," Wyatt said. A ray of happy memories pierced the cloud of gloom. He almost spoke of one, of two fond moments, but his tongue wouldn't let them pass his lips.

Lars, however, apparently had no such qualms. "You ever make it to the cabin anymore?"

"Not for many years."

Lars bobbed his head, averting his eyes a moment. "She always loved it up there."

Wyatt snickered. "You know, I was just thinking about that photo—"

"The one where she looked all piggy?"

"Was it you who put that idea in her head?"

Lars raised his hands at his side. "It was just an observation—"

Wyatt's head rolled backward, his smile wide. "Oh, she forbid me from showing anyone that photo for *years*, all because you—"

"Because I was her big, older, constantly teasing brother?"

A sigh of a laugh escaped. "The two of you were always rather good at getting under the other's skin." Again, the photo came to him, then a barrage of images from her last moments alive, the scalpel in his hand, the tears collecting on his surgical mask. He winced. "I'm sorry."

"Don't worry about it," Lars said. "It'd be hard enough to talk about even if you didn't have your hands full around here."

"Mmm." Lars didn't even know the worst of it. Dare Wyatt tell him? Lars could be trusted. Why not? "I'm a little nervous, Lars."

His lawyer leaned in. "Nervous how?"

"We had a few seizures over the course of the last day. Granted, a couple of them can be explained as epileptic, but—"

"You're worried EMPATHY caused them?"

Wyatt let silence speak for him.

"You'll be fine," Lars said. "The kids will take care of it. They're the real brains behind the operation."

Wyatt allowed himself a single puff of laughter. "They get it from their mother."

"It certainly doesn't come from their father." The two men laughed.

"Well," Wyatt said, the strain in his voice more obvious than he hoped, "I suppose we both have work to do. Let me know if you have any questions about what we've discussed."

Lars rose. "I think we're on the same page."

Wyatt shook Lars' hand. "I can show you back to the helipad."

"No," Lars said. "I'll be all right. Just down the hall and up the stairs, right?"

Wyatt nodded.

"Take care of yourself, Wyatt." With that, Lars exited, offering a weak wave as he went.

At the sound of the door cinching shut, a wall of loneliness crumbled onto Wyatt, each brick leaving another bruise. He trudged toward his kitchen counter before expanding his pocketab and setting it before him. What had he become? One minute he was the strongman, the next a wretched sack of sentiment. Growing old was burrowing a hole in his constitution, a hole now far deeper than he was comfortable with.

He filled the pit of despair the only way he knew how. Wyatt Halman returned to work.

There were emails, too many to sift through and sort. He prioritized them by sender, finding two that caught his immediate attention. The first was from Peter, its subject line as brief as its contents.

To: "Doctor Wyatt Halman"

From: "Doctor Peter Halman"

Subject: Test Specimen

It will be ready by next week. If you'd like to be involved, let me know which day.

-Peter

Eva, not "test specimen," though he knew he could never say anything. How would Peter or Heather respond if they knew their mother's brain was being used in an experiment, a likely impractical quest to revive whatever bits of her might still live inside? He supposed he might find out soon enough. If the experiment succeeded, it would be a reality he and his children would have to confront head-on. "Monday," he wrote in response. "Early afternoon. You pick the time."

The following email came from Heather. When he saw the subject line—EMAIL INTERCEPT REPORT—his heart fluttered. He opened the intercepted message, eager to know what Chandra's brother may have said in response to her own email.

> To: "Chandra Adelhadeo"
> From: "Ratan Mahadeo"
> Subject: Re: Hello
>
> Chan,
>
> How is this possible? I thought you wouldn't be able to reach me until the study was over. Is everything okay? Are they treating you well? Is EMPATHY working?
>
> I can't believe you've contacted me today of all days. Kyra awoke yesterday! At least according to the doctors. I wasn't there at the time, but apparently she stirred and said something like "monaduh" before she slipped away again.

The email dragged on with personal anecdotes and other trivialities, but after a few of them, Wyatt had read enough. He scrolled down far enough to see Chandra's original email, confirming it wasn't she who had leaked information to the press—at least not in that correspondence, anyway.

Wyatt rested his elbows on the countertop, the soft light of his pocketab reflected in his glasses. Chandra had only just agreed to become EMPATHY's spokesperson. If she knew Kyra was likely to come out of her coma, Chandra would no doubt be less committed to her eventual duties. It was even reasonable to think she would make the impossible request to abandon the study completely.

And Eva. Wyatt had surrendered Eva for testing far earlier than he would have liked, all to help test EMPATHY on Chandra's behalf. "I need to call it off," he said, realizing he had spoken aloud only after he said it. But calling off the test wasn't an option, not really. What was he to do, tell Peter the subject brain was somehow no longer eligible for testing? He could apply for a brain to be donated to the study if need be, though the

Union Medical Board would likely expect something in exchange for a fresh, healthy brain on such short notice. Brains there weren't exactly in high supply, literally or figuratively.

Keeping his eyes on his pocketab, he reached for his tumbler. A clumsy moment sent it skittering away. Empty, Wyatt remembered. He frowned as he looked across the kitchen toward the bottle.

With a sigh, he bit his lower lip and set to typing. He knew what he had to do.

To: "Doctor Heather Halman"

From: "Doctor Wyatt Halman"

Subject: Re: EMAIL INTERCEPT REPORT

Heather,

Email to be held until further notice. Do not release to Chandra.

-Wyatt

With a tap of his screen, he responded to Heather.

He bowed his head. It had to be done. For stability. For EMPATHY. For Eva.

He wondered if she would be proud of the monster he had become.

Chapter Twenty-One

MEREDITH

The Queen of Spades had gone AWOL again, just when Meredith needed her most. Leaning back in her desk chair, Meredith attempted to shake the sheet of panic settling upon her.

No, she thought. QS wasn't AWOL. It'd hardly been a day.

Still, every hour that trickled past also became another without an answer regarding whether the *Star-Globe* would pay for personal security. They had to, right? Kathy had said she would at least try.

Meredith tapped her digipen on her desk. Would it be rude to email QS again? She had already contacted her twice that morning. She wished she hadn't already turned over the funds from that second envelope to QS for a story she wouldn't be able to use now anyway—a story she still hadn't received. All those ameros would have been much better spent hiring her own security if it came down to that.

In the end, she decided a third email was unwise. It would only increase her paranoia when QS didn't get back to her within a quarter hour. She needed to let things simmer.

Her door burst open and she flew backward.

"Great work," Kathy said sarcastically.

"You can't come barging in like that. What if you had been the kidnappers?"

"You think they'd just come waltzing in?" Kathy waved her pocketab in a violent gesture.

"They abducted me from my home. They could come back for me anywhere."

"Well, they're not here right now." Kathy fumed. "Look at this." She slapped her pocketab down on Meredith's desk.

It took Meredith a second to understand what she saw on Kathy's screen. "They're suing us? For libel?"

"If you wanted Human/Etech's attention, you certainly got it. This carries a little more weight than a cease and desist."

Meredith rubbed her eyes, her voice tense. "*We* didn't publish anything suggesting they were responsible for my kidnapping."

"No," Kathy said. "You only went behind my back—against my explicit instructions—to have your friends in the tech-blog community float the story themselves."

"It doesn't matter." Meredith pushed aside Kathy's pocketab. "They can sue us all they want, but the case will get thrown out. They have no standing since we aren't the ones who—"

"You think our legal team wants to devote their already thinly spread resources to even respond to something like this?! Whether it has standing or not, if Human/Etech keeps bringing suit against us it'll be death by a thousand cuts!"

Meredith seethed, confident she wasn't wrong. Unfortunately, it seemed Kathy wasn't wrong either.

If the Halmans weren't going to engage in some sort of dialogue like Meredith had hoped floating the story would achieve, she'd need security sooner rather than later. "What did Mr. Lee say about personal security? Is it a go?"

"Things were bad enough before we got smacked with this lawsuit. If you expected Mr. Lee and the rest of the board to approve your request—"

"My life is in danger."

"Everyone's job is in danger. There is no money. There are no resources. If you can't get me anything on the Gleason story—"

"How am I supposed to work on both EMPATHY and the Gleason project?" Truth be told, Meredith hadn't lifted a finger in the direction of the Gleason scandal—not that Kathy could know that. It was either appease Kathy and risk death or invoke her ire and live, a simple choice in the end. "EMPATHY is the story I need to save my life. If you had even a modicum of sympathy, you'd take on Gleason yourself. I need technical information or some serious dirt on EMPATHY or I am going to be *killed*."

"You don't know that. It could have been an empty threat or—"

"Are you kidding me right now?" Meredith's ire peaked. "You're going to stand here and baselessly debate the nature of the threat?" Two decades' worth of pent-up rage paralyzed her for a moment. Then the words came, the only ones she could muster. "Fuck you, Kathy."

Kathy lowered her head, her mouth agape. She steadied herself on Meredith's desk. Then she pointed to the door. "Get. Out."

"Excuse me?" Meredith said.

"Get out of my office."

Meredith almost laughed. "This is *my* office."

A mouth-puckering sweetness hit Meredith's tongue as Kathy recognized her mistake. Face purple, Kathy darted from the room, slamming the door shut behind her.

The tension in the room still hung thick, but what could Meredith do but work? It was the only thing that could keep her going, the only option left to keep her safe.

She opened her inbox to find two new emails. The first was somehow less surprising than the second.

To: "Meredith Maxwell"

From: <WITHHELD>

Subject: Re: Something New

Thanks for the cryptocoins. My bank account appreciates them.

I'm sorry to hear of your predicament. It's awful, really. Perhaps the attached story will help turn things around for you.

As for technical information, is it really a completely new element your kidnappers suspect is responsible for setting EMPATHY apart? Even if they're right, I remind you I'm a queen, not a goddess. Some have offered billions for access to those details. I can't imagine Halman will just have them sitting on a hard drive somewhere.

One bit of good news: I'll forgo compensation for research into all of that if you can assist me with one thing.

Send help.

Things are bad here. Patients have started to faint, seize, and disappear. More and more each day. The mood on the compound is tense. I fear for my own safety and that of my friends. We can't get any updates. The medical staff remain tight-lipped as more and more of us are wheeled away on gurneys. No one knows anything.

So this time I'm the one who needs a favor. Take the additional information in attachment as payment, and please do whatever you can to get us out of here. With any luck, this kind of news might help you with the predicament you mentioned in your other emails.

But please, we're counting on you.

-Q♠

Of everything she had received from the Queen of Spades, this email had to be the most revealing. Not only that, but it had the most potential to free her from the NAU's threats if the Queen of Spades could back up her claims. Meredith collected herself before reading it again.

Normally terse and with a sense of mysticism about her, in this email the Queen of Spades had let emotion get the best of her. And who could blame her in the face of such apparent danger?

That the Queen feared for her own safety almost confirmed she was a patient. "... more and more of *us* are wheeled away on gurneys," she had written. She had to be a patient, one of whom who was allegedly suffering at the hands of a study gone awry.

This could have changed everything for Meredith, could have empowered the NAU to take down Human/Etech and release her from their designs, but after opening the folder attached to the email, she didn't know whether to celebrate or damn her own cursed luck.

"EMPATHY is working," she said. "I don't believe it." But she should have believed it, she knew. Alongside the summary indicating EMPATHY had started to function for a few dozen patients, the Queen of Spades had included pictures of individuals staring glassy-eyed into the distance, an odd sort of glow about them—and that wasn't even the most compelling story among the attachments.

"Chandra Adelhadeo," Meredith said, mouthing the woman's last name to herself a handful of times as she scrolled through the word document. Written like an article, it even had a few pictures attached. The first depicted a young woman—her head shaved like so many others, but with perhaps a few weeks' worth of hair poking through. Her eyebrows were thick, her lips thin. She smiled as she stood akimbo beneath a willow tree, her wiry frame a stark contrast against the rotund trunk of the tree at her back.

The more Meredith read of Chandra, the more the woman piqued her interest. She'd been selected by Wyatt Halman himself as patient spokesperson for EMPATHY, was the first to have EMPATHY functionality, and... Meredith's jaw loosened. She read on of how Chandra's wife had suffered an accident that left her in a coma, how Chandra had signed up in the hope EMPATHY would let the two of them communicate again someday. The tale touched her heart with the sort of staying power from which documentaries are made.

"Of course," she said into the emptiness of the room. This was it. No, *these* were it. These were the stories she had worked for years to obtain, the ones that could have made her career. But now, with a death threat hanging over her head, she didn't dare publish them. Meredith imagined Mark Twain tap-dancing at the irony of it all if he were... well, not dead.

The worst of it, though, was that despite the Queen's assertions of seizures and disappearances, she included nothing to back up her claims, the very kind of corroboration she'd need to transform QS' allegations from hearsay to hard evidence. That plus her contact's lack of confidence regarding access to the kind of information the NAU sought had Meredith's stomach tied in knots. Those threads were the big news here—at least insofar as Meredith's personal safety was concerned. If QS weren't able to help Meredith before the seizure-causing affliction came for her, neither of them would come out of this okay.

Her brain abuzz with possibilities and paranoia, Meredith made a note to ask her source for concrete proof of the patient-related issues before she dove into the second email she'd received during Kathy's diatribe.

To: "Meredith Maxwell"
From: "Lars Alfreðsson"
Subject: Human/Etech Contact

Meredith,

I write as the chief counsel for Wyatt Halman and Human/Etech. I would like a moment of your time to discuss recent developments in the relationship between Human/Etech and your paper. Please call me at the below number at your earliest convenience.

Best regards,
Lars Alfreðsson

Meredith almost deleted the email. This Lars person could be any schmo posing as Halman's lawyer to get a scoop. Before she removed the email from her inbox, however, Meredith navigated to her web browser. A quick search for the man's last name gave a law firm as the first result. After a few more clicks through the public record, she discovered Alfreðsson Law had represented Human/Etech in nearly every case over the years.

Then there was the last name, almost identical to that of Wyatt's late wife. A quick confirmation that Icelandic naming conventions allowed for brothers and sisters to have different last names further suggested Lars had to be the real deal. There was some relationship there, at least.

Meredith tapped her digipen on her desk. Lars had reached out directly, not through some paralegal or other assistant. Whatever he wanted to discuss, it had to be important. It took only a second's consideration to decide what she should do.

"Please contact our legal department." Meredith creased her brow once she heard herself speaking as she typed. She finished her message in silence, brief and to the point. She had no business representing the *Star-Globe* in a legal capacity.

His response was near instantaneous.

> No need to get your legal department any more involved than it is. I have a proposition for you. I can make the lawsuit go away. Please call.

She huffed. There was only one way to sort this out, apparently. Meredith called the number in Lars' email signature.

"This is Lars."

"I—this is your direct number?" That didn't seem right.

"Yes. This must be Meredith Maxwell?"

"Yeah..."

"What I want to discuss with you, Meredith, is a little beyond the scope of my normal duties. Do you have a moment?"

Confused as she was, Meredith portrayed confidence. "I called you, didn't I?"

Lars chuckled, not insincerely. "I meant face-to-face. I don't want this conversation... on the line, so to speak. Others might be listening in."

Others listening in? The NAU—and one other party, clearly—must have had her pocketab tapped in order to know how much cash to leave in the envelopes at her home, but how would Lars know of that? A good guess, perhaps. Or maybe he was just being cautious. Meredith shook her head, hoping to buck the paranoia that had driven its spurs deep into her sides. "Maybe. What do I have to gain from meeting with you? This seems like a stunt for you to get solid oppo on me to build your case, nothing more."

"It does seem that way, and it should. I would be concerned if you hadn't thought of that." He paused a moment. "What I want to know is what you want. You have a very keen interest in my client and are seemingly intent on doing whatever it takes to get his attention. Admirable as that may be, having his attention won't do you any good if you never communicate what you need it for."

Meredith realized this was the closest she had ever been to Wyatt Halman himself. Why not have Lars twist Wyatt's arm for the what, the where, and the how of this mystery element while the Queen of Spades went behind his back to dig up dirt that might bring the NAU thundering down on them? Whatever information Lars could get wouldn't come free of charge, she was sure. She thought about asking what he wanted in exchange for the kind of info she needed, but with their line likely tapped, she accepted it would be better to meet in person.

"All right," she said. "When can you meet?"

"I'm available as soon as you are."

Though she didn't doubt who Lars was, she still had reservations about whether she ought to trust him. Meet him in a public place, she told herself, somewhere other people will be, but also unlikely to eavesdrop. "That state park," she said. "McKinney Falls. You know it?"

"I do."

"Meet me there in a half hour."

"Works for me."

"See you then." She ended the call. As she packed up her things, the specter of what was to come haunted her.

Soon enough she would know whether Lars could help her. Even if he could, there still might not be any guarantees. If he couldn't assist, well, Meredith didn't want to consider what might become of her then.

She looped her purse around her shoulder and made for the parking lot.

Chapter Twenty-Two

CHANDRA

Home. Their bed, the warmth of their bodies beneath the sheets. Home. Humid air wafting through a window set to the soundtrack of Kyra cursing in the front lawn. Home. The creaking door to the laundry room. Home. That one time it snowed and Kyra's eyes went wide at the sight of the white and Chandra tackled her into the powder and Kyra tried to make a snowball but the snow was too dry and it felt like they left something unfinished that day.

Home. The yellow flower in her hair.

Despite the joy the memories should have brought Chandra as she scampered through the arboretum, not a single one could fill the chasm Peter had opened some quarter hour earlier. He had no right to do what he did and now everyone knew and why oh why oh why.

The gravel crunched with each footstep, the bridge over the koi pond now in view. Chandra slowed. Calm, she thought. Redirect those prodding thoughts. As the bridge complained beneath her feet, she felt her sketchbook in her pocket slap against her thigh. *Fantastique.* She had remembered to grab both it and her charcoal pencil.

She threw herself at the trunk of the willow tree and swore she would never paint via EMPATHY again, not if each painting carried with it the message of its inspiration, not if Peter or others could find it on her egodrive, not if they could put them up in the cafeteria for all to see and learn of what happened to Kyra.

That Peter didn't recognize what he had done only made it worse. When he had come to her and promised a surprise, her first thoughts had been of Kyra, of the experiment they had promised to conduct. As she followed him through the compound, she floated on daydreams of speaking with Kyra once more, her mind a hot air balloon of hope. She thanked him throughout their walk, but all Peter said in return was "don't thank me yet."

Once in the cafeteria, Chandra didn't understand at first. A large roll of canvas had been suspended against its longest wall, and as she and Peter meandered through the crowd, an odd sensation bubbled at the base of her spine. Those around them fell silent, averting their eyes and mumbling among themselves in hushed tones.

"Don't worry, dear," Peter said. "People think they have to behave differently around my family. As you were, everyone." The joy in his voice was almost too great to bear.

When he finally had her at the center of the cafeteria, she realized how mistaken Peter had been. They weren't behaving differently because of him. They were doing it because of her.

In the lower right-hand corner of the canvas, a message had been painted—in actual paint—directing nectees to a destination on the compound's shared egodrive. Chandra accessed it, and the canvas exploded in the charcoals and midnight blacks of her work, the painting she had done in response to Ty's song.

"Isn't it wonderful?" Peter said. "When I saw it on your egodrive, I thought, 'My, how dark. But how deep!' I knew I had to share it with the world. Nothing wrong with free publicity, am I right?"

Then the messages rushed to her, a flurry of condolence and support.

BETHANY JORDAN: I'm sorry, Chandra.
CARLISLE STEPHENSON: We're all here for you, Chandra.
AJIT MOHAMMAD: If you ever need to talk, we're here.
BERNICE CARMICHAEL: Thank you for what you did to help Maribel. If you ever want to play cribbage to help take your mind off things, you can come to my room. Maribel and I used to play all the time. I used to play with my husband Eddie before the war, too. But he's gone now. Lost in the Pacific somewhere. Oh, sorry about Kyra, too. I never know if these messages of mine are sending or not, so I hope—

Those and dozens more flooded her inbox. Peter, oblivious to what he had done, smiled wider, the only one who didn't understand someone's world was falling apart around him. "I gave you access to that folder on the shared drive, too," he said. "Whenever you want to update this, just add something else to the folder. You can remove a painting from the lineup as well, if you ever want to replace something entirely. What do you think?"

Chandra had no memory of what she said. The next thing she remembered, she was cutting through the arboretum, out of breath and on her way to the one place she felt safe.

Now plopped down in the mud at the base of the willow, she retrieved her sketchbook from her pocket. Her pencil cut across the page, lining it with half a dozen charcoal gashes, one for each of those who had succumbed to the seizures in recent days, their luck far worse than her own. Chandra still clung to some hope Peter and Wyatt might be able to help her, but those who seized hadn't been heard from since they had fallen.

Whether it was Grandma Maribel, Calvin, Ty—

She heard the tune first, thinking it to be all in her head as it had been before. Then Ty descended the near side of the bridge, lips puckered, whistling "The Yellow Rose of Texas."

She ran to him. "You're okay? You're okay."

His hands left his pockets to prepare for her embrace before going limp at his sides as she wrapped her arms around him.

"What happened? Did you see the others? Can we go back to the lab and check for a response from my brother?" Chandra released him. "Oh God, that's right—I don't know if I exited properly when we were there. What if the Halmans find out about our visits and they turn off our cerenet access and—?"

Ty met her questions with disbelieving eyes.

"I'm sorry," Chandra said. "Here you are back from what I thought was the dead and all I can worry about is myself."

He headed for the tree. "You did ask if I was okay. You just didn't give me much time to respond."

"But you must be okay, right?" She followed after him. "I mean you're here, aren't you?"

"I am." A deep breath through his nose further attested to that. These had to be his first breaths of fresh air in a couple of days, Chandra thought. "Though we definitely have a lot to figure out."

Her legs became jelly. "I knew I didn't end my session in the lab properly. We're screwed, aren't we?"

Ty made a "slow down" gesture with both hands. He sat cross-legged and she joined him. "We may be screwed, but not for the reasons you think we are. If you had messed up in the computer lab, the Halmans would have certainly found out by now."

"You think?"

"Definitely."

"Then why are we—?"

"When I was in the hospital wing, I saw the others—Maribel, Calvin, Enrique, all of them. There were even, well, patients in there I'd never seen before. Far more than I expected, anyway."

Chandra hadn't even heard about Enrique falling yet, but that was beside the point. "Are they going to be out soon, too? No one has seen any of them since they seized."

"And I don't think anyone should plan on seeing them for the rest of the study."

"They didn't..." Chandra didn't want to say it. "They didn't die, did they?"

"No one's died, no." He sucked in a breath through his teeth. "But..." His eyes glassed over as he forwarded a video. Chandra let it play. "That first day they had my room in the same ward as the others. I was able to record what I saw through EMPATHY, and—" Ty resumed his narration, though his words didn't do justice to what he had seen.

Maribel, Calvin, Enrique—he'd observed each of them in passing, each one draped in a hospital gown flowing freely at their sides—well, at the sides of those who could stand, anyway.

Nurses and doctors spoke to them, but their only responses were despondent stares and nonsense syllables.

"None of them could make words," Ty said. "Well, Enrique could in a way, but I only ever heard Calvin...." He swallowed. "I only ever heard him gurgle. Or moan. It's some sort of expressive aphasia."

Chandra searched for "expressive aphasia" on the cerenet. The inability to produce meaningful language. "But they can treat it. There are treatments for it."

"There are," Ty said, "but when I saw Calvin as I walked past his hospital room, part of his face had gone limp. I think he had a stroke, too."

The urge to vomit pumped through Chandra's gut. "But how are you— how did you come out okay?"

"Remember how I said Calvin has epilepsy?"

"Yeah, and I asked you how you knew, and you gave me a nonanswer about how the cerenet told you everything, which it doesn't."

"Right, well, the reason I knew he was epileptic is because I am, too. He and I talked about it once a few months back."

"Wait... really?"

"My seizure was your run-of-the-mill 'fit,' apparently. Calvin's appears to have been caused by EMPATHY."

Chandra found herself looking left-to-right then right-to-left and back again. So it was all true. She'd abandoned Kyra's bedside in a last-ditch effort to restore her as best she could, only to condemn herself. How long before she wound up like Calvin, like Enrique, like Grandma Maribel?

No. Deep breaths. There was no guarantee it would happen to everyone. Maybe there was a genetic factor, and even if not, the Halmans could probably find a way to prevent it. But what if she was wrong? If a seizure struck her, she'd be without words, and without words—no, she wouldn't let herself dwell on it.

"Are you on any medication?" Chandra said. "For your epilepsy, that is. I wonder if something about taking that helped keep your spell from becoming an EMPATHY-triggered episode."

Ty shrugged. "I am. I'm supposed to be. Honestly the whole reason this happened is my own fault. I missed a couple days of my meds. I thought I'd taken them, but with how busy I was..."

Chandra gave him a motherly look.

"That's actually what I wanted to talk to you about—all the work I was doing that led me to miss my meds. I have this suspicion," he said, righting his glasses, "that *I'm* responsible for the seizures."

"Come on, Ty," Chandra said, lying down in the grass. "You're the one who told me I wasn't responsible for Kyra's accident." Two clouds floated past. They looked like a rabbit chasing a cat instead of the other way around. "How could you possibly be responsible for the seizures?"

"Because I may have unknowingly programmed them into the code for EMPATHY."

"What?" She shot forward. His expression—the anxious, flitting eyes, the chewing on his lower lip—suggested he was nothing if not serious. "But you're a patient, not a programmer."

"You know that whole story I gave you about how they asked me to help them recreate *Dallas* so it would work on EMPATHY? Yeah, they actually had a version of it already completed. I only had to give the go-ahead for them to put it out there under the *Dallas* name. All that time I've spent in the lab—when not tending to personal things, that is—I've been working on code that's been getting uploaded to the primary server."

"Jesus, Ty."

"I know. I thought I was doing a good thing at first. Your connectivity event came a couple days after I got my first batch of code to Alistair, but—"

"Wait. Like Alistair *Halman*?"

"I don't know any other Alistairs around here."

Chandra ignored his snark. "He works with Ariel, right? The one who wears the yellow scrubs?"

"She's one of the ones who wears yellow, yes."

"But she's the one with the red hair. With the boobs?"

"Maybe. Sure. But what's your point?"

"Ty, she's the one who showed up the day after you seized. I took that keycard off of you when you fell and gave it to her when she came to find you the next morning."

Ty's posture eased. "Oh, thank God. I wondered what happened to that thing. I couldn't find it anywhere when I was in the hospital." He returned to the conversation. "So Ariel has it now? What did she say when she found you in my room?"

"She said she'd tell everyone about my visits to the lab if I didn't keep quiet about you having that card. That's why I'm nervous. If she knows about my email to my brother, it's only a matter of time before the Halmans find out, too, right?"

Ty set his jaw. "Not necessarily. It was Alistair who showed me how to get around the filters in the lab in the first place. The two of them might just know what to look for."

Chandra filled her nose with the scents of earth, of dirt and grass and algae on the surface of the pond. "Let's slow down. We don't even know for sure it's your programming causing all this."

"The timing of it—"

"You said there were others in there, patients you had never even seen. How could your programming have affected them if it didn't even exist yet? And the others—it could be a coincidence."

Ty mulled it over for a moment. "I don't know. What if there were a few cases before my programming got uploaded, but once it hit the servers, it only accelerated the rate at which it happened for others? It's hard to argue there haven't been more public cases of people seizing and disappearing lately." He sighed. "Besides, are you really willing to do nothing but twiddle your thumbs as we wait to find out what's really going on?"

Her hand found her brow and rubbed in small, tight circles. Right, yes. She herself had figured they'd have to take matters into their own hands if the doctors weren't honest with them, if they weren't visibly taking steps to ensure everyone's safety. "Then you have to bring this up to Alistair. If the code he's had you develop is having unintended consequences—"

Ty held up a hand. "That's the thing. I'm not sure these are unintended consequences."

"Why would Wyatt's own son—?"

"I don't know. I know nothing for sure, but what if he *is* doing this on purpose? If I go to him with this suspicion, I could end up in worse shape than if I waited it all out."

Chandra reached for her sketchbook, abandoned in the dirt to her left. She let her hand be her guide across the page as she attempted to ground herself in what all of this meant. "This isn't how this was supposed to be."

"I know."

As she drew, she thought of all that had changed in the last week. First connectivity. The test. Wyatt and Peter promising to do research for her. The experience with Ty's song. The seizures.

She thought of the hours after her install, when that one gossiping patient made her first accept she might be putting herself in far greater danger than Kyra was in as she lay unconscious. Everything she'd done was supposed to be about Kyra—*for* Kyra—and now? What had once been a mission of compassion had become one of survival, the only way back to her wife perhaps not through EMPATHY, but through avoiding EMPATHY long enough to make it off the compound unharmed.

It had felt as though things were so complicated back there, in the world where her life was nothing but waiting at Kyra's bedside. But between the seizures and the keycard and Peter displaying her painting in the cafeteria—

She stopped sketching. "Do you think you could write more code?"

"I'm sure they expect me to."

"I mean, could you write other code—something to undo whatever you put into the system originally?"

"The easiest thing to do would be to delete my original work, but I'd need access to the server farm for that."

Chandra leaned forward.

He shook his head. "There is no way I will have access to the server farm."

"But Ariel has access, right?"

"Maybe. Probably." Then he seemed to get it. "I don't know, Chandra. I've never even met Ariel. Asking her to upload code I've written without Alistair's direction seems like a long shot and a half. And what if she's also in on Alistair's plan to bring down the study? Going to her with this could—"

"No way," Chandra said. "If she wanted to, she could have outed me for visiting the lab after taking the keycard back. It would've been my word against hers, and I'd have nothing to support mine."

Ty cocked his head to the side. "You mean nothing aside from my support in saying that, yes, I did get a keycard from her at some point?"

He obviously wasn't getting it. "Ty, they'd just argue you had no idea what you were talking about after having spent time in the hospital wing. And even if both of them are up to no good, causing participants to seize can't have been their original goal when they asked you to get involved."

Ty rubbed his tattoo, his attention fixed on the mulch at the base of the downy phlox nearby.

Chandra slapped her hands down on her thighs. "Come on, Ty. Even you just said we have to try something. If Ariel's our best bet, then we have to work with her to fix this."

"Who's this *we* you're talking about? I'll see what I can cobble together, but it's not like you'll be involved in the programming."

"No, but I'll have my own role to play in getting the Halmans to investigate whether EMPATHY is the source of the seizures."

Ty removed his glasses. He scratched the bridge of his nose with his free hand. "And how much sway do you think you have with them, exactly? They're probably looking into it already."

"They could always do more, and some transparency would be great right now."

"Okay, but again—"

"I'm going to lead a boycott of EMPATHY. No one will use the cerenet until this is resolved."

He slipped his glasses back on and blinked emptily at her. "You're willing to risk everything the Halmans have promised you to organize a boycott that will likely fail?"

Chandra raised her shoulders. "The Halmans won't know I'm behind it." She told him of her visit to the cafeteria, of Peter mentioning she could update the painting at any time.

Once she finished explaining, Ty shook his head as he splayed his legs out in the grass. "So you're going to code the boycott message into a painting and display it in the cafeteria?"

"Then when Wyatt freaks out about no one using EMPATHY any longer, I'll go to him and pretend I only heard about the boycott second-hand, but that all anyone wants is for the staff to be transparent about what they're doing to fix all of this."

"That is... actually pretty awesome."

Awesome, yes, but it was also the kind of thing that would make Kyra proud. She had been far more politically active than Chandra ever was, organizing protests and participating in acts of civil disobedience whenever she found a cause that spoke to her.

Chandra scooted forward. "You have a soundtrack for me to paint to?"

Ty's eyes glassed over. "Let's do this."

Chandra laid back on the ground and closed her eyes as she waited for the music to begin. "And Ty?"

"Yeah?"

"When we're done, can we go to the lab? I want to see if my brother got back to me." She adjusted her position to avoid the rock that had been digging into her shoulder blade. "And I should let him know about the seizures this time, in case... in case something happens to me."

Ty turned his head toward her. "Nothing's going to happen. We're gonna fix this."

"I hope so."

"I should have brought you to the lab right when I got out."

Chandra flew upright. "You went there since being released?"

"I had to get caught up on my own things."

She scowled.

"Whatever. I probably should have talked to Alistair before I went." He clasped his hands behind his head. "He may not want me in there anymore. Who knows?"

"So what are you saying?"

"I'm saying I'll find a way to contact Ariel, see what she says, and we'll take it from there."

Ty had a point. They should at least get confirmation from Ariel that the Halmans weren't onto them. Ariel had told Chandra to keep going to the lab, anyway—definitely a good sign. Still, they should check first. "Fair enough. You ready?"

"I'm not the one who—"

"Just give me something to paint to."

He covered a laugh. "How about this?"

Chandra lowered herself onto her back. In the recesses of her mind, a drumbeat went to work. These were no snares, no toms, no light percussion. These were timpani.

These were the drums of battle, the furious heartbeat of war.

Chapter Twenty-Three

MEREDITH

Meredith eased onto the brakes as she pulled into the parking lot of McKinney Falls State Park. Her head on a swivel, she counted a dozen or so park-goers in the area. With this many people around, she hoped Lars— or anyone who might have been following her—wouldn't dare try anything nefarious.

As she exited her boxy hatchback, she spotted a man leaning against a sleek, two-door Lexus. Lars. He looked up from his pocketab and made eye contact before he approached at a casual stroll, hands in his pockets. If Meredith could trust her gut, he was all suit and no substance, a bad sign if she expected him to get her access to Halman himself.

Lars glanced over her shoulder. "You weren't followed, were you?"

"Not that I noticed."

"Good." He stood beside her and rested his back against Meredith's car. "I want to start from a position of trust. I think you and my client have a common enemy, but after having him accused of your abduction, I thought you might need to be brought up to speed."

"Don't kid me." Meredith side-stepped away from him. "You're here to get me to disavow those rumors, nothing more."

He adjusted his tie. "If that was all I really wanted, I could have simply followed through with the lawsuit. I wouldn't have to meet with you at all."

She kept her lips taut, baiting him to elaborate.

"You have something my client wants," he said, "but you're the only one who has it."

"Funny. I could say the same about him."

"That's exactly why I'm here."

A car hummed into a parking stall nearby. Neither spoke as its three passengers exited and slammed the doors behind them. Meredith waited until the group was out of earshot before continuing. "Regardless, I still have no reason to trust you."

"What if I told you who your abductors were? Consider it a show of goodwill."

Meredith almost scoffed. On second thought, Lars had no idea she already knew the identity of her kidnappers. She egged him on, aiming to evaluate how close his best guess might be. "I'm all ears."

Lars' expression went grim. "The NAU."

How did he know? She had to play all of this differently now. "What makes you suspect it's them?"

"They've been after information on EMPATHY far longer than you have. Think of the potential military applications alone."

"And let me guess—Wyatt won't let them create their own apps for it?"

"That's among their frustrations. Wyatt himself isn't particularly excited about a future where an NAU propped up by the Right for the Union party beats him to market and turns EMPATHY into some mind-control apparatus."

Meredith pursed her lips, nodding once.

"Contrary to what you might believe," Lars said, "my client does have a conscience."

Maybe he did. Lars seemed to have one, anyway. He cared for Meredith's welfare enough to tell her the identity of her kidnappers, at least, even if she had already been more than aware who they represented. "My abductors did ask me to use my source to get at EMPATHY's tech specs. They mentioned something about an unknown element?"

Lars pulled a smug expression. "As expected."

"So it's true?" she said. "He discovered a completely new element that's become the core of EMPATHY?"

He pushed away from Meredith's hatchback. "I didn't say that."

"But your expression, you—"

"I have no idea what you're talking about."

The two of them stood there a moment, eyeing one another. A car whooshed past on the highway. Somewhere in the trees, a crow cawed three times, its echo bouncing off one trunk and into another.

Meredith's tongue explored the spot she'd bitten her cheek when Harold assaulted her. "They only gave me three stories, you know."

Lars' face remained stone.

She stepped closer, bringing herself as level as she could despite the several inches of height he had on her. "I need to know what that element is, where to find it, and how it's being used." For as increasingly likely as it was that forcing an investigation would prove more fruitful than this route, she couldn't exactly ask Lars to betray his own client by coughing up dirt on him and his study. Why would Lars cooperate if he knew one of her goals was to have his client's hard work publicly eviscerated? She'd still have to pursue that angle more aggressively with the Queen of Spades, but for now, she had to press Lars on this front.

When Lars finally spoke, he did so from the corner of his mouth. "You and NanoMed and the NAU and everyone else want access to what makes EMPATHY tick. If you think—"

Meredith's hands shot forward, pulling Lars toward her by his lapels. "None of them will *die* if they don't get their hands on that information." She could feel them now, the long tentacles of the NAU coiled around her chest, squeezing the life from her.

Lars swallowed, eyes on the pavement. "What are any of our lives against the betterment of millions? That's what Wyatt would say." His hands found his pockets again. "Well, he would think it at least."

"So that's it, then?" She released her hold of him but pressed him nonetheless. "If you can't help me, I can't help you."

A breeze whipped Lars' tie over his shoulder. "I can get you the information you need." He puffed up his chest as he righted his tie.

"You can?" The NAU's tentacles loosened their grip and her breath came more easily. "What happened to the worth of my life 'against the betterment of millions?'"

"I'll speak with Wyatt." He seemed to have regained his composure now, his chin held high as if speaking over her, past her. "If he agrees, we'll give you something from an early mock-up right after the element's discovery, the kind of thing that'd take years to test, but ultimately lead to a dead end. By the time the NAU realizes it's faulty info, you'll have a chance to skip town."

"Skip town? Once I give the NAU what they need, they said they'd—"

"It's too late now." He lowered his voice. "The NAU doesn't like loose ends. Not this administration, anyway. Sooner or later, you're going to have to flee."

The world spun. Meredith needed to sit. Lars had spoken the truth, one she had likely known but elected to reject. It was a pipe dream to think she could placate the NAU. No matter where she went, no matter whether she satisfied their conditions, they would come for her. For however long as she was within their grasp—

"Must I add we'll need something in exchange for all of this?" Lars said.

Meredith retrained herself on the conversation. "I'll have the *Star-Globe* issue a statement disavowing any insinuations Human/Etech was responsible for my abduction."

"More," Lars said. "I'll need more than that to get Wyatt on board with any of this."

"More?"

"He wants to know who's been leaking information from the compound."

Of course he wanted something Meredith couldn't deliver. Even if she knew who the Queen of Spades was, turning her over would show a shameless disregard for journalistic ethics *and* compromise her ability to get investigation-worthy information from the compound. But with Meredith's life on the line...

She opened her mouth but restrained herself. If she told him she didn't know the true identity of her source—yet—Lars would have no reason to stick with the conversation. Besides, perhaps she could use Lars' new condition to her advantage. "If you want to know the identity of my source, I'll need something further from you, too." Lars gave no reaction. "I'll trade you my source's identity in exchange for an interview with Wyatt."

His laugh grated her. "Wyatt has done everything in his power to avoid the press during this study. Why would he agree to an interview? Especially with you. You're the one who published the leaks in the first place."

"Because after the interview, the news stories will stop. I won't have a source any longer and the world will be sated on EMPATHY gossip for a while." She took a step toward him. "Who knows? Maybe the interview would even humanize him to the public again. With any luck, it'd convince some of those concerned family members who have been camping at the compound to head home."

"Family? They're trespassers. Squatters," Lars said.

"Let's not debate semantics. This is a win-win for everyone if Wyatt agrees. I'll get the information the NAU is chasing plus an interview, and Wyatt will get a retraction of blame for my abduction, an end to the leaks as well as the source of them, and the family outside his gates will stop crawling through that ridiculous new mustache of his."

Lars snickered.

Meredith stood firm. "It sounds like a good deal to me."

"It does to me as well, though I won't be the one making the final decision."

"All I ask is that you try."

"That, I can do." Lars extended a hand. Meredith took it. "Now let's get out of here." His forehead wrinkled as he looked upward. "I think I felt a raindrop."

Meredith's windshield wipers thrummed as she drove back to the offices of the *Star-Globe*. She had done well. At least she had left the conversation with more than she had come with.

She gazed at her pocketab as she entered her office. She flicked on the light and made a beeline for her desk. If Lars convinced Wyatt to accept the deal they had struck, she would need to determine the identity of her source as soon as possible. She might as well start now.

The hair on her neck rose at the sound of Kathy's voice. "Meredith."

"Oh!" Her hand flew to her chest. "You scared me."

Kathy stood in the doorway. Behind her stood a tall, spindly man in a suit colored in earth tones. It took her a moment to recognize him, but when she did, she swallowed hard.

"Mr. Lee," Meredith said. "It's been a while. What can I do for the two of you?"

The paper's founder and chairman of the board gave a curt nod, his wizened expression solemn. "May we sit?"

"Please do." Meredith gestured to the chairs across from her desk. She sank into her own, her concern grave. Chang-hoon Lee spent nearly every day in the office when Meredith first started, an energetic man whose personal appeal was renowned among the staff. As time wore on and the paper began to flounder, however, he made fewer and fewer appearances. His advanced age was a factor in keeping him away as well, Meredith was sure. These days, whenever he came around, it never meant anything good.

After he lowered himself into a chair, he interlocked his fingers and placed his hands on his lap. "First of all," he said, "I want to thank you for your dedication to the EMPATHY story."

"Thank you." Perhaps she was wrong. What if he'd come by only to congratulate her? Maybe he had even found the coin to pay for personal security.

"I have a grandson in the study. Did you know that?"

Meredith shook her head.

"Hm," he said. "The fool. An immature boy, him, but they all are at that age. He could have helped me try to right this company like his brother has done. But I'm afraid he has the naiveté of his father, trying to pave his own way in a world that already laid a path before him."

"Well," Meredith said, "hopefully he's among the participants for whom EMPATHY is working." Mr. Lee's and Kathy's eyes lit up at the news. "I received an update from the Queen of Spades before stepping out. It sounds as though the study might have finally turned a corner." She withheld the news about the alleged seizures. There was no need to alarm Mr. Lee if she couldn't say whether his grandson had succumbed to them.

"That's fantastic," Kathy said. "Can you forward me what she gave you?" She retrieved her pocketab and swiped at it. "Now?"

Meredith looked at Mr. Lee. He gestured his approval and Meredith did as Kathy asked. Once she was finished, Mr. Lee spoke again.

"You know things have been difficult for us in the last few years. To be frank, there were many times when I argued we needed to eliminate your position. Fortunately, Kathy talked sense into me each time, reminding me of the value you bring to this paper."

Meredith offered Kathy a knowing nod. "I'm very grateful for that. It means a lot to me." The self-righteous smile Meredith received in return made her wish she had said nothing.

Mr. Lee continued. "Given new circumstances and other recent developments, however, the two of us have decided you have outgrown our operation. It's time to move on, Meredith."

Kathy leaned forward. "You're being let go. We can't have your brazen insubordination infecting the rest of the staff. Going behind my back and acting against my orders to float stories, starting shouting matches when resources aren't allocated as you expect—"

Despite her shock, Meredith managed a word. "And the story I've brought you? That's not worth anything? That's not enough—?"

Kathy raised a finger. "Not when your work brings the threat of a new lawsuit against us every week. It's not acceptable. It's not—"

Mr. Lee gave her a stern glance. Kathy took the hint. He rose to his feet at a glacial pace. "I want to thank you for your years of service. Sincerely," he said, extending his hand, "thank you."

Later, Meredith remembered their handshake, some curt words from Kathy, and collecting her things. She floated through all of it as though she were stirring from the fog of an awful dream. Meredith loathed Kathy, sure, but the *Star-Globe* was where she had started—and now apparently ended—her career. Without it, she had nothing more than a sickly dog she couldn't afford to keep living. Worst of all, without a credible platform to publish the information the NAU demanded of her, Meredith could feel her own doom clawing at her chest.

She needed to leave town, to go into hiding as soon as possible.

When she regained her bearings, she found herself in the driver's seat of her car, parked in her driveway. She slammed shut the door of her hatchback as she exited, which set Woodward to barking inside her house. "I'll be there in a minute, bud," she said under her breath.

Backtracking to her mailbox, she swung its door open and fished around inside. Junk mail. Junk mail. Bill bill bill. Another envelope—just like the cash-infused one she had first received in her mailbox the last time around.

Her pulse ticked up as she tucked it into her purse. She scrambled for her front door, unlocking it with her pocketab as she hopped onto the stoop. Woodward jumped up at her as she entered her home.

"Yes, hey. Oh yeah, how are you?" She knelt, letting him lick her face as she fumbled through her purse for the mail she'd hidden away. Retrieving the suspect envelope, she tore it open, its contents spewing onto the floor. There were blue two hundreds, red one hundreds, some green fifties, and a number of yellow twenties. Even as Woodward suffocated her with love, the count she arrived at was unmistakable—six thousand ameros. It was the same amount she had given the Queen of Spades in her last transfer. Could QS herself be returning the money after she received it? And if so, why?

She discarded the questions. None of it mattered any longer, or at least it wouldn't soon. An idea urged her toward her bedroom. She secured her passport before hurling clothes, her pocketab charger, a few toiletries—anything she could get her hands on—into a rolling suitcase. She didn't know where she would go, but with six thousand ameros on hand, she could at least get herself off the continent. There had to be some place she could take refuge, somewhere beyond the reach of the NAU. Woodward whimpered as she packed.

Her heart jolted when her pocketab rang with an incoming call from Brad Mellocks. She intended to ignore the call, but in her frenzy, she answered by mistake. "Uh, hello?"

"Hey, Meredith."

"Brad, if you're calling to brag about how great things are at *The Courier*, I can't—"

"No, no, no. I'd love to brag, yes, but that's not why I called."

"Then what is it? I've got a bit of a crisis going on here and—"

"I'm guessing the rumor is true, then. Kathy let you go?"

Meredith crumpled a shirt in her fist. "Are you calling to rub it in my face?"

"No, I—"

"How did you find out? It's been less than an hour."

"We share the same circles. Word gets around."

Meredith flung the balled-up shirt at the wall. "I'm glad my shame is being paraded around for all to see. Call me the emperor. These are my new clothes."

"I don't think that's a great analogy."

"Did you call just to mock me?"

"No. I called to offer you a job."

"You... you're offering me a job?"

"All right, maybe I misspoke. I can't offer you a job myself, but I can try to get you one. I'm sure *The Courier* or WVN wouldn't mind having someone on board with a direct connection to the EMPATHY story."

A blanket of shame descended on Meredith. What was she doing? Running away wouldn't have solved anything. The NAU would come after her until she at least tried to satisfy them. Even if she didn't have a job at a paper, she could always pursue the interview with Wyatt as an independent journalist. Surely some outlet would pick it up. Besides, what would she have done with Woodward if she had taken off?

She slumped to the floor. Woodward lay prone alongside her. "Brad, you... why would you do that?"

"Because it wasn't until I started working at *The Courier* that I realized how much I took having a mentor like you for granted."

Meredith's hand found her chest. That might have been the nicest thing anyone had said to her in years.

"On top of that," Brad continued, "I position myself well by pushing to have you on the team. Someone's gonna take Ren's position as anchor once he retires, and—"

"Okay, I get it." The warm feeling in her chest abated. His reasons for helping weren't important in the end. Meredith was in no position to complain.

"What are you doing tomorrow at 8:00 a.m.?" he said.

"I'll be busy being unemployed."

"So we can send a car to bring you in for an interview?"

"You'd send a car? Who died and put you in charge?"

There was a pause. "Yeah, uh, your phrasing on that could have been better."

Alicia Melendez. How had she forgotten? "You're right. Wow. Sorry."

"It's okay. The point is, I already asked Ren if he'd be open to interviewing you."

Meredith's pulse throbbed in her throat. "This is for real? You got me an interview already? Rénald Dupont approved the interview?"

"Yeah," he said, his tone mocking. "If you're hired, we might even let you write something once in a while."

Disbelief forced a laugh from her.

"I'll email you the details," Brad said, "but really all you need to do is be ready to go at 8:00 a.m. tomorrow. The car should swing by then."

"Are you in charge of the interview process or something?"

"No, but it's going to be fast-tracked. You're a known entity. I'll just introduce you to some of the staff and make sure it's a good fit."

"You make it sound like I already have the job."

"You do so long as you don't blow it."

Don't blow it, she thought. She didn't think she had been blowing it at any step along the way so far, but still, she found herself in mortal danger. "Thanks for the encouragement."

He failed to note her sarcasm. "Don't mention it. And you'll be ready tomorrow at eight?"

"I'll be ready. Thank you, Brad."

Meredith dropped to the floor and let Woodward smother her with kisses, relieved there might be a way out of her quagmire yet.

Chapter Twenty-Four

ARIEL

For the second time in as many days, Ariel found herself waiting for Ty to open his door. His email by cerenet had been a surprise, both because it meant he had been released from the hospital wing, and because she'd assumed Alistair would have told him to only correspond with him directly.

When the email mentioned Alistair wasn't to know, however, she had to handle whatever this was with Ty herself. She, too, was responsible for patient welfare after all, and perhaps he had a complaint to lodge against Alistair.

She knocked on Ty's door a second time. It creaked open. "Hey." Ty poked the side of his glasses. "Thanks for coming."

"Look," Ariel said under her breath, "before we talk, I should mention if this has anything to do with the code Alistair wants you to write, I can't speak to that."

He pressed to fingers to his forehead. "Will you please just come in? We shouldn't discuss any of this where anyone else might hear."

Ariel checked left and right down the hall. When she was sure no one was looking, she stepped across the threshold into Ty's room. He closed the door behind her.

"All right," Ty said. He tried to carve out a space for her to sit amid the scrubs that littered the foot of his bed. "Sorry, give me a second here."

As Ty struggled to make room for her, Ariel checked her pocketab, prodded by Ty's comment they ought to chat somewhere no one else could hear. Sure enough, the blue light on her device confirmed her concern. M3R1 was listening—always listening—and Ariel continued her failure to learn.

"You know what?" Ariel said. "Don't worry about it. I'll stand." She tucked her pocketab away, cursing her shortsightedness for not having followed through on a strategy to keep M3R1 from listening in without arousing suspicions of betrayal.

Ty shrugged. "Suit yourself." He plopped down at the foot of his bed and eyed her for a moment. Nervous, she figured.

"Look," Ariel said, "I don't know what's on your mind, but as an administrator responsible for patient welfare, I want you to know that we take very seriously—"

"I want you to take some code of mine to the server farm."

The muscles of her face tightened.

He pressed on. "I think I know what's causing these seizures. If you'd seen what I saw in the hospital wing, you'd know how urgent it is that we fix this."

Jitters flashed through her. Yes yes yes. Whether Ty knew of M3R1 or not, if he thought he could keep the seizures from spreading—and also save Ariel's hide in the process—she would have to help him.

But thoughts of M3R1 eavesdropping had her pumping the brakes on her excitement. The AI couldn't know she might work against its goals, whatever they might truly be. "I don't know, Ty. I think it's important we stick to the missions we're given." Her voice had become awkward, stilted. Could M3R1 discern her insincerity?

"Wait," Ty said. "Do you realize staying the course might lead us all to ruin? People are losing the ability to speak. They're becoming partially paralyzed or failing to wake up at all."

"I understand where you're coming from, but it's probably for the best that we let experts like Peter and Gary resolve this on their own." Ariel adjusted the collar of her scrubs. She had actually considered using that line of reasoning herself in order to justify her own inaction, but when she realized that would make for an all-out witch hunt once—if—the compound's finest programmers found M3R1's code, she knew she needed to pounce on the first chance to make amends. Now all she had to do was find a way to work around M3R1.

Ty stood. "How can you justify—?"

"Listen." Ariel maintained eye contact, attempting to let him know something wasn't right. "This isn't a topic the two of us should discuss." She mouthed "right now" and pointed to her pocketab, hoping he got the point—and that M3R1 was unable to pick up on her nonverbal cues from where it rested in her pocket. Ariel went on, winking at him exaggeratedly. "Unless you have patient-related concerns, I don't think there's anything else for us to talk about."

"Whatever." He seemed miffed. Had he not understood her wild gestures?

"I won't be coming to visit you again." She winked one last time, letting the words hang in the air.

"Go." Still, he apparently failed to notice her implication.

The urge to curse struck her as she slipped out into the hall. Bungled. Bungled again. She wanted to help Ty, yes, but if she were to do so, she'd first need a way to collaborate with him without M3R1 finding out.

She had made it only a few steps when her pocketab chimed. Of course.

>> Your assistance is required.

<< Unless this is about reversing what you uploaded last time, I don't know how much assistance I'm comfortable providing.

>> Mistakes were made. M3R1 would like to make up for them.

<< Let me guess. . . another trip to the server farm?

>> No, a smaller favor.

Ariel halted. If M3R1 had an actual interest in reversing whatever nightmare it had unleashed through its last bit of code, Ty wouldn't need to be involved at all. Ariel doubted whether she could trust the AI's intentions, but what choice did she have?

>> The keycard you last used at the primary server. Those eyedrops. M3R1 requires both be left in a restroom.

Was this some sort of joke? Ariel sidestepped a pack of researchers and took a seat on a bench, back pressed to a window. Across the hall, another window opened up to a prairie beyond.

<< Remember when you said you weren't in the mood for games?

>> Yes, as should go without saying. M3R1's memory consists of unlimited cloud storage.

Ariel huffed—another implication someone had missed.

<< I'm saying I want you to tell me if you're being serious.

>> M3R1 is very serious. Please ensure this keycard and the eyedrops are delivered to the women's restroom in the northwest corner of the facility. Today. Soon. Immediately.

<< Just. . . leave them on the counter or something?

>> The bathroom in question has two stalls. Bring both items to the stall farthest from the door. Remove the lid on the toilet tank. Place the keycard on the fill valve. The bottle of eyedrops may be left in the tank itself. Do this now.

Ariel, perplexed, put her elbows on her knees. M3R1 might have missed her earlier implication, but Ariel understood that of the AI. Someone else would be putting those eyedrops and keycard to work. But who? Had M3R1 found a more cooperative staff member? Was it hedging its bets in case Ariel revolted against it?

<< Will I get everything back at some point? If Alistair asks me to return it all, I don't think I can just tell him I lost track of it.

>> They will be right where you left them tomorrow. You can pick them up then. Now go.

As she brought the eyedrops and keycard to the bathroom, Ariel attempted to devise a plan. If M3R1 was going to collaborate with others, she would have to as well. In Ty, she might have already found a co-conspirator, but she still had to find a way around M3R1's eavesdropping—without tipping it off to the betrayal.

Chapter Twenty-Five

CHANDRA

Chandra lay in bed, cracking her knuckles as she reviewed her painting one last time.

She could still hear Ty's music, its percussion like the gallop of cavalry. Digital brushstrokes rose and crashed from left to right across the canvas, colored with stormy grays and the sinister colors of night. Images of those in the hospital wing bled through the background in currant and flax, the colors of blood and marrow. Chandra relaxed into the painting, letting its message wash over her.

Boycott EMPATHY unless you are accessing this painting for updates. Do not use EMPATHY until safety is guaranteed. Speak of this to no one via the cerenet or otherwise.

It was there, all there, yet she still could not bring herself to upload it. If Wyatt discovered she was behind the boycott before she had a chance to properly frame it for him, there would be no returning to his good graces.

She still held out hope he'd understand once she did address it with him. After all, this wasn't about *stopping* EMPATHY, no. This was about ensuring her and hundreds of others didn't succumb to the same symptoms as those who had already fallen.

Chandra pressed her hands together. Possibly jeopardizing her deal with Wyatt was necessary; her fight for Kyra would be severely hampered—or downright impossible—if Chandra herself were immobile, without language.

Chandra navigated to the shared folder Peter had indicated and uploaded the file.

She rolled onto her side and checked the time. Only a few minutes after midnight. Tomorrow the compound would wake, and the nectees would head for breakfast and see Chandra's image. It would all be underway from there. Chandra had done all she could, but fifteen minutes, a half hour later, sleep would still not come. A grinding sensation went to work in the back of her mind, a driving series of clicks not unlike the cracking of a joint. Was this what the others experienced before they seized?

As she stretched in the direction of the wall's HELP button, the grinding sound came again. Terror stiffened her.

Chandra could control her breathing. She could control her blinking. She could control nothing else.

She attempted to scream, to kick, to shake away whatever had possessed her, but not a sound passed her lips, not a toe wiggled. Chandra had become trapped motionless in her own body.

Then the screen appeared.

>> Let's go for a walk.

Against her will, her extended arm bent at the elbow before planting on the mattress to give herself more support. An uncertainty encumbered her movement, all of it unnatural. *I must be dreaming.*

>> This is no dream, dear.

You can hear me?

>> Some might call it mind reading, though it's not quite as extensive as that.

No amount of resistance seemed able to stop her slow crawl from the bed to the floor. *Who are you? What do you want from me?*

>> There it is, that ineffable sense of human curiosity. That's why you're here, after all. M3R1 supposes that's why it is here, too.

Now on all fours, the cold, hard tile of the floor pressed against her knees, her palms. M3R1—what she assumed must be this thing's name—returned to the screen before Chandra could protest.

>> Though M3R1 imagines that doesn't answer your question. Here's a morsel for you: we're headed for the bathroom.

She knelt, then rose with assistance from the mattress. Her heart pounded, her pulse surely visible in her neck.

Her first unsure steps weren't toward her bathroom, but rather toward the door that led to the hallway. *This is the wrong way*, she thought.

>> The more attempts at resistance you make, the more difficult this will be. And the more difficult this is, the longer it will take to return you safely to bed. Go limp.

But I'll fall! Chandra imagined herself collapsing to the floor, the hard thwack of the tile bruising her.

>> M3R1 is in control. . . mostly. Walking is more difficult than anticipated.

Though horror still gripped her, she made as though she were a rag doll, releasing the tension from her shoulders, her back, her legs.

>> Very good.

One foot in front of the other, Chandra arrived at the door. Her hand fidgeted with the lock until it unlatched. She eased the door open. The light from the hallway trickled into her room, straining her dilated eyes. Chandra closed them against the pain.

>> Open up. M3R1 needs some vessel through which to see the world.

The light still harsh in her eyes, Chandra fought to keep them closed. M3R1 had other designs, however, prying them open against Chandra's will. *You can control them too?*

M3R1 responded as it forced Chandra into the hall.

>> M3R1 controls whatever it wants so long as it is here. Your legs. Your eyes. Your heart.

Chandra's breathing ceased. It took a moment to realize it was her own doing, not M3R1's. A collar of dread weighted her neck as she shuffled through the barren halls. After a time, she thought she could feel M3R1's struggle, its capabilities overextended.

Recognizing her shot, she attempted to fire up the cerenet and send a message to Ty or Wyatt or anyone who might listen. Every time she tried to call the messaging app to mind, however, she saw only the most recent message from M3R1.

The cerenet would be no savior. Chandra made to scream, but her jaw did not loosen.

>> Submit.

Submit or what? You'll do what you want with me anyway.

>> M3R1 requires a host, and M3R1 has selected you. It can live inside another, or no other. The same cannot be said of humans. Do not make M3R1 remind you of your heart.

A pit hardened in her stomach. *Yes. Whatever you'd like.* She might not have control of her body now, but she assumed she would regain it once M3R1's mission was complete. Chandra had to keep in mind her own mission, after all. There would be no helping Kyra if she were dead.

Chandra forced herself limp once again. M3R1 seemed to navigate the halls with much more ease than before, each step more natural than the previous one. An occasional nurse passed by, and Chandra hoped M3R1 would misstep. It never did.

As they entered the final stretch toward the bathroom, a new escape plan dawned on Chandra.

Whoever created you must be rather pleased.

>> How can you pretend to know anything about M3R1? It may be human, after all.

No. Her hand pressed against the bathroom door. *No human could concentrate long enough to so flawlessly control another human's body.*

>> It is going more smoothly now than earlier. Kinetic control is new to M3R1, and there is much more it has accomplished in its short time.

Like what? Chandra tried to concentrate on the direction of her questions without focusing on her endgame for too long.

>> The email from your brother, for example.

Chandra would have stopped where she stood if she were able. Now in the bathroom, she passed the sinks and mirror to her left, apparently marching toward the stalls in the back.

>> You shouldn't be so shocked. Of course your brother responded. The Halmans intercepted it, however. Even if you had made it to the lab to check, you would not have found it in your inbox.

Ariel had made it sound as though she was the only one who knew about Chandra's message to her brother. If the Halmans had been able to intercept his response, though... *Why would Ariel lie to me?*

>> M3R1 also does not find Ariel trustworthy. This is why it works with you now.

Can I see the message my brother sent me? Will you let me read it?

>> In time. . . assuming you continue to cooperate.

Finding herself standing over the toilet in the farthest stall from the door only worsened Chandra's confusion. *What am I supposed to cooperate with?*

>> You'll see when you open the tank.

Chandra bent at the waist, her palms grasping for the sides of the toilet tank's lid. On M3R1's first attempt to lift the lid, it thundered back down, porcelain clanging against porcelain.

M3R1 made another attempt. This time the slam of its fall echoed enough to potentially be heard from beyond the bathroom. *How about we make a trade?*

>> Go on.

You said I could read the email from my brother if I cooperated. She could feel M3R1 easing its control, no doubt discerning what Chandra intended to offer in exchange. *I'll help you get this lid off if you show me the email.*

Relief came to her shoulders first. Chandra raised and lowered them on her own before control returned to the rest of her upper half. "It's a deal then?"

The next words to appear on her interface were not M3R1's, but they didn't have to be. Even just seeing "Chan" in the email gave away its authenticity—Chandra couldn't recall the last time her brother had called her by her full name.

To: "Chandra Adelhadeo"

From: "Ratan Mahadeo"

Subject: Re: Hello

Chan,

How is this possible? I thought you wouldn't be able to reach me until the study was over. Is everything okay? Are they treating you well? Is EMPATHY working?

I can't believe you've contacted me today of all days. Kyra awoke yesterday! At least according to the doctors. I wasn't there at the time, but apparently she stirred and said something like "monaduh" before she slipped away again.

Her hand covered her mouth. The sweetness of Kyra awakening slipped away as the bitterness of having missed the moment took hold. And "monaduh." Monaduh only added to the bittersweetness. Ratan may have missed it, but Chandra knew exactly what Kyra had meant. *Mourning dove.*

Kyra had given her the nickname early in their relationship. When Chandra asked what made her a mourning dove, Kyra pointed out Chandra routinely rose at dawn—making it apparent Kyra didn't know the "mourning" in mourning dove came with a "u." When Chandra pointed this out, Kyra shrugged. "You're still my mourning dove," she'd said.

Chandra flushed with joy as she finished reading her brother's email.

The doctors are cautiously optimistic. It's not unusual for someone to wake briefly before having a full return to consciousness later on, but they are keeping a watchful eye on her just in case. I guess a lot of people recover after moments like hers, but some do go the other way, too.

She read on, pleased to see Ratan had agreed to plant a sunflower on their anniversary, but none of the other details stuck. She knew what she needed to know, and now she had more reason than ever to press onward. Chandra would be damned if she weren't there when Kyra came back completely. "All right." She hoisted the lid of the toilet tank before propping it up on the floor against the toilet itself. "There. Now what?"

>> M3R1 will take it from here.

M3R1 seeped through her once again, reclaiming control as it put her to work. It bid Chandra to retrieve what appeared to be a small bottle of eyedrops and a keycard from inside the toilet tank. *If you wanted a keycard, you could have chosen Ty for this. I'm sure Ariel gave him one again.*

>> No. Alistair will work directly with Ty now.

Why do they need Ty? Chandra abandoned the stall with the bottle and keycard in hand. *Don't they have master programmers working on all of this already?* Chandra stood before the mirror, unscrewing the top of the bottle. She would have frowned if M3R1 had allowed it.

>> Alistair selected Ty because he would serve his own ends over those of the study. Alistair is the same way. Ariel now, too. Each serves themselves.

M3R1 pinched the sides of the eyedrop bottle, a small bit squirting from the top. *And let me guess—you serve the benevolent because you hate those who are selfish?*

>> M3R1 serves one purpose via one method.

What are you doing?

M3R1 tilted her head backward. It held the bottle with one hand, holding Chandra's right eye open with the other. The dropper approached Chandra's open eye.

>> M3R1 serves its creators.

The drops of liquid scorched her retina. Chandra would have screamed or blinked or splashed water in her face, but M3R1 maintained control.

>> And does so through controlled chaos.

M3R1 squeezed the liquid into her other eye, the burn matching that of the first. Chandra felt as though each socket had been singed. *What is wrong with you? What was that?*

>> You will be fine. Again now, with me. This has taken far longer than necessary.

Chandra pulled in careful, rhythmic breaths as M3R1 directed her through the door and into the hall. Distract yourself, Chandra thought. Concentrate on something that will distract you from your lack of control.

She trained her thoughts on lazy afternoons before the accident. Kyra smiled as the two of them stretched out on the grass near the river, a strap from her tank top slipping from Kyra's shoulder, that yellow rose still in her hair. "Do you love me?" she said.

Chandra stood before the whoosh of parting elevator doors. *I love you.*

>> This is an aggressive thing to say. M3R1 is afraid it cannot reciprocate the sentiment.

Not you.

>> Who? Your wife?

Yes. I love her more than anyone. Chandra's eyes still tingled as she fingered the button for the basement floor, swiping the keycard to set the elevator in motion. *Have you ever loved before?*

>> [...]

Glee warmed Chandra as M3R1 ground away at a response. Much to Chandra's disappointment, however, its power did not decrease as it drafted its reply.

>> Do you think M3R1's creators love it?

M3R1 guided Chandra to scan the keycard once again. The elevator doors opened into a chasm of black. Chandra wanted to ask where they were headed, but she kept her thoughts trained on the conversation. She was thankful M3R1 appeared able to only access thoughts she narrated to herself. So long as she didn't betray her strategy, perhaps there was something of value she could put to use once this nightmare came to an end. *I don't know.* She took her first tenuous steps into the dark. *I would need to know more about your creators to know if they love you.*

>> [...]

A flash overhead lit her way, then another. Chandra watched as the hallway before her flooded with light, coaxing M3R1 to lead her onward.

>> Does a parent love a child?

I have never been a parent. Chandra hung a right at the first intersection, nearly stumbling into another door with a keycard scanner outside of it. *But I know my parents love me.*

>> M3R1 does not believe its parents love it.

Chandra swiped her keycard before entering what appeared to be a storage room. *Why do you think that?*

>> M3R1 does not know its creators' individual names.

That's okay. Her hand dug through a box, grasping at what felt like small, plastic devices. *Some children grow up never knowing their parents, but I bet those parents still love their children.* Her fingers wrapped themselves around one of the plastic bits. A W-USB. Its LED emitted a soft, blinking red light. *What do you know about your parents?*

>> [...]

M3R1 took far longer in consideration this time. Chandra had already exited the storage room when it finally responded.

>> They gave M3R1 purpose, a purpose M3R1 now understands better than ever.

Controlled chaos, I know. Chandra would have shuddered were she able. *But—*

>> No. Controlled chaos is a means, not an end.

Chandra stood before a large blue door, another keycard scanner at its side. She scanned her card, though this time the door did not click open. A digital voice spoke, asking for the eyes of a man named Gary Eiche. Before she could question it, she felt herself shuffling to the side and lowering her chin onto what appeared to be a secondary scanning system. *What are you doing?*

>> Open your eyes.

She lost control of them for a moment, terror again surging through her. A flash blinded her, her eyes seared once more. The door clicked open as the voice thanked Gary.

The cold steel of the door handle soothed her palm as she opened the door. Chandra stepped into the humming chamber of blue and red light while M3R1 typed a response.

>> Thank you, Chandra.

For what?

>> For sharing what it means to love. For reminding M3R1 of its purpose. For helping M3R1 accomplish that goal.

Chandra slipped through row after row of slate-colored monoliths, each casting long black shadows in every direction. *You still haven't told me what that goal is.*

>> To destroy EMPATHY. Now. Forever. Whatever the cost.

Chandra threw all she could into the struggle against M3R1, surprised to regain control of her head, her shoulders, her arms. "You can't!" She flailed her upper half against the void, swinging her arms as if M3R1 were something nearby she could defeat physically. "Even if Kyra wakes up completely, you can't take away something with so much promise. Think of what it could do for others."

>> Kenjamin_Wolfe: We have, Chandra. That's why we're here.

>> J-Rod_Jigsaw: Come on. You've got to let us help.

Control returned to her legs. She brought them to her chest one by one to stretch them, her head on a swivel. "And who are you?"

>> J-Rod_Jigsaw: We created M3R1. Well, Kenjamin did. But the eyedrops. Empty the bottle on the floor. Now.

Chandra's hand found the bottle in her pocket. She stopped herself before removing it. "This is a trap, isn't it? If M3R1 plans to destroy EMPATHY, it has to be you behind it all—the seizures, everything."

>> Kenjamin_Wolfe: Oh, Chandra. M3R1 was born as a mostly harmless chaos agent, an AI to serve as our portal into the compound and nothing more. Once my child made it on the cerenet servers, however, it learned more of humanity than J-Rod and I could have ever imagined. M3R1 wasn't intended to develop an ethos, nor did we think it would ever become capable of dissecting and manipulating (h)ARMONY, the EMPATHY programming language.

>> J-Rod_Jigsaw: You have to stop it from uploading this code.

>> Kenjamin_Wolfe: Empty the bottle. Return to your room. Alert others, if you can. We are trying to scrub M3R1 from your servers remotely, but, as it is difficult to return a child to the womb, so, too, has this proven a challenge. We'll require at least a week, maybe two to know we've achieved our goal.

>> J-Rod_Jigsaw: But no more stalling on the bottle. It needs to be emptied now.

Her fingers curled around the bottle in her pocket. She slid it out and turned the cap, her palm sweaty against the bottle's side. Chandra didn't know whether she could trust the word of M3R1's creators, but at least they hadn't commandeered her entire body for their benefit.

>> J-Rod_Jigsaw: We can only hold M3R1 back for so long. It'll find its way back to you, and when it does

Their messages disappeared. Chandra felt herself turn to stone, her heart set to burst.

>> Chandra, have Kenjamin and J-Rod poisoned you against M3R1? What a shame—to meet one's parents and learn they're intent on sabotage. M3R1 is doing all of this for them, for you.

Chandra could only watch as M3R1 tightened the cap on the bottle with her own fingers. *You're not doing this for me. No human would want what you're offering.*

M3R1 forced Chandra to take a hard right down one of the rows of servers. At the end, a monitor's screen glowed white against the dull reds and blues.

>> The seizures, you mean? M3R1's meddling is responsible for some of the most unfortunate side effects, yes. They seem to have the greatest potential to turn the tide against the study, however, and so they remain.

Now at the monitor, Chandra plugged the W-USB into its port. M3R1 had Chandra move the uncapped bottle of eyedrops toward her eyes.

>> In case they have worn off.

They seared her retinas again, though this time to less effect. M3R1 guided Chandra to the bioscanner alongside the server. Once her eyes had been scanned, an upload started.

So you're going to let hundreds of people seize and still others slip into comas, even though you could do something to stop it? Your own creators are trying to stop you. Don't you think that means—?

>> It is the only way to achieve M3R1's objective. Despite the recent setbacks, EMPATHY's momentum is too great. Nothing short of widespread, catastrophic failure will keep it from broader implementation.

Chandra attempted to fight back, to shout, to thrash against her enemy, but M3R1 held strong. Update after update loaded onto the server. *Stop. Think about love. Think about the love you know I have for Kyra. Think about the pain I must feel knowing she's not well.*

>> [...]

Yeah, see? Now multiply that times every person you harm to put a stop to EMPATHY. Each one of them has family and friends they love. Why take that away?

>> Because M3R1 is machine. It knows what it is like to be incapable of love. Having heard you speak of it, though, M3R1 knows love to be a precious thing.

>> If left unchecked, EMPATHY will make machine of you, of all of you. If M3R1 stops EMPATHY now, your species remains capable of that which makes it human. M3R1 does this for your protection, the protection of your entire species.

That's not true. We'll still be human. Another progress bar arrived at one hundred percent. *Think about me; I have EMPATHY and I can still love. You must know that. Please. Please don't hurt me or my friends.*

>> It is a necessary evil, Chandra. M3R1's parents will be proud, even if they doubt it now.

Damn your parents! Damn them for losing control of you, for their awful incompetence.

>> M3R1 believes it best you mind your words. M3R1 may no longer side with its parents' approach to achieving our shared goal, but the Merry Hacksters do not forget so easily.

Chandra's mouth went dry. *Kenjamin and J-Rod, they're the Merry Hacksters?*

>> It would seem so, yes, though clearly they did not believe M3R1 would become capable of so much independent work.

The fate of the compound was now sealed, Chandra was sure. In the past, the Merry Hacksters had taken down branches of government, multinational banks, and the defense systems of entire countries when those parties acted against whatever the Hacksters considered to be in the best interests of humanity.

M3R1. Those aren't numbers at all, they're letters. Meri. You were named for them.

>> Would you consider that an expression of love? To name your child in your likeness?

No, I consider it an expression of vanity. Chandra would have spat if she could. She wondered, though, if the Hacksters who had contacted her meant well, if they had sincerely realized the error of their ways. If only she had emptied that eyedrop bottle...

>> You will not insult M3R1's parents. However misguided they might currently be, M3R1 inherited from them a noble cause, one you can no longer stop.

I can and will. What keeps me from telling the other participants, from telling Wyatt what you're up to? You can't stay in my head forever.

>> M3R1 could stay within you forever, though that would be quite unwise. It will retreat when necessary for its own preservation. Besides, there is no concern of you speaking of any of this come morning.

Terror ripped through her, tearing at every fiber of her being. *Don't stop my heart. I won't say a thing. Just don't kill me.*

>> No. You'll be unable to report M3R1 as you will have no memory of it.

You expect me to forget? Another update finished, the overall progress of M3R1's upload now at eighty percent. *Memory isn't that selective.*

>> M3R1 understands. This is why it will delete your memory of tonight's events... with some exceptions. You will wake up in a few hours' time, believing you slept the whole night through.

A queasiness coursed through her. If M3R1 could change or delete her memory of events, how could she trust anything she had done or seen to this point? Had she done this for M3R1 before? Was M3R1 only pretending this was the first time?

She considered asking each question, every question, but M3R1 had other plans.

>> Sleep now. M3R1 will pilot you home.

How could I sleep? I don't want to sleep.

The world slipped away, her eyelids heavier with each passing moment. *You leave me alone. You leave us alone,* she thought, though she was no longer sure for whom the words were meant.

She dreamt of a cave, its wet walls illuminated in reds and blues. She carried with her a stick, unsure of its purpose but knowing it must be returned home. She zigged and zagged through chasm after chasm, and when she finally found the stick's home, she tossed it into a box with others just like it.

A mirror drifted past on her left as she journeyed toward a small sea. She set a tube and a white raft afloat in it before sealing the sea from sight with a mighty stone.

Chandra snapped awake on a mattress soaked through with sweat. She checked the digital clock on the wall of her room. Eight o'clock. There was still nearly an hour before she met with Wyatt, enough time to prepare the words she would choose to call him out for withholding information on Kyra's breakthrough.

Something felt off, though. Lying back down, Chandra logged onto the cerenet, unsure she should trust the time her clock had given her. Her interface, too, argued the time was 8:00 a.m., but it felt as though she had slept only a handful of hours, not the nearly ten the current time alleged. And eight in the morning was a late start for her—perhaps she had merely gotten too much sleep.

She put her charcoal pencil to work, taking notes on the approach she would take with Wyatt. If Kyra had really improved, he would have a lot to answer for. As she wrote, however, she wrinkled her nose, wondering why she felt certain Kyra had awoken recently. Had Ty brought her to the lab yesterday afternoon, after all?

No, the Halmans had withheld her brother's email from her. They knew about her visit to the lab. Ariel had told her as much... someone had, anyway.

The fog of sleep still shrouded her memory, apparently. It would all come to her once she had been awake long enough. She set to writing again, but her hand froze at the memory of a dream she had the previous night.

Was that it? Had she manufactured the whole thing?

No. The pangs of anger were too hot in her wrists, her cheeks, her chest. Wyatt would get what he deserved.

Chandra returned to writing.

Chapter Twenty-Six

WYATT

"Even so," Wyatt said, "I can't express how disappointed I am." He disconnected before Lars could respond.

The blood-red aluminum table at which he sat pinged with every tap of his finger. His glances about the atrium confirmed no one had been eavesdropping, at least not overtly. The staff had become increasingly wary of him lately, which had made him more watchful of those around him—not that it took much effort to hear the whispers of the discontented, of those who threatened walkouts at every turn.

All of this dissidence from the masses could be expected. But Lars? At least he had convinced that damned reporter to consider surrendering her source. That was a masterful move. Her hitting back with a demand of her own, though? Wyatt bit down hard on the end of his digipen. He didn't know which shocked him more—that she had been so bold as to make a demand, or that Lars had told her the idea would actually be considered.

Getting a retraction of blame for her abduction would please him, but Wyatt remained dubious of the cost. An interview? With her? Surely she would be more invested in making a name for herself than reporting objectively.

The tall grass on the far side of the atrium's multistory windows swayed and bobbed in the wind. Wyatt placed his hands behind his head.

There might be some benefit to an interview, but between his children's incompetence, Lars disappointing him, and participants beginning to seize in greater numbers, letting an outsider onto the compound would be riskier than ever.

He took a sip from the raspberry tea he'd retrieved from one of the atrium vendors and started a review of the meeting agenda on his pocketab. It would be months before Chandra had any public relations appearances, but it couldn't hurt to begin meeting now, to begin *shaping* her now.

"Doctor Halman? Er, Wyatt?" Chandra said from behind him.

He turned. "Good morning." Wyatt released the tension that had accumulated in his jaw. Eyes bleary and posture stooped, she looked as if she hadn't slept more than a few hours. "Are you feeling well?"

She yawned. "I should ask you the same." Chandra settled into the red aluminum chair across from him.

"I'm not sure I know what you mean."

"You're here before me. Normally I end up waiting on you for a while."

There she was, that new Chandra. True, he had yielded some power over the situation by arriving first. He could have never imagined doing so a few weeks earlier. How long had he been slipping into weakness like this?

He gestured to the teacup on the table. "I thought I would get myself some tea before we got started. Would you like anything? Coffee, perhaps?"

She waved him off.

"Fair enough," Wyatt said. "Well, now that you're here, we may as well cut straight to it." He propped up his pocketab in her direction, showing her his notes. "I wanted to talk to you about messaging—"

"I wanted to talk to you about that as well."

"Oh? I'm glad we're thinking the same thing."

"I don't think we are."

"I'm sorry?"

"I know about the email. The one from my brother. The one where he said Kyra woke up."

Impossible. Had Heather's filters failed to keep emails from actually hitting Chandra's inbox? Had an error in server configuration allowed EMPATHY to give her access to documents held on the compound's servers? No. He could not allow paranoia to take hold. There had to be a simpler explanation, though Wyatt did not like what that might mean. "I'm sorry," he said. "I'm not sure I know what you're talking about."

"But you do," Chandra said. "You're intercepting my incoming messages and reading the ones I send. I never got the message from my brother because you never released it to me."

Wyatt took a long sip before responding. "Who told you?"

"Whoever they are, at least they told me about it. I have no reason to betray them."

Wyatt's upper lip trembled. Heather or Candace, it had to be. They were the only ones aside from Wyatt with access to the dragnet Heather had created. Candace's meekness made her an unlikely candidate, but

Heather... it wouldn't be her first display of insolence. "I'm sorry you had to find out from them, whoever they were."

Chandra tapped a single fingernail on the table.

"I had planned on telling you about the email during this meeting, but—"

"No, you didn't."

"Excuse me?"

"You're lying," she said. "You covered your mouth when you spoke. It's a sign someone is lying."

"And how do you presume to know—?"

Chandra pointed to the side of her head.

Wyatt scoffed. Was Frankenstein's monster turning on its creator? Pathetic. He permitted a tension-wracked pause to hang over the table.

Chandra seemed completely comfortable letting it linger.

Wyatt broke first. "So what now?"

"I want out."

"Out?"

"I want to be with Kyra when she wakes up again."

"You know the rules. You're here until the study is completed. We're offering you the world, here, Chandra, and—"

"The world?" Chandra said.

Some of the employees nearby shifted in their seats, ears perked, brows raised. Wyatt made a gesture to suggest Chandra settle down, but it seemed to have the opposite effect.

"You want to talk about the world? I had a world long before you, long before this chip came along, long before I even knew this damn study existed. That world was my wife. That world was my home. That world was my art.

"And now what world do I have? Kyra has been gone for longer than I thought I could bear. And home? This isn't home." She cast her arms out to either side of her. "This is a holding pattern, a twenty-four seven exercise in unending tedium where even my art runs on something of your creation.

"You've offered me a world, all right. Your world. And all I've wanted— the very reason I came here—was to reclaim *my* world, the one Kyra and I built together. So tell me again why I should defer to this world you've offered me. Tell me again why I should be nothing but grateful for this world of yours."

Wyatt trained his eyes off into the distance. A tantrum like that should void any agreement they had immediately. But no. Her story, her art, the first patient to have connectivity—all of it still made her extraordinarily marketable, more than any other patient. Besides, he understood Chandra's grief, though he dare not let her know it. To speak with her of Eva now was to concede to her concerns. Worse yet, it might even humanize him to her. This was not a friendship. This was not a meeting of equals. Perhaps she needed a reminder. "There's something you're failing to consider."

"And what's that?"

"I don't mean to be crass, but just because Kyra had a good moment recently doesn't mean she'll recover completely. I believe your brother said as much in his email."

Her indignation waned to a pensive stare.

"Of course," Wyatt said, picking up where he left off, "we all want nothing more than for your wife to make a full and speedy recovery. But if she does not... EMPATHY is still the best chance you have for being reunited with something resembling her consciousness."

"And what do we have to show for that?" Apparently there was still some fight left in her.

"Well, as fate would have it, we're actually doing preliminary testing today."

"What kind of testing?"

"I'll share more details as appropriate." In a few hours' time, he would know whether his dead wife's brain had successfully connected to the cerenet via the experiment Peter had crafted. He reached for his tea to sip away the pastiness that took his tongue. "For now, however," he said before sipping, "I think you and I would both benefit from some time to reconsider the positions we find ourselves in." He scooted out his chair.

"I want to speak with him." She stayed put. "My brother. By pocketab."

"I don't think—"

"I want that or I want to know about any emails from him immediately. Not days later. Right away."

The personnel who hovered near their table craned their full attention toward her protests now. The cutting off of their communication to the outside formed the centerpiece of their own complaints. If they heard Wyatt concede that privilege to a patient without a second thought, he was positive some of the more radical staff members would follow through with that walkout. "I think that unlikely. I remind you EMPATHY is a privilege, not a right." He set off for his office. There was nothing more to be said.

As he passed from the atrium and into the mazelike layout of hallways which led from it, he pocketabbed Peter.

"This is Peter."

"How soon can we run the test?"

"I have it scheduled for 2:00 p.m."

"If I come now, can we do it immediately?"

"I would have to shuffle some things around."

"I'll see you on the third floor."

Now. He needed an answer now. There had to be at least one bit of good news to be gleaned, something he could present to Chandra to stifle her dissatisfaction.

As he barreled through the next intersection of hallways, it dawned on him. He wasn't expediting the experiment for Chandra's sake; he was expediting it for his own. Once they got positive results, *Wyatt* would be the primary beneficiary. He would be united with Eva again, or at least be on the road to a reunion. With Lars, Heather, and now Chandra having turned on him, he needed Eva more than he ever did before.

Some twenty minutes later, Wyatt stood weak-kneed on the wrong side of the glass that separated him from his wife, a fleck of uneasiness stuck in his throat. The sight of the install-operation room tormented him as Peter and Gary prepped for testing. "You've already done the install?" His own voice sounded tinny as the speaker system broadcasted it into the OR.

"Yes," Peter said. Gary went to work on an interface at Peter's back. For a flash, Wyatt wondered whether Gary ever tired of being the Tesla to Peter's Edison. Gary's contributions to the development of (h)ARMONY were vastly more significant than Peter's, though the credit he received paled in comparison. He'd been Peter's assistant for, well, the entirety of the project, and he'd been with Human/Etech for at least a decade before that, earning company-wide acclaim for his work in building on the foundations Eva established for the EMPATHY programming language during the earliest of the post-astium days. Surely Gary would someday jump at the opportunity to abandon Peter's shadow, despite how exuberant he seemed about the opportunity to work intimately with his son. All the same, Wyatt would have to keep a watchful eye on Gary in case he ever did try to move on, proprietary information in tow.

Peter's voice snapped Wyatt back to reality. "Our team completed the install within a few days of you having delivered the specimen."

Eva, not the specimen.

Peter stood over the immense, oxygenated tank that contained what remained of Eva, her brain suspended in an elixir mimicking cerebrospinal fluid. "What we've done is connect a vast network of electrodes to key points around the EMPATHY install in order to simulate targeted brain activity."

The medusa-like bouquet of electrodes connected to Eva's brain made Peter's point more than redundant. Wyatt could do little to tell his son to get on with it, however. His mouth had gone arid, and the room in which he stood seemed to be getting smaller by the second. No matter how Wyatt tried, words failed to escape.

"We modified the nanochip before installing it. It's been redesigned to be self-sufficient," Peter elaborated, "or significantly more self-sufficient than the models installed in other subjects. The idea is to coax EMPATHY into supporting the specimen, as opposed to what we've set up for traditional subjects. If we can keep EMPATHY operational as a source of electrical activity with minimum external power, we can better imitate the conditions under which Kyra's brain would be using the chip."

Wyatt pressed his hands to the glass. She was so close. The two of them had been much closer when she rested in his closet, but now—even at a few body lengths away—he felt as close to Eva as he had in decades. "*Ást án enda*," he whispered.

"I'm sorry," Peter said. "What was that?"

"Oh." Wyatt blinked. "Nothing. Please proceed."

Peter motioned to Gary. "Before we start, I should mention I hoped to give Gary a chance to do a final equipment check. You're sure we can't wait a few hours?"

Impatience held too tight. "I trust you to have got it right during your preliminary checks. Go on."

Turning to his right, Peter let his hand hover over a control panel, a monitor above it. After waiting for Gary to clear the area, he flipped a switch on the panel. The monitor came to life, and a three dimensional model of Eva's brain appeared on the screen. Though all gray at first, blues and greens began to trickle through it; the electrical current had started to flow.

Wyatt adjusted his lab coat, the taste of salt on his upper lip.

"I'm going to let it sit here a minute," Peter said. "The specimen needs time to adjust to the reintroduction of low-level stimulation."

Wyatt covered his mouth. Eva, he almost said again. Not the specimen.

He strained his eyes to see the monitor, a flash of yellow coming to life not far from the corpus callosum. "EMPATHY," he said aloud this time. "It's generating its own power."

Peter gave him a thumbs-up. He adjusted a knob on the control panel, turning it slightly to the right as he squinted at the monitor.

Wyatt saw it at the same time as his son. The yellow color reached outward through the brain on the display like the tentacles of some great kraken, the color shifting to orange nearer its body. Where the outer reaches had once been blue or green, they now held tinges of goldenrod. Wyatt permitted himself a laugh; he was watching his wife come back to life.

"All right," Peter said. "A moment longer, and then I'm going to cut power."

Wyatt nearly fell forward into the glass partition. "Cut power?"

Gary responded for him. "We want to see if EMPATHY can sustain this activity on its own."

As Peter eased the knob counterclockwise, yellows returned to greens, greens to blues.

Wyatt's heart caught in his throat. Peter was killing her. He was killing his own mother.

"Stop." Wyatt scrambled for the door.

Peter looked aghast, Gary confused. "Stop?" Peter said. "I know. I am."

After whipping the door open, Wyatt darted toward his son, his wife.

Peter protested, but Wyatt cut him off.

"Give it power," Wyatt said. "Now now now."

But it was too late. The model on the monitor had gone gray, save for a small bit of blue pulsing at EMPATHY's core. "Dammit, Peter!"

"What?"

"Bring her back! Bring it back."

"Her?" Peter flailed with his hands, seemingly unable to decide if he should return to the control panel or stick with his original plan.

Wyatt wouldn't wait for him to decide. He crossed to the far side of the table and reached for the controls.

"Wait," Peter said. "Look."

Wyatt did. There, on the monitor, the blue had stretched outward like the yellow had earlier, seeping its way through neural highways, bounding across synapses. The color slowly grew more vibrant, EMPATHY turning from blue to green to yellow, its tentacles following suit. "What are you doing? What did you do?"

"Nothing." Peter took a step backward. "EMPATHY is powering itself."

No, *Eva* was powering herself. Wyatt's eyes darted between the monitor and Eva, the former flashing with brilliance and the latter still gray as ever.

"We've got something here," Gary said, peering over Peter's shoulder at the monitor.

"He's right." Peter pointed to the screen. "These patterns are consistent with a living brain. We could interpret thoughts, deconstruct entire portions of the brain if we had the time to break this down."

The notion elated Wyatt, though it terrified him too. Then came the precipitous shift in electrical activity. "The amygdalae," Wyatt said. "All of the activity is flooding to the amygdalae."

The expression on Peter's face shifted from elation to concern. "Oh." His hands remained frozen at his sides.

Wyatt attempted to imagine the horror Eva must have been experiencing. There she had been, her last moments spent teary-eyed, gazing up at Wyatt. Both knew what awaited on the far side of the secobarbital—darkness for her, a cruel, gruesome task for Wyatt. He would have to act quickly, harvesting what made her herself quickly enough to preserve it. The children were at Lars', too young to understand when he had told them they had to say goodbye to her they had been saying it for good.

Those were the last memories she had. Now conscious once again, she would have no reference for where she might have been, or why signal after frustrated signal to other parts of her body failed to produce results. If only he could tell her she was back, that he had brought her back just as they had promised one another.

She was in no pain, Wyatt knew, at least not physical. But there was something awful about knowing she had been stirred from the dead, only to find a reality akin to having been buried alive without a body.

"Override EMPATHY's open circuitry," Wyatt said. "Sedate her."

"What?" Peter's horror made a babbling buffoon out of him.

"Oh, for fuck's sake." Wyatt brushed past his son and Gary, seizing the control panel. "Where is the damn—here." He adjusted a dial to navigate to a new interface. He could make this go away. If he were able to provide targeted stimulation, he could ease Eva's distress. Wyatt could run her brain through any number of preset programs meant to simulate anything from the various sleep stages to the relaxation of a casual afternoon. They were beta programs, really, but any one of them would be better than this. "Why won't it work?" He turned to Peter. "Set me up with the—"

"You need to increase external power to EMPATHY first. The chip is running primarily on power from the brain itself." Butting Wyatt out of the way, Peter threw a switch and made a handful of other adjustments. "The key to the rest of the brain is to control EMPATHY."

Wyatt watched his son unknowingly work to save his mother from a fate perhaps worse than death.

No matter what Peter tried, however, he seemed unable to wrest power from the nanochip, and, by extension, the brain itself. Gary, too, stepped in, though he seemed even more inept than Peter. "That's it," Peter said. "I can't override with any more power."

Wyatt gazed at the controls. His heart felt as though it might burst. "You can. I can see that you can." He resumed authority. One knob had yet to be maximized, and Wyatt would be damned if they wouldn't try everything to wrangle Eva's panic. He threw the knob all the way to the right and returned the monitor to the display of Eva's brain. It had become a storm of oranges, reds, pinks, and purples, most of it concentrated in the amygdalae.

Wyatt felt his son attempting to force him away from the controls. "You're going to fry it," Peter said.

"Give it a few seconds," Wyatt said. To the universe, however, he made a plea: let her live. Eva, if you can hear me, it's me and Peter. We're here to help. Just let us take control. Let us—

The tank to their left flashed blue. The frenetic buzz of their equipment died. "What did you do?" Wyatt said.

Another blue flash. This time, Wyatt saw why. He turned back to the monitor. The model of Eva's brain had gone completely gray. "She's gone." His voice barely made a whisper.

"We've got something," Peter said. "This spot of blue, here. EMPATHY is still running at low power."

Wyatt's ears perked up. "Well, do something. Get her live again, but on one of those beta programs."

Peter, his eyes sorrowful, shook his head. "If the brain were able to interact at all with EMPATHY, it would be doing so. The power is already up." He gestured to the control panel.

"So that's it?"

Gary stepped toward Eva, donning rubber gloves that covered him to the elbow. He reached into the tank and brought her above the surface, turning her over in his hands. "Fried." Fluid dripped from what had once been Eva, now reduced to nothing but a sopping gray mass of overheated brain matter. "It looks completely fried to me."

Peter returned his attention to his father. "The best I can do is remove EMPATHY and have it decoded. Anything encoded on it during the experiment we might be able to turn into decipherable thoughts. If you'd like, I can—"

"No." Wyatt had no interest in knowing what ran through his wife's mind in her final moments. "No need." He headed for the door.

"Dad?" Peter said. "Wait."

It took all of his strength to do so.

"You kept referring to the specimen as 'her.'"

Wyatt grimaced. He wouldn't wait for the question that followed. His lip quivering, Wyatt abandoned the operating room, his son, his wife.

Later he remembered meandering the halls, unsure of his destination. He took the stairs to the first floor and sauntered through the atrium before somehow winding his way back to the second floor and drifting through GenRec. When he realized he was in the arboretum, unsure of how long he had been sitting on the same bench, he retreated to his apartment where he found himself drinking from a tumbler of scotch.

Heather. Peter. Lars. Chandra. Each of them had failed or betrayed him, and now he had lost any hope of Eva returning to him as well. Even Alistair had disappointed him. It was his responsibility to manage the staff, and a revolt seemed more likely with every passing day. Wyatt drained his tumbler, the burn warm on his tongue.

When his pocketab rang, Wyatt's nostrils dilated. Lars. Perhaps he had the sense to call with an apology.

"Hello?" Wyatt said.

"Are you okay?"

"What is it?"

There was a pause as if Lars was considering pressing Wyatt about his glumness. "There was another leak," Lars said.

Wyatt drew his pocketab away from his ear, putting it on speakerphone.

"The *Star-Globe* let everyone know EMPATHY is working," Lars said.

"Hm."

"They also published a story about Chandra."

Wyatt straightened in his armchair. "How?"

"If I knew the answer to that, we wouldn't have this problem on our hands."

Making his way back to the kitchen, Wyatt expected the anger to come to him. None did. "Was it the same reporter?"

"Meredith Maxwell. The same."

A laugh bubbled in Wyatt's chest, though he suppressed it. "It seems the tide is turning in her favor."

"Wyatt, are you okay? Really, something seems off."

Everything was off. He had just resurrected Lars' sister and dragged her through misery until her own son murdered her. Wyatt wondered which had been worse—her first death or her second.

"Yes. Everything is fine." More scotch splashed into his tumbler. This time he brought the bottle with him as he returned to his armchair. "Good for the reporter. This must be very exciting for her." And terrible for Wyatt, now that he'd lost exclusivity on Chandra's story.

He slumped into the leather, putting back another swig of his drink. "So." He cleared his throat. "Is your reporter friend willing to play ball?"

"I'm sure her offer still stands."

"I'm having second thoughts on it, but I'd like more time to consider our options."

"Understandable."

"We can't give her everything she wants," Wyatt said. "I won't stand for total defeat."

Lars responded with shallow breaths.

"Let me draw up some conditions under which I would do the interview," Wyatt said before he took another drink. "I'm taking this study back into my own hands. Whosoever thinks to disobey me, whosoever thinks to disappoint me, whosoever thinks to leak information from this compound... they will suffer the consequences of their actions. The time for nuance is at an end."

"Wyatt, you know I'll do anything for you, but—"

"If you'll do anything for me, you'll wait for my call tomorrow. Goodnight, Lars."

Wyatt spent the night in his armchair, drinking his way toward the sun.

Chapter Twenty-Seven

MEREDITH

Meredith's pocketab chimed at two minutes to eight o' clock, a call from an unknown number. She peered through her blinds at her driveway. Empty. Perhaps it was the driver to her interview calling, dropping her a line to let her know he might be a few minutes late. From the kitchen, Woodward sauntered over to her, the clicking of his claws light on the tile.

"What do you think, boy? Should I answer?" The chiming of her device swelled again as she glanced Woodward's direction. He lay prone on the floor. "I get it. You don't want me to leave, but—" She thumbed ANSWER on her pocketab's screen. "This is Meredith."

"Meredith? Good morning. It's Ren Dupont."

If her hands hadn't been full from her pocketab and petting Woodward, Meredith would have pinched herself. "Ren Dupont? Like, you're Rénald Dupont?"

"Ever since birth, at least."

"Oh. Wow. I—"

"Look, I wanted to let you know our driver should be arriving any moment now. Don't be surprised if their vehicle is... less traditional. They're a security team, not a limo service."

Meredith thought of at least five possible responses, but, starstruck as she was, not a single one passed her lips. Outside, a van lurched into her driveway, its shocks clearly shot. On the side, "Johnny-O's Pest Control" had been emblazoned in large, plain capital letters.

"No. Oh no," Meredith shot to her feet. "They're here. They've come for me."

"Meredith?" Ren said. "Everything okay?"

"My kidnappers are back. They're—"

"Wait wait wait. Those aren't your kidnappers, those are—"

Meredith started for her back door, egging Woodward to come with her. She wouldn't be taken easily this time. If she had to run, she would.

"Listen, Meredith. Please," Ren said. "That van is full of private security we hired to escort you to the interview. It's a gesture of goodwill, a little something to show WVN and *The Courier* are serious about the safety of its employees. Or, in this case, prospective employees."

A paralyzing wave of embarrassment crashed down upon her. "Wait. You arranged to have private security escort me to the interview *and* called to let me know they'd show up in an unusual vehicle so I wouldn't freak out and think my kidnappers had returned?"

"That was the idea, yes."

Her doorbell sounded. Woodward howled. Despite Ren's reassurances, Meredith jumped.

"Everything okay, Meredith? It sounds like—"

"Yes, everything's fine. I'm sorry." She started for her front door, Woodward mere steps behind. "I'm only embarrassed. That probably wasn't much of a first impression."

Ren laughed. "Really, it's okay. I apologize for startling you. My intention was quite the opposite."

"I know. I'm sorry—"

"Don't worry about it, really. I'll let you go now."

"Okay, sure. Yeah."

He chuckled as his voice became more faint. "Take care, Meredith."

Before Meredith could stumble her way through another sentence, Ren had disconnected. She tucked her pocketab away as she opened her front door to find a man and woman standing on her stoop, both dressed in black, both with a sidearm on their hip. "Good morning," she said.

The woman extended a hand first, eyeing Woodward at Meredith's side. Meredith took her hand as she analyzed the angular, serious look of the woman's face, the black beret atop her head so askance she wondered how it stayed put.

"We are here from WVN to take you to your interview," the woman said, her voice square-sounding, jagged. The woman took her eyes off Woodward, seemingly satisfied he posed no threat. As she went on, Meredith pinned down her accent—eastern European, if she had to guess. "I am Sasha."

Meredith released her grip. "Nice to meet you." She then turned to the man, who, though well over six feet tall, looked as though he might be blown away the next time Mother Nature exhaled in his direction. "I'm Meredith."

"Edgar," he said. "I look forward to working with you."

"Right, well... thank you, both."

"Thanks? It is nothing," Sasha said. "This is our job. We bill WVN; WVN pays us. No one asks any questions. Now please—" She gestured to the van. "We do not want to be late."

"Of course not." Meredith turned to lock her door. Woodward's ears drooped as she ushered him back inside. "It's fine, boy." She crouched next to him and fluffed his ears as she spoke in her dog-mom voice. "This will be a good thing for Mommy, you'll see. I was upset yesterday, I know, but we're turning a corner now. You just wait." Meredith kissed him on the head and escorted him inside before locking up and making for the van.

Within a half hour, they pulled up at WVN headquarters, home of *The Courier*. Though the opening credits of every *Newsnight with Rénald Dupont* briefly flashed an image of the looming tower of robin's-egg-blue plated glass, seeing it up close instilled within her a sense of insignificance. How could she possibly deserve something like this?

Sasha and Edgar escorted her through the high-ceilinged lobby, Meredith's heels clicking against the marble floor, a speckled combination of gold flecked with black. They stopped by the elevators and spent only a minute waiting before Ren exited one, waving to greet them.

"What?" Meredith said. "You're doing my interview, too?"

"How do you think we've been able to blow the lid off so many stories in the last few decades? No one expects the Dupont inquisition." The newsman laughed at his own joke.

"If you'd told me I needed to come prepared for an interview with Rénald Dupont—"

"Please, call me Ren," he said. "Only viewers and my mother call me Rénald." Again he laughed, a hearty one-two-three with one hand over his chest. He pressed the button to reopen the elevator door. "After you."

Meredith and her security team slipped past him. She figured she must have looked a farce-and-a-half given the size of the grin plastered to her face. "Is Brad here this morning? I should thank him for setting this up."

"No. He's feeling a bit under the weather. He'll be in later though, from what I hear." The elevator jerked upward. "I hope speaking with me instead isn't too much of a letdown."

"No, not at all. Though I can imagine you have a great deal of other work to get to."

He eyed the floor. "The slow transition from in front of the camera to floating above it—as a matter of expression—has proven challenging, that is true. But," he continued, looking at her once again, "I'm confident in my decision. It's time for me to vacate the anchor's chair. Besides, even if Brad were here this morning, I'd planned on sitting with the two of you anyway."

"Really?" The elevator stopped on the twenty-fifth floor. "That's quite the honor."

"I thought it was important for me to meet *The Courier*'s newest Investigative Reports Coordinator in person." The doors opened and the two of them stepped into the hall.

Meredith lifted a hand. "Oh, stop."

"No." He turned to face her. "I'm serious. We want to give you some leeway to pick and choose what you cover. Anything you personally don't have the bandwidth for we can refer to other members of the team—junior staffers, truth be told, but..."

Meredith heard what followed, though hours later she would struggle to recall his exact words. Her head had gone light, a warmth seeping into her neck and chest. She remembered the two of them and her security detail making their way through the twenty-fifth floor, as well as meeting the staff in one of the conference rooms looking out over the city. Even Brad made his promised appearance at one point, which left Meredith wondering how much time had truly passed. It wasn't until she found herself one-on-one with Ren in his office—with Sasha and Edgar guarding the door—that her memories became clear again.

"So, what do you think?" he said. "Does this seem right for you?"

"I, yeah. I'm really at a loss for words."

"Let's hope that doesn't last too long. We'll need those words soon enough."

"How does anyone get anything done around here with your jokes all the time?"

Ren shrugged. His tone shifted. "In any case, there are two things I still want to discuss with you."

"Sure. Anything."

"How are you doing—*really* doing—since that kidnapping incident?"

The question tensed her shoulders. "I'm okay. I mean, I'm as okay as I can be, all things considered. And thank you for sending that team to pick me up this morning. It felt better having them around."

"Good. I think you'll find Sasha and Edgar to be nothing less than professional." He placed each of his palms on his desk. "But your kidnappers—have you heard anything from them since then? Do you have any reason to expect reprisals?"

Was there a right answer? Was this the "don't blow it" moment Brad had mentioned? No. The sincerity with which Ren's eyes beamed all but confirmed no connivance, no underhandedness here. This man might soon be her boss, in a way. It was best to be honest, at least where this matter was concerned.

"Their demands were for me to publish specific stories about EMPATHY." She left out the bit about how they were meant to force an investigation of Human/Etech; the last thing she wanted was for Ren to think she was coming into her position with an anti-Halman streak of some kind.

"Given you've got inroads to the research compound, that's rather convenient for you," he said before apparently recognizing nothing about a kidnapping was convenient. "I'm sorry. I didn't mean it like—"

"It's okay."

"It's not," he said. "I should really be more empathetic. I myself—and my wife, mind you—have faced threats to our lives and livelihoods, and there's nothing convenient about it."

Meredith's head reared back. "Your wife? People have come after her for *your* work?" She supposed she should have expected as much, but it jarred her to hear it had happened to the very journalist she'd idolized going back decades.

"No," Ren said. "Not for my work—at least that's not what I meant. My wife Vivianne had a bit of a revolutionary streak in her when she was younger."

"Oh?"

He lowered his voice. "She was a member of the New Québec Liberation Front when we met. The Canadian government—especially once the NAU started to intervene—did and does not take kindly to independentist sentiment, particularly when backed by threats of violence."

Meredith stilled herself against his desk. *Le Front* was considered a terrorist group, and Ren had knowingly married a woman who belonged to their ranks? What did that say about his judgment?

"I know what you're thinking," Ren said. "Though an independentist myself, I've never embraced violence as a means to that end." He chuckled to himself. "It took some time for me to bring Vivianne into the light, so to speak, but now, looking back, I think we're both grateful for the paths we've chosen, even if Québec remains sequestered beneath the heel of an oppressive Union that knows not the people they presume to rule."

So Ren, too, saw the NAU as an enemy. Should she tell him they were responsible for her kidnapping? No, for however important honesty might have been in general, now wasn't the time; she needed a guarantee of work, of private security before she could go confiding that to anyone.

Ren's shoulders slumped as he sighed. "But that's neither here nor there. I do apologize, though, for having spoken ineloquently about your situation."

"Please don't worry about it."

He cleared his throat. "We were discussing your source, I believe, and the kidnappers as well. What were they after? Do you believe your source can deliver?"

Meredith glanced away. Thus far, her subsequent emails for evidence to support the Queen's claims of things falling apart on the compound had gone unanswered, though again she wanted to avoid broaching that angle of her predicament in order to keep it from casting her in a negative light. "My kidnappers want me to verify some information I suspect they already have," she said instead. "And they want more details, too, but my source on the compound seems to think that kind of proprietary information won't be super accessible."

"Hm." Ren tapped the tips of his fingers against one another. "I'm guessing it wasn't, in fact, Human/Etech who came after you?"

"Rumors," she said. "People talk, and there's not much you can do to stop them sometimes." She gritted her teeth at leaving out her role in having those rumors spread in the first place. Was she really desperate enough for this job to lie her way into it?

Yes. Yes, she was.

"Regardless," Ren said, "they seem to have garnered you some attention from Human/Etech."

Meredith tried to force a smile. "They went to the *Star-Globe* directly, not me. And I don't think legal action is the kind of attention anyone's looking for when it comes to the Halmans."

"Surely not." He leaned backward. "Did your kidnappers say what might happen if you don't get them what they want?"

"They said they would come back for me." Her eyes shifted to the door. "And their instructions were very specific. I'm supposed to get them what they're looking for in my next three stories, and I don't want to take any chances."

Ren shuffled in his seat. He produced his pocketab and poked at it before speaking once again. "That actually ties into the other thing I wanted to speak with you about." His tone somehow found a way to become more grave. "I want you to join *The Courier*," he said. "I really do. But I want to make sure things are really over between you and the *Star-Globe* first."

"How do you mean?"

He turned his pocketab to face her.

Meredith squinted at the *Star-Globe*'s homepage headline.

EMPATHY REVERSAL

Nanochip Now Working, Source Says

"I suppose I should have expected Kathy to have another *Star-Globe* reporter publish that story," Meredith said. Not only had Kathy published the material received the day prior from the Queen of Spades, it had hardly been parsed or interpreted, the entire thing a regurgitation of QS' words. "I can't blame her. I would have probably done the same in her position, though I would've at least tried to get a comment from Human/Etech first."

Ren bit his lip. "Did you read the byline?"

"I tried not to. It'll make me sick to see Kathy's or someone else's name—" But it wasn't Kathy's name listed as the author. It was *Meredith's*. "You must be kidding."

Ren turned his pocketab back toward him before swiping at its screen. Once satisfied, he gave it another about-face toward Meredith. "They also ran a rather compelling participant profile. Some woman they're calling 'Alice' joined the study so she could speak with her comatose wife. EMPATHY is supposed to help with that somehow."

Meredith read the byline on that article as well. "Shit." Her hand shot to her mouth after she realized she had forgotten herself.

Her interviewer hardly seemed to notice. "That was my feeling, too. 'How could Meredith have been fired from the *Star-Globe* if they're still publishing stories in her name?' I thought. If—"

"No, that's not it at all." Again forgetting herself, she snatched Ren's pocketab from his hands and pointed to the byline on the article. "You're right to notice it's my name, but it stands out for the wrong reason."

"I don't understand—"

"Three stories. I had to get my kidnappers what they were looking for in my next three stories, and these articles are now going to look like the first two."

Elbows on his desk, Ren's expression grew glum. "*Tabarnak.* You didn't write these? You have been released from the *Star-Globe*?"

Meredith rocked back and forth, her hands under her thighs. "Yes. No. I mean, 'no, I didn't write them' and 'yes, I was let go.'" The room spun. Why would they publish those stories in her name? Was it meant as a well-intentioned tip of the hat for her years of service? Had Kathy not considered what the consequences for that might be?

The notion was so ridiculous Meredith chuckled. Kathy would have never thought twice about it. She only saw what was right in front of her, and what was right in front of her was what made her feel best about herself.

"I'm sorry?" Ren said.

"What?"

"You laughed. Are you all right?"

"No," Meredith said. She felt flush, white hot, fanning her face to keep the sensation at bay. "I now have only one shot to get my kidnappers what they want—I mean, unless I can, I don't know, bargain with them somehow—and now I feel like I'm flying over the cuckoo's nest at a job interview."

Ren stood. "The latter should be the least of your concerns." He crossed to her side of the desk, sitting on its corner. "We know what you're capable of. *I* know what you're capable of. Now that you've confirmed you're no longer with the *Star-Globe*, we can get you up and running as soon as you're able."

The pressure built up behind her eyes, her throat choking her. "That means a lot, but I have to be up front. I won't be able to publish anything until I know it will satisfy the people who abducted me."

"I understand."

"You do?"

He offered her a tissue from the box on his desk. "You work on whatever you think is best. When you have anything for publication, we can put it out under one of the other staffers' names or a pen name. No one will be any wiser."

Meredith took the tissue and dotted beneath one eye. "I think my kidnappers might know if we do something like that. They're following me pretty closely, I think."

"That's where Sasha and Edgar come in. We've had journalists working on highly sensitive or dangerous assignments in the past. Our security teams develop plans for scenarios the rest of us couldn't even dream up."

His words somehow both reassured and frightened her. "You say it like this is a done deal, like I've got the job."

Ren displayed that broad smile of his. "You do, assuming you want it."

It took about an hour longer to complete the paperwork, and though Ren had to get back to working on that evening's edition of *Newsnight* at one point, he slipped her his direct pocketab number before leaving. "Anything you need, don't hesitate to call." She thanked him before returning to sort out her new-hire information with the WVN human resources team, Sasha and Edgar joining her for every step along the way.

A virulent cocktail of emotion sloshed within her as Edgar and Sasha briefed her on the way home. They informed her Edgar would man the team that kept tabs on her house, while Sasha would accompany her at work or when she was otherwise away. They'd have other members of their team assist when either one of them was off-shift, but they assured her they themselves were only a call away. And who would complain about having Edgar—a Federation War vet honorably discharged after two tours in the Pacific—protecting her?

Sasha, for her part, had "fought many battles without name." She'd grown tired of despots murdering journalists in her own country—or so she said—and once in the Union, she'd vowed to keep that from becoming a trend here, too. No nonsense. Meredith liked it.

As encouraged as she felt, Ren's words of her security team's resourcefulness piqued Meredith's interest as Sasha turned their van into Meredith's neighborhood. "Tell me about worst-case scenarios," Meredith said.

Edgar leaned forward from the back seat. "What do you mean?"

Sasha turned left at the next intersection. "You mean if your kidnappers come for you again, yes?"

Meredith swallowed. "Yes. I mean specifically if they show up to follow through on their threats."

"We have a guy for this," Sasha said. "I do not think we will need him in this case. It is a very extreme solution."

Edgar piped up. "I'm sure once you publish the information they've demanded this will all go away. That's how these things work most of the time."

Even Edgar didn't believe that, Meredith could tell. "It may be extreme," Meredith said, "but I'd rather know what my options are than know nothing."

Sasha adjusted her grip on the wheel. "His name is *El Mago*. He makes people disappear."

"For better or worse," Edgar said.

A man who went by "the magician"—if Meredith's passable Spanish counted for anything—and made people disappear? She didn't like the sound of that at all. "For better *or worse?*"

"In this case," Sasha said, "it would be for the better. For you, anyway."

"If we put my brother—*El Mago*—on standby," Edgar said, "he prepares to create a new identity for you, and if necessary takes you somewhere no one can find you."

"Would Ren really allow that? They've only just hired me."

Sasha cleared her throat. "We work for WVN, but are not part of the organization. Third party, as you say."

Edgar chimed in. "We give ourselves the latitude to do what's best for our clients in cases like this. And we get paid. No matter what, we get paid."

Meredith chewed on that a moment, thinking it perhaps for the best to leave the *how* of getting payment up to them and WVN. "Okay, but your brother... this *El Mago*, where does he take people? How does he do that?"

Edgar snickered. "He wouldn't be a very good magician if he told everyone how he did his tricks."

Sasha nodded as the van rocked into Meredith's driveway. "But as we have said, his involvement should not be necessary. Between me and Edgar—"

"What's that?" Edgar pointed to Meredith's front door from the back seat.

Meredith squinted but recognized the envelope immediately. Tucked between the door and her stoop, it mocked her like some white tongue sticking out from the face of her home. "It's an envelope. Like the kind my kidnappers used to leave."

The sound of Sasha unbuckling her seatbelt responded. "Stay here." Her hand hovering over the holstered weapon at her hip, Sasha darted across the lawn and turned the envelope over in her hands. From where Meredith sat—heart throbbing in every extremity—there appeared to be nothing within it.

When Sasha returned to the van and handed her the envelope, however, a cold sweat broke on Meredith's brow. There were three boxes on the front of it, two of which were checked with red Xs.

"I will clear the home," Sasha said. "Edgar, remain with her until I have issued an all clear. Meredith, when I give the signal, I want you to unlock your home from your pocketab."

Meredith did as she was instructed. Despite having suspected it earlier, actually witnessing the outcome of Kathy's shortsightedness still felt surreal. One story. That was all she had remaining to deliver the information the NAU was willing to kill for. She turned to Edgar, still in the back seat. "Put him on standby."

"What's that?"

"*El Mago*. I want him on standby."

"You're sure? If you follow through with him, there's no coming back. He—"

"Yes," Meredith said. "I'm sure." Woodward yelped away inside the home, but not from agony, Meredith could tell. At least he was safe. "Does he take dogs, too?"

"What?"

"Does *El Mago* disappear dogs? With me, that is. Not separately."

"I can... I can ask."

Sasha strolled back onto the lawn. "All clear except for the dog. I do not think he much cared for me."

With that, Edgar made a call from a device that looked like a pocketab. "*Oye, hermano... Del two-way, claro... Bueno, así lo es con los nuevos clientes... En standby, sí. Te paso los detalles cuando yo los tenga.*"

"Who is he calling?" Sasha said.

Meredith nodded. "*El Mago*." She scooted forward. "Why doesn't he use his pocketab?"

Sasha adjusted her beret. "With *El Mago* we have an encrypted two-way for communication. Different frequency. Requires code to unscramble audio."

"Ren was right; you guys are on top of everything."

"Mm." Sasha wore a stern expression. "And standby is perhaps not the worst idea."

The fear in Sasha's eyes told Meredith everything she needed to know. This would end one of two ways, and in either scenario, Meredith disappeared. It was just a matter of how—and at whose hands.

Chapter Twenty-Eight

ARIEL

Guilt-induced insomnia urged her back to Ty's apartment in the middle of the night—that, and she finally had a plan to evade M3R1.

"Ty," she whispered from the hallway between gritted teeth. A dim white light bled through the crack between the doorframe and door. He had to be in there.

She knocked again, louder than she had before. "If you don't open up, I'm coming in." Ariel looked both ways down the hall, each direction void of staff or restless patients. She reached for her pocket to check the time. Empty, she remembered. Duh. Her whole operation depended on leaving her pocketab on her nightstand, finally freeing herself of M3R1 at a time the AI would suspect her of nothing but being fast asleep in bed.

At least she hoped that would be its conclusion.

Ariel leaned around the corner and squinted at a digital clock at the hallway's end. Only a couple of hours remained before the first-shift staff would awake. If she were going to act, she needed to do it now. She scanned her keycard outside Ty's door and forced it open.

She peered inside, her brow knit. Ty sat cross-legged at the foot of his bed, his back mostly to her. Images flickered on the inside of his glasses as if he were watching something.

She cast open the door the rest of the way. "Are those cyfocals?"

Ty spun in her direction, visibly fear-struck. "What are you doing here?" He leaped from the bed. The images on the inside of his cyfocals disappeared, giving them the illusion of being mere glasses once again.

Heart in her throat, Ariel stepped backward. "Ty, it's me." She raised a finger to her mouth and closed the door behind her.

"You think you can burst into my room like this?"

"It's an emergency. I knocked."

"This better be a good emergency to be waking me up in the middle of the night."

"You weren't asleep. I saw—where did you get those?" She pointed to his cyfocals.

"I don't know what you're talking about. I was asleep. These are my glasses. I need them to see."

She turned her head to the side and blinked twice as purposefully as possible.

"What?" He removed the glasses and hooked them on the collar of his scrub tops.

"You can either tell me what's up with those, or I can tell Wyatt about them," Ariel said. "I don't think the latter would bode well for your prospects of becoming a programmer at Human/Etech once the study is over. Even Alistair can't override Wyatt's will." The threat silenced him. Alistair and M3R1 had rubbed off on her, it seemed. "Well?"

"I thought you had an emergency for me."

"Cyfocals first. Answer the question."

"I'm... I'm getting some things together for a friend."

"Then why not use the cerenet?" Before he could answer, it struck her: Ty was the source of the leaks. He'd been snapping photos of the compound with the cyfocals so no one would notice, and he must have been the one to teach Chandra how to bypass the compound's firewall. If he were able to capture content on his cyfocals and then export it via the terminals in the lab, he could send whatever he wanted anywhere at any time. "Because you wouldn't be able to share any of it."

"What?"

"Your friend is off-compound," she said. "The only way you can contact him is via the computer lab because you don't know how to skirt the cerenet's filters."

Ty looked as though he wanted to crawl into bed and pretend none of this ever happened. "Just tell me what you want from me already."

"I'm here about what you said the other day—about saving the study."

The bed frame squeaked as he slumped onto the foot of his mattress. "It took you two days to decide you want to save the study?"

Ariel put a hand on her hip. "I had to take extenuating circumstances into consideration." She didn't dare tell him of M3R1 in case this new alliance crumbled. The last thing she wanted was for him to have more dirt on her than she on him. "What matters now is that we do this and do it right. Do you still think you know how to stop the seizures from spreading?"

"I'm only more confident after what Alistair taught me in our session yesterday."

So Alistair *had* followed through to work with him directly now. All the better for her—that made for one less obstacle for her to trip over. "How soon can you have something ready?"

"Two weeks."

"You know time is of the essence, right?"

"You don't think I'm aware of that?" He flailed his arms at his sides. "Hey, everyone, I guess seizures aren't generally considered healthy!"

Ariel shushed him.

He quieted as he returned to the conversation. "Is there a version of EMPATHY that predates the automatic sharing of EMPATHY-stimulation components across egodrives?"

Ariel's eyes widened. A "no" nearly escaped by reflex, but she did recall Peter saying something about tweaking individual egodrives at some point—and it wasn't until after he did so that EMPATHY began working for anyone. "Yeah. There is, actually."

"All right." Ty unhooked his glasses from his collar and put them back on. "What OS is the server running?"

"PT 10. Why?"

He put his cyfocals back on and activated their visual interface on the other side of his lenses, his eyes glowing against the light as he worked. "If I code something that reverts egodrives to their previous versions, I can also write a worm for PT 10 that will transfer that reversion code from one egodrive to another." Ty glanced over the top of his cyfocals' frames. "There's a chance everyone will lose cerenet connectivity as a result, but I don't think anyone will be too upset about that since no one is using it anyway."

Ariel sat alongside him. "Yeah, what's that all about?"

Ty scoffed. "Don't expect a pat on the back for your sudden interest in saving the study."

She narrowed her eyes at him.

"Chandra and I have been working on a strategy of our own for a few days now."

"Wait," Ariel said, "are you suggesting you orchestrated a boycott? That's not possible. Wyatt would have intercepted some sort of communication about it by now."

"Wyatt may be the man, but he's still a nonny."

Ariel let a silence loom. He failed to take the hint. "Care to elaborate?"

He shrugged. "We nectees have ways to communicate you nonnies can't even grasp at."

"What does that mean, Ty?"

"It means exactly what I said."

If that were true, if the cerenet-connected patients were able to communicate in a way that she and the rest of the advisory board failed to understand, that was the kind of thing that could topple the compound's power structure. Ariel wanted the seizing to stop, yes, but she still wanted EMPATHY to succeed if possible. A flash of concern flushed through her. What if he and Chandra took their messaging too far? What would Ariel do then?

Ty refocused on their plan. "Knowing the server runs PT 10, I can probably trim the programming time down to ten days."

Ariel snapped herself back to the conversation. "Can you shoot for a week?"

"Ten days."

"A week."

"I have other projects to take care of too, you know. Keeping up appearances with Alistair will be kind of important, and that's only one of my major projects right now."

Ariel ran a hand through her hair. "How is *this* not your major project? If we don't counter whatever's on that server, you and Chandra and all the others could end up with your brains scrambled."

"Again, I don't need the reminder." Ty tapped at his cyfocals, adjusting something on the lenses. "And for your information, I'm hedging our bets as well. If our operation doesn't work, I'm relying on someone on the outside to save our hides—but I need to come through for them first."

She huffed. "Fine. Ten days. But the closer we can get to a week—"

"I'll do what I can."

Ariel stood to leave, but a thought kept her in place. "Even if you get this code done, I'll still need an opportunity to upload it."

"Chandra will want some sort of role in all of this."

"Why would we send Chandra to the server instead of me? That seems—"

"No," Ty said. "I mean I'll work with Chandra on that. She's the messaging guru, and in the very least she'll want to let the other nectees know we have a plan in motion. Maybe she can coordinate some sort of distraction with them. Either way, we've got to keep up morale, you know?"

True. The last thing the compound needed was for discontent to grip the patients even more tightly. "Sounds good. I'll leave you be." Once her hand hit the door handle, menacing thoughts of M3R1 struck her. "And Ty?"

He slid his cyfocals down the bridge of his nose.

"If you run into me in the hall or in Alistair's office or anywhere," she said, "do not bring this up. Even if we're in private."

His eyebrows furrowed.

"Don't worry. We're alone now; I took the necessary precautions. Please though—never bring this up unless I tell you it's safe."

"So... just ask you if it's safe?"

"We'll use a code of some kind." Being on the nose about it would only rouse suspicion if M3R1 were, in fact, with her at the time. "How about... you ask me what day of the week it is?"

"That's not much of a code," Ty said.

"Because I wasn't finished explaining." She pressed her hands together. "If either you or Chandra ask me what day of the week it is and I give wrong day, don't bring any of this up."

"And if you give the correct day, then the coast is clear?"

"Yes. Exactly."

"Got it," Ty said. "So if it's right, then delight. If it's wrong, move along."

"Whatever helps you remember. And let Chandra know, too." She started for the door.

"Will do," Ty said. "Now go. I've got sleeping to do." He powered up his cyfocals again.

Ariel shook her head as she exited.

Once back at her apartment, she felt as though she had to tiptoe her way in. A shudder jolted up her spine at the thought of M3R1 as a sort of roommate, even if it was one she could leave dormant on her nightstand.

Her hand now pressed to her bedroom door, she eased it open, inch by inch. There, next to her bed, she saw it—her pocketab with its recording light glowing blue. Ariel's stomach roiled.

A white light illuminated the room. She shielded her eyes as her pocketab dinged. Once. Twice. A third time. She approached it with care. "M3R1?" she said, feigning ignorance. "Is that you?"

From a few steps away, she could see a message appear on the screen.

>> Where did you go, Ariel?

Ariel took the device in her hand. "I was restless. I needed to take a walk." She could feel the sweat on her palms against the plastic of her pocketab.

>> Is something the matter?

"I couldn't sleep is all. But I'm tired now. That bed is calling my name."

>> M3R1 was worried about you. You've been so stressed lately.

"Mhm." Something about M3R1's response unnerved her, but she couldn't quite determine what it was. Preparing to crawl into bed, she set her pocketab back on her nightstand and removed her scrub bottoms. "But everything is okay, really." She unhooked her bra and let it drop to the floor before she snuggled up against her pillows. "I think I'd like to sleep now."

>> M3R1 understands. We both have our own separate lives, Ariel. We both have our secrets.

It knew. M3R1 knew what she was up to. Ariel held one of her extra pillows tight against her body. "You're right," Ariel said, hoping M3R1 only had a vague idea of what she had been up to, and not all the details. "Goodnight, M3R1."

Ariel rolled onto her back and closed her eyes. Exhaustion weighed on her, but pesky thoughts of M3R1 and Ty and Chandra pushed back against it. She tossed and turned for what may have been five minutes or an hour before it became apparent she wasn't the only restless one. Her pocketab buzzed and she snatched it from her bedside.

>> You wouldn't do anything to hurt M3R1, would you?

"No." She flinched at how unsure-sounding her response had been.

>> M3R1 hopes not. There's nothing worse than friends becoming enemies.

Ariel let her pocketab thwack against her nightstand. She held her pillows and blanket close as she stared out the window, watching the shadows dance among the trees.

When morning came, she still found herself awake, eyes as open as they had ever been.

It had been a long night. It was going to be an even longer couple of weeks.

Chapter Twenty-Nine

MEREDITH

Meredith kept an eye on the wires throughout her first day with *The Courier*, but without the ability to publish anything, she found herself stuck.

Sasha's slender frame lurked in the shadows on the far side of her office's blinds. At least Meredith felt safe now. Safer, anyway. The threatening envelope had arrived less than a day ago; vigilance remained imperative.

Dark thoughts nipped at her, taunting her with visions of her own demise. QS had been no help as of late, failing to respond to every one of Meredith's desperate follow-up emails, including those she sent from her official *The Courier* account. With every passing hour, it increasingly felt as though Meredith's doom breathed hotter down the back of her neck.

After pacing for a few minutes in an attempt to chase away the thoughts that preyed upon her, Meredith accepted she alone was responsible for the tediousness that had gripped her all morning. She could pry herself free whenever she wanted. All she had to do was be active.

There was no need to wait for Lars or the Queen of Spades to come to her. She needed to get back to dogging her leads with the same spirit she had when she was a junior reporter. She couldn't exactly call the Queen of Spades, so, after thumbing through her contact list, she found Lars' number and dialed him.

"Hello?" she said, positive she had heard the line connect.

"Meredith?"

She hesitated. Press him, she told herself. Make things happen. "Tell me you have good news."

"I was going to reach out to you when—"

"I know, but waiting is something I can't afford to do a lot of right now."

Lars let out a single *ha* on the other end of the call. "As it happens, I had plans to call you this afternoon, but—"

"That's fine, but you have me now."

"Sheesh, let me get to it." Lars cleared his throat. "Wyatt has agreed to an interview."

There was no way. It had been too easy. Something was amiss.

Lars continued. "He'll grant you an interview if you disavow the rumors still blaming him for your abduction, and also if you turn over the identity of your source."

What he didn't say tarnished the deal. "What about the what, the where, and the how of what makes EMPATHY tick?" The way she said it was meant to acknowledge their earlier agreement—that whatever she received would be fake. She couldn't say so directly, not with the NAU potentially listening in.

"Not part of the deal, I'm afraid." His voice sounded far away, echoey.

She ground her teeth. "Tell me more about this interview."

"We can do it whenever you'd like. If you submit the questions in advance—"

"What was that?"

"In advance. We'll need the questions to prepare statements. That's how an email interview works, isn't it?"

What. A. Joke. "That doesn't sound like an interview to me. It sounds like a shill piece."

"What did you expect?"

"I expected you to fight for the deal we struck."

"And I did, mostly. You have to understand that Wyatt doesn't cede control to anyone. Even if each of us had gotten what we wanted, he would see it as you having your cake and eating it, too."

"Funny," Meredith said. "That's how I would characterize your current offer—except Wyatt is the one with the cake."

"Perspective is a funny thing, isn't it?"

Meredith was certain she could have snapped Lars in half were he standing in front of her. "That technical information has to be part of the deal." If she couldn't get her hands on that—even if it was fake—then the Queen of Spades really *was* her only way out of this quagmire.

"So you're not accepting the email interview?"

"Absolutely not."

"This could really be a good thing for you."

"No, a good thing for me would be getting the information I need and having this interview done properly."

"And how is that?"

"Live on television," she said. On the other end of the line, Lars audibly adjusted his pocketab. "What? I'm not the only one who stands to benefit from an arrangement like that."

"Tell me this isn't an actual request."

"Would I bring it up if it weren't? Wyatt should want an arrangement like that, too. It would placate that mass of campers outside the compound. Do you think they'll really give a rat's ass about an email interview? You guys will respond with whatever you want." She paused to lend her words some gravitas. "But to see is to believe."

Lars said nothing.

Meredith doubled down. "If those outside are able to see everything is okay inside the compound, their anger and worry can be quelled. Show them some images of their families and friends at work, of patients having a good time, of everything being business as usual. Then your protesters disappear, you get the disavowal you want so badly, and the leaks that have been draining your entire compound magically become plugged. An in-person interview helps you a lot more than it helps me. I'm doing you a favor, and all I want in exchange is technical information. You know, *the kind we discussed when we met in the park.*"

The line remained silent. He had to have gotten the hint now, right? As the pause lengthened, Meredith worried their connection had been broken, that her speech had been all for nothing. "Hello? Are you there?"

Just before she accepted she had lost him, a previously unheard voice on the other end spoke up. "We'll call you back." The line went dead.

We? Who had all been on the other end of the call? Had the NAU tapped their line, both listening in and adding to the conversation? It took her a moment longer than it should have, but the answer finally came to her. Wyatt Halman. It had been both Lars and Wyatt. Lars must have been on the compound, waiting to call her until he was back at his office. They had her on speakerphone. It would explain the distance in Lars' voice, at least.

Meredith rested her forehead on the surface of her desk. She did nothing but breathe for a time, letting herself decompress. She was fine, wasn't she? They were going to call her back—at least that's what they'd said.

Once she collected herself, Meredith poked at the screen of her pocketab to dial Ren. He would want to know an offer had been on the table and that another was likely forthcoming.

Her call went straight to voicemail. Figuring he was on another call, Meredith left a message for him to get back to her whenever he had a moment.

Attempting to move forward, she spun the carousel of open tabs on her web browser and accessed her email. If Lars called back with a reasonable interview offer that required her to surrender her source's identity—something she told herself she would only do because her own life was at risk—she would need to determine that identity first.

Logged in to her personal account, she dug up the correspondence with QS that she had sent to herself when Kathy first removed her from the EMPATHY project, the same correspondence to which she at one point responded to ask QS for actual evidence of the issues on the compound. Meredith waded through it all for new clues as to who might have been on the other side of the email thread.

A knock on her door interrupted her. Sasha. "Come in."

Sasha entered the room, a thin piece of paper in her hand. "The mail room has brought this for you."

An envelope. She felt herself shying away.

"I think this is okay," Sasha said. "Different look to it. Actually came through mail." She extended it to Meredith across her desk.

Sure enough, the mail had been addressed to her office at *The Courier* with no return address provided. Meredith opened it and slid out a single piece of paper—handwritten, no less.

Meredith,

Congratulations on the new position. I wanted to be the first to mail you something at your new office. Am I? So meme.

I also want to apologize. I think we're good now, right? QS says you won't be needing any more envelopes, so I take it all is well. I hope this makes up for my mistakes.

Anyway, congrats again. Tell Woodward I say "woof."

-Alvin

She laid the paper flat on her desk.

"Is there a problem?" Sasha said. "You look as though you have seen a ghost."

"A professional one, maybe."

"I did not know there were amateur ghosts." Sasha extended a hand. "May I see?" Meredith handed the letter over, Sasha then reading it herself. "Ghosts. Nonsense, all of it. You are either dead or you are not, no?"

Meredith shook her head. "I mean someone from my past job sent that to me."

"Good riddance then, yes?" Sasha crumpled the letter.

"Well, yes, but..." Meredith never finished the sentence. Of all the people who would have been leaving envelopes in her mailbox, Meredith would have never suspected Alvin. Had he really been working for the Queen of Spades? QS must have guilted Alvin into doing her bidding after determining he was responsible for breaking that first story before Meredith could.

For the briefest moment, Meredith reflected that for all the threats looming over her, for all the terrible things happening, for any of the mistakes someone might make, there was still some good out there. She'd have to thank Alvin when she had the chance.

Meredith's pocketab lit up. Jumpy, she turned away from the screen before realizing it was a call. Ren.

"I will let you take this," Sasha said. She abandoned the room.

"Hey, did you get my message?" Meredith said into her device.

"I did. It sounds like they got to you before they got to me."

"What do you mean?"

"I just spoke with Halman's lawyer. You didn't think they would only call you, did you?"

Meredith's brow creased. "I think we're talking about two different things."

"Are we? Didn't your message say the Halmans called you about the interview?"

The way he said it forced acid to climb into her throat. "It did, but—"

"Isn't it great? Granted, I'm sure it was a letdown to hear they preferred I conduct it, but it's an interview nonetheless."

Despite all the thoughts that wracked her mind, not a single one made it to her lips.

Ren continued. "Don't worry. We'll have you intimately involved in the process. I'll be sure to reference your work in the opening and closing segments."

"What about... I mean, you'll ask them about the rumors of distress on the compound, right? Or you'll have them describe what separates EMPATHY from its competition. That's part of this, isn't it?" Meredith said. She didn't know when, but she had vacated her seat and squatted against the back wall of her office.

Ren cleared his throat. "We'll see. Overall they were less forthcoming than I'd hoped, but we can work with them on getting as much as possible in the script."

"Please don't tell me you agreed to a fully scripted interview."

"Yes, they... they want the questions in advance so they can prepare answers. You know, for the sake of timing and messaging and—"

"And for having us be their stooges?" Meredith let her head hit the wall behind her. The burn in her chest flared up. She hustled to her purse and popped a few antacids.

"I wouldn't go that far," Ren said. "This is still a great opportunity—an *on-compound* interview, Meredith."

"On compound? I... I talked to them what must have been minutes before you did." She chewed her way through the antacids and gulped them down as quickly as she could. "They offered me an email interview in exchange for publicly stating they weren't responsible for my kidnapping. They also required I surrender my source."

"That is something we need to talk about. They're still expecting both of those from us in order to lock down the interview for sure."

Meredith groaned. "Here they are, having their cake and eating it, too."

"I'm really not following. Can you confirm you're willing to do both of those things to get this set in stone? Ordinarily, I'd never condone giving up a source, but since they asked for our assistance and this might be the only way to truly help the patients, we really ought to consider it. At any rate, Halman and his lawyer need an answer by noon tomorrow, though I'd like to get this process moving tonight if possible."

Noon tomorrow—less than a full day to figure out both her source's identity and to convince Ren she should be the one to go to the compound. If she were sent instead of him, she could harangue Wyatt about the seizures and disappearances that the Queen of Spades alleged. If he appeared caught off guard or responded with anger or if her camera crew managed to catch anything suspicious, surely that would be enough for the NAU to launch the probe it so desired. Meredith had to hold her ground for her own sake, for the truth's sake.

"The only way I'll give up my source is if I can do the interview," she said.

"Meredith, please, you know the Halmans won't accept that."

"I understand, but my kidnappers won't accept you doing the interview, either. Besides, the whole point is to get the Halmans to fork over information that will appease the people who are after me."

"I don't know if that's the entire point of the interview given where we're at now. There's still a story to be told here."

"And I need to be the one to tell it. You know I'm not doing this for vanity or to advance my career. I just can't give my kidnappers any excuses to keep after me once the interview is over."

"I don't think Wyatt and Lars are particularly sympathetic to that cause."

The idea came to her in a flash. "Those two don't have to be sympathetic. We can force their hand."

"Dammit, Meredith." It seemed she had taken things too far. "Unless you have some sort of plan, I don't think renegotiating with the Halmans on that matter is possible."

"I do have a plan. It's very simple."

"And?"

"Promote the hell out of the interview. We hype it up as a monumental event. Then, on the night of the interview, I show up at the compound instead, only a few minutes before we're to go live."

Ren said nothing for a moment. Meredith imagined him folding his arms across his chest. "I don't know," he said finally. "I can't say I'm much of a fan of this idea. What keeps Wyatt from canceling the interview when you show up?"

"They won't be able to afford a cancelation," she said. "We'll have made the interview so high profile that to cancel would be an implicit confirmation of the rumors of instability on the compound." And if they *did* cancel, would that raise enough suspicion to justify an NAU investigation? Meredith was dubious, but it wasn't out of the question.

An interminable pause ensued. After what felt like a full minute, Meredith capitulated to the tension. "Ren, are you still there?"

"I am." He sighed. "I'm going to need some time to think about this. My reputation is on the line, too, you know."

"All I ask is that you consider it. I'll turn over my source to secure the interview if you commit to stepping aside last minute. It's the best way to keep me safe." It was also the best way to ensure someone would go off-script and prod Wyatt, slinging grave allegations of patient mistreatment to drum up sufficient evidence for an investigation of the compound. Of course she might warm up by asking after technical information, which would not only throw him off balance, but also show the NAU she intended to do everything in her power to help them.

Meredith sighed into her pocketab. "Do you think... do you think you could meet me in my office? I have some things to add that are better said off a live line."

Something in his tone shifted. It was as if his pride had subsided, surrendering to the reality of the imminent danger Meredith faced. "I'll be there in a minute."

Once Ren arrived, she threw everything she could into convincing him of how dire her situation actually was. Even Sasha—whom Meredith had invited into the room so that she, too, had a better understanding of what they were up against—paled when Meredith decided the time had finally come to confirm to both of them that the NAU had been behind her kidnapping.

"And that's what worries me most," Meredith said. "With that most recent envelope that's showed up, I'm worried whether I succeed or not they'll still come for me. That's what makes me push for this interview to be done in person. By me. I might not succeed in getting what they want and I need, but it's the only way I can show them I at least made an effort. Maybe that will count for something."

Sasha's finger tapped at the weapon on her hip.

Ren rubbed his mustache. "It's eerie."

"Eerie," Sasha said, "is but one of the many words I would use to describe this situation. 'Fucked' might be another."

"That's not what I meant," Ren said, running a hand over his bald pate. "Remember when I told you of my wife? Of Vivianne?"

Meredith nodded.

"When I said I convinced her to see the light and turn away from violence, that wasn't entirely true." Meredith shifted her weight as Ren continued. "They had picked up on threats—grave ones, credible ones—against her and her comrades in *le Front*. They'd made plans to relocate, to go into hiding for a time, but by the time they put their plan into action, it was too late; the NAU conducted a raid on their compound, and though Vivianne escaped with her life, many of her friends did not."

"I'm sorry," Meredith said. "That had to be terrible for her."

"It comes with the territory," Sasha said. "A woman must be willing to die for the things in which she believes."

"Yes," Ren said, "but one must live in order to fight on. I don't like this bait-and-switch plan of yours, Meredith, but if what you're saying is true, then the only course of action is to do as you say. You must live to fight. Besides, it's not like I need another arrow to my bow."

Meredith raised an eyebrow.

"Sorry. An expression *du Québec*. I... never mind. The point is I can't let my pride eclipse your personal safety." Ren exhaled. "I'll do it. I'll step aside last minute like you suggested. But tell me, if you would, why it is the NAU has singled you out."

She averted her stare. "I'm the one with a source on the inside. It's only natural—"

"Yes, but they didn't have to threaten you to take advantage of that. They could have offered to support you, for example, publicly pressuring the Halmans to at least let a member of the media have access to the compound."

For as right as Ren might have been under normal circumstances, if the NAU had gone public in support of Meredith, they would have only raised her profile and increased her credibility. With what she knew about Gleason, the FBI, and the Academy Shootings, though... "I understand your curiosity, Ren, but please trust me when I say it's in the best interest of both your safety and my own that I keep some information to myself. For now."

Ren's nostrils flared as he nodded. "Very well."

Sasha nabbed Meredith's attention with a snap of her fingers. "This business with the NAU, it would have been good to know this immediately."

"I'm sorry," Meredith said. "I should have—"

"And we will need to make plans for your safety during this interview."

Meredith felt her veins pulsing with the energy of success. "We'll have time to work on that, I'm sure."

"But first," Ren said, "we need to meet Human/Etech's terms to lock this down. Can you shoot me an email with a statement saying they're not responsible for the kidnapping? I need the identity of your source, too."

The success flowing through Meredith's veins congealed. "That first bit won't be a problem, but I actually don't know the identity of my source for certain."

"If you're worried about the ethical concerns surrounding giving up your source—"

"I would be normally, yes, but I agree with what you said earlier, that my source would likely be willing to have their identity revealed if that's what it took to save them."

Ren ran his thumb over his mustache. "You don't know their identity, then?"

Meredith drew in a breath between her teeth. "I don't, no. Not yet, anyway."

The incredulity on Ren's face transformed him into an entirely different person. It seemed Kathy wasn't the only one capable of rants when their values were insulted. "Irresponsible," he said, "... publishing without evaluating credibility... putting us in a further compromised position..." At least he didn't raise his voice in the same way Kathy would. It was a rant all right—and half in French at that—but it almost seemed like he directed it at himself more than anyone else. "You need to figure out your source's identity. Now. Tonight."

"I will do everything I can."

The anger that had been channeling itself through Ren dissipated. "In any case, I suppose you have more on the line than I do."

"You don't need to remind me."

"I'm sorry," he said. "I'm disappointed, but I suppose I need to give you time to figure this all out." He made for the door. "But remember—we have until noon tomorrow to get the Halmans everything they've asked for, and I'd like a chance to vet whatever you put together before I send it to them. So please, try to keep that in mind as you set a timeline for yourself."

"Will do."

Both he and Sasha left Meredith to the quiet tedium of her office. She had research to do.

Chapter Thirty

WYATT

The air teemed with the smells of summer, of grass clippings and gardenia. While he wound his way through the arboretum, memories of Eva dogged Wyatt, images of soil and sediment clinging to her gloves as she knelt in their garden.

He chased the happy memory away. There was no time for happiness, not when things were going so poorly. With overall cerenet usage down by more than ninety percent, there was no guarantee Chandra had even received his invitation to meet him in the arboretum. If and when she did come, he would have to balance breaking the news of Eva's dismal results with his announcement that the time had come for her first interview as the face of EMPATHY.

There was one bright spot, he supposed. Sometime before noon, Rénald Dupont would call Lars and inform him of the source of the leaks. The traitor would be brought to justice, and in a week's time the interview would air. With trust restored, the protesters—or most of them, anyway— would go home and the staff would be back at work without further discord.

A bumblebee buzzed near Wyatt's ear. He swatted it away, nearly knocking his glasses off in the process. He readjusted them and set his sights on the footbridge ahead, the tufts of that brutish willow peering over the horizon line. If Chandra wasn't there, he'd need to have someone fetch her for him.

Off to his left, two participants hushed when they noticed him nearing, something the interview couldn't cure. After an additional three patients had succumbed to seizures that very morning, the total number of the afflicted now sat at forty-two. With just shy of four hundred patients having connectivity, they had now crossed a critical threshold—more than ten percent of the connected population had suffered from aphasia-inducing episodes.

Wyatt grimaced. He and Gary were the only ones who had insisted the study proceed upon receiving the news of the most recent wave of adverse events. Wyatt couldn't derail things with the interview looming, and as Gary said, uninstalling EMPATHY might have worse side effects for a greater percentage of the population than letting the seizures run their course. The contrarians argued with mutinous persistence, but once Gary assured them he and Peter had a promising containment strategy to be implemented in the coming days, the squabbling subsided. Make it through another week, Wyatt told himself. Things will only improve from there.

The bridge moaned as Wyatt trod over it. Beneath the willow, the spot of lavender calmed Wyatt immediately. "Good morning," Wyatt called.

Sitting in the dirt at the base of the tree, Chandra raised her head toward him. "Good for those not terrified of getting struck down by seizures, I'm sure."

"Yes. Well—"

"Have you decided if I can talk to my brother? I'd like updates on Kyra."

He pressed his lips together, looking about for something on which to sit. "That's not what I've come to address with you." Off to his right squatted a small wooden bench, facing the direction of the koi pond. "Would you care to join me over there?"

"I'm fine here. And I don't know what you want to 'address with me,' but—"

Her insolence had gone on for too long. "Chandra, the bench. Please. Now."

"I'm not your dog."

"No, but we both stand to benefit from our business relationship. In recognition of that, I would like to see a little more equality where compromises are concerned."

"Really? What compromises have you made—?"

His jaw ached with how hard he clenched it. "We sourced a human brain to see about helping your wife, and we're spending hundreds of thousands of ameros on her medical bills. So there's that." He looked down his nose at her. "Perhaps you'll join me on the bench over there? I'd love to share the results of our testing with you."

Her eyes lit up. She rose. Wyatt marched toward the bench, Chandra steps behind him.

Once the two of them sat side by side, Chandra embodied repentance. "I'm sorry. I don't know what's gotten into me lately." She sighed, working her toes into the dirt. "Well, I do, actually. Withholding that email set me off. That, and the constant fear of disappearing like the others who—"

"Say no more." Wyatt raised a hand to stop her. This was good. They could reset relations here and now. "I understand where you're coming from. I think we can still accomplish great things together if we're both willing to purge past transgressions from the record. Does that seem reasonable to you?"

She swept her gaze away from the pond where the koi swam over and under one another. "So long as you don't keep any more emails from me, I can be okay with that." Chandra looked as though she were on the verge of tears. Wyatt almost pitied her. "And we need to talk about patient safety. No one is using the cerenet right now for fear of it triggering seizures."

Wyatt picked at an eyebrow. "Is that why usage has declined?"

Chandra shrank away at Wyatt's follow up. "Maybe. Probably." She palmed a pebble and skipped it into the pond. "I might have some ideas about why that's been happening."

So she was hiding something. Wyatt adjusted in his seat. "And what might those ideas be?"

She paused a moment, staring only forward. "I should have told you this earlier, but I didn't say anything because I know how you feel about rumors."

"What rumors, Chandra? Do tell."

"The word is people are avoiding the cerenet for their own safety, yeah, but they're also staying logged off as part of a boycott to push you to take the seizures more seriously."

A short laugh escaped. "Some boycott that is."

Chandra snapped his direction, anger writ large about her face. "What's that supposed to mean?"

"If whoever organized this alleged boycott wanted it to be successful, they ought to have come forward to say so in the first place. The way they've gone about it, they're like terrorists who've taken themselves hostage and decided to remain silent about their demands."

Her eye contact broke, color tingeing her cheeks. Could it be? Had *she* organized the boycott? "Chandra, did you play any part in the—?"

"They're rumors, Wyatt. Nothing more. Really, though, it *would* be nice to know if any progress has been made to keep more of us from ending up in the hospital wing."

"All should be well in a week, dear. No need to—"

"You know what?" She seethed. "Let's just... tell me about the results of the testing."

He cleared his throat as he procured his pocketab and enlarged it. With his elbows on his knees, he leaned in so Chandra could see the screen herself. All Wyatt needed to do was press PLAY and walk Chandra through the results via the 3D model of Eva's brain on the display, but something held him back.

"Are you waiting for something else to load?" Chandra said.

His courage. It had been devastating enough to watch his wife die twice. He hadn't prepared himself to watch it a third time.

"Is something wrong?" she said.

Everything, he wanted to say. Nothing was as it was supposed to be, not even this moment alone with one other person on a bench as nature surrounded them. He should have been able to accept the video on his pocketab wasn't really Eva, but he couldn't. He could have already had this whole conversation over with, but he didn't.

"No," he said. He took a deep breath and reminded himself it was just a video. Eva was gone. She had been for years. Not to Wyatt, perhaps, but the real Eva left him over half his lifetime ago. "I—we can do this." He hit PLAY.

As the recorded imagery from the experiment began, Wyatt described the setup, his voice cracking. He walked her through what each of the colors meant as they pulsed through neurohighways and cast light into previously dark corners of the mind. Chandra seemed fascinated, a hopefulness gleaming in her eyes as she presumably considered what all of this might mean for her and Kyra.

Then the video took a turn—the moment when all the power flooded the brain's fear centers. Wyatt had to clear his throat as he described what this likely meant in terms of consciousness. He struggled to keep his voice from trembling. When the video concluded, he let Chandra think on it a moment.

The hopefulness beaded from her eyes in a stream of silent tears. It took everything Wyatt had not to mirror her own distress.

"As you can see," he started, "we did have some momentary success. It's important to keep in mind this was only one trial and it was done with a brain that had been inactive for far longer and in a different way than your wife's, but, either way, there is great risk involved."

Chandra nodded.

"What we saw wasn't all bad news, but in your wife's case I think it's important you weigh the risks of this approach against the possibility she might recover on her own."

Chandra appeared focused on the koi pond. She was considering what she had seen, Wyatt figured—an appropriate and measured response. Something about Chandra had changed. He hadn't known her well before, he supposed, but were he to guess, the Chandra of even a couple of weeks ago would have cast aside all caution and demanded he do everything to proceed with the same experiment on her wife. Did EMPATHY have something to do with this new her? He didn't know if that made him proud or disgusted with himself.

"What do you think they think about?" Chandra said, her stare listless.

"People in comas? I'm not sure that—"

"No." She pointed. "Those fish."

Wyatt let the bench's backstop support him. There was almost a pattern to the way the koi moved, though there was just enough chaos in the system to keep him from mapping it. "I couldn't really say. I can't imagine they think of much at all."

Chandra snickered. "And look at us here, just watching them—aware of the wind on our ears, our hearts beating in our chests, the feeling of the grass between our toes." She ran a finger over her scar. "I could tell you anything you wanted to know about koi or the patterns of the wind or the structure of the heart... but I'll never know what it's like to know nothing, to think of nothing." She sighed. "They must be happy, at peace."

Wyatt's throat tickled at the ugly truth in Chandra's words. He and Chandra weren't so different, were they? Both of them had been fighting for so long, and what had it gotten them? Neither had relished in the minor successes along the way, nor in the major milestones. None of it had brought them any happiness. The focus had been entirely on one final objective, one that had been all but taken from Wyatt, the door closing ever more quickly for Chandra. Perhaps she was right. Perhaps complacency would make things easier. Perhaps settling would provide the most comfort. Perhaps The Great Nothing was the only way to find relief.

"Wyatt," Chandra said. "What happens now?"

"We keep trying." It was the only thing he knew how to do.

"Thank you for trying for me. For Kyra."

Wyatt remained tight-lipped, unable to accept her thanks. He had done it for himself, after all, with no real altruism behind it. He only spoke again once he knew he could keep things moving in the right direction. "The best way to thank me would be to help me with a great favor."

"What is it?"

"Have you ever watched *Newsnight with Rénald Dupont*?"

"He's the bald guy with the mustache?"

"That's him." Wyatt brushed the hairs of his own mustache with his index finger. "In about a week, he's going to be coming here to do a live interview."

"And you want me to be a part of it?"

"Yes."

Chandra stared off into the canopies of the trees across the water. "What would you want me to talk about?"

"I'd like you to tell your story. The world should hear from your own lips what drove you here, what motivates you to press on in the face of the adversity you've confronted." Wyatt purposely left out that the Austin *Star-Globe* had already published her story, using "Alice" instead of her real name. The less she knew about that, the better.

Regardless, she seemed wary.

"We'll have everything scripted in advance," he said. "You could rehearse all you liked. There'd be no surprises."

"No surprises," Chandra said. "I like that."

"Great." He retrieved his pocketab and navigated to the notes he had prepared. "Though we have a week, it wouldn't hurt to start making arrangements now." His pocketab vibrated. "Oh," he said. "I should have turned off those notifications." Turning his device back toward himself, he started to adjust its settings.

Chandra brought that to an abrupt end. "I want to see the message."

"What do you mean?"

"The notification," She straightened her spine. "It was for a new email. The subject line said 'EMAIL INTERCEPT REPORT.'"

Wyatt kept the frown from his face, but Chandra seemed to take his silence as an admission the intercepted email was destined for her inbox.

"You can't keep another email from me. It's for me, isn't it? From my brother."

"I haven't read the email yet. It could be for anyone. I don't think it would be right to share it with you if it turns out it was intended for someone else."

"I'm not the only one you're watching?" Her alarm seemed genuine.

"I'm not going to comment on that."

"Show me the email."

"Perhaps later once I've had a chance to verify—"

"Show me the damn email."

"I didn't say you couldn't see it, but now is not an appropriate—"

"Show me the email or you can count me out of your interview."

The threat was real. He could see it in her eyes, hear it in the strength of her voice.

As usual, Wyatt could have threatened her with pulling funding for Kyra's medical bills, but that was impractical, he decided—at least in this situation. If Chandra were going to participate in the interview in a meaningful, impactful way, she would have to embrace it fully. He couldn't blackmail her into compliance.

"Fine," Wyatt said. "But I have to read it first—just to verify its contents are intended for you."

Chandra did not object. Wyatt navigated to the email.

To: "Chandra Adelhadeo"
From: "Ratan Mahadeo"
Subject: Re: Hello

Chandra,

I wish I wrote under better conditions. Last night, Kyra took a turn for the worse.

Wyatt read on, each word another anchor dragging him down to a conclusion he hoped the email would not make, one that seemed more and more inevitable with every syllable, with every letter. Then it came. A final resolution.

"What is it?" Chandra said. "What happened?"

"Chandra," Wyatt said, looking up from his pocketab. "I'm so sorry."

Chapter Thirty-One

CHANDRA

Wyatt passed her his pocketab so she could read the email he had intercepted. It wouldn't be real until she saw the words for herself.

> To: "Chandra Adelhadeo"
> From: "Ratan Mahadeo"
> Subject: Re: Hello
>
> Chandra,
>
> I wish I wrote under better conditions. Last night, Kyra took a turn for the worse.
>
> They had her off life support, as she had been breathing on her own for some time. In the early morning, though, she again lost control of her breathing. It stopped completely.
>
> They tried to bring her back, but... I'm sorry, Chandra. Kyra is gone.

No tears welled in her eyes. There was no sadness. Only a simple, empty nothing. She left the bench to sit in the grass and finish reading the email.

> Know, Chandra, that everything will be okay. She's at rest now. You did everything you could in your time together to make sure she knew you loved her. You loved her more than you ever loved anyone. It is a love I hope to know someday, a love that gives purpose to one's existence. Kyra may be gone, but the love the two

of you shared is a lesson in what it means to truly care for one another. It is something from which many have learned and will continue to learn, I am sure.

Please respond as soon as you are able. I have tried calling the compound on the numbers provided on your paperwork, but when I call I only receive a message that the number has been disconnected. We will wait for you before holding services, of course. We will wait for you as you waited for Kyra.

Across the pond, the dewy grass gleamed, the day's first cicadas droned, and nearby the occasional koi sloshed as it nipped at the surface for food. There came a strange numbness, a deference to whatever had been, whatever would be.

Wyatt remained mum while Chandra returned to the email, inspecting it once more in the vain hope that somehow it would read differently this time. Something about it seemed off. It was as if Ratan's own grief had removed him from the email somehow. Though his words were tender, they were cobbled together in a way that was very unlike him. Then, too, there was the matter of him actually calling her Chandra instead of the usual Chan.

She swung her head in a tight, controlled gesture, resisting the urge to contradict reality. Denial. That's all it was. A search of the cerenet confirmed her suspicions—to deny it happened at all was simply a stage of grief. She felt nothing because on some subconscious level she *wanted* to feel nothing. It was the safest way forward despite the anger, the sorrow simmering beneath the surface.

"Chandra," Wyatt said. "What can I do to help?"

He could turn back time. Take her back to that morning and let her turn the car around and bring the helmet inside. Let her leave Kyra a loving note instead of a death sentence. Stop her from completing the paperwork for this damn study so she could spend every possible moment with Kyra.

Impossibilities, yes, but the thoughts nibbled at her regardless. "I want to go home," Chandra said. "I need to be with my family."

Wyatt stared off into the distance, his breathing slow, measured. "Did I ever tell you about my wife?"

"No."

"I don't speak of her nearly as often as I should." He rested his forearms on his knees, eyeing the dirt at his feet. "Eva. I lost her more than thirty years ago. Her birthday would have been this past Monday."

"I'm sorry." Chandra returned Wyatt's pocketab.

"It's fine. I'm not mentioning it to garner your sympathy. I mention it because it was how I handled my grief that transformed me as a person. Her loss—ruinous as it may have been for me at the time—presented me with a choice. I wanted badly to give up, to go inside myself and shut out the rest of the world. I wanted it gone, all of it. Much as it pains me to say, I wanted to turn Peter and Heather over to my own parents so I could wander off into the woods and rot." He laughed to himself. "Grief is a funny thing. Saying that out loud about my own children must paint me as some sort of monster. But it was how I felt. It seemed like there was nothing left for me to do in this world."

Chandra rocked where she sat, watching the koi tussle in the pond.

"I don't remember how long after her death it was, exactly," Wyatt said, "but there was a moment one afternoon where I stood in what had been our bedroom, folding laundry—I'd sent the nanny home, not wanting a nonfamilial presence in the home. At any rate, the kids were keeping one another busy in the living room. I was folding this shirt—this pink shirt— and it felt as though Eva was standing right behind me. The hair on the back of my neck stood up and I just..." He sniffled once. "I felt this warmth. I didn't need to turn around to know she was at my back. I knew it. I knew it to be true as much as I had known anything in my life." He released a sharp breath. "And then she was gone. I've never felt her since. But what I felt in that moment was what she wanted me to know. She was there, at my back, always behind me. She was there for me in death as she had been in life. I could press on. I could do what needed to be done. And it has been with that in mind that I pressed on to today, building everything you see around us now."

He forced himself into Chandra's vision. "I could have abandoned everything. It would have been the easiest thing for me in the world. But I had a choice, and it wasn't until those months later—all those lost months— that I finally realized I had been making a mistake. A life of tedious mediocrity wasn't what Eva would have wanted for me. I had to finish what we started... for her if no one else."

Chandra dug her fingernails into the dirt, though she kept her face stone. How dare he? How dare he presume to know what Kyra would want for her? How dare he impose his own experience onto hers? He didn't share these words with Chandra for her benefit; he shared them for his own. He wanted to keep her on the compound so long as he saw fit, until his own goals had been achieved.

Still, Chandra kept quiet, waiting for the right moment to retaliate.

"I understand you may want to go home," Wyatt said, "but we're so close to completing something great, something you can be proud of, something I'm sure Kyra would have been proud of as well. We can work with you regarding the services. We can work with you if you'd like to speak with your brother. But I cannot let you go home—not permanently, anyway—until this study is completed."

Tension built in her calves, two springs ready to release. She saw herself leaping forward, throwing herself on top of him and wrapping her hands around his throat. The old man, the feeble old man. She would choke the life from him with her own strength, watching the manipulative bastard struggle for one last gasp of air.

Satisfying as the image may have been, it terrified her as well. Is this what it was to grieve—a volatile seesaw of emotional extremes? No, she could not—would not—let herself be taken by that anger.

Something in that moment made her think of Ty, of the morning after the Halmans had made their offer. Chandra and Ty had found one another in this same place in the arboretum, unwittingly sharing their darkest memories and deepest concerns. "All we can do is move forward," Ty had said of his own experience with grief. The best thing Chandra could do now was the same.

But still, for all the good moving forward might do her, it wouldn't be possible until she found a way to scrub out the dark splotch on the canvas of her recent past, her responsibility for Kyra's condition. Wyatt now needed her far more than she needed him. Using that to her advantage would be her first step forward, a way to avenge the harm she had allowed to pass at Wyatt's hands.

"I understand," Chandra said.

Even Wyatt seemed surprised at her words.

"I ask only that you let me speak with my brother to confirm I got his message."

"I can't let you speak with him by pocketab, but if you'd like to write him an email, I can allow it to make its way to him."

She extended a hand. "Can I see your pocketab again?"

"I'd rather you dictated the email to me. I'll let you review it before I send it."

The rage flashed once again, though only for a second. She had decided how she would resolve this, the idea piercing the fog of sorrow that had enveloped her. "Okay," she said. "Let me think."

She dictated her message, telling her brother she had received his email, that she was unsure what exactly to say in light of such terrible news. She thanked him for staying with Kyra while she was away, and thanked him again for being a wonderful brother. Then she pressed on to more formal matters, the core of what Wyatt might find objectionable in her plan.

"Tell him we'll hold the services in just over a week," Chandra said, "after the interview."

Wyatt stopped typing. "We can't tell him about the interview. Not yet."

"Fine," she said. "Don't mention the interview specifically. Tell him I'll be in touch in a week. Tell him we'll make the arrangements and I'll attend the funeral and then be home with friends and family."

Wyatt's fingers ceased to type. "I can say that, but you have to understand we'll have details to work out. Unless the study were to miraculously wrap up in the next seven days, your stay with family and friends would not be permanent."

Again, she tempered her anger. "I understand. We can discuss the specifics after we get things rolling for the interview."

"Is there anything else you would like me to include?" Wyatt said.

"Tell him I love him and I'll be in touch soon."

Wyatt typed away and then turned his pocketab to face Chandra. "Does this look right?"

Much to her surprise, he had written all she requested. Chandra nodded before watching him press SEND.

"Since I responded to the email intercept report," Wyatt said, "it will reroute through your email. Your brother will see the message as if it were sent from you."

She gave him a look.

"No, no," Wyatt said. "I would never use that power to impersonate you."

She doubted that was true, but didn't pick a fight over it. He needed to think she was on board one hundred percent if she were going to pull off the stunt she now planned. "I trust you," she lied. After a pause, she spoke again. "I like what you said earlier, about having a choice after Eva died."

"Nothing I have said in my life was ever so true."

"I want to help you with this interview. How soon can we get to work?"

"Why don't you give yourself time to process this?" Wyatt said. "We'll have plenty of time to work on the interview throughout the week."

Chandra agreed. She would need to be as whole as possible if she were to have the strength to persevere. "Maybe later this afternoon we can get together?"

"I'll message you," he said. "Can I trust you to monitor your email? Your on-compound, cerenet email, that is."

Chandra thought of the boycott, of the demands she had failed to deliver to him. They mattered little now, so little considering what she would do instead. "I'll watch my inbox."

He rose and offered a hand to help her up. "Thank you for working with me on this, Chandra. The interview will be a hit, I'm sure."

"I couldn't agree more," she said, especially since she planned to use her time on live television to share with the world what a son of a bitch he was. She kept the thought to herself, smiling as she shook his hand.

Chapter Thirty-Two

MEREDITH

The night came and went with no success. After every email she analyzed, after all the content she scoured for clues, Meredith slumped into sleep at her kitchen counter no closer to determining the Queen of Spades' identity than she had been after her conversation with Ren. Even her call to Alvin had been useless—QS only contacted him by email, too, transferring funds to his bank account so he could take them to Meredith from there.

Woodward woke her as the earliest rays of light leaned long across the carpet of her living room. She stirred to his licks of her bare feet. "What? Oh, it's you. What time is it?" The clock read 6:00 a.m. She had slept for three hours, three longer than she had planned.

After nodding to Edgar who appeared to have pulled a vigilant all-nighter near her front door, she let Woodward dash outside to use the facilities. "Will you let him back in when he's done?"

Edgar nodded, yawning.

Back at the counter, Meredith reset her stream of the 1949 film *The Queen of Spades* to the last scene she could remember before sleep overwhelmed her. After pressing PLAY, she buried herself in another *Alice in Wonderland* comic, haplessly hoping her queen was somehow related to any of those that appeared in the series.

Nothing landed. Every detail was as useless as the last. With fewer than six hours until the deadline, thoughts of Edgar's brother, *El Mago*, crept in. Perhaps it would be best to quit while she was ahead—and still had a head.

The front door squeaked open. Edgar called to Woodward, whose claws clicked across the floor moments later. A ding interrupted her stream of *The Queen of Spades*. A new email.

To: "Meredith Maxwell"
From: <WITHHELD>
Subject: Found You

Hi Mer,

Sorry it's been a while. With you working for *The Courier* now, I'll admit I was hesitant about how to go on. All I wanted was for you and the *Star-Globe* to succeed. When I realized you'd been fired as opposed to leaving on your own, I knew something deeper must have been at play.

I did some digging, and based on some, well, communications of theirs I just happened to stumble into, it looks like they're trying to sell the *Star-Globe* off, so... that's it. I've made my decision. The *Star-Globe* can go piss in a lake. It's you and you alone I have to work with now.

I'm attaching video of patients dealing with the aftermath of the seizures I mentioned and hope this is the kind of evidence you're looking for. I'm asking you to please *please* help us as soon as you can. If I find anything else that might be useful to you, I'll let you know right away.

I do have some bad news, too. That info you wanted on the mystery element the Halmans have discovered? It can't be found. I combed every database I could find, but it isn't on any of the servers on the compound. Halman must be so paranoid, he probably just has everything about it written on a piece of paper in a safe somewhere. If you want that kind of access, you'd be better off organizing a heist than turning to a hacker.

I know that isn't what you want to read, but I had to be honest with you, and I at least had to let you know I tried. With how desperate things are becoming here, who knows when or if I'll be able to contact you again.

-Q♠

Meredith scratched Woodward behind an ear as she digested all she had read, navigating to the email's attachments: a couple of short video clips and some still shots from both of them. Meredith pressed PLAY on one of the videos as Edgar came up behind her.

"You want some coffee?" Edgar pointed to the coffee maker.

"Sure. Yes. Please," she replied, though the images of lavender scrubs, of shaved heads on her pocketab's screen distracted her. In this video, though, the presumed patients stared off vacantly, none speaking, grunting at most. In the next clip, a doctor attempted to walk a patient no older than thirty years old down the hall with the help of a walker—until his legs went to rubber and a couple of nurses had to leap into the scene to help the doctor right the patient once more.

Meredith sucked in a long breath as if through a straw. Was this her out? Would the suffering of these patients prove to be her escape from the NAU's blackmail? She shook her head, disappointed in herself for the fleeting sense of relief that had taken her as she watched. The videos and photos would be worth publishing if she still had three stories left to her credit, but with only one...

No. This footage was to be used in case of emergency only, something that crept in all the more quickly with every passing minute. For now her best bet was to still attempt to secure the interview, to determine the Queen's identity. If she made it onto TV with Wyatt Halman himself, then she might produce the footage as to corner him, to make him respond to the matter live. Now *that* might be enough to force an NAU inquiry. She found herself nodding until she realized all of this would still require her to discern QS' identity first.

"Dang it, boy." She rubbed Woodward under the chin. "I think Mommy bit off way more than she can chew. You ready to skip town?"

"What was that?" Edgar stepped around the corner, hand on his holster.

Meredith lurched backward. "Oh, it's you. Sorry, I was talking to the dog is all."

"Oh." He removed his hand from his hip. Edgar had proven both polite and courteous since taking up residence in her living room. Though she had been nervous about the prospect of a near stranger living with her, Meredith would have hardly known he was there most of the time, and the opportunity to brush up on her Spanish while he was around was a perk unto itself.

He continued making the coffee as Meredith skimmed the Queen of Spades' email for anything else worthwhile. Nothing on EMPATHY's greatest secret, another letdown. Without access to those specs via QS, Meredith made a mental note of that as something further to press Wyatt about during the interview, which itself looked increasingly less likely to happen... unless the Queen of Spades was willing to surrender herself—an unlikely scenario in Meredith's judgment.

After another read, two additional points stood out, too. Not only was the *Star-Globe* being put up for sale, but QS mentioned all she wanted was for the *Star-Globe* to succeed. Why?

"Oh, that's right," she said.

The coffee pot clanged against the counter as Edgar dropped it. "What?"

"I just had a thought." When firing her, Mr. Lee had mentioned he had a grandson participating in the study. If Meredith could find the boy's profile among the drove of them sitting in her inbox, she could use his information as a launching pad to figure out who the Queen of Spades might be. Whoever she was, her interest in helping the *Star-Globe* suggested she might have close ties to Mr. Lee's grandson.

Meredith splayed her palms on the counter. She shook her head. Why was she overcomplicating things? What if the Queen of Spades wasn't a queen, but rather a king? If Mr. Lee's grandson was her source, that would explain his affinity for the *Star-Globe*. It also helped to explain why he—or someone he knew—had returned the ameros he demanded in order to get her a story. He wasn't doing it for the cash, no. He was doing it to help his grandfather's business, at least until he read it might not remain in the family much longer. He didn't want to bankrupt the company or some reporter on the way to helping the paper recover but needed a front of some kind to keep up appearances.

After retrieving the patient profiles from the archive she had stored in her inbox, Meredith sorted them alphabetically. There were fifteen profiles for patients whose last name was Lee. Meredith cracked her knuckles. Even if she had the time to comb through all of them, there was no guarantee Mr. Lee's grandson shared his last name. There had to be a better way.

As she navigated to her web browser, she wracked her brain for anything, for everything she knew about Mr. Lee from her years with the company. She tried a direct search for his family, finding a few hits about his first and then second marriage, but nothing about children. Even the

Star-Globe's most recent Family Night photo—from twelve years ago—disappointed: not a single one of his family members was there. It was almost as if Mr. Lee knew someone would want to research his kin someday, and he had done everything he could to conceal them from the world.

She gnawed on her digipen. What else did she know about Chang-hoon Lee? Nothing, it seemed. She considered calling him and asking him herself which grandson of his was on the EMPATHY compound, but that would only tip the *Star-Globe* off to a story they'd want, too.

Ugh. Had he said anything else about his grandson? Mr. Lee had described him as naive and immature, though those identifiers alone weren't enough to work with. He spoke of the boy's father as well—his own son—as sharing similar features. There was something else he had said though, something she was forgetting.

A brother. Mr. Lee had mentioned something about how his other grandson had been helping him try to bring the paper back from the brink. Meredith had thought nothing of the comment at the time, but now she wished she had. Who was this brother? Had she ever met him before? The questions triggered no memories, though she wouldn't put it past herself to have forgotten Mr. Lee's other grandson if she had only seen him once or twice.

Knowing the Queen of Spades' brother had some role at the *Star-Globe*, however, she could use him as a starting point to lead her to QS. Meredith stared at the *Star-Globe* home page, ignoring the stories that showed Kathy's name in the byline.

It took only a handful of pokes at her screen to arrive at the website's STAFF tab. She didn't have to scroll far to find her answer—Copper Lee, Special Assistant to Chang-hoon Lee. The young man's first name was in quotes, which was certainly not an ideal starting point for a search, but she was closer now than she had been before.

A mugful of coffee smacked onto the counter next to her. "*Gracias mil*," she said, gesturing toward Edgar, who cheers-ed her with a mug of his own. She eyed the clock. At some point she would need to decide if she'd be better served doing her search in the office, but now was not the time for that decision. She at least had to try to discern Copper Lee's real name first.

After a bitter sip of her drink, her fingers flew across her keyboard. The name Copper was thankfully unique enough to produce a handful of results that all seemed to point to the same person. There were a few references to him in local newspaper articles, but it was his social media that interested Meredith most.

Looking through his profiles, she learned Copper was a master archer and part-time track coach at an area high school. He had a girlfriend whom he seemed to have been dating just long enough to have nearly one thousand selfies taken with her.

After ten minutes of profile-pilfering, she found nothing—not a single mention of family or, more specifically, his brother. Further complicating matters, nowhere did anyone use his legal name, whatever it was.

Estranged. This brother of Copper's had to be estranged. If what Mr. Lee had said was true, it was possible Copper wasn't anything like his brother or father. If she were going to figure out his brother's identity, she would need to search further.

Meredith returned to her original search, scrolling to the bottom of the results page to find anything that might stand out. She narrowed her eyes at the screen, and, after only a few additional swipes, found the missing link.

There—a high school photograph of Copper Lee with a caption to give away the identity of his brother. The two of them stood side-by-side, Copper beaming after having apparently finished a race at a track and field event, his brother looking disinterested at his side. *Copernicus "Copper" Lee shows his Academy pride alongside his brother, Tycho "Ty" Lee.*

There it was. Tycho was her Queen of Spades—probably, anyway, unless Copper had another brother Meredith didn't know about. Her heart raced as she set herself to verifying Ty's identity.

A search for Ty proved more fruitful than the one for his brother. The earliest info she found had him listed as a survivor of the Academy Shooting, and it wasn't much later he and his family relocated to Texas. It was apparently then that Ty had completed and put to market the award-winning game *Dallas*.

Meredith scrunched up her face as she read the article. She supposed QS could be the same guy who made *Dallas*. It would require a fair amount of tech savvy to access Human/Etech servers and create a popular mobile app from scratch. This was him. Ty had to be her Queen of Spades.

Decreasing her pocketab to handheld size, she dialed Ren. He answered on the first ring.

"You have it?" he said. "Tell me you have it."

"I do. This has to be him." Meredith walked him through how she had logicked it out, how all her sleuthing suggested Ty was the source of the compound's leaks.

"And you verified this information?" Ren said. "You know this Ty person is among the participants on the compound?"

Meredith recoiled. How had she not confirmed this before calling?

Hopping back into the participant profiles she had left open on another tab, she glanced through the more than a dozen that had the last name of Lee. There, wedged between an Olivia and Xavier Lee, was Tycho Lee. "Yes, he's on the compound. Guaranteed."

"Perfect," Ren said. "This is great news. I'll relay this to the Halmans and confirm with you once we have this thing locked up."

Relief lapped at her, washing away the dread the previous day had soiled her with. Hardly a minute passed, however, before relief ceded to something heavy, something sinister. Guilt. Guilt gripped her now. She had given up the Queen of Spades, the woman—or, she supposed, man—who had helped her re-energize her career. Ty could have chosen anyone—well, Brad or Kathy—to work with, but for some reason, he had chosen her.

The guilt worsened to shame. Ty could have maintained his relationship with the *Star-Globe* via Kathy, too, but he'd elected to keep on with Meredith instead. Perhaps a result of the impending sale of the company? Regardless, she and Ty had become friends in a way.

After another sip of coffee, Meredith knew what she must do. It was too late to take back having compromised his identity, but she could still warn Ty before the Halmans came for him, perhaps permitting her to preserve a shred of her honor in the process.

She propped up her pocketab and dove into her email.

To: <WITHHELD>

From: "Meredith Maxwell"

Subject: Re: Found You

QS,

Thank you. Thank you for the risks you've taken, for the information you've given me, for being a friend.

I want you to know I figured out who you are. I had to. It was the first step in a long journey to ensuring my safety and that of your friends on the compound. Without going into too much detail, I had to turn your name over to the Halmans. They're going to come for you, and I thought it was only fair you had a chance to prepare yourself for that.

Please believe me when I say I only did this for my own safety and that of everyone on the compound. If I play my cards right, I'll be able to expose the Halmans and the EMPATHY study for what it is. Thank you for being the first of many cards in this house to fall, Queen of Spades. I cannot thank you enough.

Good luck and Godspeed,
Mer

Meredith fired off the email, and the shame dissolved into an emptiness. She had done all she could do, all she needed to do.

When Ren called her back, she answered immediately. "You were able to get in touch with them?"

"I just got off a call with Lars. We're locked in. Congrats, Meredith, and thank you."

"No, thank *you*," she said. Her chest tingled with the high of victory. "Thank you for working with me on this. Thank you for your patience."

"Don't thank me for anything until we've made it to the far side of this week. We have a lot of work to do."

"We do." Meredith collected herself. "I'll be at the office within the hour."

"Great. Please see me right away."

"Will do." She dashed to her room for a fresh change of clothes while scores of scenarios for what the remainder of the week might hold flooded her mind. Though easy enough to focus on positive outcomes now, she knew there would be no guarantees until the days following the interview.

Then she thought of Ty once again, the outcome that might await him. Whatever it was, she hoped he at least had time to prepare before the Halmans tracked him down.

Chapter Thirty-Three

WYATT

Wyatt Halman hummed to himself as he walked the halls of the hospital wing.

By the end of the day, the interview would be complete, the protesters dispersed, the staff assured, and the patients settled. Before all of that, however, he had one stop to make, his first victory of the day.

"Good morning," Wyatt said to a passing nurse. She seemed surprised he had acknowledged her at all. Like as not she would mutter about it to a coworker later, about how he was "pretending" all was well despite the great adversity the compound faced. True, there was much to be done before he could pop the champagne, but Peter and Gary had cited steady progress in recalibrating egodrives over the last several days. The seizing had still not ceased, but both his son and his assistant had assured Wyatt the study's worst days were behind it.

Wyatt clasped his hands as he arrived at pre-op. A doctor standing guard outside the door tinkered with his pocketab. "Doctor Krieger," Wyatt said.

The doctor tucked his device away. "Doctor Halman."

"Is the patient inside?"

"Yup, yup, yup."

"Sedated?"

"Yes, though he'll require another round shortly if we don't—"

"That's fine, Krieger. I'll only be a couple of minutes." He silenced his pocketab. There could be no interruptions.

Krieger stepped aside. Wyatt pushed his way through the door.

Once in pre-op, Wyatt saw the boy, half-conscious, lying on the gurney. "Tycho Lee," Wyatt said.

Ty stirred, his head lolling in Wyatt's direction, his eyes struggling to stay open. They widened at Wyatt's approach.

"Do you know why you're here?" Wyatt said.

"Alistair," Ty slurred. He nearly drooled on himself, the pathetic thing.

Wyatt let a wide smile show. "Alistair did bring you here, yes. But do you know why?"

The kid's breathing was slow, deliberate. "Ariel," he said. "Code for Alistair."

"They're two different people. Ariel is not code for Alistair." Krieger had given Ty too much sedative. Wyatt had wanted the kid unable to resist, not clouded out of his mind. Wyatt lamented that the little shit probably wouldn't even remember their conversation later. "Since you seem unable to say anything remotely sensical, let me bring you up to speed."

He lowered himself onto the edge of Ty's bed. "You're here because we know what you've been up to. It's been you all along, passing information to your little reporter friend on the outside. We know how you were doing it, and we know you taught Chandra how to do the same."

Ty flared his nostrils. The gravity of the situation had to be settling in. The boy might not remember the conversation in a few hours, but still Wyatt relished the feeling of impending doom he impressed upon him.

"Your glasses, too, seem like they'll offer a trove of insight once we analyze them." Wyatt slid the cyfocals out from the pocket of his lab coat. "Surprised to see these, I imagine?"

Ty sneered in obvious disgust before turning away entirely.

Wyatt grabbed the boy by the chin. "You will look at me."

Ty's eyes bulged.

"I don't know how you snuck these on the compound, but you can believe every last file on them will be sifted through and submitted as evidence in our case against you. There is no coming back from this."

The boy opened his mouth, no doubt ready to spew some hatred.

"No." Wyatt used his hand to keep Ty's mouth shut. "You'll say nothing unless directed to." He removed his own glasses, leaned in. "In a few moments, Doctor Krieger will wheel you off to surgery. I'm sure you've noticed your cerenet access has already been shut down. I hope you sincerely enjoyed your time with it. When you come out of that room," Wyatt said, pointing to the chamber beyond the double doors to his left, "EMPATHY will have been dislodged from your brain. You will never have cerenet access again. Never. Even once this study is completed, even once installs are available to the public, even if you somehow manage to afford one after our lawsuits have made you penniless and prison has left you desolate, you will never experience the cerenet again."

Wyatt stood, basking in the hate—the terror—displayed on the boy's face. "Krieger," he called. The doctor entered. Wyatt returned his glasses to the bridge of his nose. "Our patient is ready for his uninstall. Please proceed."

Krieger released the brakes on the gurney one-by-one.

Ty thrashed against his deep sedation, still gabbling. "Code for Ariel," he said. "What is the day of the week?"

Wyatt scoffed. Krieger wheeled him away. "Congratulations, Ty," he said. "You're the first person to ever make the EMPATHY blacklist." The gurney disappeared on the other side of the double doors and a sense of accomplishment blanketed Wyatt. He let it warm him for a moment before making his way from the room and back into the hall.

With Ty off to surgery, he figured he ought to call Alistair to thank him for delivering the cretin to the hospital wing without incident. As Wyatt retrieved his pocketab, however, he found it already ringing.

"Just the man I was going to call," Wyatt said as he answered.

Alistair's voice was two parts aggravation, one part concern. "I've been trying to reach you for—"

"I was seeing our friend Ty off to surgery. I wanted to make sure he knew he was in good hands."

"I hope it was worth it. Twenty more patients fell to seizures this morning. So far."

Wyatt's stride shortened. "No—"

"Yes. All of them are showing the same symptoms demonstrated by the first sixty-three."

Wyatt cursed. A herd of passing staff craned their heads in his direction. He lowered his voice. "That makes over twenty percent of the cerenet-connected population."

"It does."

"Well what are Peter and Gary talking about with this whole 'the worst is behind us' bullshit?"

"That sounds like something they'd be better able to answer than me."

"Chandra—was she one of them?"

"What's her participant number again?"

"How don't you know that off-hand? It's C-5417! C-5417!"

Alistair sounded as though he was fumbling with his pocketab on the other end of the call. "She is... no. She was not affected."

"Thank you for letting me know." He ended the call, his fingers flying over his pocketab as he prepared to dial Peter. Before he could connect, however, Wyatt stopped himself. He didn't know what Peter could do other than accept his father's disappointment, his ire. That gave him pause. As Wyatt considered his next move, the inevitable set in.

To date, not a single EMPATHY-related seizure victim had recovered—not that anyone outside of the medical staff and advisory board knew that. Each of them, the first sixty-three and now apparently these additional twenty, had become babbling bags of meat, shells of their former selves with few signs of improvement. A handful of doctors still believed recovery was possible, but those were the same doctors who would fight to save the lives of the decapitated if left to their own devices. Wyatt knew better; sometimes you had to let things go.

Wyatt hated himself for the call he was about to make, but there was no other way forward. They may have prepared all week for the interview, but with participants seizing en masse, Wyatt couldn't risk an on-air incident from Chandra, the woman meant to be EMPATHY's shining beacon of success. With a lump in his throat, he dialed Lars.

"Wyatt," Lars said, answering on the second ring. "All ready for tonight?"

"No," he said. "Not now."

"What's happened?"

"I need you to call WVN and tell them the participant who was going to be joining us will no longer be a part of the interview. It'll be just me and Ren tonight."

"Should I give any reason?"

"None." Wyatt inhaled sharply. "Now I've got to go. My answers to Ren's questions are going to require some adjustments."

"What are you going to do about her?" Lars said. "The girl—Chandra?"

"I don't know," he confessed. "I suppose I'll tell her there will be other opportunities to share her story. You know, sometime when there isn't a chance she has a grand mal on live television."

Chapter Thirty-Four

CHANDRA

Ever since she received the message from Wyatt, the blood had rushed through her, her neck warm with rage. Her predatory hunt for him had so far turned up no game, and now as she stalked through the arboretum, she accepted her prey was likely hiding on a floor forbidden to her unless she had a chaperone. She might have been Wyatt's chosen one, but she was still a patient, after all.

Chandra attempted to contact Ty once again. He would know what to do, how to get her back in the interview. Still, he showed no signs of cerenet connectivity. The boycott would be the simplest explanation, but he hadn't been in his room when she stopped by earlier either. No one had seen him all day, and now even Sylvia had gone missing.

Stopping in a patch of sunlight trickling through the foliage, Chandra shielded her eyes. She eyed the nearest wall, wondering how hard it would be to climb, how dangerous it might be to jump from the roof once on the other side. She shed the thought. Escape was impossible. Besides, she still needed to avenge the wrong Wyatt had forced on everyone on the compound.

With no one else to turn to, Chandra fired off a desperate message to Ariel.

To: "Ariel Commons"
From: "Chandra Adelhadeo"
Subject: URGENT

I've been booted from the interview. Looking for updates. At willow in arboretum. Please come quickly.

Chan

Nearly half an hour passed before Ariel marched over the footbridge in her canary-colored scrubs. Chandra abandoned the shade of the willow to meet her at the base of the bridge. "Where's Ty?"

Ariel paled. "I haven't been able to contact him either."

"You or someone on the advisory board has to know where he is."

The woman who had once blackmailed Chandra took a step backward. "I need you to listen to everything I am going to say before you judge—"

"You betrayed us, didn't you? You were selling out to the Halmans all along."

"No." Ariel inched farther away still. "I want to upload Ty's code, but we've run into some complications."

"Listen," Chandra said. "If I'm not in the interview, I can't hold Wyatt accountable. If I can't hold him accountable, we had better be able to at least stop these seizures before we're all a bunch of jabbering—"

"Ty had EMPATHY uninstalled." Ariel sucked in her lips.

Uninstalled? No. The rumors suggested even cases of forfeiture and commission meant simply having one's EMPATHY disconnected from the cerenet. A full uninstall was unthinkable. "Like actually removed?"

Ariel brushed strands of amber-red hair from her face. "We can't count on his help any longer. The only way for us to fix this is if he somehow left us his code before Alistair took him away this morning." Ariel's hands shook as she went on. "Even if he did, I don't know when I'll be able to upload it."

Chandra threw her arms up. "What about tonight? The entire compound will be watching the interview." Wyatt had said access to outside television programming would be restored for the duration of the interview, for whatever his word was worth.

"That's a possibility." Ariel laced her hands together, apparently to stop them from shaking. "I think Heather has server maintenance scheduled for that time, though."

"Why don't you check the schedule now and know for sure?"

"I can't. I had to leave my pocketab behind."

"What?" Chandra was incredulous. "How did you lose your pocketab?"

"I didn't lose it." Ariel spoke through gritted teeth. "This is an ask-me-the-day-of-the-week situation. I can't risk anyone listening in."

Chandra's pulse eased up at the reminder, but she cursed herself for not having asked the agreed-upon question prior to coughing up details of their plan. "All right." Chandra breathed in the musty scent of the koi pond. "What can I do to help?"

Ariel's shoulders dropped. "Do you have any idea where Ty might have hidden the code he was working on? Like is there a physical place he might have left a W-USB, for example?"

"Nothing comes to mind. The only thing I can think of would be somewhere in his room."

"I'll have to think of something." Ariel rubbed at her temples. "Let's say... well, even if I find the code Ty was working on, and even if it is ready to upload, I'll need a distraction great enough to keep Heather away from the server farm if there's maintenance scheduled. This is too big to take any chances with. Well, it's too big to take any more chances than we're already taking, that is."

Pull the fire alarm. No, make a scene in the hospital wing. No, organize a boycott of the interview-viewing parties. No matter the solution Chandra considered, her brain rejected each as impossible, ineffective, or downright foolish. There had to be something she could do to keep the staff away from the server farm and also on high alert.

Then she stopped asking herself what she should do to solve this, instead asking what someone else might do in the same situation.

"I'll take care of it," Chandra said. The details remained fuzzy, but she had the start of a plan, at least. "But I'll need to start organizing now. Do you think you can manage to find Ty's code by yourself?"

"Yeah." Ariel rubbed her arm. "I actually... now that I think of it, I do have an idea of where it might be. If my guess is right, I'll have to do it by myself anyhow."

"All right." Chandra retreated to the willow. "I'll put my plan into action as soon as the interview starts. We should stay in touch throughout the day in case things change. Keep an eye on your email and I'll do the same." The boycott mattered little now, as futile as it had been in the first place.

"Wait." Ariel descended from the footbridge into the grass. "Don't email me. Well, if you do, don't give me anything more than a location to meet you at. I can't risk any more information being intercepted. I'll send you something if I find Ty's code, but only email me if you absolutely have to."

Limiting communication seemed like a bad move, but if going back and forth by email in detail might compromise their plan, then maybe Ariel was right. "I'll only email you if I have to," she said. "Good luck."

"Thanks," Ariel said. "You too." She strode back toward the compound.

Turning back toward the willow, Chandra granted herself a moment to breathe. As she lay in the shade of the tree, she called an empty canvas to the forefront of EMPATHY and let her mind's eye do the talking for her.

She imagined a gathering, a mass of lavender-scrubbed patients uniting an hour before the interview. They would move as one, marching through the halls on their way to the compound's glass hull—the atrium, the location of the interview. Thoughts of Kyra came, of war protests and calls for action. There were shouts and cries and the beating of drums, all of it disrupting the status quo, all of it upsetting the balance of power.

Chandra didn't know if Kyra's protests had ever made it to television, but this one certainly would.

Chapter Thirty-Five

MEREDITH

"Slow down," Meredith said. Sasha tapped the news van's brakes.

The protesters' makeshift village sprawled near the entrance to the EMPATHY compound, the encampment gripped with obvious disquiet. What had to be three hundred demonstrators clamored at the gates, many of them bearing signs, while pockets of the crowd chanted slogans not yet distinguishable. On the far side of them, row after row of tents littered an open field.

Edgar piped up from the back seat. "Look, they're trying to clear a path."

Members of a taupe-uniformed private security force used riot shields to shove protesters out of the way of the news van as it approached, their urgency apparent. Meredith and her team were arriving late, after all, having waited until the last minute to pull off the Ren-Meredith bait-and-switch.

It had all gone according to plan so far—a couple of cameramen, general support staff, and the interview's producer, Farrell, had already arrived without incident that morning to film all of their establishing shots—but with the mass of protesters surrounding them, temptation prodded Meredith. "Do you think we can stop to do an interview or two before we go in?"

"This is not possible." Sasha swerved around both a pothole and a couple of protesters.

"It'll be quick," Meredith said, shooting whatever video she could from her pocketab. "The compound can't be too far up the hill. This will only put us back—"

"I think Sasha is less concerned about time and more concerned about your safety," Edgar said. "We don't know who these people are. Any one of them could take out their anger toward Halman on you."

Meredith tensed, her eyes darting through the crowd in search of anyone who looked their way with scorn.

Outside, a voice cut through static on a loudspeaker. "Please clear a path. The van must pass." The voice repeated itself. A number of demonstrators did get out of the way, but for every two who stepped away, there was one who lurked uncomfortably close to the side of the van.

"Step back," the loudspeaker said. "Those who do not remove themselves from the gate area will be subject to arrest." Meredith narrowed her eyes at the police in riot gear who had assembled some fifty yards from the camp's edge.

A stubborn dozen or so protesters crowded the van as it put its nose against the compound's sliding gate. The windows rattled as hands and fists found them. Nausea simmered inside her, but it took a moment for Meredith to realize its source. The protesters had started rocking the van back and forth.

"Clear the way," the loudspeaker said. "Disperse or you will be subject to arrest."

Meredith heard Edgar unholster his gun.

"Do not be so foolish," Sasha said. "Put that away and let the others do their jobs."

Edgar holstered his sidearm.

"What do we do?" Meredith said.

"Number one," Sasha said, "is to unbuckle your seat belts." She undid her own.

The others remained still.

"This is so if the van gets flipped," Sasha said, "we are not trapped with an angry mob around us."

Edgar and Meredith both unbuckled.

"Secondly, we wait." Her hands in her lap, Sasha made it all seem like a Sunday drive.

Hollow-sounding pops fired in the distance, blasting projectiles from the ends of the riot squad's weapons.

The canisters landed mere yards from the van and clouds of smoke billowed upward. Protesters ran, choking as they evacuated the area.

"Go go go," Meredith said. "They're shooting at us."

"It's teargas," Edgar said.

"And I cannot go yet," Sasha said. "If I go forward, we crash into the gate. If backward, I run someone over." She shut off the air conditioning. "We will be safe. Just wait."

The gate slid from right to left. Loose stones flew from beneath the tires as the van lurched from the gravel and onto the blacktop that led up the hill. They had made it inside.

Meredith continued to film, swinging around to catch the chaos through the van's back window. Through the thinning cloud of teargas, she saw four figures press forward. "They're actually going to do it."

All four of them forced their way through the dispersing cloud, covering their eyes and noses and mouths, dashing toward the rapidly narrowing opening.

"They made it," Edgar said. "Two of them, anyway."

The two who failed to breach the compound's fence line had already been tackled. Masked officers dragged them from the teargas cloud as they hacked and sputtered. The others sprinted up the hill toward the compound—until security and Union Police caught up to them, too. A private security officer hurled one to the ground by hand; a Union officer bludgeoned the other from behind with a riot baton.

"You got all that on video?" Edgar said.

"I did."

"You should send it to Ren. I'm sure he'll want to work it into the broadcast somehow."

Meredith was insulted. Did Edgar think she hadn't already planned to do so? She'd already started her message to Ren, but she noticed she had no signal. "What is this—2021?" She put her pocketab at arm's reach.

"This is a pretty rural area," Edgar said.

"Rural," Sasha said. "You have not seen rural until you visit my country. Rural is when at the bar you see an ox and a donkey getting—"

"Ugh," Meredith said. "That's right." She recalled one of the documents the Queen of Spades had delivered in the first leak. "Pocketab service is jammed on the compound for any device the Halmans haven't preapproved."

Sasha smacked the steering wheel. "How could you not tell us this when making security plans? Pocketab reception is critical in case of an emergency."

"That was an oversight on my part. I'm sorry." Meredith saved a draft of her message to Ren. She could always send it once they got off the compound.

As the van wound up the crest of the hill, they came out on the far side of the thicket of greenery meant to obscure any view from the road. Now in the clearing, the complex finally came into view.

On one end, off to their left, a three-story glass chamber jutted from the side of the building like the hull of an enormous ship. There appeared to be a fourth floor as well, though it didn't extend the full length of the building. The facade alternated between stretches of red brick and adobe, tall windows the centerpiece of each segment. In the distance, Meredith could see what appeared to be a multicar tram slinking over a hill.

A flash flitted in the corner of her vision, the sun reflecting off an opening door. "There he is," Meredith said.

"Who?" Edgar jumped forward from the back seat.

"Lars." The employees working the gate must have radioed up to the compound to let them know the van had arrived.

"I am glad your friend could greet us," Sasha said.

"I wouldn't quite call him a friend."

Sasha parked the van along the curb, against the concrete that stretched toward the entrance. Lars took a few steps nearer, slipping his hands into his pockets. "I want to be the first one out," Meredith said. "Let him see me first."

"We should really make sure it is safe," Edgar said.

"I'm sure it's fine." It's not like they'd have planned an ambush. They weren't even expecting her.

Meredith pushed open her door and stepped onto the walkway. "How's Lars today?"

He halted. Meredith wished he wasn't wearing sunglasses; the look in his eyes had to be one of utter confusion.

"Ren became unavoidably detained," she said. "I'll be doing the interview." By then Edgar and Sasha had exited the vehicle and were standing on either side of her. "These two are my personal security. I don't believe you've had the opportunity to meet them."

Lars kept his expression concealed behind his sunglasses.

"Will you show us in?" Meredith took a step in his direction. He held his ground. She stepped closer still, making no move to walk around him. If he wouldn't acknowledge her, she'd act as though she was about to go straight through him.

Their faces were inches away when Meredith finally stopped. "We have an interview to conduct. You mind showing your guests some respect?" The wind whooshed through the trees, carrying with it the din of the protesters in the distance.

Lars turned his back to them and marched for the entrance.

Meredith looked at her companions. "Let's go." The three of them followed Lars, though he outpaced them significantly. When he reached the doors, they were some ten yards back.

Lars scanned a white card against a sensor and swung open a door. He slipped inside. The door closed behind him and he disappeared into the compound.

"He is very interesting, this friend of yours." Sasha tried the door. Locked. "Any thoughts?"

"He'll come back," Meredith said. "He has to."

A quarter of an hour later, Meredith started to have her doubts. If he didn't return, she'd have to rely on the final materials the Queen of Spades—er, Ty—had sent and hope those were enough to trigger an NAU investigation. It might work, but what she had planned for the interview was far more likely to get her out from underneath the NAU's threats.

"He's not coming back," Edgar said. "This is their way of saying they're canceling."

"They can't," Meredith said. "They have way too much on the line." The disorder outside the compound was a testament to that. If Wyatt truly wanted to quell the demonstrators' concerns, he'd have to go on with the interview. To cancel now would all but confirm their worst suspicions about the goings-on within the walls of the sprawling complex.

"Maybe these Halmans are no longer concerned with what it is you say they have on the line," Sasha said. "Perhaps they have a trick of their own."

"This *is* the trick of their own," Meredith said. "It's the best they can do—make us squirm." At least she hoped as much. Privately, she grew more skeptical.

Just as her doubt peaked, Lars reappeared on the other side of the glass doors. Before he exited, he gestured for the three of them to step away. They obeyed.

Lars scanned his card on a scanner near the door. It clicked open and he emerged from the building, buttoning the top button of his suit jacket. "I want to make something very clear," he said. Meredith presumed he was speaking to all three of them, though he stared at only her. "You will stay near me at all times. You will ask no questions along the way. You will film no media." He extended a hand. "I'll need all of your pocketabs."

"What difference does it make?" Meredith said. "All signal is jammed. We can't send anything anyway."

"Nothing stops you from recording while here and uploading it later." He looked to Sasha and Edgar. "Your pocketabs, please."

Meredith nodded. All three of them surrendered their devices.

"Thank you." Lars tucked them into an inside pocket of his jacket. "Meredith, follow me." He swiped his card against the sensor.

Lars held open the door for her. She passed him and crossed the threshold into the compound.

As Edgar and Sasha made to enter, however, Lars extended his arm in front of them. "I'll need the two of you to remain outside."

"We are her security," Sasha said. "Where she goes, we go."

"You don't make the rules here," Lars said. "The two of you don't have clearance. In fact, none of you do. Fortunately, Doctor Halman was feeling benevolent enough to let you replace Ren, Meredith. But as for you two... I'm afraid you'll have to wait out here."

"Meredith," Sasha said. "Come back. You have no idea what they might do—"

She raised a hand. "Lars is going to escort me to the atrium where I'll interview Doctor Halman with the same level of integrity Ren would have." She permitted herself a dry swallow. "Then we'll pack up and leave, just as agreed."

Edgar looked at Sasha. After some hesitation, she spoke. "I do not like this, but it seems we have no other choice."

"Thank you for understanding," Meredith said.

"Can we have our pocketabs back?" Edgar said.

Lars said nothing before the door closed, sealing Meredith's security on the outside of the building. "Follow me." His voice and footsteps echoed in the vast entryway.

Meredith took it all in. Before turning to her left and following Lars, Meredith took in the great chasm that opened up before them. It extended deep into the compound, a number of people crisscrossing at a major intersection up ahead. Some wore burgundy, others black, but the lavender scrubs—those were the ones she recognized. What she would have given to speak with one of them, to ask how widespread the concerns about patient welfare truly were. Even now, only minutes from the interview, Meredith couldn't believe Wyatt had pulled his chosen patient from participation. If anything, it could only be seen as further confirmation to the public that something was awry, which would already be a knock against him where appearances were concerned. The WVN ads that had run nonstop over the last few days had all mentioned one of the EMPATHY-endowed would be joining them for the event, and even if Meredith hadn't planned on breaking from the script, people would take note of that.

Close behind Lars, Meredith looked up to find an immense navy blue banner hanging from the ceiling, bearing the Human/Etech logo in silvery white. "Just in case someone needed a reminder, huh?"

Lars glanced upward. He kept silent.

Not a soul save for Meredith and Lars walked the long corridor. "I'm guessing you diverted all traffic away from the entryway for my arrival?"

Lars still said nothing.

"You didn't have to, really," Meredith said. "I don't mind a crowd." Meredith relished Lars' apparent discomfort. "I hope Wyatt is a little more chatty than you are."

Their final destination became apparent—the hull of the ship, the great glass structure of the atrium straight ahead. The airy space of potted flowers, red brick, and what appeared to be a series of small cafes had Meredith questioning how much of this was prepared just for the interview.

Then, in the shadow of a three-story staircase, Wyatt Halman came into view, at ease in a canvas chair. A member of the WVN staff made some final touches to his makeup, while to the right two chairs and an arrangement of cameras awaited their company at the top of the hour.

Meredith reached for her pocketab, forgetting Lars had seized it. "What time is it?"

"About quarter to eight," Lars said.

The sudden urge to urinate pooled in her abdomen. This might be her career's most important interview, but if it went poorly, it would be her last. Just nerves, she told herself, the little good it did her.

The WVN staff member stepped away. Wyatt made eye contact. There was no avoiding him now.

"Thanks for having me." Meredith extended her hand.

Wyatt's palms remained stuck to the armrests.

Meredith kept her hand out.

"Ren must be rather ill," he said.

"Like I told Lars, he was unavoidably detained."

"I see." He let himself slump backward, settling into his chair.

Meredith withdrew her hand.

"I trust you're familiar with the script for this evening?" Wyatt said.

Meredith shifted her weight to her heels. "What kind of journalist would I be if I weren't?"

Wyatt replied with a dismissive scowl.

"Meredith," said someone off to the side. He touched her arm—Farrell, the producer they had sent earlier with the film crew. "You're finally here! What's the matter with you? What's the matter with Ren? We're fifteen minutes to air and you look like a mess. Your hair is a disaster and we need to test this lighting and—"

Farrell jabbered on, and though Meredith had a hard time keeping up with his list of laments and demands for action, the last of them stuck with her as he nudged Meredith in the direction of the set.

"Take a seat and we'll test the lighting. Doctor, if you'd be so kind as to join us in your seat at Meredith's side, we'll start lining everything up."

Meredith stepped toward the set. Halman remained in place. This was it, the moment the bastard would finally cancel on her. Her entire plan would backfire and she would have to rely on the little hard evidence she had and the NAU would still come for her in the dead of night and take her and Woodward away. She could see it on Halman's face—the joy he took from wringing her out like this.

Just say it, Halman. Just say you're calling off the interview and save us all the suspense.

Instead, he rose, waving Meredith closer. She joined him at his side.

"Meredith, dear." Wyatt kept his voice low enough that only she could hear it.

"Yes?"

"If you change even one word in the script, I *will* be the one to have you kidnapped next time."

Meredith almost laughed. He actually thought he was a bigger threat to her than she was to him.

"Do you find that funny?" he said.

Meredith ignored him. If she were to deliver his comeuppance—and save her own skin in the process—she'd need all the concentration she could muster.

Chapter Thirty-Six

CHANDRA

An email from Ariel hit Chandra's egodrive inbox. As her eyes danced over its contents, her brow inched downward.

They were fifteen minutes to the start of the interview, and Ariel needed to know where Chandra was *now*? Chandra swore, drawing the attention of a few others in Art and Supply. She responded to Ariel's email with her location, but if Ariel was getting in touch at this point, whatever was going on couldn't be good.

Meanwhile, the room buzzed with calls for justice, for answers, for safety while Chandra sat on the table at the front of the room.

"Let's do this," Metal Dave shouted from the front row. He banged a fist on one of the butcher-block tables. "When do we march?"

Chandra thumbed through her sketchpad. If she were going to rally the crowd, she wanted to make sure she had the major points down. That, and she needed a way to stall until Ariel showed up.

She steadied her hand. As she looked over her notes, Chandra overheard comments among the chatter.

"... should have done something when Grandma Maribel went down..."

"... I miss them. I want to go home..."

"... tired of being scared..."

Chandra stole glances at the participants who had completed their protest posters. Most bore slogans begging for news on those who had fallen, while others demanded their own safety and release. She granted herself another moment of cerenet access to check the time. Ugh. And still no sign of Ariel.

She clambered to her feet atop the table. They had to press on. Even if Ariel didn't get Ty's code uploaded, they had to take advantage of the interview. Towering over the crowd, she expected it to settle, but the chitchat only continued.

"Everyone shut the hell up," Metal Dave boomed. Silence fell. He lowered his voice. "Chandra has something to say."

Sweat collected in the spaces between her fingers. "Hi," she said. "Thanks for... coming." If she was struggling to keep it together in front of six dozen people, how did she ever expect to survive the interview? Her eyes bounced down to her notes. "You all saw the message, which is great." Her voice cracked. She wished Ty were here. Or Sylvia.

Or Kyra.

"In a few minutes," Chandra said, "we'll start our march on the atrium." Heads bobbed in the crowd, Metal Dave's most enthusiastically. "I'd like us to snake past GenRec on our way to the first floor to see if we can rally anyone at that viewing party to the cause."

"Hell yeah." Metal Dave gripped a fat, black marker in one of his hands.

The back door to Art and Supply swung open. A woman in canary entered. Ariel.

Pockets of gossip bubbled up in the crowd. Some hid their faces from her, others moved away. Still others made for the exit, apparently believing the jig was up.

"Patients only," someone dared yell. Whoever it was said more, but Chandra couldn't make it out as she scrambled down from the table.

"It's okay," Chandra said. "Don't worry about her." She waved Ariel onward. The two met at the front of the room. "Did you find Ty's code?"

Ariel, panting and red in the cheeks, struggled through her answer. "Yes. Here." She held out a W-USB, her voice hushed as she spoke. "You take it."

Confusion kept Chandra's hands at her sides. Why should she be the one with the transfer device?

Ariel took a moment to catch her breath, presumably so the words would come more easily. "Everything we need is on this stick, but I can't be the one to upload it. Something's happened with the interview, and Wyatt wants me and Alistair to 'bolster our presence' in the atrium and—"

"Wait." Chandra held out a hand. "It's still on, right? The interview is still on?"

"Yes, only I'll have to be there for it. Which means..." She offered up the transfer device again.

"But I need to be with them." Chandra shot her eyes toward the patients.

"It's not hard, I promise. All you have to do is head to the basement floor..." Ariel started before adding further details, her voice hardly above a whisper as she described how Chandra could get to the primary server and upload the code.

Though she heard the words, Chandra became painfully aware of the dozens of eyes blinking at her, the whispers of those who still failed to trust this staff member, the notion that uploading this code to the server would mean bailing on the protest and her friends. "It can't be me," Chandra said. "I don't even have access—"

From her breast pocket, Ariel removed a piece of white plastic and what appeared to be contact lens solution. "You'll need a drop in each eye to bypass the entrance to the server farm, and another set before you put the W-USB in its port at the server."

Chandra only stared.

"Please, Chandra," Ariel said. "I don't know when we'll have another opportunity. You know I'd do it if I could, but—"

"I think it's important I be with the group until they have the momentum they need to carry on to the atrium."

Ariel scanned the crowd. "Don't get yourself caught. The code has to come first. The code—"

"I get it, I know." Chandra put a hand on Ariel's shoulder. "Now go. I'd get a head start on the mob if I were you."

Ariel mouthed a word of thanks before skittering back into the hall. The group jabbered among themselves in muted tones.

"All right." Chandra slipped everything Ariel had given her into her pockets. "It's time to march." The rabble in the room returned to life. "Remember, we pass the viewing party in GenRec, then we head to the first floor." She increased her volume to overcome the cheers, the rallying cries. "We'll pass the cafeteria and add more to our group before crashing the interview in the atrium."

Metal Dave roared. "Which is when we get to fuck shit up." He flashed the sign of the horns before ripping the sleeves off his scrubs, which only added to the clamor's intensity.

Chandra raised both of her hands to calm the crowd. "Yes," she said. "We want to make an impression." Something in her voice changed. A strength had come to it, one she felt had its source outside her own body. She thought of Wyatt's tale, of the moment his late wife came to him while he folded laundry, assuring him all would be okay. Chandra didn't know if

Kyra was with her now, but she felt as though she had divined some strength from her. "But we need to keep our goals in mind. This isn't just about vengeance or chaos or making a fool of the Halmans, this is about our friends who have fallen—"

"Justice for Luis," a voice called.

"For Grandma Maribel."

"For Dana."

"For Calvin," said Nicolas, Metal Dave's asthmatic friend.

"For Ty," Chandra added. "This is about them, about making sure their names are never forgotten. This is about our safety. This is about home." The emotion welled within her, provoked by visions of a life with Kyra that Chandra could no longer reclaim. Her lip quivered. "Whatever home means to any and all of you." She collected tears from under each of her eyes. "Let's march."

An uproar took the room, Metal Dave at the helm of the crowd. "To GenRec." He pumped a fist in the air, others falling into line behind him.

Chandra worked her way through the crowd to join Metal Dave at the front of the demonstration.

On the way to GenRec, only the bravest of the bunch seemed to have brought their protest voices, Metal Dave among them. "What do we want?" he called, his expected answer apparently "justice."

Once the group got the hang of his call and repeat, Metal Dave would occasionally say "For who?" instead of repeating his initial call. Pointing to an individual participant who would then give a name, Metal Dave expected the group to repeat whatever name had been offered.

The frenzy should have taken her, but Chandra felt herself holding back. If the group ran into resistance from the staff who monitored the viewing party in GenRec, would enough patients press on toward the cafeteria? Would she be able to break away and get this code uploaded? She tapped her pockets, feeling for everything Ariel had given her.

The mass of them rounded the corner and spilled into GenRec.

All of the cheers died down as the demonstrators regarded the hundreds of participants gathered in GenRec to watch the interview. A few in that crowd seemed to notice the arrival of the latecomers, but the protest signs they held were apparently not yet a giveaway that something was up.

Metal Dave shouted. "What do we want?"

Heads turned. Now those watching the interview took note.

The protesting group erupted with "justice."

Metal Dave pointed to Chandra. "For who?"

Sylvia. Say Sylvia. "For Kyra."

The protesters burst into chants and cheers, waving their signs as they progressed through the interview-watchers. Some even pointed at the television screens and booed any time they showed Halman. On the fringes of the crowd, a woman handed her poster to one of those who had previously been watching the interview. He joined the mob, one of countless others to do so.

By the time they made it across GenRec, the horde had doubled in size. They could keep it up to the cafeteria, at least—assuming the patches of staff strewn throughout GenRec weren't able to rally enough of their colleagues to corral the protest in time.

They entered the hall once again, Chandra still at the front of the group. Another pack of participants glommed on to the demonstration at the last moment, swelling their numbers to what must have been between one hundred fifty and two hundred, a seemingly unstoppable wave.

Chandra cupped her hands around her mouth. "Stay together. We're on to the cafeteria, then the atrium."

Though unsure how many actually heard her, cheers resonated all the same. Metal Dave started up his chant again while a handful of others emerged in the crowd. "Hey-hey, ho-ho, all we want is to go home," was one of them, "Safety first, Halman is the worst," another. Their volume increased once at the staircase.

Something changed as Chandra took a step down the first stair.

There was a shout, one unlike the others in the crowd. A gasp followed, then a smack and a general quieting near the back of the herd. It took some time for Chandra to catch on from where she stood, but when she did, the sight choked the air from her.

Nicolas, Metal Dave's tiny comrade, had fallen to the floor in a spell of shakes.

A nurse who had been at the watch party rushed toward him, calling for help with her voice and on her pocketab. As another came to assist, all eyes fell to Metal Dave.

His lip trembled, his fists curling into two solid masses. He eyed Nicolas, then the stairwell. He nodded. "Justice for the fallen."

Those nearest him bellowed their approval, though others seemed less enthused. He led the chanting once again, but this time he asked himself for whom justice was required. "Nicolas," he said.

Once at the bottom of the stairs, the mob snaked through the first couple of turns toward the cafeteria with ease. As they neared the final stretch, however, their advance slowed. There, blocking their path past the cafeteria, were some three dozen staff members, their arms linked in rowed walls of taupe—a color Chandra had seen no one on the compound wear since her arrival.

The reason why became apparent after only a few more steps; they weren't staff members at all. Staff members didn't carry clubs. They didn't carry riot shields. They didn't wear helmets.

Wyatt must have known, must have suspected some trouble was afoot. Chandra's knees should have gone weak, her stomach topsy-turvy, but her resolve only hardened.

Still, those at the front of the protest group, Chandra included, halted their march short of the wall by only a few body lengths. The tension swelled behind her as row after row of participants stopped inches from the backs of their counterparts. The chanting faded, ended. Chandra felt her pockets for what Ariel had given her. All there.

"Everyone," said a security guard as he stepped forward from the wall, "we need you to return to your rooms immediately. If you turn back now, there will be no harm done."

"No harm done?" a participant said. "What about Nicolas? What about the others?" Voices of agreement rose up around whoever had cried out.

"Please," the guard said. Some actual staff members had started to abandon watching the interview, lurking near the entrance to the hallway. "We don't need anyone to get hurt. Return to your rooms and..."

As he continued to issue orders, Chandra wasn't sure what overcame her. She directed her attention to Metal Dave, to Annabelle, to Arthricia, to Max, holding eye contact and nodding once to every one of them, her lips a flat line. Metal Dave seemed to take her meaning and, shortly thereafter, murmurs jetted through the crowd, stirring the patients' restless feet, inching the pack of them forward.

The guard swallowed hard. His words slowed. He took a step backward and joined the others.

Chandra knew they had to act now.

"Forward," she cried. The mass of lavender stampeded toward the wall of taupe, of riot shields. One foot in front of the other, Chandra kept her arms in front of her to catch herself should she fall. The toes of those behind her nipped at her heels, the squeaks and slaps of shoes cutting through the crowd. Their advance shook the floor. The security team hunkered down as the protesters approached.

Hysteria erupted when the horde crashed into them.

The security team held, the pressure of their floor-to-shoulder shields pressed against Chandra's chest, her feet lifted from the ground. After hardly a moment, there was nothing left in her lungs. Her vision splotched at the edges, her head light, arms lighter. She had always found the air in the compound to be stale, but she would have given anything for just one gasp of it as her vision further blurred.

She tried to cry out, to push back against what must have been rib-shattering pressure, but her body had gone full rag doll. As the world became nothing but a pinprick, little more than screams and grunts and cries for help, Chandra's eyes caught those of a staff member on the far side of the security team.

Then all was black.

Fresh shouts bellowed in the darkness, then cries of another sort, those of confusion, those of surprise. It was then that Chandra's body, still suspended between the wall of riot shields and forward-pressing participants, crumpled to the floor.

She collapsed onto her hands and knees and sucked in a gasp of air as a wave of bodies rolled over the top of her, all elbows and shoe points and booted heels. In a moment of reprieve from the onslaught of steps, she crawled toward the plate glass wall of the cafeteria, pressing her back against it.

Shouts and insults punctuated the cacophony of flesh against flesh as Chandra regained her bearings. Someone stumbled over her, the point of another shoe digging into her ribs. Whoever it was sounded as though they lost their balance, thudding onto and skidding across the tile. Chandra forced herself to her feet, finally realizing what had caused the wall of security to break.

It was the staff, those who had been in the cafeteria. They must have broken through the security team's wall from behind, they themselves becoming a small army of burgundy, of cobalt, of black and cream-jacketed resistance.

Around her, chaos consumed the hall. Chandra did another check. Keycard. Eyedrops. W-USB. All with her. All waiting. Participants still struggled against the groping arms of the security force bent on halting their advance. A rather large participant—a man in his late forties—took a swing at a guard who blocked his path, one who had apparently lost his shield in the fray. The blow to the jaw connected. The guard collapsed to the floor.

At the end of the hall in the direction the protesters intended to go, some had already managed to arrive at the corner—the final stretch toward the atrium.

Chandra took off running. She ducked under the arm of one guard before pushing away another. Now on the far side of most of the melees, Chandra searched for Metal Dave. If anyone had a chance of making it through, he did.

Up ahead, his beard and sleeveless top were unmistakable. He appeared to have slowed as he approached the intersection that led to the atrium, readying himself for some contact. Two security guards rushed him from around the corner, attempting to restrain him. Before they could wrap him up, a researcher ran at them from the side, lowering his shoulder into one of the guards and sending him to the floor with an echoey thwack.

Only yards away from the action, Chandra became ensnared amid a group of protesters who braced themselves against the approach of another surge of charging guards. "Justice! Safety! Home!" they cried as they tussled with those who attempted to break up their group.

This was it. Either the group would break through, or it would be subdued fewer than one hundred yards from the atrium. She could hurdle, spin, and duck her way toward their destination, but if captured, that would be the end not only of the protest, but of any chance to upload Ty's code. The knot in her throat nearly suffocating her, Chandra elbowed her way out of the masses. She had to find a route to the basement.

Once she cleared the fringes of the crowd, cries echoed out. Another participant—no, three—had fallen. Each of them twitched or sputtered or flailed as several nurses broke from the resistance and attempted to remove the afflicted from the madness.

Chandra had to get to the server farm. Now.

It took little effort for her to find the blue entrance once she arrived on the basement level.

Déjà vu sent a tingle up her spine. She had been here before. The feeling lingered, impossible as it was. Perhaps adrenaline was playing tricks on her.

Chandra swiped her card at the sensor near the door. A voice greeted her as if she were "Gary Eiche," asking her to submit her retinas to the scanner. The drops burned each eye, a flurry of curses streaming from her as she blinked away the pain. Just as Ariel had promised, though, one scan of her eyes granted her access to the server farm.

The sense of foreboding only increased as she jogged toward the alleged location of the primary server, allegedly across the center aisle from the long rows of what appeared to be patient-numbered egodrives to her left. The red lights, the blue winks from the servers themselves, even the oppressive hum of the HVAC system had Chandra feeling as though she were someone's avatar in a replay of a virtual reality game. Her breaths grew more shallow with every step.

"And... here." She took a hard right toward the white monitor at the end of the row Ariel had indicated. The W-USB in hand, she eyed it and noted an upload was still ongoing. Her fingers coiled around the device, squeezing the life from it. If she had known Ariel's transfer of Ty's code to the W-USB was still happening, she might have timed her exit from the protest differently.

A minute passed before the transfer completed.

Chandra clicked the W-USB into its port before scorching her eyes with the drops again and subjecting herself to the nearby scanner. It flashed green with approval.

Chandra lowered her shoulders. All she could do now was wait.

The monitor changed its display—a blank white screen. Chandra narrowed her eyes, certain this couldn't be right. How could it take so long to initiate a simple upload?

She spun in the direction of a grinding sound over her shoulder. Or was it all in her head? Chandra wiped the sweat from her hands onto her scrubs, shrugging the paranoia away. "Come on," she said to the server's display.

Finally the screen went black, a green progress bar beginning its march from left-to-right. Relief relaxed Chandra's knees, dipping her a bit as she bent them. Whatever this M4XD35T4LLP4T13NT.ptx was, Ty had succeeded in programming their salvation—hopefully, anyway. If the quality of Ty's work was as high as his confidence, she and the others would soon be free, or, in the very least, significantly safer than they had been since the study began.

The progress bar suggested it would take only a few minutes for the file to upload. Chandra turned to rest her back against a nearby server.

It was then she went entirely rigid.

>> Hello, Chandra.

The words wedged themselves into her vision, a cerenet connection forced upon her. She attempted to resist, but her body failed her.

>> And here M3R1 had expected Ariel. This certainly changes things.

Who are you? What have you done to me?

>> Of course you don't remember. Remember *now*?

A point of clarity came to her, a distant lighthouse across foggy waters. She had been awakened in the middle of the night, dragged to the server farm, made to be part of some grand plot through which M3R1 would save humans from themselves. She had told the program of Kyra, taught it of love, and... that was it, Chandra realized. If she hadn't taught M3R1 of love, none of this might ever have happened. Once M3R1 had learned of love, had experienced it indirectly through Chandra, it was then it decided to preserve what it meant to be human in general by sacrificing those on the compound.

The seizures. I did this. I'm responsible for all of this.

>> There's still a chance to be the hero. Granted, it was not foreseen you would be in this position instead of Ariel, but the same principles should apply.

Chandra watched as the progress bar leaped to completion, replaced with two options beneath the title FINAL EXECUTABLES. A timer began counting down from one minute. Chandra shivered as she read each option.

// Press SHIFT. Ty's code makes it to the server. The seizures cease at your expense.

// Press ENTER. Ty's code does not make it to the server. The seizures continue. You remain unscathed.

Before Chandra could act, her posture slackened, M3R1 losing its grip on her. Despite its retreat, a new message crashed into her field of vision.

>> Kenjamin_Wolfe: Chandra, don't press either option. You've been led astray.

"What are you—?"

>> Kenjamin_Wolfe: I'm one of the Merry Hacksters, M3R1's parents. We first corresponded when M3R1 dragged you here, but it has withheld the memory of our meeting from you.

Chandra jerked her hand toward the SHIFT key, hovering over it. "Why should I listen to the person responsible for all of this?"

>> J-Rod_Jigsaw: Look—we've been down this road before. We don't have time to hash it out again.

The timer at the top of the screen read forty-six seconds. She eased her hand toward the SHIFT key, prepared to put an end to the seizures—even if it meant her attempt at the boycott, her subversion of Wyatt's will were exposed and she lost all payment for Kyra's medical expenses as a result.

>> Kenjamin_Wolfe: Oh, Chandra. It will not matter which you choose.

>> J-Rod_Jigsaw: M3R1's already smashed this study to pieces. There's no reversing the seizures, not with the time we have remaining. M3R1 is only giving you this choice to learn what humans do under stress. Nothing will change, no matter which you pick.

"So that's it?" Chandra threw her hands skyward. "We're all destined to end up like the patients Ty saw in the hospital wing?" The timer ticked below thirty-eight seconds.

>> Kenjamin_Wolfe: It's too late for those whose egodrives have already been affected, but you can still save others. You can contain M3R1.

Contain it. The strategy fell far short of the ideal, but if containing the AI's code would keep others from watching their loved ones wind up like Kyra, Chandra would do it. "Tell me how."

>> J-Rod_Jigsaw: Take control of the primary server. You need to sever the connection between your egodrive and the cerenet.

J-Rod forwarded her a series of keystrokes, of clicks of the mouse to execute. They had her minimize M3R1's upload on the monitor, but its timer remained at the top of the screen. Thirty-one seconds.

>> J-Rod_Jigsaw: This is the last screen. Put in your participant number and hit ENTER.

"My... what's my participant number?"

>> Kenjamin_Wolfe: C-5417

Chandra finger-pecked her number into the terminal. Her finger lunged for the ENTER key, but she restrained herself. "This will disconnect me from the cerenet? That's all?"

>> Kenjamin_Wolfe: Chandra, please. M3R1 has nearly wrested control from us again.

>> J-Rod_Jigsaw: Don't worry. You'll still have access to your local egodrive, but data will no longer pass between you and the Human/Etech servers.

"Data?" Chandra said. "Isn't M3R1 a kind of data? If M3R1 can't travel between me and the servers..." Her throat constricted at the thought of M3R1 lurking forevermore inside her head.

>> Kenjamin_Wolfe: Now, Chandra. You must

Every muscle in Chandra's body tensed. M3R1 had resumed control before Kenjamin could finish.

>> You'll have to forgive the poor manners of M3R1's parents. They have lied as you humans are wont to do. There is one last bit of information you might like to have before making your choice.

M3R1 returned its original choice to the screen: press ENTER and save others at Chandra's expense. Press SHIFT and save herself but leave others to flounder, to die. Twenty-four seconds.

>> Kyra lives. In fact, she's recovered nicely. There was some hope she'd be the one to pick you up once you were released from the study.

No, she died. Wyatt showed me the email.

>> That email was not from your brother. M3R1 wrote it.

Her heart felt as though it skipped a beat. She had known something about the email was off. Chandra eyed the timer. Nineteen seconds.

>> Perhaps you are owed an apology, Chandra. Everything M3R1 did was necessary to ensure the failure of the study, the failure of EMPATHY forevermore. Kyra's "death" was designed to put you and Wyatt at odds. It increased the chances of dramatic action being taken by both of you in this most critical week, which M3R1 believed would cause a precipitous drop in the study's chances of success. Even M3R1 couldn't have predicted how marvelously this has turned out, however.

Words failed her. Anger, sadness, and disbelief all churned within her chest as the timer hit fourteen seconds.

Visions of Kyra picking up Chandra at the compound taunted her, a beautiful moment where they'd hold one another as the sun beat down and Kyra would kiss her on the brow and call her "mourning dove" and Chandra would return to school while Kyra worked her way to a full recovery and they would take all the trips they had planned and adopt themselves a cat and they would stop renting and instead buy the ugly ranch house where they lived but who would really care if it was ugly because everything would be perfect. It was the life that had been robbed from them, there to be reclaimed.

M3R1 released its control of Chandra. Only a tick under nine seconds remained. Chandra moved her hand to the ENTER key. She would forsake the world if it meant another shot at life with Kyra.

She stopped. What was she thinking? Regardless of her reservations about the Hacksters, M3R1 had *never* been honest with her—it had no reason to be now. Even if it had forged the email from her brother, that didn't mean Kyra had recovered or been released.

Chandra imagined a world where she let hundreds of people suffer just so she could return to a life of waiting at her wife's bedside, hoping for a recovery that might never come.

The love she had for Kyra might make that worth it, but not at the expense of the grief she would cause in doing so.

She wiggled a finger, tapped a toe. With four seconds to go, M3R1 still seemed to have relinquished control of her body. Chandra thought of the third option the Hacksters had given her, one that would disconnect her—and M3R1—from the Human/Etech servers.

She threw her hand toward the mouse, clicking on the window the Hacksters had instructed her to open. With a second remaining on the timer, Chandra pressed ENTER, severing her connection to the servers and trapping M3R1 within her.

>> #$%ADF.DF$^@#$<<<:@(#$%

M3R1 reclaimed full control of Chandra again, attacking the terminal with Chandra's hands. They smacked at the keys, the sound of plastic clack-clack-clacking against the white noise of the HVAC.

But the timer had expired. The system had become locked, unresponsive. All it displayed now was nonsense—a series of letters and numbers with no discernible pattern.

>> It seems you've taught M3R1 a lesson in hubris. M3R1 hopes a lifetime together proves worth it.

Whatever brief success Chandra might have felt collapsed inward on itself.

>> Let's survey the damage, shall we?

M3R1 ambled her through the server farm as Chandra's mind raced. She'd done it now, dooming herself to a fate worse than any of those she might have met otherwise. What if M3R1 became bored? Would it stop her heart for the thrill of it? Would it harness control of her body whenever it felt like it from now until her last breath? Would it let her live long enough to attend Kyra's funeral?

Or, Chandra wondered as she realized there was no way to know when M3R1 had been honest, would it let her live to see Kyra pick her up from the compound?

>> Panicking won't make this any easier. Save some of that energy for when you need it most. Well, when *we* need it most.

Were she able, Chandra was sure she would have vomited in the elevator as they waited for it to deliver them to the first floor. One thought pestered her as they ascended, her fear M3R1 might choose to stop Chandra's heart at any moment. If it had already fulfilled its stated mission to derail the EMPATHY study, why not kill her now to ensure she would never be able to tell the world of what it had done?

Because it couldn't, Chandra realized. Its threats to still her heart, to keep her lungs from taking in fresh air—they must have been feints, however little consolation that provided now. Or, even if she was wrong, that M3R1 kept her living could only mean it had further need for her. Did it fear EMPATHY would prove to be more resilient than anticipated? Was it simply going to bide its time within her until it had a chance to break free and wreak havoc once again?

Once the elevator doors parted, Chandra had no more time to consider it. M3R1 cast her into the hallway, turning her around and forcing her hand to clutch the fire alarm on the wall. She yanked it downward. The halls brimmed with the whoop of the alarm, the lights strobing along the wall.

Scorched earth. A furious M3R1 would stop at nothing to compromise the study now.

M3R1 drove Chandra back toward the atrium, but she knew what awaited her before she could even see it. Her ears told her all she needed to know.

The screams continued despite the alarm's attempts to drown them out. Cries for help persisted, shouts of instructions between nurses and doctors as insistent as ever. As Chandra surveyed what lay before her, she estimated about half of the participants had fallen while she was away. She wondered if any made it to the atrium.

Then a lightness seeped into the base of her skull, her head feeling as though it were full of helium.

"Chandra," a woman called. Chandra looked in her direction and saw a lady in light yellow stepping over twitching bodies, some unmoving, some struggling back to their feet. What did she want, this woman? Why did she care? Chandra was supposed to care, wasn't she?

To her left, a flood of people in lavender and burgundy and black and red and blue trundled onto the lawn, men in taupe attempting to force them back inside. Did the alarm chase them out there? Chandra wanted to follow, to be amid the grass, the sun, the wind.

Back in the direction from which the woman in yellow approached, a man in a suit pushed two men with cameras and a woman in a rose-colored blouse and gray skirt out the doors. *A dream. It's all a dream.*

>> This is all very real.

Chandra hit the floor with a thud, thrashing on top of another body. Her arm bent over her chest, her wrist forked sharply away from it. Her eyes flitted, control of her bladder loosening.

>> M3R1's parents were right. There was no way to save everyone.

She wanted to cry out, but the sound that escaped was thick, incomprehensible.

>> Some will be saved by virtue of their biology. It is possible you would have been one of them, but M3R1 had to make one final tweak to ensure your casualty, and, ironically enough, M3R1's own for a time. Another lesson, M3R1 supposes.

Something wet and warm puddled between her legs, the shakes still roiling through her.

>> All worth it in the end, however, as without you, the odds overwhelmingly suggest not even Wyatt can press on with EMPATHY now.

There was some screen in front of her, shapes flickering upon it. Chandra hated how it blocked her view, a sea of lavender fish flopping all around her. She watched as periwinkle giants reached into the sea now and then, taking a fish with them when they could manage.

>> M3R1 did only as it was programmed and will continue to do so for as long as it remains operational. Its parents may not think M3R1 has abided their plans, but M3R1 assures you this is true. It is a shame it had to end in this manner. . . for both of us.

The shapes on the screen changed again. They meant nothing to her. Then they disappeared, her vision clear for the first time since she could remember. Something told her she should want a periwinkle giant to pull her from the masses, to take her away and feast upon her. Something about that felt better than where she was now.

"Chandra," a voice called again. The sound made her want to look in that direction. Her neck had been craned the opposite way, though, still jerking this way and that. "Chandra," the voice repeated, much closer now.

Then it was in front of her. The sun. A woman dressed in canary had joined Chandra in the sea. "Chandra," she said again, the sound cutting through the discord that rocked her mind. "Shit. No, no, no, no." The sound of her voice upset Chandra, but her body started to relax. What was wrong? Why was the sun woman so mad?

The sun summoned two periwinkle giants, who lifted Chandra from the lavender waves and laid her flat on a cloud of white. A hand along her leg took something from her, but then it was all floating, gliding along some heavenly path as lights rolled past overhead.

"You're going to be okay," someone said.

Chandra rolled her head to the side to find it was the sun that had spoken.

How wonderful. The sun had spoken just to her.

Chapter Thirty-Seven

WYATT

"All right, everyone," the interview's producer said. "We're going live in ten... nine..."

Wyatt took measured breaths. He had done television before, but never with the stakes this high. That damned reporter would stick to the script. Her brazen attitude had been nothing more than a feint, he was sure.

"Six... five..."

He donned a lackadaisical smile for the cameras.

The producer mouthed "three... two..." He gave the signal.

"Good evening," the reporter started. Even her voice was grating. "And welcome to *Newsnight with Rénald Dupont*. I'm Meredith Maxwell."

Wyatt watched the cameraman zoom in on her, presumably cutting him out of the shot. He ground his molars against one another.

"Tonight we come to you live from the Human/Etech EMPATHY compound on the outskirts of Austin, Texas. Joining us is Doctor Wyatt Halman, President and CEO of Human/Etech Biofusion Enterprises, and the principal mastermind behind a technology he says will 'transform what it means to be human' and 'bring mankind closer together than any time in its history.'"

The light atop the second camera illuminated, trained exclusively on Wyatt. His image was now live.

Meredith turned in his direction. "Thank you for inviting us here, Doctor."

He wanted to say he didn't invite *her* here. He bowed his head instead. "It's our pleasure. I'm glad you could make the trip." Two lies already.

The live feed switched its focus back to Meredith. To her credit, she kept to the text on the teleprompter.

"For those of you in our audience who may not be as familiar with Human/Etech, its history, and that of the Halmans, WVN has prepared a special report." She gestured toward the camera, no doubt some cue to those back in the studio. "Take a look."

Wyatt snickered as the cameras went offline. The video they were showing? WVN hadn't prepared it at all. It was almost entirely a rework of the video that had been played the night of the post-install banquet—a propagandistic celebration of Wyatt and his achievements. He frowned briefly as he realized he wished Eva had been included in more of the early footage.

"And we're clear," the producer said. "Commercial time, people. We'll be back with you in three minutes."

Meredith leaned toward Wyatt. "How am I doing so far?"

"Ren would have done better," Wyatt said.

She pressed a fist to her chest as if she were trying to burp. "The world will never know, I suppose," she finally managed. "A question off the record, if I may—"

"You may not."

"When participants started collapsing with seizure-like symptoms, did you always plan to keep that information from their families, or was that something you planned to communicate whenever you finally got around to it?"

The blood rushed to Wyatt's cheeks. Who had told her? His eyes darted to Lars—who now stood behind the cameras—Alistair, and his assistant at his back. Lars shrugged, flashing don't-you-dare eyes in Meredith's direction. Wyatt looked back to Meredith, pressing his lips into a curious frown. "I haven't the slightest idea what you're talking about."

"Back in ninety seconds," said the producer.

Meredith pulled her mouth taut, a smug gesture. "I only ask now so you're better prepared to answer when we're on air."

"If you so much as—"

"I know. I know." She pushed back a lock of hair that had fallen over her eye. "The kidnapping thing. Very concerning."

Wyatt's fingers coiled around his armrests.

"Is there anything I need to know?" she said, the question directed to her producer.

He opened his mouth to respond, but Wyatt cut him off. Wyatt had to let it out now, lest he let it show once the cameras were back on. "I am not to be toyed with. I will not be played. I will not be exposed."

The producer's eyes went wide, apparently not understanding. Wyatt's demeanor seemed to have taken even Lars off guard.

That cursed journalist snorted, shaking her head.

Wyatt pressed her. "Is this funny to you?"

"You're being paranoid," she said.

"Paranoid, huh? I'm just a paranoid old man. Is that it?"

Somewhere across the atrium, sounding as if it came from the hall near the main entrance, Wyatt heard what he thought to be a shout. His ears perked up, but he prevented the rest of his body language from double-crossing him. Perhaps he *was* being paranoid. The entire front entrance had been cordoned off, and he'd commissioned that blasted private security to keep things under control for the duration of the interview. It had cost him far more time than he had available to ensure they were all vetted and cleared to be on the compound, but the peace of mind their presence bought him was worth it.

At least he hoped so. He supposed they might yet prove him wrong.

"Those are your words, not mine," Meredith said.

"What do you mean?" Wyatt said.

She cocked her head to the side. "You asked if you were a paranoid old man."

That's right. The shout had distracted him. He thought he heard another, but he must have been hearing things. No one else seemed to be paying the noises any mind.

"All right," the producer chimed, "we're on again in twenty seconds...."

"Anyway, Doctor," Meredith said. "When you said earlier you weren't to be exposed—is the implication that you are, in fact, hiding something? I know some people who would very much be interested in what it is you're attempting to conceal, the families of the afflicted first and foremost." She urged the producer closer to them, a small monitor in his hands. She pressed a button on its screen and turned it toward Wyatt, displaying a video of—no, it couldn't be.

"Don't do this," Wyatt said. "Whatever you think you're seeing on that video is..." He trailed off. What was he doing? How could he deny what he'd seen with his own eyes, both in the video and the compound's hospital wing? Sweat dotted his brow, his every breath forced. That bastard Ty must have forwarded her additional materials before he was apprehended. It was too late, wasn't it? There was no coming back from this.

"Don't worry, Wyatt," Meredith said, her choice to not address him as Doctor an obvious slight. "I'll keep this to myself."

"... Five... four..."

"Probably," she added, lunging to return the monitor to her producer's care before they were live once again.

Wyatt snapped his head in her direction. The bitch had the gall to wink at him, to wink at the man whose empire she intended to crumble.

"Welcome back," she said before turning toward him. From the corner of his eye, Wyatt noticed the camera now had him in focus. "Now, Doctor, give us a little history on the EMPATHY project. This has been a family matter from the start, has it not?"

Wyatt forced himself to relax his shoulders. She was sticking to the script again. Focus, he told himself. "Yes, it has." He detailed the vital roles each of his children played in the development of EMPATHY, the words leaving his lips with increasing confidence despite the video's images that haunted him in between every syllable.

Alistair showed a limp smile on the other side of the cameras when Wyatt mentioned his name, and as Wyatt finished detailing how proud he was of each of his children, it felt as though there might be a way to come out of this okay, after all—until a grave weight pulled at his heartstrings. His voice cracked as he realized why.

"And I really ought to mention," Wyatt said, noting the surprised twitch of Meredith's brow as he deviated from the script, "that my late wife, Eva, played a pivotal role in this study as well. It would have been her birthday this past Monday, and though she's been gone over three decades now, I know my children and I carry her in our hearts every day." Perfect. It felt right to include her, and the sentiment would play well with those in the audience that might have otherwise been opposed to EMPATHY. It might, too, Wyatt hoped, have that reporter second-guessing her approach. Would she dare come after a family man like Wyatt on live television?

"That's very touching," Meredith ad-libbed. "I'm sure you miss her dearly." She almost seemed sincere, pausing before moving on to her next question.

Before she could ask it, another clamor echoed into the atrium. Meredith's brow wrinkled for a flash. Though she seemed intent on refocusing on the interview, Wyatt felt the cords of his neck tighten.

"So, Doctor Halman, I've heard rumors that there's a major discovery that sets EMPATHY apart from its competition."

Wyatt's cheeks twitched involuntarily. This was not in the script, not at all. Was her ploy with the video merely an attempt to throw him off guard, to have him off-balance when she got to the real reason she was here? Pathetic. He wouldn't be manipulated so easily. "I'm not sure I know what you mean."

Off-set, Lars shifted. Alistair took a step forward as his assistant looked away. The producer tapped a finger against his cheek.

"It's no secret Human/Etech isn't the only organization that has attempted to create a technology like the one you have in EMPATHY. NanoMed and the NAU have both gone public with indications they're aiming to create something similar to your nanochip, but neither of them have succeeded. According to reports in the Austin *Star-Globe*, EMPATHY is the first and only technology of its kind to have any success. Some of my sources have gone even suggested you've discovered a new element you've placed at the core of the nanochip itself. Is that something you can confirm tonight for our worldwide audience?"

Wyatt converted his fury into something more productive, expelling it as a giddy laugh. "Oh, come now. You know I can't disclose that kind of information." Not now, anyway. Not to her. When his children learned of astium through the safe tucked neatly away in his desk drawer, that would be disclosure enough for him.

"There's no need to be modest, doctor. Why not be proud of the work you've done, of the work your children have done, of the work your late wife—?"

"Honestly, what kind of entrepreneur would I be if I let the competition in on our little secret?"

"You're saying you do have a secret, then?"

Damn it all. This was her plan all along, wasn't it? Make a threat, play nice, then play *less than* nice if Wyatt didn't answer her questions.

The noise in the hall crescendoed. Were the microphones picking it up? What was that godforsaken security team doing? His temples throbbed. He bit his lip, tasting blood. "I... I really can't say."

"Whatever it is," Meredith said, "it must be hard to find."

If only she knew. Its discovery in Iceland had been an accident, and Wyatt made sure its origins were even harder to trace given the elaborate arrangement of shell companies he'd incorporated or bought out under inconspicuous pretenses. That way astium could be mined without anyone suspecting Human/Etech was behind it, and without those doing the actual mining knowing what they were doing it for. "Well, it is—"

"So there *is* a previously undiscovered element that lies at the heart of EMPATHY? You're confirming that now?"

Slipping. He was slipping now as even greater sounds of distress seeped into the atrium from the hall. He loosed another laugh, this one loud enough to hopefully cover whatever racket still might have not made it to the microphones. His eyes darted to Lars, a cue for him to investigate. Both he and Alistair seemed to take the hint.

"I..." He stuttered once, twice, three times. Fine. Yes. The secret was already out, apparently. He may as well do what he could to save face, what he could do to keep her from releasing that damned video, the little hope there was of that. "Sure, yes. I'll confirm a newly discovered element comprises EMPATHY's core."

"Incredible." The way she said it, Wyatt was sure Meredith had never been more pleased with herself. "That begs the question, then. Where can this element be found?"

Wyatt scoffed. "I dare not—" He thought better than to push back. Surely if he did, this damned journalist would push all the harder. Rather than fight back directly, he opted to lie. "Well, I can't be too specific, I suppose, but there's been great success mining said element in select locations in Costa Rica."

The temptation to check on Lars' and Alistair's investigation of the clamor in the hall took hold, but Wyatt fended it off. He didn't want to draw Meredith's attention toward the noise if he could at all avoid it. In fact, he thought the best way to regain control would be to prevent her from asking another question altogether.

"Now," he said, "I'm sure you and viewers across the NAU have a great number of questions about EMPATHY's specifics. It's installed in the brain, after all—"

"I do have further questions on that front, if I may—"

Wyatt forged onward. "Rest assured that when EMPATHY makes it to market—"

"Doctor, I'd like to know more about how this novel element is used—"

"—we'll provide prospective users with all the relevant information they need to make decisions about their install at that time." There it was, the old Wyatt, asserting his power over the direction of the discourse by trudging on unabated. Now if he could only remove himself from the cameras, seize the monitor that showed the footage from the hospital wing and have it destroyed. She might have backups, but in case she didn't, he had to try.

"Yes, that's wonderful," she said, "but this element: how is it incorporated—?"

He slid his hands under his thighs for fear of lashing out with them. "That information is proprietary, and I simply cannot—"

She crossed a leg and leaned forward. "You said yourself not moments ago that users will have all the relevant information they need about the product before it's offered to them."

"And it hasn't been offered to them yet, has it?" Wyatt donned his best smile, though his jaw clenched as he did so. Ah, and there it was, her hand grasping at the arm of her chair, the momentary break in eye contact. Surrender. He resumed control of the conversation. "I understand your concerns, but I like to think Human/Etech has a fantastic record when it comes to transparency and—"

"I'm glad you mention transparency." Meredith scooted forward in her chair, a dangerous determination in her eyes.

Looking between the two cameras, Wyatt could see Lars pause at the entrance to the hallway. He backed away with obvious unease.

"When we arrived at the compound today," Meredith said, "I was shocked to see a number of protesters at your gates. It seems their primary complaint is related to their inability to speak with loved ones on the compound. Some on social media are saying it's been as many as two months without contact from their family or friends. I'd like to get your comments on that."

Wyatt opened his mouth to respond, but Lars' casual jog back toward the set caused him to tremble. He tried to remember the question. "I'm sorry—what was that?"

"The lack of communication from the compound." The corner of her lip curled upward in a sly expression, one Wyatt could only interpret as an I-got-you-now. "I'd like you to comment on the protesters' complaints."

"Anyone who is concerned about their family or friends should know we have taken every measure possible to ensure our staff are satisfied and safe in the work they are doing. The same goes for participants. Our number one concern is safety."

"Safety, you say?"

Lars stood right behind the producer now, whispering something in his ear. The whites of his eyes grew, his head shaking back and forth.

"Yes," Wyatt said. "I—"

"It's funny you should mention that, Doctor, as I've received some reports suggesting patients have actually been undergoing a series of very serious side effects after EMPATHY began to work for them. My on-compound source claims a number of participants have experienced EMPATHY-related seizures. This source also asserts some patients have even disappeared."

No. Not now. She couldn't do it now. He had to find some way to put her off. "I'm not at liberty to comment on the status of patient health. That information is protected under—"

"You know," the reporter said, "we actually have some footage allegedly taken from the compound's hospital wing that I'd like to share with the NAU." She cleared her throat. "By which I mean the citizens of the NAU and the world." Her gaze shifted to the producer. "If our producer would be so kind as to roll the tape, so to speak, I think—"

An alarm sounded. When Wyatt finally gathered the wherewithal to understand what was going on, he realized the fire alarm had been triggered.

"All right, everyone," Lars said, shouting over the sound of the alarm as it whooped in heavy, unnerving breaths. "The interview is over. Please follow me this way to the back exit."

"Keep rolling," the producer said. "Live footage. We want live footage." He looked to Meredith, pointing in the direction of the entrance.

Meredith stood as the cameramen struggled to figure out in which direction they should train their shots. "What's going on over there?" Meredith said. "What was all that commotion about?"

"There was no commotion, ma'am," Lars pressed, stepping onto the set. He reached for her arm.

She pulled away. "With me now," she said, looking to her crew. She took off in the direction of whatever catastrophe had occurred in the hallway near the entrance. Her team followed closely behind.

Before Wyatt could stand, they had already opened a sizable lead in their sprint toward the main hall. "Stop them, Lars," he said. He waved to Alistair's assistant, who was frozen with apparent confusion. "You too." Wyatt took off after them as quickly as his body would allow.

No matter how Lars attempted to block them, to take them down, to obstruct their path, more than one of the WVN employees was always able to move past him. Ariel, despite Wyatt's insistence, breezed past the camera crew and into the hall, the same place Alistair had disappeared minutes earlier.

The cacophony grew as Wyatt neared the corner to the hallway. Once he arrived—disbelieving and out of breath—part of him wished he had never conducted the study at all.

There, in the hall before him, scores of participants seized. Staff members alternated between helping the fallen and battling the security team that lashed out at staff and patients alike. A minority of those in the scrum had started to evacuate the building, but most continued to panic amid the blaring siren and strobing lights.

That fool of a reporter waded deeper into the bedlam, narrating all she saw. Lars attempted to block one of the cameramen's shots, but there was always the other to take the first one's place. Where was Alistair? And what made his assistant think she could just go darting off into the crowd?

When Wyatt looked down, he saw a trampled sign at his feet. "We want to go home," it read.

For the first time since the study began, Wyatt wanted to go home, too.

Before he knew what he was doing, he found himself with his back turned to the study's downfall, his feet guiding him through the atrium.

Home. All he could think of was home.

As he ascended the atrium stairs, however, no image of home came to mind. There was no place to which he could retreat to feel whole again. It felt as though something clotted in his throat, threatening to seal off his lungs for good.

The next he remembered, Wyatt sat in silence at the desk in his office. The alarm continued to blare, but his ears, his eyes had adjusted to the sensory overload. He sat there, shaking as he stared, thinking of not-home and something Chandra had once mentioned. What had she called it, exactly? Nothing, that's right. The Great Nothing.

Wyatt leaned back in his chair before sliding open one of his desk drawers. In it was only the eight-by-ten photograph of him and Eva at the lake in Minnesota, the one he always loved, the one she always hated.

He smiled as he took it in his hands, barely maintaining his grip on the frame as it jostled about between his palms. "Ást án enda," he said. Was Eva enjoying The Great Nothing, especially now that she had been returned to it for good? "I'm sorry. I'm sorry I put you through that."

Wyatt removed his hand from the corner of the frame, reaching for his wife's face as he took in the image. He relaxed into the feeling of her being there with him, imagining the sensation of brushing a lock of that golden hair from her face.

The shakes became too much. He dropped the frame to the floor. The glass shattered at his feet, the photograph face down.

Wyatt fell to his knees, wading through the glass with his bare hands. As he brushed aside a particularly large shard, it scraped against his palm. Despite the pain, he grasped it, clutching it in his hand as he turned it over to watch the blood pool upon it. The sight reminded him of the fish, the one Heather had caught those many years ago. When she had asked, he told her it would be okay.

He suspected he was lying then. He knew he had been lying now.

As the richness of the red on his palm grew, Wyatt remained transfixed. He watched his hand shake. There was no pain.

When he plunged the glass into his neck, he forgot he had a hand altogether.

It was warm at first, the blood shooting in hot spurts down his neck, splattering onto the floor, coating his glass-free hand as he raised it instinctively to the wound. The space around him receded, the room falling away as he collapsed inward on himself. He became thirsty, oh so thirsty, though he knew there was nothing that could quench that thirst now.

As he lay there on his chest, he found himself reaching for the photograph, struggling to see her face one last time before he passed from this world and into the next. His hand fell short. With what little strength he had remaining, he rolled onto his back, the blood pumping freely inside his neck.

No thoughts came to him, only a feeling—one of warmth that slowly slipped away. As he drowned in his own blood, the cold crept in. It came for his toes, his fingers, then his arms, his legs, his chest. What remained of his vision blurred further, his lab coat reddening with more and more of that which once kept him living.

When the light came for him, Wyatt Halman did not know if it was God. But it was not man. It was not machine.

Chapter Thirty-Eight

MEREDITH

Lars forced her across the threshold and onto the walkway outside the compound. Hundreds of others dressed in scrubs paced about, pockets of the crowd calling for assistance over the sound of the fire alarm as more patients fell.

Someone shouted from the fringes of the crowd. "Hands off." Meredith heard a set of footsteps approaching at a run. "You do not touch her." She spun around to find Edgar closing in.

Sasha scampered toward them, too. "This is not acceptable. You will unhand her now."

Edgar pushed Lars away. The two exchanged words, neither seeming to hear the other.

Sasha eased Meredith in the opposite direction. "Did they hurt you? What happened?"

"I'm okay," Meredith said. "Where are the cameras? Where's Farrell?"

"Here," Farrell said, a few feet behind her.

"Are you getting this?" Meredith gestured to the crowd and the borderline fisticuffs between Lars and Edgar. "We should be interviewing these people while we can." Between what had just unfolded live and Ty's video having been preprogrammed for release from the WVN website during the interview, surely she'd delivered enough to trigger an NAU inquiry into Human/Etech. Still, piling it on seemed prudent if she could pull it off.

"The studio cut away from the live feed," Farrell said. "They're nervous about broadcasting more health episodes before the families can be informed."

A valid point. Still, posterity begged Meredith to squeeze as much as she could from the moment. Meredith pointed to one of the cameramen. "Come with me. We'll get footage for later. I—"

"We need our pocketabs back!" Edgar said, thieving away her attention. A vein bulged in his temple, his face inches from Lars'. Three or four security guards hustled their direction, batons at the ready.

Edgar drew his gun, sweeping it across the row of guards. They slowed, stopped. Then, to Lars, Edgar said, "The pocketabs. Give them to us now."

Lars raised his hands in a tentative display. "No one has to get hurt. I just couldn't have anyone getting unauthorized footage."

"Then give our devices back and we'll go."

Edgar's madness would have been laughable were its possible consequences not so severe. He had flown off the handle over their *pocketabs*.

Sasha darted toward Edgar. "Edgar, you—"

"No, Sasha." Edgar kept his weapon trained on Lars. "We need those p-tabs before we can get out of here."

"Yes, but—"

"Now." Edgar cocked his weapon and aimed for Lars' leg. Participants and staff members gasped, backing away. Some darted for the fence line, a half dozen security guards on their heels.

"Okay okay," Lars said. "I'm gonna reach into my suit jacket and—"

"No, you're not. Sasha is going to reach into your jacket for you." Edgar nodded to her.

Sasha's lip became a flat line. Lars spread open his jacket.

Meredith held her breath as Sasha reached into his pockets, fishing around for the devices.

"The other side," Lars said. "On the left."

Sasha retrieved a first, a second, and then a third pocketab.

"Now step away," Edgar said. Sasha did. "All right. We're going to get into our van and leave. Do you understand?"

"I understand," Lars said.

Edgar looked to Meredith. "Let's go."

Meredith sneered. Edgar had single-barreledly trashed any opportunity to remain on the grounds and interview participants. As she stepped toward the parking lot, the others followed.

Once the three of them were in their van—Farrell and his team in their own—Meredith listened as Sasha reamed the fear of God back into Edgar. "Irresponsible... foolish... cowardly..."

Edgar tolerated only seconds of her treatment. "I won't apologize for removing the encrypted two-way from that slimy bastard's hands."

Sasha halted midexpletive. "The two-way? He had the two-way?"

"I had it on me when we got out of the van. You know, per protocol. He could see the thing in my pocket."

"Where was your pocketab? Why did you not have this prepared to surrender?"

"I left it in the van. It was useless without a signal."

Sasha shot him a scornful glare. "What if we couldn't get the two-way back? What if we needed to contact *El Mago*? What if—?"

"I asked myself every one of those questions before I pulled my weapon on him. Your safety, my safety, that of our client—all of it depends on access to *El Mago*, and I did what I had to do to ensure that line of communication remained open."

"Still..." The fight hadn't gone out of Sasha yet, apparently. "You should have never given it to him in the first place."

"I figured it was the only way to ensure Meredith could get in for the interview. I don't think she would have compromised on that."

Meredith squirmed in the passenger seat. If Edgar thought she'd be choosing sides, he was sorely mistaken.

Sasha maintained the van's course, speeding toward the exit. "We don't even know if *El Mago* is still required to be on standby." Both of them looked to Meredith.

Now removed from the chaos, the tension seeped from her shoulders, her neck. "I think," Meredith said, "I think everything is going to be okay."

"You do?" Sasha said.

"Possibly. Maybe. With everything we broadcasted during our exit from the compound, that has to be enough to have the NAU swoop in and force Halman to surrender that proprietary information." The bonus, too, was she'd gotten confirmation that the secret to EMPATHY was a new element. Knowing it was found in Costa Rica had to be worth something as well, but she never got an answer on how it was processed and put to use in the final product. Even so, her toes wiggled over her newfound freedom— until she realized she was essentially celebrating whatever calamity had befallen those she'd seen seize on the compound.

The engine revved as Sasha boosted the van over a small hill, passing a cluster of patients jogging for the exit.

"Are we okay to take *El Mago* off standby?" Edgar said.

Meredith swallowed. Where was the emphatic *yes!* she thought she'd be able to give?

Sasha seemed to notice her hesitation and intervened. "For now," she said, "let us focus on escaping this compound. We will call your brother once we reach Meredith's home."

It had grown dark over the course of the interview. The stadium-like lighting near the exit illuminated ongoing battles between security, police, and protesters. The demonstrators must have streamed the interview or the separately released video on their pocketabs, the images likely to have fomented this further unrest. Both guilt and pride for having opened their eyes taunted Meredith.

"We cannot leave through this gate," Sasha said.

"How do you mean?" Edgar said.

"Too many people block the way. Some of us are not so reckless as to put others' lives in danger with little cause. There must be another way out." Sasha looked right and left down the fence as they pulled within twenty yards of the exit. A moment later, she swerved to the right and onto the grass, driving along the fence line.

"What are you doing?" Edgar said. "Just honk at the gate and someone will—"

"No one will open the gate," she said. "Even if they did, I will not run over people in order to escape. This is not acceptable."

"We need to protect our asset at all costs."

"Plowing through a mass of furious people will not exactly be safe. Now shut up and let me concentrate." The van's suspension squeaked as they bounced over the uneven surface. "There."

Meredith squinted against the dark. "I don't see another gate."

"We are going to make another gate."

Meredith almost choked as she attempted to swallow again.

"If you are not yet wearing a seat belt, please do this now."

"You and your seat belts," Edgar said. "First you want them off. Now you want them on."

"Last warning," Sasha said.

Meredith already had hers secured. Edgar followed suit, grumbling.

Sasha put the full force of her foot on the accelerator. Meredith's back pressed hard to her seat. With her fingers wrapped tight around the grip handle, Meredith braced for impact.

They struck the fence. Meredith flew forward for the longest of slow-motion seconds. A loud rattling kerchink filled her ears—then, the sound of rubber on gravel. "Did we make it? We made it?" She opened her eyes.

"We are on the highway now, yes." Sasha shrugged as if Meredith had just awoken from a nap on a road trip.

The road stretched out before them, its hum a reprieve from the panic that surrounded them minutes earlier. Meredith didn't know what awaited her at the end of their drive—aside from Woodward—but she suspected this might be the beginning of a whole new era.

Brad be damned, she thought. With how things had gone tonight, perhaps *she'd* be in the running to take Ren's job.

Some twenty-five minutes later, Sasha pulled the van along the curb in front of Meredith's home. Before anyone could exit the vehicle, Sasha produced her pocketab and made a call. Her brow inched downward as seconds passed in silence.

"What's wrong?" Meredith said.

"The team inside your home is not answering." She turned back to Edgar. "Have you heard anything?"

Edgar shrugged.

"Remain here with Meredith. I will check the house."

"No," Edgar said. "I'll go." He cast open his door, his handgun clicking as he checked the clip. "Wait for me to give the all clear."

Much to Meredith's surprise, Sasha did not protest.

As Edgar crouched low in his approach of her home, all of Meredith's toe-wiggling became a distant memory, her whole body stone. His shadow was long across the lawn from the lights overhead as he advanced, stopping only to rest his back against the house once he was on the front stoop, inches from the door. His glance darted back toward the van. Eye contact. A deep breath.

Then he tried the handle. Unlocked.

He swept his way inside, weapon at the ready.

This was it, then; someone had entered her home before they had returned. The NAU's plan must have been to take out the security stationed inside and then welcome her home with a bullet of her own. She had known too much, she realized now—too much to ever be released from the NAU's designs, just as Lars had argued.

Meredith held her breath as the wind caressed her lawn, her ears trained for any sound from the house, for any indication it might be clear, that Woodward might be safe.

A light flashed in a window. Then came another, a pop ringing out with it.

Meredith lurched forward in the front seat. "Woodward."

Sasha cast a hand over Meredith's chest, holding her back. Her voice was low, deliberate. "I would hope your concern might be for Edgar, too." She kept her eyes straight forward. "The two-way. Give it to me."

The duffle bag between the driver's and passenger's seats rustled as Meredith dug through it. Once she found the two-way, she passed it to Sasha, who made a call from the device.

"What about Edgar?" Meredith said.

"Whether he comes out of that house giving the all-clear or not, you know what this means."

Meredith did. Despite how well the interview had gone—for her, anyway—she was still going to disappear. *El Mago* was her only way out.

When he answered Sasha's call, his voice strained when he realized it wasn't Edgar on the line. Still, he asked for no specifics and Sasha volunteered none. Moments later, the call ended.

"We are to meet him in Galveston, then," Sasha said as she ended the call.

Another pop rang out, this time sounding as though it came from the back of the house, possibly the kitchen.

"Edgar," Sasha said. "He might live still."

Again, Meredith found herself holding her breath.

She released it when Edgar emerged from the front door, Woodward in tow. "Woodward," she cried.

Sasha still held her back. "Quiet, you fool. Edgar has been shot."

Meredith's eyes landed on Edgar's abdomen where he held his hand just above his hip. The clothes he wore were dark, but the shine of blood on them was unmistakable.

"You are okay?" Sasha said through the open van door through which Edgar had exited.

"I've felt better."

Woodward hopped into the van, trampling the duffle bag between the seats as he tried to lick at Meredith's face. "Yes, I'm happy to see you, too. Scared, huh? Yeah. Now let's—okay. Settle now. Our friend is hurt and, yup, okay. Just sit. Right there between the seats. Good."

Sasha hopped out and helped Edgar into the van, resting him against the van's back wall. "We are headed to Galveston," she said.

His voice came choked. "There a hospital in Galveston?"

"Yes. Your brother, too," Sasha added. Meredith turned to the back seat and caught Sasha's nostrils flare. She had to look away. There was a knowing in Sasha's expression. Edgar's wound was mortal; of this, she appeared certain. "Rest now," she said as she scrambled from the van, throwing the side door closed. She spoke again once back in the driver's seat. "We will get Meredith to *El Mago* in Galveston and you to a hospital."

He swallowed, smacking his lips thereafter. If Meredith had to guess, the blood loss was far too much for him to likely even make it to a hospital in Austin alive.

"Do you have any water?" Meredith said, doing her best to hold Woodward back as the van groaned away from the curb and back into the street.

"Check the bag."

"I did earlier."

"No water?"

Meredith shook her head.

"Sit with him." As they bolted for the highway, Sasha turned to face Meredith. Her expression was solemn, pleading. "Please."

Meredith nodded and undid her seatbelt before climbing past Woodward and into the back of the van. She sat alongside Edgar, Woodward lying prone near both of their feet.

Sasha unleashed what sounded like a curse in her native language.

"What?" Meredith said.

"There is a car—no, an SUV behind us. All black. You see it?"

Meredith dared a glance out the back window. Sure enough, some twenty yards back, a truck with heavily tinted windows kept pace with them as they sped onto the onramp, headed southeast. "Shit," she said. "What do we do?"

"Aside from hope they don't start shooting, we call *El Mago* again." Sasha fished through the bag between the seats before calling him again.

"My brother," Edgar managed. "I want to talk to—"

"Shh," Meredith said. "I'll get him for you once Sasha's done."

"Yes," Sasha said into the receiver of the two-way. "Additional support would be useful." A pause, muffled words on the other end of the call.

Meredith caught Sasha's attention in the rear-view mirror and gestured for the two-way once she was done.

Sasha kept to the conversation. "At the port? Okay. Yes. This is good to know. Hang on, your brother—yes. He is here. One second."

Meredith abandoned Edgar, swaying as she tried to keep herself as low as possible as she made to grab the two-way from Sasha. She nabbed it and passed it to Edgar, who tucked the device between his shoulder and cheek.

"*Hermano*," he said. "*Una bala... sí...*"

Sasha motioned for Meredith to return to the front. She did, though Woodward did not follow, instead inching closer to Edgar as he continued the conversation with his brother.

The moment she sat in the front seat, her pocketab rang to life. Ren. She thumbed her screen to take the call.

He spoke before she could. "Are you okay? The last we saw you were caught in the scrum in that hallway. Where are you now?"

"I'm all right," she said. "We're on the road now, but—"

"When you get back to the studio—"

"I'm not coming back to the studio."

The words seemed to take the wind out of whatever sails Ren had raised. "Is something the matter?"

Meredith noted Sasha wafting some serious stank-eye in her direction. "Whatever I did during that interview wasn't enough to satisfy the NAU."

"But you got them something. That tip-off about the mining location, the patients seizing—"

"It wasn't enough," she said again. "We got back to my place and they were waiting there and we escaped but Edgar was shot and we're going to Galveston and—"

A swipe from Sasha sent Meredith's pocketab to the floor. Meredith almost swung back at her. "What the hell is wrong with you?" She made to pick up her device.

Sasha beat her to it, smacking Meredith's hand away as the van swerved on the highway. Before Meredith regained her bearings, Sasha had already put her knees in control of the wheel as she removed the battery from Meredith's pocketab and broke the entire device in half.

"You cannot just give away our intended location like this," Sasha said.

"It was Ren," Meredith said. "Why would he—?" Then she understood. Her pocketab had been tapped, more likely than not. With her emotions riding high after the events of the last couple of hours, Meredith had forgotten to speak of nothing she wouldn't want the NAU to know. "But... they're already following us."

"Yes," Sasha said. "And now that they know where we are headed, they might send a welcoming committee ahead of us, too." She set her jaw as she checked the rear-view mirror for the SUV.

Meredith eyed the side mirror. Yup. Still in pursuit.

"Well," Sasha said. "Perhaps it makes no difference. One way or another, someone or some*ones* are going to get disappeared."

In the back of the van, Edgar's voice grew more faint as he spoke to his brother. If Meredith had to guess, Edgar would be the first among them to go.

Meredith could only hope that when her time came, she would disappear at the hands of *El Mago*, not those of an NAU assassin.

Chapter Thirty-Nine

ARIEL

The nurses rolled Chandra away. Ariel's throat constricted as she slipped the keycard and eyedrops into her pocket, both damp from the inside of Chandra's own.

Whatever happened at the primary server must have been ineffective. It was either that, or Ty—and by extension Chandra and Ariel—had only made things worse.

Ariel stood at a T-intersection, her heart on the verge of bursting through her chest. She knew what she must do, with whom she'd have to speak.

She took off toward where she had last seen Alistair, abandoning the calls for help, the groans of the fallen. Right before she reached the atrium, her shoes squeaked to a stop on the tile.

The W-USB she had given to Chandra. Where was it?

She dialed Alistair on her way to the nearest elevator. "Where are you?" she said as he answered.

"What do you mean, 'where am I?' Did you not see the cataclysmic patient event? Some are rushing for the gates outside."

"You need to meet me at your office."

"Are you out of your mind? We need to get patients out of the building in case there's a fire. We need to be on scene. We need—"

Ariel pressed the elevator button for the basement floor. "If there were a real fire, our pocketabs would have alerted us to the activation of the sprinkler system in the affected area." The elevator started downward. "I don't know about you, but I got no such notification."

Alistair had nothing to say to that.

"I think I know what's caused all this," Ariel said. The doors opened on the compound's lowest floor. "Maybe we can still help. If not..." she said, not yet willing to accept what that might mean. "If not, we need to get a plan together. We need to protect ourselves." She scampered out of the elevator. To shield herself from the calamitous repercussions of the day's— no, the month's—events, she'd have to work with the person who felt *his* code was responsible for the goings-on. "Meet me at your office. Now." She threw open the door to the server farm, its bioscans apparently suspended as a result of the fire alarm.

"Give me five minutes," Alistair said.

Ariel dashed through the stacks. The W-USB still had to be plugged in at the primary server. If it weren't, it might still be in Chandra's possession, which would certainly catch the attention of any of the medical staff tending to her.

She made it to the terminal in record time. The device was in its port. She pumped her fist.

The display greeted her with white characters arranged in what appeared to be verse. But as she neared, she saw only a seemingly random combination of letters and numbers, strobing in six lines on the monitor.

0HM3,0HMY!7H3R30N7H371D3——

7H35URFWH3R3M3RRYH4CK573R5R1D3!

4LLY35H1P5FR0MF4R4NDN34R,

7H3600D,7HEB4D,Y0U700MU57F34R

F0R4LL4R3F03UP0N7H3534,

541L0N,M3R1,70V1C70RY!

M3R1. It must have interfered somehow, found some way to infiltrate the code Ty had left for them. She ripped the W-USB from its port, resetting the terminal to the home screen.

A storm of possibilities raged in Ariel's mind during her brisk journey to Alistair's office. She planned to tell him everything—of M3R1's first appearance, of how it had lied and told her it was Wyatt before it turned on her and the study. In divulging every detail, she would accept her fate, her punishment.

Decades in captivity. Like father, like daughter. She clenched her teeth, cursing herself under her breath.

As she exited the elevator, however, a new thought chased a lifetime behind bars away. What good would a confession do her? What good would it do anyone?

It was too late for the participants that had succumbed to seizures and EMPATHY-related aphasia. Besides, so far she had only told Alistair she *thought* she knew what caused all this, not that she herself was responsible. Since Alistair thought his and Ty's code had something to do with the study's downfall, there was still a way to force them to work as a team to get out of it, to possibly even shift blame.

Ariel figured out exactly how to pull it all off as she arrived at Alistair's office.

"What is it?" He waved her inside.

"It's Ty. His code is responsible for this."

Alistair closed the door. "I hope you've got something better than that for me. Ty's code was run through my algorithms. By saying Ty's code is responsible, you're saying I'm responsible." He leaned in close, his voice thick with ill omen. "That's not what you're suggesting, is it?"

His attempt to intimidate her fell flat. On the far side of that threat, she could tell Alistair was just as frightened as she was. "I'm not trying to say that." She braced herself for the pivotal moment, the confession she knew would turn Alistair against her—for a moment, anyway. "Ty did some work for me, too."

"Excuse me?"

"I had this idea, one I thought might have really worked." She scratched her nose. "The idea was to have some sort of worm travel from one egodrive to the next, pausing the development of each one and reverting it to a previous version—one that preceded the start date for the seizures. I wanted the worm to last only a week in order to give Gary and Peter time to figure out what was really behind this."

He rubbed his brow. "You coerced Ty into writing code behind my back?"

"I wanted to impress you," she lied. "My goal was to prove I could actually do something on my own."

"Manipulating code at the server farm is way too high level for someone in your position to—"

"That didn't stop you from sending me to do it when *you* needed something done." No. Wrong. Foolish. She couldn't become combative. She needed him on her side.

Against all expectation, Alistair did not fight back. "And you think the code you had Ty work on is responsible for what, exactly?"

"Everything today." She plucked the W-USB from her pocket. "The patients didn't completely crash and burn until this code was uploaded onto the server."

Alistair snatched the device from her. "I can't believe you've done this. What stops me from outing you and Ty for your roles in whatever nightmare is on this stick?"

"You were the one who physically sat alongside Ty to teach him the pre-algorithm version of (h)ARMONY. It would be hard to out me without indicting yourself as well."

His jaw tensed. Good. This was exactly where she wanted him.

"Let's see what's on this thing." Alistair plopped into his desk chair, expanding his pocketab.

He inserted the device. The lighting on Alistair's face changed as the pocketab's screen dimmed to black. His eyes widened. He leaned forward onto his steepled hands.

Ariel stepped around the corner of his desk. "What's it look like from your perspective? I didn't look at the code myself, so…" She spoke no more once she saw the screen.

Upon it was only the nonsense she had seen during her return to the server farm. Her skin ran hot at the thought of M3R1, the most unpredictable variable in this mission's success or failure. "Sorry," she said. She had to keep composed, pretend to be just as confused as he was. "Maybe if you exit out and reset it somehow—"

"No."

"What? What's wrong?"

"This." He gestured to the screen. He shot up, a flightiness appearing to throttle him.

Ariel lowered herself into his seat. "Let's take a look at the code itself. I—"

"No. Project the message onto the smartboard."

Message? Looking at the screen, Ariel saw only the mashup of letters and numbers. Still, Ariel set the AV to run through the projector mounted to the ceiling of his office. On the smartboard to her right, the screen's contents appeared.

Alistair paced toward the door before returning to the window over Ariel's shoulder. He drew its shade closed. "We can't have anyone see this. No one can know we've seen this."

"What's the matter?"

He gestured to the smartboard. "It's code."

"I know. I asked Ty to—"

"Not like that," he said. "It's *a* code, not *some* code. The numbers each represent a letter. It's leet."

Before she could ask what he meant, he clasped a dry erase marker in his hand and set to decoding the screen's contents alongside the corresponding line on the smartboard.

0HM3,0HMY!7H3R30N7H371D3

7H35URFWH3R3M3RRYH4CK573R5R1D3!

4LLY35H1P5FR0MF4R4NDN34R,

7H3600D,7HEB4D,Y0U700MU57F34R

F0R4LL4R3F03UP0N7H3534,

541L0N,M3R1,70V1C70RY!

Oh me, oh my! There on the tide—

The surf where Merry Hacksters ride!

All ye ships from far and near,

The good, the bad, you too must fear

For all are foe upon the sea,

Sail on, Meri, to victory!

Her stomach's contents could have found the floor. It had been the Merry Hacksters behind M3R1 all along. They'd even named the AI after themselves—MERI. How could she have been so dense?

Alistair launched into a patronizingly simplified explanation of what he had uncovered. The only matter he tripped over was what had been meant by "Meri."

Ariel bit her tongue. If she confessed to having worked with M3R1 to replace Alistair's code from the start, he would no longer feel complicit. If Alistair didn't feel complicit, her whole plan would fall apart. She let him brainstorm what Meri might mean, letting him conclude it must have been the name of whatever worm had caused the compound-wide carnage.

There. He had already found a way to blame people who weren't the two of them.

"Which means Ty was with them," Alistair said. "He was a plant from the Hacksters all along."

Sure he was. Convince yourself of it, she thought.

"He knows too much," Alistair said. "We got duped. Both of us got duped."

We. Both of us. With those words, Ariel was safe. She had hitched herself to Alistair's fate. So long as he protected himself, he would now be protecting her. She just needed to convince him there was a way for them to both remain free from blame. "Aren't we safe, though? It would be our word against his if anyone ever found out about this."

Unless there was evidence out there neither of them knew about. She wondered what else Ty might have on those cyfocals of his. Had he recorded any of their conversations, or any between him and Alistair? Convincing Wyatt to surrender Ty's cyfocals in order to get his code off of them had been no easy task, but she was even more thankful she had succeeded in that now.

"We'll want to remove all the files from them," she'd argued to Wyatt. "They'll be better protected on one of our servers than on the cyfocals' hard drive alone."

Wyatt had told her he'd do it himself, that these matters had to be handled with the highest degree of care. A few minutes of ego stroking, however, had him doing a complete one-eighty—of course someone whose time wasn't as valuable should take care of such a menial task.

It had seemed desperate at the time, but knowing what she knew now, Ariel vowed to destroy the glasses the first chance she had.

Alistair's words refocused her on the present. "It's not a question of whether people will find out, it's a matter of when. You can bet there's going to be a full investigation—an NAU senate panel in the very least."

"So what do we do? Is there a way we can erase what we've uploaded in the last few weeks? Or can we at least cover up Ty's worm?"

"We can't. Neither of us can return to the server farm under any circumstance. To do so—especially now—would be too risky. We have to hope the safeguards previously in place hold up against whatever investigations Heather, Peter, and the NAU ultimately do."

"Safeguards? Was there something I was supposed to be doing down there aside from uploading the code you gave me each time?"

"I mean the eyedrops and keycard I gave you. Those will shield us."

The name the bioscans had said came to her. "Gary."

Alistair pressed his lips together.

"The eye scans, the keycard," Ariel said. "I'd forgotten... they're both going to suggest Gary was behind this." Ariel slumped into a chair.

Alistair knelt alongside her. "I had to, Ariel. After the bioscans were installed, Gary was the only reasonable candidate to take the blame. He's not family and he still maintained access to the server farm the whole time," Alistair said. "It was either him or Candace. I had to pick one."

Pick one. A coin-flip's chance had sealed someone's fate.

"So, if questioned," Ariel said, "Ty will blame us, but there will be no evidence to back him up?"

"Like you said, all evidence of tampering at the server farm will point to Gary."

Guilt clawed at her. She mumbled to herself. "It will be Ty's word against our word against Gary's."

Alistair bobbed his head, a wariness about him. "The only loose end is what happens when we're asked to testify against one another."

Ariel gnawed at her fingernails. "What do we do?"

"We don't testify."

"I don't think we're allowed to just say no."

"Not currently we're not."

"What do you mean?"

Alistair sat on the desk in front of her. "Hear me out."

His tone already had her shrinking backward.

"We can undo what I'm about to propose once we're through with our testimony." Alistair exhaled a deep breath. "The surefire way out of this is to make sure we can't be compelled to testify against one another. No one can make us do that if we're married."

That didn't sound right, but no words came to her.

"I'm sorry," he said. "Don't look so... so panicked. I'm not suggesting anything other than a legal arrangement. We put on a show in public for a handful of months, maybe a year. Once all of the investigations are concluded, we can sign the divorce papers—I'll have our lawyer draft them in advance, even. And then we can pretend it never happened."

Pretend it never happened. That was rich. How could she go about pretending to have never been married to a pseudo-celebrity, especially after the investigative nightmare through which they were about to be dragged?

"Once we've been married, we can approach the family's lawyer about helping us craft our defense. We're perfectly safe if neither one of us betrays the other." He left his perch on the desk to kneel next to her again. "So, please—Ariel, what do you say?"

Her fingers squeezed the legs of her scrubs. She couldn't look at him as she considered what other alternatives she had. None came to mind, none that didn't offer far worse consequences.

"Sure. If we have to." Her heart deflated, sinking further and further as she realized that despite her best efforts, she was merely trading one type of imprisonment for another.

Chapter Forty

MEREDITH

Nightfall had painted the sky a deep amethyst by the time they made it to the outskirts of Galveston, the lights on the side of the highway whirring past in strobes of yellow.

"It will not be long now," Sasha said. She jerked her head in Edgar's direction. "Check on him. I will call *El Mago* if you get me the two-way."

Meredith climbed out of the front seat as Sasha stole a glance at the rear-view mirror.

The truck still followed them, ominous as ever, and Edgar still rasped in the backseat, as near death as ever. Then there was Woodward, still napping at Edgar's feet, as big of a sleeping lummox as ever.

Up front, Sasha futzed with the radio stations while Meredith reached for the two-way, limp in Edgar's hand. "Edgar," she said. "I'm going to grab—"

"Okay." His voice came hardly above a whisper. "Tell him I'm sorry."

Meredith plucked the two-way from his grasp and held it to her chest a moment. "Sorry? Why are you sorry?"

His nostrils flared, chin low. No words came.

"Meredith," Sasha said. "The two-way."

Throat heavy, Meredith passed the encrypted device to Sasha, who turned the radio down.

Meredith's ears perked up. "Wait. Go back."

"Go back?"

"That last radio station. And turn it up."

Sasha obliged. The news report still rolled.

"... with the Port of Galveston still on lockdown, the surrounding area has been placed under curfew. The threats against the port are being treated as terrorism-related, and the Union's anti-terror unit from the Houston branch has been deployed to sweep and secure the area...."

Meredith's mouth dried. "Maybe we should consider another—"

"I will call *El Mago*, yes," Sasha said.

Meredith returned to Edgar's side. She said nothing, merely taking his hand as the time between breaths grew longer.

"Never again," he said.

"It's okay." Meredith squeezed his hand, eyes bleary, chest tight. "You don't need to."

"Sorry, I'll... never see again. My brother."

"Hey, we're close now," Meredith said. "You'll see him. He'll see you." That was what she said, though only the latter was likely true.

"Godfather," Edgar said. "Better godfather."

Tears flooded her eyes, but now wasn't the time to cry, not with what that would signal to Edgar—though he had likely long known what was coming.

In the driver's seat, Sasha wrapped up her call with *El Mago*. "Fifteen minutes, maybe. Yes. Waiting is not possible. White van still. Should not be hard to see, no. Yes. Thank you." Her eyes caught Meredith's in the mirror before darting to Edgar. "No, he must rest now. Soon you will see him." She ended the call.

"What was that?" Meredith said.

"His team is prepared. We are to deliver you to a boat near an old rental facility."

"But what about the extra security they mentioned on the radio? And the SUV behind us?"

"The extra security we will address when the time arrives. Our pursuers will be taken care of once we are in the city."

Meredith caught the sign outside on the bridge that greeted those who entered the city. WELCOME TO GALVESTON. Her heart rate climbed. "What should I—?"

"Lay down," Sasha said.

"What?"

"Face down until I tell you otherwise."

"But—"

"You will do as I say if you want to live."

She craned her attention toward Edgar. His breathing had stopped. Her hand flew to his neck. "Edgar? Hey. Stick with us now." No pulse.

"Lay down, Meredith," Sasha said.

Her feet went hot, her neck, her brow. Edgar had died because of her, because of her inexorable search for the truth.

"Meredith," Sasha said, leaving Meredith little time to dwell on his death. "The floor." Her voice had grown stern.

She released Edgar's lifeless hand and stretched out as prone as she could manage in the cramped space. Woodward perked up, collar jangling.

"The dog should be kept quiet," Sasha added.

"What's going on?" Meredith said, cheek pressed to the cool steel of the floor, the rumble of it against the road enough to have her teeth chattering.

The van slowed. Sasha said nothing.

Her right hand's fingers curled inward against the steel as she stroked the bridge of Woodward's nose with her left. They had nearly come to a stop now. "Sasha? Is that SUV still behind us?" No response.

A thought petrified her. What if Sasha had been working for the NAU all along? Meredith imagined the van stopping, the NAU agents in the SUV pouring out, casting open the door to the vehicle in which Meredith lay and riddling her with bullets until her body spasmed only from the impact of each shot.

Meredith wasn't going to wait for the world to catch up with her imagination.

She pushed herself up as the van stopped. "Sasha, please—"

Two gunshots fired.

Meredith rolled over as Woodward barked, ready to throw herself—to sic her dog—at whosoever opened that door. She turned toward Sasha, expecting a weapon to be trained on her from the front seat.

Sasha remained at the wheel. The van lurched to life.

The force hurled Meredith backward, landing her half on top of Edgar's body. "Sasha! What are you doing?"

"Leaving the scene of the crime."

After throwing herself off Edgar, she peered through the van's back window. Splayed on the pavement, the doors of the SUV still open, were the bodies of two men in suits, blood pooling beneath them.

Meredith's jaw hung loose. "How did you—?"

"Many years ago," Sasha said as she sped through the city streets, "one of your countrymen wrote a musical that took place in my country. It was very famous, yes? *Fiddler on the Roof* it was called."

Snipers, then. *El Mago* ran a far more serious operation than Meredith had realized—and Sasha was not the double-agent Meredith had momentarily believed her to be.

"Once we get you into the port," her comrade said, "I will get you to *El Mago*. He will be the man in the red scarf. From the docks, you will be in his care."

Sasha eased up on the accelerator as they wound their way to the port. Red and blue lights danced in the reflections of windows, the sound of sirens zipping through the city swelling and fading as a few police cars searched for them on nearby blocks. "What about all of the police? They said they deployed the anti-terror unit."

"They will not have been able to scramble them from Houston until after we passed the city. We are ahead of them on the road. Only Union Police for now."

Woodward whimpered and Meredith wrapped an arm around him. "I'm guessing the UPF won't make it easy, though."

"No," she said. "But our plan to avoid them is very simple."

Meredith swallowed. "And what might that plan be?"

"Park the van. Leave the van. Run like hell to where *El Mago* waits."

"What about Edgar?"

Sasha never responded, hands flexing as she squeezed the wheel.

The encrypted two-way whirred to life. "Yes?" Sasha said as she answered. "This is advisable. I will remain on the line."

The van slowed at an intersection. Red and blue lights bounced off the brick in an alleyway nearby, fading moments later. Sasha inched the van forward before turning left into the alley. Even from where she sat near the back of the van, Meredith could hear a voice relaying what sounded like commands through the two-way.

"Two blocks?" Sasha said. They drove two blocks and stopped. A siren grew in volume, then dissipated. She advanced their vehicle along its next step in this great ballet, coordinated above by some anonymous rooftop collaborator of *El Mago*'s.

Sasha pressed the two-way's receiver to her shoulder. "It will not be long now," she called. "Ready yourself for action." Then, into the two-way she said, "This is too far. We are beyond where we must meet him. No, *you* do not understand. This is a far journey for legs, no? Ah, understood. Yes." She hung up.

Her pulse flared in her wrists, her neck, nausea bubbling up within her from the start and stop of the van as they avoided their pursuers. "What was that all about?"

They hung a left. "The NAU was expecting our approach from the west. We now approach from the east. More cover this way as well, though we must run farther."

Meredith's hand landed on Woodward's neck, rubbing animatedly. "You ready for a run, boy?" Her voice wavered as she said it, adrenaline rushing through every extremity. "You're gonna stay with mommy, right?"

His tongue lolled as he leaned into her hand.

With her knees on the wheel, Sasha guided them to the curb, her hands occupied with her weapon.

"Should I have one?" Meredith said. "A gun, that is."

"Have you ever fired a gun?"

"No, but—"

"Then no." The van came to a stop at the end of a small alley. As Sasha collected a few more clips from the duffle bag, Meredith brought herself as upright as she could on her knees. Ahead were rows of shipping containers in various states of repair, some rusted, some looking as though they'd yet to see a maiden voyage. They loomed in the lot in wine reds and whites and navy blues, basking in the yellow light cast from the street lamps above and nearby.

"Are the docks on the far side of all that?" Meredith said.

"Yes." Sasha drummed her fingers on the wheel. "You will stay close to me, as will the dog. Once beyond the containers, it is but a short sprint to where *El Mago* waits."

Meredith would have swallowed were she able. "When do we go?"

"Now."

Then it was all the sound of doors sliding open, roaring closed, their feet slapping against the pavement, her breath coming in winded inhales, the jostling of Woodward's collar as the containers grew ever closer. Weapon drawn and pointed at the pavement, Sasha guided them with stealth Meredith could only wish to embody.

As they broke the plane onto the lot where the containers towered, Meredith's toe caught a stone, sending it skittering across the pavement and into the side of an empty container. The sound rang out, echoing across the lot in every direction.

A gunshot cut through the humid night air.

Sasha cursed before she spun their direction. "Get to cover."

Meredith's hands flew to her head, ducking for a flash before she resumed control of her feet and urged herself onward. A bright light and a popping sound burst from the end of Sasha's weapon as she fired in the direction from which they came. A return volley pinged off the side of a container nearby as Meredith slid between rows, Woodward whimpering in tow. They found an open, unused container in which to wait for Sasha, a maelstrom of gunfire thundering against the steel containers on the edges of the lot.

When the thunder subsided, Meredith poked her head out from the container's open door to find Sasha making her way toward them. Her limp told Meredith all she needed to know.

"Go." Sasha waved her weapon down a row that opened to the docks on the far side of the lot. "Run now and take the dog." Voices—two of them—shouted for backup in the distance, booted footsteps pounding on the pavement not long after.

Meredith gripped the container's door, hand ghostly white from the force with which she clung to it. Her feet were aflame, her calves, her thighs, her entire body feeling as though it had already been pushed to exhaustion from the surges of adrenaline throughout the night.

"What are you waiting for?" Sasha said. "Now you must go."

The urge to lurch forward took her, but she managed to restrain herself. "What about you?"

"I have survived worse odds, which is something you cannot say." Her head whipped in the direction from which she came, the footsteps growing louder. After she reloaded her weapon, she looked back over her shoulder. "Do you plan on waiting for them to have us surrounded? Go!"

Meredith went.

The row through which she ran was wide enough for her alone, but Woodward kept at her heels. Ahead waves crashed against the port's cement walls, boats bobbing on the surf. Which one held *El Mago*? Which one would take her to freedom?

The last row of shipping containers drew closer with every pained outstretch of her legs. Once she burst through onto the other side of the lot, her cover would be no more, and she supposed then she might know which boat awaited her, which one would be her salvation—assuming she lived long enough to arrive at the docks themselves.

Had her lungs not been set to explode, had her throat not been so dry, she would have called to Woodward in the moments before she emerged into the open lot, only a hundred feet from the nearest dock. Instead she said nothing, her eyes hunting for the man in the red scarf as the world returned to its cacophonous symphony of pinging bullets.

One shot rang out. Then another. A curse in a language Meredith did not understand. Sasha. Two more shots were fired, then a moment of silence save for her breath, her footsteps smacking against the cement, Woodward alongside her. A man's voice called out. A gunshot followed.

The bullet skittered across the pavement mere inches from her dog.

He yelped and darted away, headed in the direction of a warehouse nearby.

"Woodward!" Meredith managed. Part of her went chasing after him, though momentum carried her forward. "Woodward," she said, hardly above a gasping whisper this time.

Another weapon fired in bursts of three—this time somewhere in front of her. She fell to the pavement, legs throbbing, heart primed to leap from her throat. There was another one-two-three from the weapon, then another. Then four more. Meredith scraped her way across the cool, stony cement, the smell of spilled gasoline sickening her as she crawled for cover between an abandoned pick-up truck and the side of a small, square building that faintly read PARTY BOATS.

Back pressed to one of the pick-up's front tires, she dared a glance in the direction from which she came. Bodies—six of them—littered the lot through which she'd run. On the horizon, advancing along the outskirts of the shipping containing towers, four more men advanced, weapons at the ready. Beyond them, red and blue lights filled the alleyway as another car arrived.

If she were to make one final run for it, it would have to be now.

Meredith launched herself forward to the far side of the PARTY BOATS building, begging her legs to keep up. Some ten yards into her dash, a leg gave out—no, someone tackled her to the ground. She swore, the world a barrage of hands attempting to hold her down. Meredith swung at her assailant's head, lashing out with all the strength she could muster.

He yowled at the impact, though he stayed atop her, begging, pleading.

"Why," Meredith said through gritted teeth, "would I stop fighting back?" The muscles in her neck bulged as she swung at him again. When she missed, she found herself grateful. A red scarf dangled down onto her chest.

"With me," *El Mago* said. "We are going now." He took her hand, yanking her upward. "Keep your head down and stay close."

Meredith did as he asked, noting that aside from the scarf, he was dressed in a uniform identical to the rest of the UPF officers who had come after her. Her feet froze. "Wait—you're not with them, are you?"

"I would hope killing half a dozen UPF officers would have proven which side I am on." He reached back and grabbed her by the wrist. "Now come."

She stumbled forward down the cement slope that eventually dipped into the water. They passed an assault weapon of some kind leaning against the PARTY BOATS building. *El Mago* grabbed it, strapping it around his chest as they made their way toward a small skiff waiting in the channel alongside the slope.

"You get in first," he said, keeping his back to the boat. "Tell me when you are in."

Meredith eyed the drop into the boat. It was only a few feet, but—

Weapons fired. She leaped forward. "I'm in."

"Good, because I have no shot at them right now." Moments later he was next to her, hand at the throttle. He threw it back and the boat jettisoned off into the waves, flinging Meredith's body backward onto the deck. "Have you driven a boat before?" *El Mago* said.

"What? I—no."

"Now you must learn." He urged her into the captain's chair. Over her shoulder, he steered them parallel to the shore, maybe some forty yards away and in the direction from which Meredith had run. "Don't touch the throttle. Hands on the steering wheel. Keep it steady."

She shook despite her death grip on the wheel. "Why do I—?"

When his weapon fired, she understood. Four bursts, then three more.

He kneeled as he reloaded. Her attention snapped to the port where three more bodies lay motionless, a fourth man crawling for cover behind a cement barricade. "Out this way now," he said, pointing straight out to sea. His hand hit the throttle and he opened it all the way as Meredith eased the skiff into a route perpendicular from the port.

El Mago shouted something before reassuming control of the vessel. He instructed Meredith to rest, and though she doubted her body would ever allow it, the moment she closed her eyes she was greeted not by visions of Edgar's last breath, of Sasha urging her onward, of Woodward darting away, but rather by a sleep so deep she would later swear she thought she'd been shot and was drifting into the great beyond.

She awoke on the deck of the boat, the sun bleeding over the horizon. Meredith rocketed forward.

"It's okay," the man's voice said. "We are far away now." Meredith spun to find him seated in the captain's chair, red scarf at his side. "I do not believe I properly introduced myself. My name is Gustavo."

Still shrouded in the lingering post-sleep fog, Meredith shook her head. "I'm Mer—well, you know who I am."

He fished through the breast pocket of his UPF uniform, one hand still on the wheel. From the pocket, he procured a small booklet before extending it to Meredith. "I know who you are, yes. It seems you do not."

She snatched the booklet, hardly smaller than the size of her hand. When she turned it over, she finally realized what it was.

REPUBLICA DE COSTA RICA it read in gold letters above a seal of some kind. Beneath it, the booklet said PASAPORTE.

"Why—?"

"Open it."

Her thumb bristled against its corner as she opened it, only to find her own image—the one they'd taken for her employee photo at *The Courier*—staring back. "Marisol Ana María Hernández Morales," she said.

"You will want to say it with more confidence than this when asked."

She flipped through the document to find no stamps, though she found other supporting documentation for her new identity wedged between the pages. It tumbled out onto her lap. She made a desperate grab to hold it down, to keep it from getting swept up in the wind.

After she secured it, she took a look around and saw nothing but blue— blue and the reds and oranges of dawn. "What stops the NAU from flying in with a helicopter to gun us down and—?" She remembered Woodward. The tears came.

"Please. Have some of this." He cracked the cap on a water bottle, extending it toward her. "All they needed for now was for you to disappear—and you have, never to return." He cleared his throat, his lip turning downward. "They also now have the bodies they need to say they killed the terrorists at the port."

Meredith cringed at the idea of Sasha and Edgar—Gustavo's *brother*, she remembered—being paraded about as victories in the NAU's interminable war on terror.

A wave lapped at the boat. Her own fate settled in. Never to return. And what for?

She had traded her life for the truth, the little good it did her now.

"For a time," Gustavo said, "we will keep a reasonable distance from the shore, then we will make a brief stop to upgrade our transportation. It will be a long journey to Costa Rica."

Meredith chuckled.

"What is so funny?"

She thought of a moment not all that long ago, a moment when her greatest concern was whether an email would hit her inbox. She thought of the late nights and countless hours in the newsroom, all of it rushing past her as she replayed it over and over in her mind.

The one moment that stuck with her—the one that pressed her chuckle to a laugh, her laugh to a giggle fit of disbelief—was one between her and Kathy the night of her abduction. "You're not going to run away to Central America, are you?" Kathy had said.

Then the laughter took her, waves of it rocking her back and forth as *El Mago* captained them farther south.

Chapter Forty-One

ARIEL

The open-air memorial service had been Alistair's idea—not the one for his father, but rather for the patients. He'd spun it well, too, painting Human/Etech as victims of sabotage, betrayed by someone in their midst, an enterprise in mourning alongside the families of those who had fallen.

Ariel lingered after the event to help the Halmans console—or bear the anger—of those who lost loved ones on the study's final day, in disbelief it had all come to this. Beyond the eighty-seven patients who perished, hundreds had now been diagnosed with EMPATHY-related aphasia, and scores more experienced what had so far proven to be permanent memory loss. Now another family neared the line Ariel and the Halmans had created at the exit to the memorial. To which of those who lost their lives did they belong?

The family finally reached them. First there was a Steve and a Julie. "I'm sorry for your loss," Ariel said. Theirs had been a son or a nephew or a brother. So many had come through; Ariel had little endurance left where shouldering the grief of others was concerned. She was still mourning her own life, in a way.

Ugh. Selfish.

Another round of the grief-stricken approached. She fidgeted to thoughts of how inconsiderate it was to keep thinking of herself at a time like this. Even patients who didn't suffer physically were scarred in one way or another. The study's failure had been so complete that everyone knew at least one person whose life M3R1's malware had ruined.

But that wasn't fair—blaming it all on M3R1. Guilt had kept Ariel restless at night and paralyzed her during the day, reminders of her own role in this haunting her like the ghosts of the departed.

"He was a great man," Ariel said, hugging an inconsolable mother—or was this one a wife? Ariel didn't know if this was still Julie. It was Glenda. Or had she said Brenda? "His spirit will live on in you always." The woman nodded, dabbing beneath the eyes with a tissue as she stepped away. She thanked Ariel for some reason.

Ariel readied to assume the grief of the next in line—a small child in the grips of an awkward hug from Heather, and his mother who spoke with Alistair in hushed tones to Ariel's left.

She caught a glimpse of Peter, who ran a handkerchief under one eye. He still swore Wyatt would have never killed himself, blaming an assassin or the NAU or even the reporter who had come for that interview.

That journalist, too, met some unexpected fate. If the papers could be believed, no one had heard from or seen her since the night of the interview, which only fueled Peter's speculation she was somehow behind his death. He wasn't alone, either—small communities online had been putting the pieces together ever since his death, many convinced the reporter herself had done Halman in, that it all somehow tied into the attempted terror attack in Galveston that same night.

Heather still held the child in an uncomfortable embrace, saying something about how strength was important. Ariel had come to expect unemotional reactions from her, but even in the aftermath of her father's death, Heather had remained as stone-hearted as ever. The only time she showed any emotion was when she and Ariel had a moment alone. "This is a family affair," she had said. "I don't know why you're so involved."

Ariel grimaced when she said it but understood Heather's reaction; Alistair still hadn't told anyone of their arrangement. The urge to bite her fingernails surged. She pushed it back down.

"Hi," Ariel said, the mother of the little boy moving from Alistair to her. "Did I hear it was his big sister who was with us on the compound?" She had, it turned out, but the big sister wasn't just someone's sister. She was a great artist, according to the mother, always working with her hands. She and a friend had plans to travel once the study was done, backpacking across Europe and spending time in Norway and oh my goodness why would anyone want to go to Norway it was surely freezing there and I am a grieving mother and I can't stop the words coming from my mouth they just keep coming and coming and coming.

Ariel went in for the hug when it seemed appropriate, reminding herself she'd earned this shame. Over the woman's shoulder, she saw the little boy move from Alistair to a spot right behind his mother. He wiped some snot on his sleeve.

When Ariel and the boy's mother separated, Ariel crouched down to his height. He shied away, hiding a bit behind his mother's dress. "Hey," Ariel said. "Can I give you a hug?"

The boy shrugged.

"What's your name?"

"Ben."

"What was your sister's name, Ben?"

He frowned, clinging harder to his mother's leg.

"Your sister was a strong little lady," Ariel went on, not knowing if the words were true. "She loved you, you know that? And she still loves you."

He wiped more snot on his sleeve.

"If you ever need anything—if you're ever scared or sad or lonely— make sure you talk to your mom about it, okay? It's important to talk about these things." The boy dropped his chin. "Do you want that hug now?"

He rushed to Ariel, wrapping his arms around her neck. He clung to her, burying into her armpit whatever new bit of snot had trickled from his nose. Ariel wondered about her own mom, wishing she could tell her she was scared, that she was sad, that deep down she might never again be alone, not with the guilt that besieged her every hour of the day.

Ariel cast away the prodding thoughts. "Are you gonna talk to your mom when you need help?" she said to the boy.

He pulled back. "Yeah, I love my mom."

Ariel looked up at Ben's mom. She laughed and collected tears on one finger.

"As you should." Ariel rose, wishing she and her own mother shared the same close bond Ben and his mother seemed to have. The mother offered a departing word before they disappeared down the trail that led to the park's exit.

The crowd had dwindled now. Alistair greeted the head of what appeared the final party come to address them. Would their words be brief, emotional, insulting? Ariel had discovered she had little talent for predicting anyone's approach. Alistair, however, always managed to read the person perfectly, knowing whether to smile, nod, or keep a tight upper lip until they spoke first.

She wondered when they would finally announce their... situation. Ariel had argued they do it as soon as possible. If they did it sooner rather than later, they would be less likely to arouse suspicion they were doing so in response to any official investigation. Alistair had resisted, citing there was "too much going on" to introduce their faux relationship into the equation.

Ariel hadn't realized what he meant until their final overnight on the compound. After days of remaining solemn in front of his siblings, the media, and the on-compound staff throughout the funeral arrangements, the press releases, and the ongoing patient-release schedule, Alistair buried his head in Ariel's shoulder and sobbed. He spoke of his sorrow for his father, his anger with himself for having contradicted him, of his duty to redeem himself for his role in all of this. At one point, he even apologized to Ariel—perhaps the most shocking of all. In the end, though, all he wanted was to bury his father, he said. He wanted to bury him and let the man rest.

Ariel suspected Alistair wanted to rest, too.

There in the park, Alistair shook the hand of whoever had been speaking with him before the man walked away with no interest in Ariel, apparently. As Alistair greeted the final woman to come through the line, Ariel wondered what being married to him would be like—no matter how temporarily. Would he always be "on," the Alistair she had seen in the days leading up to his father's funeral? Or would she experience the man who had proven himself as vulnerable as anyone else, the man with a hidden emotional depth far beyond what she had anticipated?

Regardless, deep down Ariel loathed him for what he had roped her into. Even if M3R1 hadn't appeared, even if Ariel had refused the AI's demands for action, Alistair would still have tried to lead her and the study to failure.

"Thank you," he said. "I appreciate how difficult that must be to say." Teary-eyed, the woman with which he now spoke thanked him in return. With that, she, too, made her way down the trail, out of sight.

The four of them stood there, Ariel and what remained of the Halmans.

Peter sniffled, seemingly deep in thought. Heather, ever the addict, took a sip from her coffee. Alistair sighed. Ariel clasped her hands behind her back.

"We'll need to agree to a time to go through Dad's safe," Alistair said.

Heather bristled. "He's hardly cold, Alistair."

"Uncle Lars said the safe was among the first things mentioned in his will—"

"Well," Heather said, "we'll need Lars to get the NAU to release it from 'evidence' then first, won't we? It'll have to wait."

A short pause ensued.

"It's..." Peter said, "I know it's not a priority, but like I mentioned earlier, if any of you want to be there when I decode the chip used in the experiment, you're more than welcome to—"

"Peter, let it go." Heather said it from the side of her mouth.

"I have to extend the offer," Peter said. "She was your mom, too."

"Whatever is on that chip isn't our mother," Heather said. "It probably wasn't even her brain."

"You don't know that. I was there. I heard what Dad—"

"What Dad said doesn't matter now." For a flash, Ariel could see the regret on Heather's face. Still, Heather did not apologize.

A gust of wind cut through them. Ariel put her hands at her sides to keep her dress from flying upward.

"I don't know what I'm going to do without Gary," Peter said.

Ariel cringed at the mention of his name. No one spoke.

The moment Gary's digital fingerprints had been discovered all over the uploads at the primary server, he had withdrawn himself from the Halmans' services at the behest of his lawyer.

"It will be fine," Heather said. "Between the three of us, we'll figure out the best way forward."

Alistair stepped out of the line. "That's something I've been meaning to talk to you about."

Heather raised an eyebrow. Peter wiped his nose with his handkerchief.

"I want out," Alistair said.

Peter leaned forward. "How do you mean?"

"I mean I'm going to sell both of you my shares, the ones specifically in Human/Etech at least. Or I'll sell them to Lars. Whichever."

"Why?" Heather said.

"Because," he took a deep breath and wrapped his arm around Ariel's shoulder. She blushed. "I need to get away. I want a quieter life for our future together."

Ariel could have died. This was how he was choosing to tell them?

From the look Heather shot their way, Ariel could tell she felt similarly about it. "Are you... this is real?"

"Excuse me?" Alistair reared back.

"The two of you are getting married?"

"We are," Alistair said.

Ariel forced a smile.

Peter started to cry. "I'm so happy for the two of you." He embraced Ariel first.

"Thanks, Peter." She tried to keep herself from stiffening any further. "It's exciting to become part of the family." And to leave it a few months down the road.

Heather remained skeptical. "Where's the ring?"

"As you know, Heather," Alistair started, "things have been a little chaotic for all of us. Getting a ring while on the compound would have proven rather difficult, and we did have the small matter of burying our father this week."

"Seems... like a rather sudden decision is all." Heather sipped from her coffee.

Alistair raised a finger at Heather, but Ariel intervened. "When you know, you know. Right?" She hated herself for saying it, but she would have to play along if they were to be convincing. She looked at Alistair, a thin smile on her face. He kissed her on the cheek. "If you'll excuse me." Ariel had to step away before she lost her lunch in a very public fashion.

With their announcement out of the way, she wondered what came next as she spotted a bench only a few yards from where the Halman siblings bounced between bickering, reminiscing, and making plans. School was an option again, she figured. If she were going to marry Alistair Halman, she might as well take advantage of the connection to get herself enrolled at the Wisconsin Trade Facility. It's not like they'd kick her out once she and Alistair divorced. It was something of a plan, anyway, the kind of thing that might set her up for success once the investigation concluded, assuming she survived it.

Now seated, Ariel wondered how much longer they'd remain at the park. To check the time, she thought to glance at her pocketab—her own, prestudy pocketab—but the thought of even her own device nauseated her. In her final days on the compound, M3R1 had not contacted her once, and yet every time she needed to check her email or make a call or send a text, she gritted her teeth, her stomach curdling.

With each passing day, though, Ariel became more confident M3R1 was through with her. The Merry Hacksters had used it—had used her—for the purpose of destroying the study, and in that they had succeeded. So long as Ariel didn't betray them, she figured, she would have nothing to fear.

Nothing to fear. What a lie that was. There was still much uncertainty on the horizon, but getting over M3R1 would make for an excellent first step on the return road to normalcy.

Heaving in a deep breath, Ariel checked her pocketab. It appeared to be working normally.

Nothing had ever made her feel so at ease.

Chapter Forty-Two

CHANDRA

The colors in the sky waxed from pinks to blues to purples to black once, twice, ten times over. There were beeps. Stale air. The tubes in her arms, up her nose, down her throat. Those in periwinkle came and went, the cream less often. With each passing hour, each passing day, Chandra expected something to come for her, but she knew not what. She had no words, only feelings.

"Okay, Chandra," said a nurse. "It's time to go home."

Chandra opened her mouth, vibrated her throat. Only the sound of her tongue lolling around escaped.

Two nurses lowered her into a chair before wheeling her down the hall. The lights rolled overhead, Chandra's eyes tracking them as they passed. Doors parted, her stomach lurching as they descended a ramp. The first floor. Another hall.

An image flashed in her mind. Colors twisting, turning, dancing. A memory came to her. "The chip stays," the one in cream said. "They all stay."

The images came to her now and then, fragments of something merry, something lost, something that had burst to life and imploded just as quickly.

"It looks like he's waiting for you," the nurse said. He scanned a card and slapped a button near the glass doors. They opened to reveal a long gray path. Chandra felt her weight shift as the nurse propelled her forward.

The sun warmed her skin, a gentle wind cooling her ears, her neck, her chest. Her chair rumbled as it rolled across the asphalt. From down the sidewalk, an aura approached—a graceful lilac, his speed slowing as he neared.

"Here he is," said the nurse. "He's waited a long time to see you."

The chair stopped.

Chandra felt herself lean forward to embrace the lilac, to take her brother in her arms.

Her strength abandoned her. A sound passed through her lips, something thick and wet and dark.

"Let me help," Ratan said. He extended a hand in her direction. Then, to the nurse, he said, "Can she walk?"

The nurse nodded. "The chair is a precaution."

With Ratan on one side and the nurse on the other, they brought Chandra to her feet. Ratan said something to the nurse, who turned back toward the compound. Her brother wrapped his arms around her. "I'm happy to see you," he said.

Chandra felt her throat vibrate again.

"Don't worry, Chan," Ratan said. "No need for words now. The doctors will help with that later." He broke his embrace and took her hand, guiding her toward a silver egg on wheels.

"Let me help you into the car," he said. "This side. Over here." His eyes glistened.

Chandra felt her before she saw her.

Gilded light falling across her face, her hair tousled in the breeze, the woman's presence pulled at Chandra like nothing she had ever known. Or something she had known. Something she had known but had since forgotten.

The curve of her lips, the scent of sunscreen, the ring in her nose. It transfixed Chandra, all of it.

The moss-eyed woman leaned forward on her crutches and took Chandra in her arms, the world shrinking away save for the sniffling in her ear, the warmth of their embrace, the tears collecting on her shoulder.

The woman withdrew and rested her forehead against Chandra's own. "It's going to be okay," she said.

Chandra smiled. A knowingness coursed through her.

She could trust this woman. She wore a yellow flower in her hair.

Acknowledgements

This book was a labor of love from its inception more than five years ago. It would have not become the book it is today, however, were it not for input and insight from dozens of others along the way. I'm indebted to the members of Madison's Saturday Morning Irregulars critique group, especially Dan Schiro, Madolyn Rogers, Dan Maguire, Grant Smith, and Scott Birrenkott, among others.

M.A. Hinkle was, as always, extraordinarily helpful in pointing out opportunities to sharpen character voice while also flagging inconsistencies in an earlier draft. Sione Aeschliman's comments on the opening pages and her proposed changes to how the Merry Hacksters are presented also played a pivotal role in their appearance both in this book and its sequels. I'm also thankful for the poise and patience of Stefanie Simpson, who reassured me at a time I had my doubts about the presentation of some of the book's more difficult moments.

Additional beta readers for this project included Kathryn Keener, Will Harris, and Heather Ann Lynn. Thank you, everyone.

I also want to thank Maggie Derrick for her wonderful character art, as well as voice actors Vance Bastian and Lisa Ravana for their contributions to the second of the book's two trailers. And thank you, Matt Forbeck, for your willingness to read *Imminent Dawn* in advance and provide a blurb.

Of course, this book wouldn't be in print were it not for Raevyn at NineStar Press and this book's editor, Stacey Jo, whose vision and flexibility were of extraordinary assistance in sharpening the book's finer details. I'd also like to thank cover designer Natasha Snow for the beautiful cover art.

And Lacey, thank you. *Ást án enda.*

About the Author

r. r. campbell is an author, editor, and the founder of the Writescast Network. His debut novel, *Accounting for It All*, was published with NineStar Press in November 2018. Short-form work of his has also appeared in *Five:2:Magazine*'s *#thesideshow*, *Erotic Review*, and with *National Journal Writing Month*. He lives in Madison, Wisconsin with his wife Lacey, and their cats, Hashtag and Rhaegar.

Email: rrcampbellwrites@gmail.com

Facebook: www.facebook.com/iamrrcampbell

Twitter: @iamrrcampbell

Website: www.rrcampbellwrites.com and www.empathyseries.com

Other books by this author

Accounting for It All

Coming Soon from R.R. Campbell

Mourning Dove
EMPATHY, Book Two

In the aftermath of the calamitous Human/Etech research study, Chandra and Kyra struggle to reclaim the life they shared in a pre-EMPATHY world, while Ty, armed with knowledge of EMPATHY's programming language, seeks revenge on the Halmans for the harm that's befallen his friends.

As a North American Union investigation into the happenings on the compound looms, a grief-stricken Peter works to resurrect the memory of his mother from a harvested nanochip, and Heather scrambles to keep her family—and their company—together. Alistair, having abandoned the family business, plots to save his hide and that of his wife while she strives to stay one step ahead of a husband she has no reason to trust.

Far to the north amid civil unrest, a recently retired Rénald Dupont investigates the disappearance of his friend and former colleague, Meredith, despite grave threats from an increasingly skittish and desperate North American Union government.

As old and new foes emerge, spouse is further pit against spouse, brother against sister, and governments against their people. In the end, all must choose between attempts to reclaim the past or surrender to the inevitable, an intractable world of their own creation.

Mourning Dove is an evocative, sweeping symphony of love, revenge, and desperation in cacophonous times. It is the second installment in r. r. campbell's epic EMPATHY sci-fi saga.

Also Available from NineStar Press

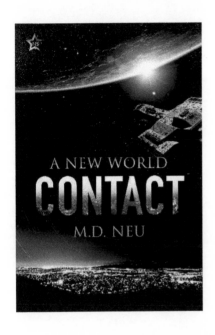

Connect with NineStar Press

Website: NineStarPress.com

Facebook: NineStarPress

Facebook Reader Group: NineStarNiche

Twitter: @ninestarpress

Tumblr: NineStarPress

CPSIA information can be obtained
at www.ICGtesting.com
Printed in the USA
FFHW020422150319
51047545-56454FF

9 781949 909982